CONSUMED

Blood Ties Series

A.K. ROSE
ATLAS ROSE

Triggers

Please be aware this is a **dark** romance series, especially this one. You knew the end was coming. That it was going to be terrifyingly dark and full of violence and love and desperation and you aren't wrong. But there are special considerations with this book.

It touches on pregnancy and potential loss, so please be aware going into this. The usual suspects also play out: Violence, gore, murder, stalking, as well as family and love and desperation and a fight to the absolute bitter goddamn end. You'll hurt, you'll smile and find new characters you're going to love as we explore more of this world together. As always take care of your well being. I cannot wait to bring you so much more.

Atlas, xx

ONE

Helene

"AGAIN." HUNTER GRUNTED BEHIND ME.

I shoved off the ground, wincing at the stab of pain in my side. It'd been days since we escaped Coulter's mansion of hell and I was still recovering. I looked over at Thomas, at his black eye and the way he still favored his leg. We were *all* recovering. But that made no difference here...not when there was a war to finish and those we loved to protect.

Again.

My thighs tensed, driving my boots into the rocky ground as I lunged forward. Thomas was a heartbeat behind, but it didn't take him long to surge ahead. His strong shoulders tensed, hands fisted, pumping through the air as we tore along the side of the mountain house and around to the steep incline.

Hunter called this training.

I called it pure, goddamn torture.

"FASTER!" He bellowed behind us. *"LIKE YOUR DAMN LIFE DEPENDS ON IT!"*

My damn life, huh? How...about...yours?

My pulse was booming, my breaths a billowing blast from the furnace in my chest. Still, I drove myself upwards, crying out when my foot slipped on the rocky surface, pitching me forward.

But Thomas was there, grasping my arm before I plunged off the rock face to my death. He held me steady until I gave a nod, meeting his gaze. A tremor raced with the connection. For a single heartbeat, the world seemed to stop. His lips parted. That hard rush of breath caught before he glanced at the fall behind me.

Then the magic was shattered, leaving Thomas to lunge, digging his sneakers into the slick surface and driving his muscular body upwards.

And I followed.

My heart was racing, trapped between fear and lust—living with these men. Both were sure to kill me.

He slowed at the incline, and it wasn't the first time. I looked upwards, to where Riven waited, his bare chest heaving, sweat glistening on his skin. But those dark eyes were all for me, gripping me in that ravenous stare.

I drove myself upwards, digging my toes into the shale surface and pushed forward. They were what I ran for...what I bled for...what I sacrificed *everything for.*

Thomas matched my strides, his thick thighs bulging under his cut-off sweats as we made it a quarter of the way, then pushed to half. I couldn't do it...I couldn't—

Riven lifted his hand, leaving it outstretched in the air toward me.

Fuck.

I pushed harder, unleashing a roar as I raced toward him until he wrapped his arms around me, stopping me cold on the small rise.

"Easy, Trouble." He murmured, holding me against his chest.

"*TIME!*" Hunter roared below.

"You...*made...it.*" Thomas braced his hands on his knees, then looked up at me, that same hunger burning in his eyes.

I had to force myself to look away. My damn knees were shaking hard enough as it was. "*Barely.*" I gasped and lifted a shaking finger to point down the mountain. "He...he's going to kill me."

Riven straightened, his chest heaving. "No, he won't, Trouble. He loves you."

I looked back down to the bottom of the mountain, to where the towering outline of one of the biggest men I'd ever seen in my life cast a long shadow across the ground. He loved me. They *all* did. I glanced around, that fear still trembling inside me. I wasn't sure why they loved me...or how.

But I was learning.

I licked my lips, wetting my mouth. "Again?"

Thomas shook his head. "Not for me. I'm about to have a damn heart attack."

Riven jerked his head toward the house. "You guys go ahead. I'm going to grab my gun and hit the range with Hunter."

He wiped the sweat from his palms on the back of his pants. Tight, ribbed stomach muscles drew my focus. He was leaner now, harder on himself in the days since the attack. Almost punishing himself when he barely ate and ran almost all the time. Unless he was shooting with his brother.

He gripped the back of my neck and pulled me closer before he kissed me. Salty lips smashed against mine. I opened my mouth, dropped my guard, and gave myself to the sensation.

The sharp breeze snatched at my hair, cooling the sweat on my skin. My nipples tightened, that heady rush brewing like a storm inside me, until he broke away, staring into my eyes.

"You okay?"

I took a second to search my thoughts before I answered. "Yeah."

"Good." He hinted a smile, then stepped away. "I'll see you later."

"I'll see you later." I repeated.

But he was already gone, striding away along the edge of the ridge as Hunter headed in the same direction from the base.

Thomas watched me for a second, then turned, moving slow enough down the ridge for me to catch up. My foot slipped, leaving me to skid and run until I reached the bottom.

"Showers?" I asked, but I didn't wait for him to answer, just strode toward the house.

I was aware of him, his steps crunching behind me, his breaths at my back as I opened the back door and headed inside. I yanked my shirt over my head as I kicked off my sneakers, pushed them aside, and headed for the front of the house and the stairs.

Thud.

Thud.

Thud.

I climbed, stopping at the top of the stairs before I turned around. "Thomas...I..."

He grabbed me and his powerful hands gripped my chin as he stared into my eyes. I could melt in them, searching the glistening soft brown for the sparks that ignited. My lips parted as I waited for him to lean close and press his soft lips to mine.

But he didn't. He just waited, like he always did, hovering in the corner of the room or in the doorway, watching me with Hunter or me with Riven and Kane. He was always watching, always waiting...always...*yearning.*

"I'll go shower." He said carefully, lowered his hand, then slowly stepped away.

The pang in my chest was instant, watching him walk away like that...like he...deserved the pain. I opened my mouth to speak, but he was gone, stepping into the room at the far end of the hall, the hiss of the shower coming seconds later.

I made for Riven's room, working the hooks of my bra, then shoved down my shorts and peeled off my socks. The hot water was soothing, running over my shoulders and my hair. I washed and shampooed, then switched the water off.

I ached for him.

I looked toward the door, knowing he was in there feeling the same for me. *So why the fuck won't he give in?* My pulse raced and my breaths deepened. I licked my lips, telling myself my hunger had been sated with the others. I ran my fingers through my damp hair, then dropped them to my breasts, remembering last night.

God, they'd sated me.

Still, The Priest.

The Priest wouldn't give in.

He lingered at the edges of my subconscious, like a tiny burr in my shoe. I needed this burr, desperate to pluck it free from where it was nestled deep in the soft padding of my mind. These were my favorite shoes, ones I'd longed for my entire life.

"That's it." I dropped my hands and strode out of the bathroom, naked.

Until I stopped.

On the floor next to the bed were the cuffs Riven had used on me when he'd chained my ankles as well, until they'd spread my knees wide, leaving me exposed. I couldn't get out of them, and if I couldn't, maybe they were perfect for...

"Him." I whispered. My pulse raced as the image of him bound filled me.

I snatched them from the floor and walked into Thomas' room, watching him step out of the bathroom as he toweled his hair dry, with one wrapped around his waist. A quick glance around his room and I grabbed the hard-backed chair pushed out from behind his desk.

"Helene." He murmured. "What are you—"

I dragged the chair with me, stopping in the middle of his room. "Sit." I commanded.

His confusion shifted as his gaze met my stare, and in that instant, a desperate longing gave way between us. His lips parted, a rush of breath escaping. I left the chair, carrying the cuffs with me. My fingers trembled as I ran them along the chain to the cuffs. One snap and I closed one around his wrist.

A deep, shuddering moan rumbled in the back of his throat. I moved to his other hand, pulled them behind him, and snapped the cuff shut.

"Sit." My demand was breathless.

I hadn't realized how exhilarating this would be. To have a powerful man like Thomas so...controlled. He took a step, barely needing me to guide him, and sat on the chair, the towel parting to expose those strong thighs as he did. I looked down at the soft hair there as I bent to one side of the chair and grasped the other end of the chain with its own pair of cuffs.

He jerked as I pulled, bowing his shoulders back to clasp the other pair around his ankles. "Your brother used these on me once. Did you know that?"

He met my stare as I rose, those amber eyes brighter than I'd ever seen them. One shake of his head and I knew...he wanted this. I'm not like the others. His own words echoing in my head. We'd shared a moment in hell trapped in the tunnel under

Coulter's mansion. A moment when he'd revealed how he couldn't handle a feather-light touch.

But this—I looked down to where the outline of his cock grew bolder under the parted towel—this he liked a lot.

"You want to pray for me now, Thomas?" I murmured as I moved around the front of the chair to the other side and knelt. "Or do you want to pray for yourself?"

His eyes fluttered closed.

"After all, it's what you do best."

I'd heard him at night, spending hours on his knees, desperate for whoever he believed in to protect those he loved. My name was repeated...*often*.

He flinched as my breath brushed his thigh.

That sound came again, wounded and desperate, rumbling in the back of his throat. Half a whimper...and half a purr.

I reached down and slid my fingers along the taut muscles of his stomach until I grasped his hard cock. "Go on, Priest, pray."

"Please." He whispered and opened his eyes. "Please..."

TWO

Thomas

"PLEASE," I WHISPERED.

Need.

Need.

Need her.

Crave her.

Don't give in.

Don't give...

She dropped, moving into my view. I turned my head, unable to let her see...*how much she truly affected me.*

"It's okay," she murmured softly, her hand wrapped around my cock.

I'd tried to fight this, tried to fight her. But it was too much...too much...*too much.*

"Look at you." She clenched her grip, and I twitched with the sensations.

The roughness of the towel against my skin.

The strength of her fingers around my cock.

"Hands bound, knees spread, just like I was," she murmured.

That thick vein twitched, shooting electricity all the way to the head. I was going to come like this, bound, helpless...completely at her mercy. "I...I can't," I whispered, that feeble fight inside me trying one last time to pull away from her.

"Shh..." She pressed her fingers to my lips.

I opened my mouth on instinct, and my sick need finally won out. Her finger slipped inside. But the sensation had me reeling. The feel of her soft flesh against the edge of my teeth made me wince until she yanked down, opening my mouth further.

"That's it." She stared into my eyes, then glanced toward the bed. There was my collar, white, starched, sitting on the end. She pulled her finger out of my mouth and leaned over, her body stretched out in front of me.

God, she was beautiful.

The bruises on her side were a gruesome blue tinged with yellow-green. I could almost make out the shape of a fist against her ribs. But she was here, surviving, grabbing the collar from the bed, and turning back to me.

"Open," she commanded.

I could only obey.

A tremor raced as I lifted my gaze to hers. But instead of panic and the overwhelming need to escape, I felt a peacefulness, a sense of...*belonging*—her perfect lips curled at the edges—*belonging to her*. That smile widened. One just for me. Every cell in my body reacted, making me yield to whatever she wanted.

The hard creased fabric of the collar slipped between my lips. I bit down, feeling the collar pull tight against the edges of my mouth, leaving only the heavy gasps of my breath behind.

"You like this?" she asked.

I nodded, tugging at the binds around my wrists, testing their hold.

She reached up, gently fisting a handful of my hair. "Tell me," she commanded.

"Yes." The word was muffled and strained.

One yank and she pulled my head backwards. The wounded sound that tore from me wasn't human.

"Christ, you're beautiful," she whispered, looking down at me. "When you're mine like this."

My cock twitched, and my ass clenched, aching to thrust. This was where I belonged, under her touch and control. She looked down. But I couldn't look away, fixed by her focus as the towel wrapped around me shifted. Cool air tickled as it danced around the warmth of my body. Her breath caught before she slowly reached down. Her fingers grazed the length of my cock as she swept the covering aside.

I'd never allowed a woman to look at me like she did.

Until now.

Now my spine bowed, the cuffs around my wrists and ankles pulled taut as I thrust my hips harder, desperately aching for her touch.

She bent and lowered her head, the strands of her damp hair falling to smack my bare thighs.

Warmth wrapped around me. Wet, slick warmth that trailed along the thick shaft then slipped around the head. I unleashed a whimper and opened my eyes, looking down. But all I saw was her head.

"I...I want to watch you." I croaked.

She pulled away, lifting her gaze to mine before she moved between my legs and knelt. "How's this?" She lowered her head once more and opened her mouth.

Dear God in Heaven...

My thighs tensed, my balls quivered, watching as she gripped the base and slid my cock all the way inside her mouth. My eye twitched as I slid along her tongue to push against that soft flesh at the back of her throat. Her breasts pushed against my knees. I strained in reflex and my fingers twitched, desperate to touch.

I made a muffled sound against the collar that was a gag in my mouth, until she eased her hold.

"Your breast," I urged. "In my mouth."

She lifted her gaze, meeting mine. But she never moved, just skirted her tongue around the ridge of my head, then dragged the tip all the way down. The vein pulsed as the overwhelming need to fuck made me pant.

The gag was forgotten. She had other things on her mind.

"Whimper for me, Priest," she said, shifting her focus as she licked and sucked, dipping low to draw my balls into her mouth.

"Oh, fuck..."

Her cheek twitched with a smile. I pulled against the cuffs, but I had no control here. No way for me to take it either. I was completely at her mercy. A shudder tore through me at the thought. I licked my lips. "Whatever you want, My Queen." I dropped my head backward. "Whatever you want."

She rose, her hands moving to each side of me. "I want your ass on the floor and your head back against the bed. That's what I want. I want your tongue inside me as I ride your face. What do you think about that?"

"Yes." I moaned, dragging my teeth against the soft flesh of my lip.

She rose, then moved around behind me. One *snap* of the lock and the cuff fell free. I pushed myself forward. My knees were shaking so badly they barely held my weight. I slipped to the floor in front of the chair, looking up at her.

She dragged the chair aside and stepped around it. The last feeble hold of the towel came away, leaving me naked as I squirmed on the floor. Helene looked down at me, desire burning in her eyes.

"Head back, Thomas." She demanded.

I pushed my shoulders back as she moved toward me, her fingers spearing through my hair as she pressed her body against me. I turned my head, kissing her thigh. This wasn't like before when my emotions got the better of me. This was...easy.

She fisted my hair and tugged backwards, forcing my gaze to hers. "You sure you want this?"

My cock was so rock hard I thought I was going to come. "I'm about to make a mess of myself if you don't."

She looked down, and my cock jumped. Christ, one look from this woman and I lost myself. She moved against me, lifting her knee to one side of the bed, opening herself to me. I looked down at the soft, pale flesh of her inner thighs.

Faint silver razor marks marred the flesh. She'd cut herself, releasing all her pain and anger out on her own body. The moment I saw them, I knew she was the one. I lifted my gaze, meeting her stare. The one who would make me fall in love. She released her grip, leaving me to lean forward until I brushed my lips across her skin.

She let out a soft sound, almost a sigh.

Such a tiny thing.

I wanted more of that.

My lips moved, gliding across her abdomen until I lowered my head, brushing the soft hair of her mound.

"Higher," I murmured.

She did, lifting her knees higher and pushing forward until my head pressed back on the bed. All I saw was her, pale flesh, soft brown bush. I tilted my head, opening my mouth and licked, finding her warmth. She was still too far away. "Closer."

She pressed harder, giving me what I wanted. I pulled against the cuffs, tugging hard until the links snapped taut.

This was what I wanted. Her scent invaded my lungs. Her taste lingered on the tip of my tongue. I was desperate for more. I bent my head, pushing my tongue along her slit until I hit the tiny ridge of her clit. Her hips jolted forward, pushing me back.

I sucked, drawing a whimper from her, but it wasn't enough. "Ride me, Helene. *Ride.*"

Adrenaline kicked through me. I knew she was looking down, watching me as she slowly and gently bucked her hips forward. It was all I needed. I lowered my head, spearing my tongue deep inside.

"Oh, fuck." She moaned and reached down, grasping my hair.

Oh, sweet Jesus, Jesus.

That's it.

That's so it.

I dragged my tongue upward to croak. "Use me."

She did, clenching her grip, forcing my head back down to where she wanted my tongue. I licked and sucked, my cock pulsing as she grew wetter. Fuck, she was beautiful. She was so goddamn beautiful. I closed my eyes, my chest throbbing as well as my cock.

Hunger consumed me. A kind I'd never felt before, making me moan like that last lick was my dying breath. I swallowed the taste of her, desperate for this woman to invade every inch of my body and felt her push harder, grinding her perfect pussy against my mouth before she jerked away.

Her eyes were wide. Hard, panting breaths rose and fell.

"I want to fuck you." She gasped.

"Then do it."

Her body trembled as she slowly sank to the floor and straddled me. I'd watched her fuck my brothers. The savage desperation she had with Riven. His hands around her throat, or buried in her hair. Her on her knees for Kane. His cock thrusting into her mouth...and the tender moments with Hunter as he guided his body inside her.

But this was different. She reached down, grasped my thick length, and seated herself down, allowing me to slide all the way in. Her eyes closed and her head dropped backward as she ground her hips, rocking forward to push me even deeper.

This was me on my knees for her.

"Oh fuck, Thom." She moaned and opened her eyes, holding on to my stare.

But I was coming apart. My legs pushed as wide as the chains would allow. My fingers spread wide, desperate to touch her.

"Bounce." I groaned. "For the love of God, bounce."

She did, rising only to slide back down *hard*.

"*Ohhh.*" I groaned. "*Again.*"

She did, slamming her body against mine and thrusting forward until I rubbed that spot inside her.

"Oh..." she wailed, dropping her head forward, thrusting harder. "*Godddd.*"

Her core clenched around me, pulsing and milking until stars exploded behind my eyes. She wrapped her arms around my shoulders, crushing me, and still it wasn't enough. My pulse pounded louder as I turned my head, drawing in the scent of her.

I was in love with this woman.

Maybe I hadn't been at first, but this need was roaring louder than I'd ever experienced before.

"I...I want more of this," I whispered.

She eased backwards and stared into my eyes. "You do?"

My heavy breaths fluttered her hair. "I do."

Her smile was instant.

"Well, that was...*different.*"

I jerked my gaze to the doorway, to where Riven leaned against the door, watching us.

"Riven." I jerked my hands, testing the links of the chains.

"Don't get up on my account, brother." He moved that possessive stare at Helene. "I'm just glad you're on board now. I want you to fuck her. I want you to love her."

He pushed off from the frame and strode forward, looking down at her. He reached out, brushing the hair from her face before he met my stare. "Now you understand what we're fighting for. This..." he brushed his thumb across her cheek. "This right here is everything."

THREE

Helene
_____

"*T*HIS RIGHT HERE..." RIVEN LOOKED DOWN AT ME AS HE brushed his thumb along my cheek. "Is everything."

That pang ripped across my chest with his words. There was nothing like the love from this man...so controlling and consuming, one I'd never felt before. To find one like him was almost impossible.

But to find four?

That could only be fate.

"I know," Thomas murmured, drawing me back to him.

I still straddled his body, his cock now soft inside me. Still, my core pulsed from the work of his tongue. I reached around, unclasping the cuffs one by one, before I reached behind me to his ankles, letting the chain fall away.

"We have to go," Riven murmured, and lifted his other hand with his cell.

Thomas pushed upwards. "Now?"

Riven gave a nod.

"Do we have a lead?" Thomas asked.

"We have *something*." But it was that look in Riven's eyes that worried me, especially when he turned that careful stare to mine. "We leave in thirty."

I turned to Thomas the moment Riven headed for the door. I knew my priest had seen it, as well. The glint of fear, and the apprehension in his brother. Riven didn't *do* apprehension. He was all fury. All rage. Unleashing everything like a goddamn tornado.

"Is this it?" I asked him.

"I dunno." He searched my stare. "But it's something."

He held my hips as I pushed upwards, while Riven's heavy steps ricoched along the hall.

"Do you need...can I help?" he asked awkwardly.

I just smiled, reached out, and ruffled his hair. "It's okay. I got this."

I bent down, grabbed the cuffs, and took a step before stopping. "You good with the chair?"

There was a chuckle, one I loved hearing before I headed back to Riven's room and went toward the bathroom. The shower was hissing, the steam already filling up the room.

"There's a lead," I said carefully, stepping back into the shower with him.

He scrubbed his hair, sluicing the shampoo from the strands before he lifted his gaze as rivulets of water ran down his forehead to cascade alongside his nose.

"More like a potential lead, or a problem."

"A problem?"

He washed, scrubbed under his arms, and ran his hands over his chest before he stilled. "Look...just, stay with me or Hunter, okay? You'll be okay...I promise." He reached up to cup my face and leaned in, kissing me. "Your cunt looked good on my brother's face, Trouble. I hope to see it there more often." Then he dropped his hands and stepped away, leaving me alone in the spray.

I washed again, scrubbing between my legs before I switched the water off. I wasn't on the pill and thanks to that piece of shit, that *dead* piece of shit, I could now get pregnant. I would have at least...until my lovers took matters into their own hands. I hadn't even asked them to do what they did. Still, I went with them, sitting in the waiting room while each of them went in and walked out with legs wide apart twenty minutes later.

We came home that day. I took care of each one as they lay back on their beds with a cold pack nestled against their balls. There was ice cream and smoothies, back rubs and gentle kisses. But that was just over a week ago...and now...now you'd never know they'd had any snip at all.

It was a big thing.

For me.

But not for them.

Drawers closed in the bedroom. I hurried drying once more, but by the time I stepped into the bedroom, he was gone. I grabbed underwear, then pulled on jeans and a t-shirt before socks and my boots. There was something wrong with this. Very wrong.

I headed downstairs, meeting Kane and Thomas in the entrance as Hunter came from the rear of the house with a duffel bag over his shoulder.

The zipper was open, black steel shone from inside. I knew an arsenal when I saw one. "Expecting trouble?

"Always," Hunter answered, and headed out.

This was strange. I glared at Riven, but he didn't stay, just headed out after his brother, leaving the rest of us to follow.

"What the hell is going on?" I hissed to Kane.

He stared straight ahead and muttered. "Who the hell knows."

It looked like I wasn't the only one left clueless.

We walked out, climbed into Hunter's Hummer, and yanked the doors closed. My stomach clenched as we left the safety of the compound. Behind these walls, we were safe and the outside world, with all the terror waiting for us, ceased to exist. But I knew more than anyone that the outside world was hunting us and it was only a matter of time before it found exactly where we were.

Kane reached across the seat and grasped my hand. The smile he gave me was quick and careful. I wanted to smile back at him, but I couldn't, not until I knew what we were dealing with.

Stay with me or Hunter, okay?

Riven was expecting trouble. They both were.

But if it was that dangerous, then why meet at all?

I pushed my spine against the seat, my thoughts returning to my sisters.

That's why we'd meet.

For them.

In the weeks since the attack at Coulter's mansion, Vivienne had returned home. She was due to give birth any day now. London and the sons were beside themselves with worry, watching her every second of the day and night. We were racing her body, desperate to find where Hale and that fucking bitch Melody hid behind the rest of the Order's Sons, to destroy them before my niece and nephew were born into this world.

They deserved a world where they were safe.

A world where they knew nothing but love.

Not this world...not yet, at least.

"Turn here." Hunter said, drawing my focus.

One glance along the street filled with razor-wire-topped fences, casually lurking armed guards, and massive dogs, and I knew instantly where we were. It was the same compound where they'd brought the other Daughters the day we were taken from the Order.

Hunter's men lived here. They trained and hunted, scouring the dark web for men like Haelstrom Hale so we could take them out one by one when the Order fell. It was falling now, but with Hale gone, there was no coming back of the Order... the old one or the new.

Headlights splashed along the steel gate. It slowly rolled open. We headed into the compound, but before we could even get out of the four-wheel drive, Ollie, Hunter's new second-in-command, strode out with a phone in his hand.

"The meeting's been moved." He said, handing the phone through the window.

"What the fuck do you mean, moved?" Riven snapped.

"Exactly what he says." Came the careful male voice on the other end of the line. "Now drive."

Riven jerked his gaze down to the cell in his hand. The car was silent. Not even a breath...from me, at least.

Daughter?

The faint word echoed in my mind. The memory of that night in Coulter's mansion pushed in. I tried to shake it off, focusing instead on that voice. I knew him...*somehow?*

"Take Madison south all the way to the Juncture." Came the stony instruction.

Hunter shoved the Hummer into gear, then punched the accelerator, pulling us back out of the compound and into the street. One hard glare toward Riven, and we shot forward. Silence filled the vehicle. All we had was the throb of the engine and the sound of the tires as we made for the Juncture.

"Take Wilder, then First Street to Prefect North. There's an alley between the dry cleaners and a closed down accountants, take it."

Hunter's jaw flexed. He didn't like this. None of us did.

But we had no idea what we were here for.

Headlights blurred from the oncoming cars, casting a kaleidoscopic view as we turned. The rain grew harder, pummeling the windshield with heavy drops. I shook my head, glancing at Kane and Thomas. It was too eerie, too similar to that day...*the day I'd stepped in front of Riven's car.*

"Here," came the growl on the other end of the line.

We were turning before I knew it, pulling into the darkness of the alley.

"To the end. I'll be waiting."

The Hummer slowed, pulling into the tight space.

"Goddamn fucking games," Riven muttered as Hunter stopped the four-wheel drive.

The headlights glinted off a steel door at the end of the alley. One that opened...

Hunter climbed out. His hand moved to his side, but Kane and Thomas didn't move...not even when Riven followed Hunter, climbing out of the car with his gun in his hand.

My focus moved to that door as shadows spilled around a lone male as he stepped out and took a step toward us.

A cold, unforgiving shiver raced through me once more.

I knew instantly who he was.

Daughter?

I shook my head. "No…" I jerked my gaze toward Riven as he moved toward the Son. The one from Coulter's mansion…the one trained by the Order. "Riven…*stop!*"

I yanked the handle before lunging out. My pulse was booming as I hit the pavement.

"*Riven!*" I yelled.

But it was too late.

Headlights filled the alley behind me as the dark sedan pulled in and killed the engine, blocking us in. He was making a mistake here. He was making a *deadly mistake.*

"It's okay," Riven called as the Son stepped forward, those dark eyes moving to me.

But he wasn't okay.

"Daughter." The icy tone echoed behind me.

I spun as the rogue Son stepped closer and gripped my arm. His gaze went to the dangerous male standing at the door before turning back to me. "You weren't thinking about running again, were you?"

My breaths raced.

Panic moved through me as I met the unflinching stare of a killer. He was the one from Coulter's mansion. The one who'd lifted his foot and tripped the guard as he lunged for me.

"You," I whispered.

"Me," he said carefully, lowering his gaze. "I see you have clothes on this time…*pity.*" He met my stare. "You looked good, bathed in the blood of your enemies."

FOUR

Riven
_____

SHE SHOULDN'T BE HERE.

The Son's dark eyes glinted as he looked her up and down, standing still as the rain fell. "I see you have clothes on this time. Pity. You looked good bathed in the blood of your enemies."

I took a step forward, not caring about the rain falling into my eyes. "You wanted to meet." Forcing the words through clenched teeth. "So let's fucking meet."

The Son's lips curled into a smile before he slowly looked my way, then casually sauntered straight past me, heading for the open door of this fucking place.

These goddamn Sons.

They were starting to piss me the hell off.

Helene's eyes were wide, her gaze fixed on him. Maybe this whole goddamn meet was a bad idea after all? I turned toward the open door as Hunter moved. But there was only one way to find out.

"Trouble." I turned my head and murmured over my shoulder. "Remember what I said. Stay with Hunter."

She didn't even argue, which said a lot. Instead, she headed for my brother, sinking into the shadow he left behind. It was a bad idea bringing her here. Part of me hated myself for using her one last time. But I'd be a fool to think we'd win this war without every man or woman who was willing to align with us...and that included the Sons, even if they came for her alone.

I headed deeper into the building, kicking an old sewing machine as I made my way inside. I glanced down, then slowly looked around. Rusted mechanical hangers hung overhead, a bank of ancient sewing machines, and what looked like the remnants of a steam press ran along the wall.

"So, we're here." I tore my gaze from the machines of the abandoned dry cleaners and scanned the room, finding no one else but us.

What the fuck?

My attention was drawn to the far end of the room to where I swore I saw a shift in the shadows, until the Son from the alley stepped out of the shadows behind Helene. My lip curled, watching the bastard flank her side, drawing her focus.

"Four men," he said quietly, his attention solely on her. "That's all you brought with you?"

There was a tremble in her body, drawing my attention to how her wet fucking shirt was stuck to the swell of her breasts. All I saw was her racing breaths and it was all because of that *motherfucker* right there. That...walking, talking, cold-as-fuck machine who seemed to have some kind of control over her.

A control I didn't like.

Not one goddamn bit.

"I didn't realize it was a fucking interview of the strength of our numbers." I jerked a glare to Hunter as the Son lifted his hand, his curled fingers reaching for her cheek before my goddamn brother finally moved.

What the fuck was this Son's deal?

No...

Not this one.

She belongs to us.

My own words came roaring back from that auction room in Coulter's mansion as they'd tried to take her then, just as they were trying to take her now.

His attention snapped my way. "Everything is a *goddamn interview.*"

I took a step closer. "You wanted us here, so we're here." I tried not to look at her, to see the way she looked at him, like she was somehow in a trance. "Now, tell us what we want to know... *where the fuck is Haelstrom Hale?*"

He fixed that unflinching stare on me. "You think you can win this war?"

"We have so far." My words were cold, leaving no room for doubt.

There was a *humph* before he glanced at Helene and took a step backwards. "You need more men, Principal, if you're planning on surviving." He gave a shrug, his gaze fixed on the woman I loved. "Either way, know she will be protected."

Helene went deathly still. Hunter, on the other hand, stepped in front of her, blocking the Son's view.

"Give us Hale's location." I stepped toward him. *"Give it to us now!"*

Lightning flickered outside, the neon flash shining through the open door to the alley. Movement shifted in the corner, drawing my focus for barely a fucking heartbeat. But by the time I looked back, the Son was gone.

"What the fuck?" I stepped forwards. "Where did he go?"

He was gone. Like nowhere to be seen gone.

I raced to the steel door that led to the alley, yanked it wide, and rushed out. Even the car parked behind the Hummer had disappeared like it hadn't been there at all. Like none of them had been.

"Fuck!" I roared as rain fell into my eyes. Thunder snarled overhead, unleashing my frustration into the sky. I spun around, finding Hunter in the doorway. "They're gone." I headed back toward them. "They're all fucking gone."

"So what now?"

I shook my head as my cell vibrated, giving a *beep*. I didn't even have to look at it to know who it was. Heavy breaths consumed me as I waited for that savage hunger to ease. "We leave."

I headed back out into the pouring rain, feeling like a goddamn failure. I didn't do *failure*. Not like this.

"Riven!" Helene called my name. I winced and kept walking. But she was so goddamn stubborn. Her boots smacked on the pavement as she ran. *Boom...boom...boom.*

"Hey!" She grabbed my arm, yanking me around.

"What?" I barked. "What the fuck do you want, Helene?"

She stopped, her eyes widening. Her throat muscles worked hard as she tried to swallow her pain. But she couldn't. It shone in her goddamn eyes. I looked away. Her perfect, fucking eyes. I racked my hands through my sodden hair as rivulets of water ran down my temples and stuck my shirt to my body.

She was affected by these Sons in a way I couldn't understand. Did she fucking want them, was that it? Was she somehow genetically modified to want them over...over someone like me?

That nagging thought just wouldn't leave me alone. It wasn't about Hale in that moment, or the fucking goddamn war we were staring down the barrel at, it was about her. *It was always about her.*

I spun around and my hand instantly moved to her throat as I pushed her against the side of the Hummer. But there was no strength in my grip. My thumb stroked the base of her throat. "Do you want him...him. Do you want him over me?" I asked carefully.

But inside I was bellowing the words *DO YOU WANT THEM OVER ME?*

Raindrops smacked against her cheek before they raced to her jaw and fell away. Still, she didn't answer. Just stared at me with those dark-colored eyes. The small shake of her head was a lie. I knew that.

"I...I don't know," she said carefully. "I don't want to, but I feel drawn to them somehow. Like I'm supposed to want them."

"Do you?" I searched for the truth. "Do you want them?"

If she said yes, what then? My pulse was thundering.

"No," she said, that stare fixed on mine. "I want you. I want you and Hunter and Kane and Thomas. That's who I want..."

My knees shook, causing me to fall forward and collapse against the car. I dropped my head to her shoulder, pressing against the warmth of her body.

"It's going to be okay," she murmured, her fingers sliding through my wet hair as she held me.

My voice was a croak. "I don't need your sympathy."

"It's not sympathy, Riven. It's love."

I froze, then slowly lifted my gaze.

"It's love, you stubborn fool." She wrapped her arms around me, pressing her cheek to my chest.

My heart was racing as I closed my eyes. To die in this goddamn battle was one thing, but to lose her...that was un-fucking-bearable.

She just refused to give up, didn't she? Always fighting for my goddamn heart or my soul. I looked down at the wet strands of her hair and the paleness of her skin and that ache inside my chest howled in desperation.

Beep.

My cell vibrated in my pocket, drawing my focus.

"Come on." I captured her chin, forcing her gaze to mine. "Let's get you out of this fucking rain."

I opened the car door, holding it as she climbed inside. My brothers followed. The engine started the moment Hunter was behind the wheel. But it was that empty building we left behind that drew my gaze. I turned my head, finding the open door.

Why ask us here if the Sons already knew we didn't have enough to fight Hale? What was their fucking goal? Something crawled inside me, remembering the way he'd looked at my woman. He was testing us, poking and prodding, finding out exactly how far we were prepared to go.

I turned, rounding the rear of the four-wheel drive and opened the door, climbing inside. I guess all the talking meant nothing. It was time to show them.

"St. James'." I yanked the door closed behind me.

"We're going to see Vivienne?" Helene asked.

I gave a nod, finally pulling my cell from my pocket. "We are, Trouble. We are."

I glanced at the screen.

London: We're all here.

I typed out a response. *We're on our way.*

Then hit send.

It was time to show everyone.

FIVE

Helene

DO YOU WANT HIM OVER ME?

The question still lingered as I climbed into the Hummer. I answered him, but Riven didn't believe me. I knew that because he refused to meet my gaze as he closed the door.

Thud.

Water ran down the sides of my nose. Thomas and Kane were quiet beside me. Even Hunter flicked those dark eyes my way, watching me in the rear-view mirror. He said nothing as Riven climbed into the seat, just shoved the four-wheel drive into gear and pulled back out of the alley.

I didn't want the Sons.

Adrenaline surged inside, making my pulse race and my thoughts freeze. It wasn't desire...but it was *something*.

"You okay?" Thomas murmured beside me.

I looked his way, desperate for solace, and found love. I didn't want those others. But how could I describe that pull toward them? It was like gravity was lopsided, like somehow my balance was off and I felt myself falling whenever they were around.

I didn't want them.

I turned away, staring at the bright lights reflected in the puddles on the edge of the road. Vivienne would know how this felt. She'd know exactly what to say. I lifted my gaze as we left the towering buildings behind, making for the quiet residential streets where those who had money lived.

It was a Mafia neighborhood. Dark sedans sat on street corners. Armed men paid to keep watch for trouble. We were trouble. I was, anyway. I glanced at the back of Riven's head. Trouble for them. That panicked fluttering in my chest grew bolder. Trouble for them and everyone else who loved me.

We turned once more. My focus shifted to the massive, opulent house at the end of the cul-de-sac. Flashes of memories invaded and terror followed as we pulled up alongside the curb and parked. A black Mustang was parked in the driveway...was Ryth here as well?

I fumbled for the clasp on my seatbelt and yanked open the door, shoving it wide as I clambered from the vehicle. But Riven never called my name, just let me race along the driveway that ran down the edge of the path until two armed gunmen stepped out from the corner of the house.

"You're clear to go in, Ms. King." One gave a nod and stepped to the side. "Mrs. St. James is expecting you."

Mrs. St. James.

I doubt I'd ever get used to that. My little sister was now a married woman. I forced a smile and made for the back door, yanked it open, and rushed through. *"Viv! Vivvv!!"*

Movement came from the doorway to the kitchen. Guild stepped out, carrying a tray of coffee and two neat sandwiches. He lifted his gaze. "Helene."

I glanced around. "Is everything okay? Where is everyone?"

"They're in the gym."

"The gym?" What the fuck...

He started walking. But the creak of the door behind me and the heavy steps that followed drew my gaze. Riven and Hunter stepped in. Kane and Thomas followed as I turned back and started walking, hurrying to catch up to Guild as he made for the east wing of the house.

"What the hell is going on in the gym?"

"You'll need to see it to understand," he muttered.

Riven and Hunter caught up as we strode along the hallway, all the way to the end.

"Over there!" Vivienne called out. "Carven...you're doing it wrong!"

I stepped into the doorway of what used to be a fully equipped gym to find...chaos.

A blow-up pool sat in the middle of the space. Vivienne stood next to it with a pissed off look on her face. Carven carried the biggest punching bag I'd ever seen heaved onto his shoulders to carry it where I wasn't quite sure. I glanced at Ryth, holding her baby, and Nick and Tobias, who were not even trying to cover their smirks as Viv waddled toward Carven.

"What's going on here?"

She stopped, then slowly spun around. Her smile was instant, highlighting the dark circles under her eyes. "What do you think?" She waved her hand around the room.

I stepped closer as Carven gave a grunt and heaved that bag into the corner of the room and dropped it with a *thud*. "It's..." I started, looking around the room trying to understand exactly what I was looking at. "It's lovely."

Viv scowled, then followed my stare. "It's not lovely, Hel...it's a birthing room."

I jerked my gaze to hers and my eyes widened. "A birthing room?"

"Yeah." She said slowly, concern creasing her brow. "You know." She waved her hand over her massive belly. "Where you give birth."

Ryth just chuckled before she handed over my nephew to Tobias and headed our way. She still walked slower, favoring her side. But she was alive...and with us. I opened my arms as she neared and wrapped one arm around her, waiting for Viv to step close and complete the circle. She did, all belly and the scent of Chanel.

I closed my eyes, my arms wrapped around my sisters.

My...sisters.

I'd waited for what felt like a lifetime for this moment. I'd dreamed about it, ached for it, and for a long time watched as it slipped through my fingers as I lost my sisters to the Order.

Still, I'd fought. I'd fought for them when I no longer had the strength to fight for myself.

Riven cleared his throat gently behind me.

Now I didn't have to fight alone.

"Riven." Nick's deep voice followed.

"Nick...London." Riven answered.

I lifted my head and opened my eyes as the *birthing room* was filled with men armed to the teeth. The plastic pool, covered with cartoon palms and beach balls, half filled with water looked so out of place here. A terrifying reminder of just what we were up against.

War...

And my sister's body.

"The meet," London started. "Want to tell me exactly what happened?"

"Nothing happened." Riven drew everyone's attention. "They seem to have decided we're the losing side."

"Motherfuckers," Tobias muttered. "Fuck them, we don't need them."

"Don't be an idiot," Kane snapped. "Of course we need them, take a look around the room. *We need everyone.*"

Riven glanced my way, anger and desperation shining in his eyes. Everyone saw. Including my sisters. Viv gave my hand a nudge, forcing my gaze to hers.

What happened? She mouthed.

I looked to Ryth. To the dark circles under her eyes and the permanent look of fear, and shook my head.

Viv smacked my hand even harder this time. *Don't lie to us.*

I was acutely aware of Carven, and Colt as he slipped into the room, carrying an armful of blankets and pillows to drop beside the pool.

The Sons. I mouthed, meeting my sisters' stares. *That's what happened.*

Ryth scowled, but Viv stiffened, her breath catching. She knew...

They tried to take you?

I started to shake my head and stopped. Did they try to take me? Yes, the answer was yes. But not by force. *Do you want him over me?*

"They want something," Kane continued. "We just need to find out what that something is and use it to our advantage."

"We *know* what they want," Hunter growled and glanced my way, and everyone else in the room followed.

Heat burned my cheeks. My stomach clenched. Betrayal was a heavy burden to wear. I didn't like it, not one goddamn bit.

"I don't want them." The words slipped free. "I don't know how many times I need to say it, but I'm saying it one last time and I'm hoping you'll remember this. *I. Don't. Want. Them.* I don't want any of them and I don't understand the hold they seem to have over me."

"Over *us*," Vivienne said quietly, lifting her gaze to London, then to each of the sons. "We all feel it."

It was Carven and Colt who reacted the most. Carven stalked to her, that hunger glinting in his stare. "Like a pull of gravity or a memory of each other. One we can't place. But we know it and we feel it."

He neared her, flanking her side. She was mesmerized by him as Colt also headed straight for her. She cupped Carven's cheek, staring into his eyes. "Yes."

My pulse raced at the sight of them. That connection. That desire raging inside them. Ryth's cheeks burned before she looked at Tobias and Nick. I wasn't sure she'd ever faced the Sons, not really. Not when they had their sights set on you.

But I had and I didn't like it one bit.

"If their aim is to find the Daughters, then we use that to our advantage," Kane murmured.

"They want them," Carven answered, staring into Vivienne's eyes. "They can't help themselves but want them. It's undeniable."

"So then we need to figure out how to get them onboard," London answered. "And we use you and Colt to do it."

Carven lifted his gaze, that twinkle of desire dying instantly. There was no love lost between the twins and others of their kind, men born into the Order and programmed to hunt and kill.

"Then we need more men," Carven answered. "They need to see we're the ones to align with. We need more men and we need more guns. That's how you'll win them over. We have to do the things we've been afraid to do. We have to lie and cheat and steal. We need to do whatever it takes to get every man and woman on our side."

Movement came from the doorway as Caleb slipped in, wiping the back of his knuckles with a handkerchief before slipping it into his pocket. Tobias and Nick looked his way. The nod he gave them wasn't lost on me, nor Ryth, as she took a step away from me and headed straight to him.

"Then we have a lot of calls to make," London said carefully.

Caleb wrapped his arms around Ryth, and leaned down to kiss her. But his lips didn't find hers. Instead, he moved to her ear, whispering something the rest of us couldn't hear. She stiffened, then jerked her gaze to his. I saw panic before she smothered it with a forced smile, then glanced my way.

What the hell was going on? She said nothing, only turned her gaze back to Caleb.

"We recruit anyone else willing to stand by our side." London said.

"And anyone else, we force them," Riven added. "We've been the bad guys before. But this...this is personal."

The entire room was utterly still. Not even the draw of a breath pierced the silence. Then in an instant, London turned around, found Vivienne, and gave a nod. "Playing the good guy was never my strong suit anyway."

Vivienne gave a soft, sad smile. I watched them, and the way they were so fiercely protective of her reminded me of my own life. I turned back to find Riven, then Hunter and Kane...but Thomas wasn't here. I glanced around the room. Caleb was gone, as well.

"Okay. That's that. We keep in touch and make sure everyone is updated. Let me know if you need anything."

"Same goes for you," Nick added, and glanced Riven's way. "Both of you."

We all moved, but I was the first to head for the door, leaving everyone else behind. Something was going on and it involved Thomas. I headed back along the east wing hallway to the foyer of the house, hearing voices coming from the kitchen.

I stepped inside, finding Caleb and Thomas standing on the other side of the middle island. Thomas' gaze was lowered, but Caleb's was fixed on him.

"What's going on?"

Thomas jerked his focus my way, his cheeks red.

"Nothing," Caleb answered, giving a smile as he patted Thomas on the shoulder. "Just catching up with Priest."

"It doesn't look like nothing to me, Caleb." I stepped closer. "I think you forget who you're dealing with here."

All of a sudden that smile died away, leaving the stare of a dangerous man behind. Caleb had been mysteriously absent these past few weeks. My sister made excuses, but I knew they were a lie. Caleb Banks was up to something and now he seemed intent on drawing the man I loved into whatever he was up to.

I wanted to know what it was.

"Water," Thomas muttered and turned away, went to the refrigerator, and yanked it open. "That's what I came for."

His hair was still damp. His white shirt was still so wet it stuck against his skin. "Haven't you had enough of that?" I asked as he let the door close and screwed the top off the bottle.

One large draw and he swallowed. But I wasn't buying this for one minute.

"C?" Tobias called his brother from the doorway. "You ready to head out?"

"Yeah." Caleb answered, giving me a smile, then flicked those dark eyes to Thomas. "Talk soon, yeah?"

Thomas just lowered his hand, met the lawyer's stare, and nodded.

They left, leaving their lies behind.

They wanted to hold to their schemes and their lies, that's fine.

We've been the bad guys before. Riven's words repeated. He had, that was for sure. I took a step, moving closer to my Priest and dragged my fingers through his hair, finding those beautiful brown eyes. But not my Thomas. He wasn't anything like the others. I wrapped my arms around him and pressed my cheek to his chest, knowing all that was about to change.

SIX

Thomas
_____

"Thom...you're quiet, buddy."

I jerked my gaze upwards, finding Hunter's stare in the rear-view mirror. Voices settled around me. The soft, bass-filled tone of Riven lingered as our headlights cut through the dark and we headed back to the sanctuary of the mountain house once more.

"You have a say in this, too," Riven added. "This affects all of us."

"I..." I said, my mind slow to shift gears, suddenly conscious of the weight of her stare.

Helene...

Hale.

We need you. Are you ready to hunt?

I tried to hide it. Tried to fight it. Tried to wrestle with the weight of right and wrong that weighed down my soul. "Don't know."

"You don't *know?*" Riven snarled. "What part of any of this is unclear for you?"

None of it.

I closed my eyes.

None.

Of.

It.

To act in self-defense was one thing, but to openly go to war and commit murder was a whole other thing. I wrestled with that demon. My fingers were in the beast's mouth, yanking down on its pointed fangs, opening that gaping hole wide. I could look all the way down its throat to the festering pit of its belly, into the depths of the darkness that waited for me.

It snarled and growled. Those bright red eyes fixed on mine, desperate to swallow me whole.

"Leave him." Hunter hit the turn signal and braked. "He has to come to terms with this on his own. Just like the rest of us have had to."

He glanced at me in the rear-view mirror once more. That intense stare from my brother implored me to do exactly what he said...come to terms with it. He pulled into the driveway and killed the engine. But the truth was, I wasn't sure if I could.

To react in the moment to defend yourself and those you love was one thing...but to hunt, to hurt and kill, was something else entirely.

We need you. Caleb's words echoed in my head. *You, me, and Benjamin Rossi. You can get us into places we can't go without you. But it's...it's dangerous.* A shiver raced up my spine at the words. *It's dangerous and bloody. Are you in, Priest? Are you ready to hunt?*

Are you ready to hunt?

I climbed out of the Hummer, glanced at Riven's gray Audi parked on the other side, and followed the others as they headed inside. Their voices carried, but I heard nothing. I was still locked in an embrace with the Devil. Red glowing eyes pierced mine. *Are you ready to hunt, Priest? Are you ready to... huunnnntttt.*

My footsteps hit the stairs, climbing after the others.

Helene stopped at the head of the stairs. She spoke, glancing my way. I didn't stop. Just gave her a nod. "Goodnight," I murmured and headed for my room, closing the door quietly behind me.

The chair still sat in the middle of the room I used, like a reminder of just how far I'd fallen.

Unseen ties tightened around my wrists.

Pray for me, Priest.

My pulse sped at her words. I turned, lifting my gaze to the doorway. *Pray,* that's exactly what I needed. I spun around, finding the white clerical collar on the end of the bed, my own bite marks still imbedded in the starched fabric. I grabbed it and my jacket from the desk and headed for the door.

They were gone by the time I stepped out. Their voices carried from Riven's room further along. But there wasn't a flicker of jealousy. Only desperation haunted me tonight. I gripped my jacket and hurried down the stairs.

Leave him, Hunter's voice replayed as I made for the front door, punched in the code, and waited for the locks to disengage before I slipped out. The locks gave a *thud* behind me. I hurried to Riven's Audi in the drive.

Movement came from above. The blinds shifted. The shadowed silhouette of my Hunter filled the window. I turned back, knowing he watched me as I climbed into Riven's car and pressed the button to start the engine. The keys were in the console. The sleek sports car was now used for trips into the city and war. I couldn't forget that, could I?

I met my own haunted stare in the rear-view mirror as I shoved the car into gear and backed out, turning hard before heading for the gate.

I was going to say no to Caleb.

I'd almost made up my mind.

Still, that Devil continued to plague me, wrapping long taloned fingers around my throat so he could stare into my eyes. *Are you really going to turn your back on your family? Are you going to turn your back on her...the woman you love?*

I jerked my wide eyes from the mirror, fixing them instead on the white line that blurred at the edge of the highway as I pushed the car harder, driving back into the city once more. My pulse was booming as I turned, taking the on-ramp deeper into the city, heading for the one place that gave me solace.

St. Sebastian's.

I turned the car again, took the off-ramp, and dipped low until I caught the glimpse of the bell tower through the trees.

YOUR GOD WON'T SAVE YOU HERE, PRIEST!

London St. James' roar boomed inside my head. I clenched the wheel, stilling the shakes, and turned into the street, pulling up at the base of the wide stony steps in front of the sandstone building. I sat there for a second, staring at this place of worship. A place that'd given me sanctuary and also the place of my near-death. Shadows hung at the looming bell tower, but the face of it was bright, illuminating the colored stained glass image of Jesus Christ.

It was that image that made me move to open the door and called me to step out. I moved in a trance, hitting the fob on the keyring to lock the car behind me. My boots echoed as I climbed and fixed my collar, buttoning it in place before I slid my jacket on.

I wanted to be present here, to fall to my knees and beg for guidance.

There was a war coming for us. One that wasn't going to stop until there was no one left to fight. I needed to make sure I was on the right side here. The only side salvation would allow. I gripped the curled black iron handle of the heavy double doors and pulled. Hinges creaked, and softly lit candles flickered at the front in the sanctuary. I pulled the door closed behind me and headed for the light.

This place was more than a haven. It was my one shining light in a world of darkness. Helene's face rose. I winced, swallowing down the weight of guilt. It should be her, but it wasn't. It was here amongst the hand-carved pews and the scent of frankincense and myrrh.

This was the first church I'd been assigned to. Father Peters had been hard and relentless. A massive man forced into a small, twisted frame. He'd had Multiple Sclerosis for four years by the time I'd asked to be sent here to be closer to my brothers. He couldn't walk by then and was confined to a wheelchair. Still, I'd taken care of him, staying in the rectory at the rear of the church. The same rectory I'd sought out after being beaten almost to death. When Father Peters passed, it had sent a shockwave through the community...and me.

He was the one person who'd understood me.

He'd never touched me.

Never talked down to me.

He made me work day and night helping people, until the work helped me. I'd told him about Melody, about the night of her abduction, and now the information my brothers had found. Information that pointed to a place called The Order.

He knew about The Order, knew the men who controlled the power, as well. His last words were a warning to me, *they are not men of faith.* They were not. But what man truly was now? Was I a man of faith?

I didn't know.

Not anymore.

"Thomas?"

I jerked my gaze to the confessional booth as a man stepped out. "Father Cassius."

His brow furrowed with concern. "A little late to be working, son."

I forced a smile, glancing at the candles. "Not working, Father. Just...seeking guidance."

"Ah," he motioned to the front pew. "I was just about to close up, but I have time to sit if you want to talk to me about it?"

I shifted my gaze to the confessional, wrestling with that Devil inside.

Are you ready to hunt?

My knees trembled as I stepped closer, leaving me to grasp the edge of the wooden seat before I sat down. Warmth closed around my hand as thick fingers squeezed mine tightly. I recoiled inside, desperately fighting the need to wrench my hand back, until finally he pulled away.

Shivers raced along my spine. "My soul is in trouble."

"Trouble? What kind of trouble?"

Get her to the table.

Let's see what four million dollars gets you.

Helene screamed and thrashed inside my head, fighting the men who pushed her head against the table and forced her legs apart. That shiver inside me turned to a quake of rage. "I find myself having thoughts of harm, especially to those who harm the people I love."

"That's only natural to have those thoughts. It's the whispers of temptation that come from the Devil. You know that."

I lifted my gaze to his. "And what if they're not just whispers?" *What if...they were screams?*

No!

NO!

Get off me!

GET THE FUCK OFF ME!

Father Cassius gave me a soft, careful smile. "I think you're stronger than you think. After all, you're here, aren't you?"

"There's bad men out there, Father." I whispered. "Real bad men and they want to hurt and keep on hurting. They're evil. They're so fucking evil they make my skin crawl. They need to be stopped. They need to be..."

You ready to hunt, Priest?

He flinched at my outburst. "Listen to me. You need to forget about them. You need to listen to your faith. Your place is here, within these walls. *That* is your purpose. *That* is your future. Turn your back on all others except for God, including your brothers. Only God will lead the way...his way."

A two-way radio hooked to his belt flicked to life, crackling faintly before he snatched it free and pressed the button to turn the volume down.

"His way is the only way," Cassius repeated, giving me a ghost of a smile. "Now, I really must go. It's late."

I gave a nod as I watched him rise, the two-way clutched in his hand. I'd never seen a priest with one before. "Thank you, Father." I lifted my gaze and met his stare. "I appreciate your words."

He gave a nod. I could still hear the sound from the device, the sound faint, so faint, before he turned away and headed for the door that connected to the rectory. His steps hit harder, moving faster. I tried to drag my focus away, forcing my attention to those flickering candles.

Candles others lit when they prayed.

My knees no longer shook when I stood.

Cassius's words took hold. He was right. This wasn't my battle to fight. No matter how dangerous this became, I wanted to find our sister, to ease that weight on my soul. But this...this was different. This was...*sin*.

I stepped forward, picked up a long, tapered candle, and lifted it to the flame.

But that two-way nagged at me. The way he'd snatched it free, the look of almost terror on his face as he'd fixed his eyes on mine...because, for a second...before his finger pressed down I was sure I'd heard the words *please, help me*.

My head turned on instinct, finding that door shrouded in shadows. A door I knew as well as my own heart. I placed the unlit candle down and took a step. The urge to walk to that door was overwhelming. My hand reached for the handle, and before I knew it, I was inside, closing the door behind me.

There was no sound at that moment. Only the steady thudding of my pulse in my head. I walked along the dark hallway that led to the house in the back.

"*No...no, please no!*" A woman's cry came from deeper inside.

"*You fucking whore. You dirty, sinful fucking whore. Do you know what God does to filthy whores like you? Filthy fucking*

51

Daughters. He saves them, that's what he does. Now wider...
WIDER!"

I froze, stopping in the middle of the hallway.

Whack!

A muffled shrill scream followed.

"Filthy fucking cunt. It deserves to be beaten. Open your legs,
Daughter. Open them or I'll shove this cane all the way in your
ass."

Revulsion rocked me. My gut clenched. My gaze fixed on that
doorway at the end. The one where the faint light shone from
inside. My hands curled into fists as I moved forward, until I
reached out and gripped the black iron handle, the one which
mirrored the entrance to the church.

Soundless.

The door swung inward.

The sight before me rocked me to the core.

He didn't see me.

His back was to the door. A woman lay on the bed, each ankle
tethered to the posts so her legs were spread wide. The cane in
his hand shone with blood as he raised it once more. All I saw
was that blood.

"Dirty fucking Daughter. Dirty goddamn whore," he said,
staring at the bleeding mess between her legs. *"You're all the*
same. Every single one of you. All the goddamn same!"

I reached out and grabbed the heavy gold cross sitting on the
dresser as he drove that cane down, carving an arc through the
air. Then I lunged and swung the cross.

CRUNCH!

The impact was sickening, slamming into the side of his head, throwing him sideways. His blow still hit, though, whipping into the soft flesh of her inner thigh. The woman moaned around the tape that'd come away from her mouth.

I inhaled, then glanced at the priest who clung to the bedpost she was tied to and felt that resounding quake of rage.

"God will show me the way," I said, my voice low and sinister. "That's what you said. *God will show me the way.*" I looked down at the heavy gold cross in my hand, now marked with blood. "I think I see the way now, Father. I think I see the way."

Are you ready to hunt now, Priest?

I clenched my fist around the cross, then looked at the unblinking eyes of the woman in front of me. Her legs spread, her body a goddamn mess.

Cassius lifted his head and turned his gaze toward me. Blood ran in a rivulet down his temple and fell into a crease as his eyes widened. "No," He hissed as I lifted the cross once more.

You ready to hunt, Priest?

I plunged the cross down, this time into the middle of his face.

CRACK!

His head snapped backward, blood spurted out of his nose. A front tooth cracked, falling into his mouth.

"*NO!*" He lifted his hands to protect himself. "*NO! NOOOO!*"

I drove that cross down again. His face became the face of so many. Hale, Coulter, and all those men who'd pushed Helene onto that table and spread her legs.

"You will *never touch her again!*"

Swing.

CRUNCH!

Swing.

CRUNCH!

Cassius slumped to the floor. Still it wasn't enough. I kept hitting, kept fighting. It wasn't the Devil who had hold of me. It was myself. The Devil was me. It was always me. Blood arced as I lifted the cross. There was no gold left now. Just a shimmering mess of red.

I sucked in hard breaths and pushed myself upwards, my gaze moving to the woman on the bed. *Daughter* he'd called her.

"Easy," I croaked and stumbled to her side, my hands moving to the ties at her ankles.

Flashes of the cuffs Helene had clamped around my own body came back to me. But that wasn't like this at all. I tugged them free and her feet hit the bed before her thighs clamped together. She was whimpering in pain and fear as I moved to her mouth.

"I'm not going to hurt you," I whispered. "I'm going to...*save you.*"

Those words beat like a drum inside my chest. I tugged the tape free, then moved to her hands, untying the bonds.

"I'm going to take you to someone who can help," I murmured as she turned on her side and tried to pull her knees to her chest.

There was a lot of blood on the sheets. The sight of that made me goddamn rage. I pulled my cell free and pressed the contact.

"Who's this?" Caleb answered on the second ring.

"It's me." I fixed my gaze on her. "I'm in...but first I need a favor from you."

"What kind of favor?"

"A damaged one."

SEVEN

Helene

A CREAK WOKE ME INSTANTLY. I OPENED MY EYES, MY pulse booming from a nightmare I couldn't quite remember. Somehow, I was glad for that, knowing whatever waited for me in the darkness wasn't something I wanted to face...not yet, at least.

Creak.

The sound came again. I sat up, leaving the warmth of Riven's bed behind. He was still snoring, deep in that faraway place. But there was a nagging feeling that called me, forcing me to climb out of bed and make my way to the bedroom door.

The moment I cracked it open, I saw him. Thomas, slowly making his way up the stairs. I moved out of the doorway, quietly closing the door behind me.

"Thom?" I whispered, my barely focused eyes fixed on the bright red blood splattered over his face and across the white clerical collar hanging from his shirt. "What happened?

He froze, almost at the top of the stairs, and lifted his gaze. Those once warm brown eyes were haunted, fixed on mine. Still, he said nothing, just held my gaze for what felt like forever until he climbed the last stairs to stop in front of me.

"You don't have to worry about me anymore." He lifted his hand, the edges of his nails stained with blood. Still, I didn't move as he grazed the back of his fingers down my cheek. "I found my calling. I know what I have to do."

Those words scared me. That and the emptiness in his stare made all the fear resurface.

"They have to pay," he said quietly. "They all have to pay."

He turned away then, leaving me behind, and went to his room. It wasn't until the door closed that I moved. I jerked my gaze to the door as that darkness inside my mind crept closer.

Memories came with it. Like a terrifying storm that rolled in carrying all the horror I tried not to remember. Hands reached out. Fingers clawed, desperate to drag me back to that nightmare. The one that waited, lurking in the shadows.

I forced my gaze away, my knees trembling as I reached for the railing and slowly made my way downstairs and into the kitchen. I needed to keep myself busy. I needed to do...*get her on the table.* I closed my eyes and gripped the counter as the terror pushed in.

"Coffee," I whispered. "That's what I need."

I pushed away, wrenched open my eyes, and spun around to find the filter and the coffee, then set to work filling the pot. Steam rose seconds later, filling the kitchen with the heavenly scent. I poured a cup, splashed in some creamer, and lifted it with a shaking hand to my lips.

I know what I have to do.

They have to pay.

Thom's words rose as I swallowed.

They all have to pay.

But when a face rose from my memory, it wasn't Thom's...it was my father.

They have to pay.

They all have to pay.

Screams invaded. Flickers of my memory. I could almost feel myself falling as they'd pushed me from that stage to the floor littered with men and women ready to buy and use.

Let's see what four million gets us! Melody's cry was followed with bellows of cheering and laughter. My pulse thundered as I remembered their hands forcing my face against the table. My legs were forced wide, fingers pushed between them. But it was the faces that stayed with me. Faces that blurred and sharpened...focusing on one in particular.

"No." I shook my head.

Low voices moved in, desperate and pleading.

"No."

"Helene, baby, it's me. It's Kane. Come back to us."

The touch came against the back of my hand. I jerked my eyes open and wrenched my hand away to find Kane, Riven, and Hunter staring at me over the middle counter.

"Trouble," Riven murmured. "Baby, you're scaring us."

"I know what I have to do now," I whispered the same words Thomas had. "I know where I have to go."

Not once did they look away. Each of them nodded.

"You tell us where you want to go and we'll take you." Hunter stepped around the corner of the counter, moving slowly. "But know this. You will never be alone, nor will you be at their mercy. Never again."

"Never again," Kane echoed.

Out of all the demons of my past, my father hurt the most. His betrayal cut so deep I didn't think it would ever heal.

"He has to pay." Tears filled my eyes as I met Hunter's stare. "They all have to pay."

The mountain of a man scowled down at me. "And they will, believe me. They will."

He wrapped his arms around me. Riven and Kane watched from the other side of the counter. But they knew...they knew.

Hunter held me until my body stopped shaking and the tears dried. I lifted my head and met his stare. No words were needed. I knew now what I had to do. I left the rest of my coffee behind and walked upstairs, but before I headed for Riven's room, I stopped and quietly opened Thomas' door. He was passed out face down on the bed. His arms were hugging the bunched-up comforter.

He looked peaceful, content, a stark contrast to the tormented man he normally was. I turned around, my hand on the door handle, then I stopped. His clothes were shoved into the small plastic wastepaper basket in the corner of the room. The sides of the basket were bowed out, the blood-splattered shirt shoved all the way down, his jacket on top. But it was the clerical collar that had stilled me. Bright red spots marred the white. I focused on it, finding the small indents of where he'd bitten down earlier.

They have to pay.

"They will," I whispered. "They sure will."

I closed the door, leaving him to sleep, and headed for the bathroom in Riven's room, turning on the hot water and stepping into the spray. Just like Thomas, I knew what I had to do now. Purpose filled me, steadying my movements as I washed, then turned off the water and stepped out.

Riven was dressed when I walked into the bedroom. My clothes were laid out on the bed. Black jeans, black shirt, and sturdy boots.

"I thought you'd appreciate not worrying about—" he started.

I rushed forward, wrapping my arms around him, pressing my cheek against his chest. "Thank you."

I'd never had this...someone to protect me, to care about me and stand with me, even in the darkness. *This is love.* My own words came back to me as I tightened my hold. He brushed my hair, smoothing the strands.

This was love.

I straightened, then hurried to dress before tugging on my boots.

"YOU SURE YOU'RE ready for this?" Kane asked, lifting his gaze to my father's expensive three-story modern Tudor.

"No," I answered honestly, opening the door. "But I'm doing it anyway."

The place felt deserted, soulless somehow, even though the sun shone and the wind blew, swaying the wall of wild bamboo that grew on the east side of the gardens, leading to the expansive private retreat at the rear. But it was the house I wanted, the house I needed. Because if there was anywhere my father would be, it was here.

I closed the gate behind me and walked up the long, sloping flight of stairs to the frosted glass entrance of the single black door.

I pressed my thumb on the keypad and held my breath, almost expecting the light to stay red with the ultimate betrayal. But it didn't. The light turned green and the lock released, allowing me to turn the handle and step inside.

It felt like a dream coming back to this place, especially after all that'd happened. All the lies and the betrayal and the sick alliances with men my father had sworn to destroy. Had I ever really known him, the man others knew as King, or was my entire life nothing more than a lie?

I moved through the foyer, heading deeper into the house, before I turned.

"Trouble," Riven called my name cautiously.

I guess he had a right to be cautious. There was an eeriness about this place. A feeling that it was a little *too perfect*. Light cascaded through crystal clear windows, giving you an illusion of brightness, but that feeling didn't last, not when you turned into the hallway and lifted your gaze to the room at far end.

The meeting room, my father called it.

But it was the one place where we truly came together. I kept walking, stopped at the keypad, and pressed my thumb against the sensor. If there was a point of shutting me out, it was this one. The information we gathered in that room was all we had.

Click.

The light turned green and the locks disengaged.

Only, he hadn't shut me out. I swallowed the tremor of hope and pushed down on the handle, then stepped into our own seat of command. In my head, I still saw wall to wall maps, photographs, and a timeline of events. I saw Haelstrom Hale's face in black and white sitting on top of the long list of men and women who'd become the players in that vile institution called The Order.

But that seat of command wasn't what I stepped into now.

"What the fuck?" Riven muttered behind me.

At first glance, it looked like the place had been tossed, that somehow my father's estate had been broken into and this one room had been destroyed. I stepped further inside.

"Hunter, search the perimeter." Riven commanded.

But I shook my head, staring at the mess of strewn photos and trashed furniture. One chair was even embedded into a wall.

"Don't worry," I said carefully. "The place hasn't been trashed."

"What?" Riven stepped deeper into the room, scanning the utter destruction. "So, this is normal?"

Normal?

No.

No, it wasn't...

I moved forward, finding the shattered screen on the large monitor mounted on the wall, then the upturned desk below it. Something had happened here. Something...painful. That's what I saw...pain.

I moved deeper into the room, then headed to the one thing that hadn't been disturbed, the drawn reproduction of DNA strands. Three of them, to be exact. The image was of big, muted colors against a background of the galaxy.

This is you and your sisters.

Your DNA, Helene.

Your's.

Vivienne's.

And Ryth's.

You're my entire world. Don't you know that?

"Helene?"

I shook my head, trying to shake his hold free. I'd come here to confront him. To demand answers, not to torment myself even more with the lies of the past. But that's all this place was, a goddamn lie. I winced, ground my teeth, and lifted the framed image from the wall, staring at the safe embedded in the wall behind it.

The stainless safe shone, drawing Riven's focus even more.

"What's in it?"

I punched in the sequence, day, month, me; day, month, Viv; day, month, Ryth.

Click.

"Flash drives mostly." I murmured, staring into the empty space. "Well, usually."

There were no drives, none of the bundles of cash my father stashed everywhere. There was nothing but a single yellow envelope with a note attached.

"What the hell is that?"

"I don't know." I reached up, grabbed the envelope, and pulled it out.

I'm sorry.

My father's neat scrawl was written on the note attached. My pulse skipped, forcing me to lift my gaze. Riven's eyes were fixed on mine. Those dark eyes shimmered with fear and excitement. He knew it was something. Because it was... something.

I looked down at the unsealed flap, the sticker tape still in place. "Shit."

My fingers trembled as I reached inside.

Medical Report for Weyland King.

D.O.B...

I let my gaze move down the page. This wasn't just any report— I glanced around the room, finding the utter destruction. Then turned to the only untouched thing in the entire room—so it couldn't be anyone other than my father. Who else would leave this for me to find?

CAT Scan evaluation, Glioblastoma Multiforme, Grade IV.

"Grade four?" I whispered, fumbling for my cell to punch in the details Glio...Glioblastoma Multiforme.

I stared at the information as it filled the screen.

Glioblastoma is a fast-growing, aggressive brain tumor that invades nearby brain tissue. GBM is a devastating brain cancer that can result in death in six months or less if untreated. It's imperative to seek medical care urgently.

"Six months?" The words were a squeak. My stomach rolled and heaved. I crushed the report as I braced my hands on my knees. *"Six months? Six fucking months?"*

"Give it to me."

I handed over the report, focusing on the gray carpet at my feet and the corner of what looked like a list of names.

"Jesus Christ," Riven moaned.

Movement came behind us. Riven handed the report over to Kane, who read it quickly. "This could explain a lot."

I lifted my gaze, straightening. "What do you mean?"

There was a sincerity in his stare. "If you had six months to live and three daughters to save, what would you do?"

What would I do? In the world of Haelstrom Hale and that festering pit of vipers. "Everything."

I looked around the room, finding deep gouges in the walls before I looked at that chair with the leg embedded in the wall. This wasn't the room I remembered. I looked down at the note still stuck to my hand and unfurled my fingers.

I'm sorry.

He knew I'd come here, knew I'd open the safe and find this. I couldn't imagine how desperate he must've felt! I crumpled the note in my fist and brought it to my chest. *What the fuck were you doing, dad? And why the hell didn't you confide in me?*

"This report is over six months old." Kane said. "Did you know about this?"

I shook my head. "No. I knew he was having tests, but he told me it was just routine." I lowered my gaze to the three strands of DNA all entwined against the backdrop of a galaxy. *You're my world, Helene. I want you to know that. You and your sisters mean everything and there isn't anything I wouldn't do to protect you.*

That anger and rage I'd carried into the house trembled and suddenly fell away. I'd wanted to hate him for what he'd done to me and what he'd failed to do. But how could I hate what I didn't understand? *Six months. Six goddamn months.*

I didn't understand any of this.

Not one bit.

Beep.

Riven reached down, grabbed his cell, and stared at the screen. "Looks like we need to head back into the city. St. James has some guys he wants us to meet."

"What guys?" Hunter asked.

"Fucks me. Some men who are willing to lay a lot of money on the table...men who deal in diamonds."

I jerked my gaze upwards. "Diamonds?"

Riven met my stare, those dark eyes twinkling already. "Yes, Trouble. Diamonds."

EIGHT

Riven
_____

Six months...that motherfucker had known about this for six fucking months? I lifted my head and glanced into the rear-view mirror to Helene, to find her staring out the window. I wanted to say something, anything to ease her goddamn pain. But I couldn't. I couldn't do a damn thing but push the accelerator all the way to the floor and head to the meeting.

But...goddamn him.

I turned from her reflection and focused on the road.

Goddamn him all the way to Hell.

I lost myself in the streets of the city as I made our way to a bar downtown. I turned into the almost empty rear parking lot and pulled into a space near London's Audi.

The Sons.

I killed the engine and climbed out of the hulking, slowass piece of shit and closed the door. I took the opportunity to scan the lot, the exits, and the cars parked in the shadows. They were out there, watching, waiting. At least that savage blond-haired motherfucker. The beast one would no doubt be at home...protecting the one person they all cared about.

Sister to the woman I was one day going to marry...my Helene.

I opened the back door, watching for movement as she stepped out. My pulse sped the second she was near, just like it had the moment I'd climbed from my car and saw her lying in the street. Because I was going to marry her. She belonged to us, but it was my ring she was going to wear. By hell or high water, it was my ring, our name...our future where she'd find herself. I wasn't going to let her slip away from me. Not again.

"This the place?" Kane asked.

"It's where he told me," I answered coldly.

Hunter took a step, scanning the parking lot and the alley, no doubt picking up on the same details I had before...

"Cruz," St. James' deep rumble came from the rear of the dark club.

I turned around, reached for her, and placed a hand on her lower back, guiding her toward London. We knew nothing about these assholes. Nothing apart from the name Lawlor.

We headed for the door and stepped into the darkened club.

"You want to tell us what this is about?" I muttered, scanning the dark tables.

"Just keep walking," London commanded.

Four men and a young woman waited at the rear of the club. The men didn't turn when we approached, but the woman did.

She was young and fresh faced, with innocent eyes...one by one, the heavy hitters turned, cutting me with a cold, dangerous stare that reminded me too much of St. James. I glanced back at the woman, poor bitch. She wouldn't stay innocent for long.

"I'd like to introduce you to the Lawlor brothers," London started. "This is Baron." He motioned to a chisel-jawed motherfucker with a hard stare. "Royal, Atley, and Wolfe. This is Helene, Riven, Kane, Hunter, and Thomas Cruz."

They said nothing. Just a nod my way before Baron shifted his focus to Helene. "Ms. King." He reached out his hand for hers. I fought the need to tighten my grip.

But she took his hand, giving him a smile. "Mr. Lawlor...Lawlor Diamonds, right?"

His smile widened, but those shifty fucking eyes flicked my way like a goddamn snake. "Yes," he answered, giving her his full attention. "Are you in the market for one?"

Then my goddamn hold did tighten. I cleared my throat and stepped forward, moving my focus to the young woman who stood quietly between them. A woman who looked awkward as hell amongst the towering assholes in crisp, unbranded suits. No, there was no Armani with these guys. I turned my focus back. I doubted you'd find a single brand in their entire wardrobe. It was all allowed with these men. All perfection molded around their heavy frames.

I smiled, shifting to her once more. She trembled, her heels tottering like she wasn't used to wearing them. "You look frightened, don't be frightened. I'm sorry, I missed your name." I reached out my hand.

Her eyes widened before jerking to Baron, then the others. There was a tic in Baron's jaw before he swung that fake-ass motherfucking smile my way. But I saw the real look under the lie. Revulsion. Hate rippled in his stare. The motherfucker hated me and for the first time in my life, I didn't know why.

"Cloe, why don't you take Helene and show her the gem London just purchased for her sister? I'm sure she'd love to see it."

"For Vivienne?" Helene's voice rose. "Oh my God, show me."

No woman could resist beautiful things.

Especially if it was in secret.

But that fucking asshole was playing us. No, he was playing *me*. I stepped closer, lowering my voice. "You got a problem with me, motherfucker?"

"Gentlemen," London murmured. "Not here."

I jerked my focus to London. What the fuck was going on here?

But London didn't give me anything other than his steely stare as the young woman reached for Helene's hand. "You have to see the four-carat pink diamond. It's my personal favorite."

Helene didn't want to leave, glancing from London to Baron, then to me. I gave her a nod. "It's okay."

She didn't like it, but she allowed herself to be guided to the bar, just out of earshot. I waited until the young woman unrolled the black velvet pouch and spread the jewels out, the sparkle reaching us here.

"Through here," London said carefully and turned away, heading toward a door that connected to a separate seating area through a glass wall.

From the corner of my eye, I caught Helene glance our way before the young woman touched her arm, drawing her focus back. I followed London and these rich assholes into the room, my brothers close behind.

Lawlor took a seat, leaving London to stand on the other side of the table.

"You might want to close that." Baron glared at Thomas, who was the last inside.

My brother glanced my way, waiting until I gave a nod. He wasn't wearing his black shirt and clerical collar. Strange, but now wasn't the time to ask him why. I turned around as the door closed. Through the glass, Helene looked our way.

I strode forward, bracing my hands on the end of the table to glare into the asshole's eyes. "Want to tell me what the fuck is going on?"

"We need to know one thing before we start," London said carefully.

My cheeks burned as I waited. "What?"

"Did you rape Helene?"

I flinched, then jerked my gaze to London. "What the fuck did you say?"

He winced, then settled into that cold-heart-bastard act he'd perfected.

"Did you drag her into a room at The Order?" Baron growled. "And hold her down while you and your men took turns?"

What.

The.

Fuck?

Ice cold rage plunged all the way through me. Baron glanced her way, finding her as she turned around, watching us. It took all my strength not to lunge over the table and—you know what? *FUCK. THIS!*

I cocked my fist back, driving hard and fast over the table. London and my brothers hurled themselves forward, but they were too late.

Crack!

My fist glanced off the smarmy asshole's cheek. I grabbed his shirt, wrenching him forward until his eyes grew savage and dark. "Say that again," I snarled. "And you're a fucking dead man."

"*Come on!*" London yanked me away, throwing me aside. "Get control of yourself. Jesus Christ! It's not him who's saying it!"

I tugged my shirt, drawing in hard breaths. "What the fuck are you goddamn saying?"

"This morning I received a text from Hale." Baron stared me down, his cheek reddening. "A video actually. One where you and your men brutalized that woman out there."

I stopped, instantly feeling the warmth bleed from my body. "A video? What fucking video?" He never moved. I jerked my glare to London. "What goddamn video?"

"Show him," London said, watching my every goddamn move.

But I didn't care about that...all I cared about was her. A video of me and my men? Did he mean my goddamn brothers? It was consensual. It was all fucking consensual. There was no way I'd hurt her. No fucking way.

I looked through the glass wall to her. She was watching us, her back to the young woman now, totally absorbed by what was going on in this room. She couldn't know. No fucking way did I want her dealing with this.

I turned back to the big-mouthed fucker as he pulled his cell free and brought up the messages.

All I saw was a number. No name...that meant no contacts.

But the moment he opened the message to the video, it wasn't the one I was expecting.

"No...NO!" Helene screamed.

"Turn it off!" I growled as rage plunged through me.

"NO! NO NOOOO!"

"Get her on the table." I said on the screen.

Only it wasn't me...IT WASN'T FUCKING ME! I lunged, slapping the cell clean out of his hand. "I said, TURN THAT FUCKING THING OFF!"

One of the other Lawlors eased backwards in his seat, his smug smile just itching to meet my fucking fist. "I told you this bastard was for real. All the fucking rumors were true."

Don't lose your shit.

Don't lose your shit.

"You think that was Riven?" Kane stepped forward, then bent down and grabbed the cell from the floor.

I shook my head. "Don't...don't waste your goddamn breath."

"Please, by all means..." the asshole called Wolfe muttered. "Waste it."

"You know," Kane said in his doctor's voice. "You're right. We're wasting our time here."

"He's sent that to everyone." Wolfe's eyes glinted, watching my every move. "Everyone knows you dragged her to that room and you held her down while your men violated her. You're dead after all this is done. You get that, right, motherfucker? You're...fucking...dead."

I froze as every vile sin I'd ever committed came to take its pound of flesh. I'd known one day they'd all come back and drag me into the hell I deserved. I closed my eyes. But not this... please, God, not this.

"What's going on here?" Helene slowly asked.

I slowly opened my eyes, staring at the bastards.

No one looked her way...they couldn't.

My words were husky and raw, burning all the way down. "You don't want to be in here, Trouble."

She stepped closer. Please, for the love of God, don't touch me. I'd break. I knew that. I'd fucking shatter into a million pieces with the simple brush of her hand and weep like a goddamn child.

But she didn't touch me. Instead, she stepped closer. "If I'm going to be the topic of conversation, don't you think I deserve to at least be in the room?"

"You don't want this conversation, Helene," London answered. "Trust me."

She snapped her gaze toward him. I knew that look...by the way he winced, so did St. James. "Trust you? You might be my sister's husband, London. But please don't overstep our friendship."

He visually blanched, adjusting himself before he nodded.

"Now." Helene turned back, eyeing the cell in Kane's hand. "Someone explain to me what's going on."

"We have evidence that Riven attacked you while you were at The Order." Baron started. "That he...that he and his men dragged you into a room and brutally assaulted you. We came here to find out the truth."

She stilled, not even her chest rose. There was nothing but silence, until finally. "You think...you think Riven would do that to me?"

Baron shifted uncomfortably.

She wrenched her gaze to London. "You? Do you think he did that to me?"

"There's a video." London murmured and shook his head. "One that shows Riven's face as the attacker."

A sound escaped her, low, wounded, devastated. She closed her eyes for a second before opening them. "I *was* raped at The Order. I was dragged into a room and held down on a table. But it wasn't Riven who did that. He—" she met my gaze.

I clenched my fists, desperately needing to tear something apart. The world, yeah, the world would do. Anything so she didn't have to relive that fucking night once more.

"He saved me," she finished. "In more ways than one. Coulter is the man who attacked me. He is the one you should be interrogating. Oh, that's right," she said coldly. "You can't... because I killed him."

Jesus, she was strong. Stronger than I'd ever seen in my entire life.

I remembered that day after she'd been hurt at The Order. The one when she walked into the cafeteria and looked in the eyes of every bastard who'd hurt her, right before she spit in Coulter's face. They couldn't break her then. But they were still trying.

They were still goddamn trying.

"Don't you want to see the video?" Atley Lawlor asked carefully.

She snapped her focus toward him. "If you were raped and it was doctored to look like someone you loved did it, would you want to look at it?"

He stilled, then slowly shook his head. "No, I wouldn't."

She gave a slow nod, then turned to London. "You know us better than anyone. For you to think Riven or any of these men would do something like that is pretty goddamn low, London, even for you."

"I didn't mean—" he started.

She lifted her finger, stopping him cold. "You did, and you damn well know it. Now," she swung that savage glare back to the diamond brothers. "I don't know you and I'm assuming you don't know me. If you did, you would've come to me first, instead of going after those I love." She gripped the table and leaned down. "Now, I hope we've cleared up any confusion you might have."

Baron's eyes twinkled and his mouth curled up at the edges. "Yes, ma'am."

"We need your help." She pushed up, looking everyone in the eye. You'd never know she'd just found out her father was living on borrowed time. "So, I'm willing to overlook this, if you are. Let's start afresh." She reached out her hand. "Helene King, daughter of Weyland King, partner of Riven, Kane, Hunter, and..." she looked his way, giving my brother a soft careful smile before turning back. "Thomas Cruz. It's very nice to meet you."

NINE

Helene

"Is everything okay now?"

I turned back from where Riven paced the floor outside that room, raking his fingers through his hair.

"I don't know," I answered, finding her wide blue eyes waiting when I glanced her way.

Cloe bit her lip nervously, one corner of her mouth twitching in a smile. She was out of place with these men. That thought had crossed my mind before, but now it was all I could think about. "What's your deal, anyway?" I asked carefully. "What's a nice young woman like you doing with dangerous, powerful rich men like them?"

They weren't nice businessmen.

Not at all.

Not after what had just gone down.

"You wouldn't believe me if I told you," she answered quietly.

There was fear in her tone, clear enough to make my cheeks burn. She was clearly out of her depth with these men. One look at the flyaway strands of her hair and the awkward way she moved, and you knew she wasn't made for this world. None of us were, really...but certainly not her. It was more than her adorable round cheeks and curvy body. There was an innocence about her, a gentleness that wasn't going to last long.

I gave her my full attention as I gently placed my hand on her arm. "Word of advice, Cloe. Get out now while you still can. This isn't a world where someone as sweet as you survives, not without being eaten alive in the process."

She swallowed hard, then glanced to where the Lawlor brothers stood with London and my men. "I fear it might be too late for that."

I winced, my stomach sinking with her words. "Then at least let me put my number in your phone. If any time you're in trouble, you can call me."

Her lower lip trembled and the shine in those blue eyes made me feel sad for her. "Why would you do that?"

I gave her a smile, even if it trembled a bit. "Because us women need to stick together, that's why."

She smiled back, then reached into her pocket and pulled out her cell. I typed my name and number, saving it under HK, hoping like hell she'd reach out to me if things ever got bad for her. I liked her. She was kind, gentle, and far too goddamn innocent for this world.

"Hey." Riven growled, then stepped in front of Baron, leaning down, murmuring something in his ear.

Whatever it was, it was met with a glare of savagery from Baron.

"Cloe." Came a deep baritone call as he looked her way.

She snapped her head upwards to meet Baron's stare.

"Time to go."

One nod and she slid from the stool at the bar, her ass squeaking against the leather before she landed. She reached over, grabbed the velvet bag full of stunning diamonds, and flicked her gaze my way. "Thank you for talking to me. I hope... I hope one day we get to meet again." Surprisingly she stepped close, wrapped one arm around me, and pulled me in for a hug to whisper in my ear. "I can't leave, not yet."

My eyes widened as she quickly pulled away, gave me a shy smile without meeting my eyes, and darted away, her heels clicking. Baron Lawlor met my stare over her head as she hurried toward him. One cautious nod my way and he reached out his hand, instantly finding the small of her back before they turned and made for the rear of the bar.

I stood there for a few minutes, watching them as London left. But Riven didn't look my way, nor did he call my name. He just turned around and walked away. I jerked my gaze to Kane as he watched him, then turned to me, lifting his hand.

I made for the door, meeting them in the hallway.

"He's hurting." Kane murmured as Hunter shoved the back door open. "So be gentle."

My breaths raced and my pulse thundered as I stepped out into the parking lot. The sleek black Bentley was already driving out. I glanced at the customized license plate, DMND1, then turned away, ignoring London's Audi as it followed the Bentley.

"Riven," I called as he yanked open the driver's door.

He stopped but didn't look at me.

"Hey."

Now he turned. Those dark eyes were cold and stoney, full of rage.

"Talk to me."

"Talk, Helene. What do you want me to say?" he said coldly.

I flinched, then yanked open the back door before climbing inside.

"How I can ease your pain," I said to the closed door.

"You can't." Kane captured my chin, turning my gaze to his. "This is the game we're playing. Hale will do everything he can to discredit us. We knew that."

My throat thickened and ached. I did know, but that didn't stop it from hurting. Kane dropped his hand, then climbed into the back seat. Tears threatened, blurring the parking lot through the windshield. Riven met my gaze in the rear-view mirror before I looked away.

He started the car and pulled out, but instead of turning back to the highway, we headed toward the commercial estate and the compound that Hunter's men occupied. When we got there, the place was empty. There were no Hummers or Explorers in the yard, no neat rows of boots outside the door.

We pulled up and climbed out. Hunter headed for the main command building, with Riven close behind, disappearing as I closed my door behind me.

"They're searching, aren't they?" I asked, turning my focus to Kane.

"Yes." He lowered his gaze to mine. "Everyone is out searching."

We followed Hunter inside, hearing the chatter coming from the intel room.

"Who else has this?" Riven's cold demand reached me as I neared.

A young former Marine sat in front of the bank of computers. It was the same soldier Riven had sat with the day he'd learned about the Sons. The goddamn Sons. It all came down to them.

"It's been showing up on different servers. More in the last five minutes and it's..." the soldier glanced my way. "Growing in popularity."

Oh, God.

I froze in the doorway. My stomach rolled and churned until I was going to be sick. "That video is out there?"

Riven gripped the edge of the desk and bowed his head. "He wanted this. He wanted...this." He lifted his head, rage visibly quaking through his body. "Goddamn him."

He shoved backwards and turned, striding out of the room past me. I reached for him, my fingers brushing his shoulder. But he never stopped, just kept walking, leaving us behind. Hunter watched him leave, then met my gaze.

"Hale is going after him." I couldn't keep the pain from my voice. "Painting him the monster. He's going to ruin him, isn't he?"

"He's going to try." Hunter answered.

"He doesn't care about himself." Kane shifted his gaze to me. "He cares about you."

That hurt. Like a knife to my chest kind of hurt. Kane shook his head and walked away. Hunter leaned forward, talking in hushed tones to his mercenary. Thomas just stood at the back of the room, his body crammed into the corner like he couldn't get away from us...like he couldn't get away from here.

"Just call me with any updates," Hunter said finally.

Any updates.

He meant if it's found all over the goddamn internet.

I closed my eyes and felt the world tremble.

"Baby?"

I opened my eyes to find Hunter in front of me. "You want to go home?"

Home...

Images of the chair embedded in the wall and documents strewn all over the place filled me. Then my empty apartment, left vacant, with the cheese now surely molded in the refrigerator. Or my childhood home. Echoing hallways and lonely nights spent studying images of young girls I'd never known...girls who shared my blood.

Where *was* my home?

Was it there, or at the mountain?

I didn't know. Not anymore...

Still, I followed when he headed out, and climbed into the back seat. The wind picked up, whipping Riven's hair as he strode toward the four-wheel drive and climbed into the passenger's seat staring straight ahead as Hunter slid behind the wheel. Riven never spoke, never flinched. It was almost like he wasn't even there.

He was already hunting, tracking down Hale in the dark recesses of his mind and dragging the honed edge of a blade across the bastard's throat. The four-wheel drive backed out and headed out of the city, leaving the traffic far behind.

Still that heaviness plagued me, as did the silence in the car. No one spoke, no one made a sound, just stared straight ahead as the mountain drew closer. A brush came across my finger, slowly, controlled, comforting. I looked down to where Thomas' hand met mine, then lifted my gaze to his. Still, he didn't glance my way, just kept that stony stare straight ahead with his warm fingers pressing against mine, until we finally turned into the shrouded driveway and stopped at the gate.

Then he pulled away.

For some strange reason, even though I was surrounded by the men I loved and who loved me, I was lonely. The car stopped and Riven was out first, leaving us behind as he strode toward the mountain in the distance.

"I should go after him." I yanked the door handle.

"Don't," Kane said quietly. "He'll come to you when he can."

I climbed out and closed the door behind me, watching him climb the incline where we'd trained before he disappeared. Leave him. That's what Kane wanted and, as Hunter headed for the gym and Thomas turned toward the house, that's what I did. I didn't have much choice.

"Thomas!" I called, but he didn't stop, just punched in the code and stepped inside.

I threw my hands into the air. They were all walking away from me...again. It felt like before, when we were separated and not just by distance. They'd pulled away from me and they'd pulled away from each other, which left us vulnerable.

"Not again," I murmured.

"What?" Kane asked.

I turned to him and met those piercing green eyes. "I said, not again."

I headed after Thomas, quickening my steps until I pushed through the door.

"Thom! Thom, wait!" The steps were a blur as I took them two at a time. I could hear him on the landing, catching sight of him with his hand on the handle as I reached the top. "Wait," I gasped, sucking in deep breaths. His head lowered like he was consumed with pain or guilt. I stepped closer, reaching for him. "It's okay. Listen to me, it's all going to be okay."

"No...it isn't."

The rage that rippled through those words made me freeze. It wasn't pain he was feeling, not hopelessness or rejection. It was cold, unflinching, tearing from the deepest pits of his soul. He whirled around and met my stare.

There was no warmth there, no soft, careful comfort. There was no awkwardness either, no nervousness as he looked everywhere else but at me. Thomas was kind, careful. The closest thing we had to goodness and to salvation. But this man...this man standing in front of me not only held my stare, but he gripped hold of it, clutching it like it was his salvation.

Was that it?

He'd lost his faith?

I looked at the black t-shirt he wore, remembering his collar and jacket tossed into the trash in the corner of his room.

"They have to answer for their sins, Helene." He took a step toward me. "I will make them answer."

"What are you saying?"

The door below closed with a thud. I could hear Riven talking to someone, drawing my focus away. But I couldn't allow that. Thomas was hurting, tearing himself apart.

"Talk to me." My voice cracked. "Tell me what you're planning to do."

"What the fuck do you mean, you don't want to talk to me?" Riven's voice rose. "My war? My goddamn war? I'm not sure if you're aware of this, Rossi. But this isn't just *my* war we're fighting here. Wait...what? What the fuck are you talking about? Rossi...ROSSI!"

I stopped and turned around, watching Kane and Hunter as they followed Riven up the stairs.

"Motherfucker!" Riven snarled, his cell clenched in his fist as he stepped toward me on the landing.

"What is it?" I whispered.

His eyes were wide, as though he couldn't believe it himself. "He wants nothing to do with us, can you believe that? He, Mr. Fucking Mafia himself, wants nothing to do with me?"

That couldn't be right. Desperation thrummed inside me until I felt panicked and afraid. The Rossis were as much a part of this as we were.

"It's the video." Riven spat the words. "It's the goddamn video. He believes it was me."

"No." I whispered. "He can't...he wouldn't."

"But he does," Riven answered. "He does."

TEN

Tobias

"WHAT DO YOU MEAN, WE NEED TO GO UNDERGROUND?" I hissed into the phone.

The voice on the other end was quiet and...*guarded*. "Just that," Benjamin Rossi answered. "It's time," he said and a chill raced along my spine. "It's time to go, son."

"You're not telling me a goddamn thing here, Ben." Anger filled me, but I tried to keep it leashed. "And where the hell is my brother? I know he's been out at night for you, doing things he won't talk about. Tell me what the fuck is going on."

I'd tried to keep my voice down, still she'd heard me. Her shadow spilled across the doorway and my body reacted to that alone, making my pulse race as every cell in my body came alive. My stepsister still had that effect, drawing my focus as she stepped into the doorway. Her intense stare found mine as she reached up and brushed her hair behind her ears. Her once long auburn hair was shorter now, making her look even younger than she was.

I turned away, giving her my back. "Give me a goddamn reason."

"Not like this," Ben said quietly.

"Then when?"

"First, get Ryth and the baby out, then I'll text you the address on the burner. I have to make sure Kat and the baby are safe. They're my priority now. You get that, right? I have to look after my own."

I froze, the fight dropping away instantly. *Kat...Kat was in danger?* "Ben, talk to me."

"The burner, son." His thunderous steps sounded in the background, his rushed breaths telling me he was running. "Get the burner. I'll talk soon, okay?"

"OK—" I started, not liking this one goddamn bit, but he was already gone, leaving me whispering to an empty line.

"What is it?"

I closed my eyes and gathered myself for a heartbeat before I opened them and turned around to meet her piercing stare. "We have to leave."

"Leave?" Her eyes widened as panic moved in. She jerked her head to the room at the end of the hall. The room where Nick and our son were. Not just our son...*my son.*

I moved forward, reaching out to grasp her shoulder. "Yes, baby. We have to leave now. Pack your things, we'll get Ali, just take whatever you need." I stepped past her, hurrying for the end of the hall as I called over my shoulder. "*Now*, baby, please."

Go underground, some place no one can find you. Go there now...

Benjamin's words rang in my head, punctuated by the heavy thud of my steps as I pushed into a run, tearing through the open door of Ali's playroom. Nick jerked his head upwards, tearing his gaze from the laptop screen before he glanced at our sleeping son.

"You wake him, T, and I swear to God, you'll be the one up all damn night," my brother started.

"We have to run." I moved fast, cutting across the room, looking for my son's bags...*where the hell were all the bags?*

Nick rose instantly. "What do you mean, *run?*"

I stopped and lifted my gaze to my brother's. "Ben just called. There's trouble, trouble with Kat. He said to go underground, some place where no one can find us."

There weren't any arguments. He didn't even need clarification, he just reacted. *"Princess!"* my brother roared. "We have to leave now!"

Ali flinched on his foldaway cot. I left the bags and his nappies and toys behind, moving to him as he opened his eyes and unleashed a wail. He was so small...so fucking small and vulnerable. If my heart sped when Ryth was near, it fucking ripped in two when I touched him. He was every good fucking part of me and Nick and Caleb and Ryth all wrapped up in a tiny body. There was no way I wasn't protecting him with all I had.

I have to look after my own.

Ben's words surged to the surface as I slid my hands under Ali's perfect little body and lifted him, cuddling my son against my chest.

"I'll get the bags." Nick rushed to a cupboard in the corner of the room and yanked out three stowed getaway bags.

"His nightlight." I turned around. "Don't forget his damn nightlight."

He wouldn't sleep without it. Nick unleashed a snarl and lunged for the damn thing as I clutched Ali to my chest and raced for the kitchen. I grabbed everything I could. His formula, his bottles, his sterilizer and his pacifiers. Still, there was so goddamn much.

Ryth dumped three packed bags onto the floor, then glanced my way to our son first before swiveling around. "I'll get the rest. Nick has the guns."

I gave a nod, shoving teething jelly and any other medication we might need into another bag. Nick's heavy steps invaded the kitchen. "I can't get hold of C."

"Leave him." I swept all the plungers and thermometers and the thousand other things we had for emergencies with the sweep of my hand. "We'll call him from the car."

Nick gave a nod and headed out, carrying the guns and the weapons to the rear of the Range Rover. The car was registered to a false name, as was this house. But still it wasn't enough. It was *never* enough, not while Haelstrom Hale still lived.

I have to make sure Kat and the baby are safe...

Something was happening. Something Ben wouldn't talk to me about. Whatever it was, it was bad. My thoughts returned to

Laz as I carried Ali toward the four-wheel drive and loaded his bags onto the back seat. I cradled his head as I lifted him into his car seat as Nick returned, carrying more bags. "You take Ryth and Ali, head to Margrave Street Warehouse. It's as safe as we can get right now. I'll get rid of the Mustang and follow."

Click.

Ali's seat belt snapped tight. I checked it once...twice...three times just to make sure. Still, it didn't ease that tightness in my chest.

"Hey." My brother grabbed my shoulder, drawing my gaze to his. "We're going to get through this."

"They can't take her again, Nick," I whispered my worst fears. "I won't let them."

"That's not going to happen, brother. We'll kill them all before they even come close to Ryth or our son."

I slowly nodded, but an ache settled in the back of my throat, One that refused to budge.

"Okay," Ryth said breathlessly as she heaved three bags of our clothes into the back of the four-wheel drive. "I packed most of your clothes and all of Caleb's, not like he has many anyway."

She wiped her hands on her jeans and lifted her gaze to us, stopping cold. Concern raged. "What is it?"

I shook my head.

"Nothing." Nick answered for us as he stepped close to her and brushed his thumb across her cheek. "We just need to get you and the baby to safety is all."

"As long as we're together," she said, "That's how we stay alive. We stay together."

She was right. She was always right. I shoved my hand into my pocket and pulled out my cell as I stepped away, hurrying for the house and the last remaining bags. But what I really wanted was my brother to answer his goddamn phone. I pressed his number and listened to the cell ring.

And ring.

And ring.

"Goddamn you, C," I whispered. "Don't you know we need you?"

He didn't answer, so I left a message, short and to the point. *"Call us back, asshole or the next time I see you, I'll throat punch you."*

If that didn't do it, then I didn't know what would. I walked through the house, scanning the skeletal remains of what had been our home for the last eight months, and walked out, heading to the Range Rover. Ryth was already in the passenger's seat, watching me as I opened the door and climbed in.

Nick's Mustang started with a snarl. He waited for me to start the engine before he opened the towering steel gate and backed out into the street of this quiet middle-class residential suburb. I shoved the four-wheel drive into reverse, gripped the back of her seat, and backed out after him. Only, Nick turned one way and we turned the other.

"Are you going to finally tell me what happened?" she asked quietly.

My...perfect...little...mouse. I glanced her way, reached for her hand and gripped it tightly. "I don't know myself. All I know is that something is going down with the Rossis and it's bad. Ben said he has to take care of Kat and the baby. He has to make sure they're safe."

"Safe?" Her eyes widened as I drove, taking the back streets and watching the rear-view mirror. "Something's happened."

"I agree." I knew right now Lazarus must be losing his goddamn mind. "But like the man said, we have to take care of our own."

I gave her hand a gentle squeeze and let it go, focusing on the streets as they became busy. There was no way Hale or his fucking men were getting anywhere near us. We needed a plan...and we needed to know where the fuck he's hiding.

My cell rang. I glanced at the caller ID. *Riven Cruz.* That motherfucker was lucky he was alive. If I had my way...Ryth's gaze was fixed on the screen. "Aren't you going to answer that?"

Fuck him.

I fought the need to snarl.

But I couldn't, because somehow the vile motherfucker had found some good in that black heart of his. Enough good to make Ryth's sister fall in love, at least. With a growl, I leaned forward and swiped to answer the call. "What do you want, Principal?"

There was silence on the other end of the line.

The name hurt.

Or pissed him off.

I was good with either of those.

"Benjamin Rossi," he started. "Has he contacted you?"

My gut clenched tight. I wanted to tell him to go to goddamn hell before I answered any of his questions. But one look from Ryth and I clenched my jaw. "Yes."

"And he told you it was me, I assume?"

"Assume all you fucking want." My anger spilled over.

"It wasn't me." His voice broke. "Do you hear me? It *wasn't* ME. I'd never hurt Helene like that. I'd never...never hurt her like that. The video was doctored, made to look like I was the one who hurt her. But I wasn't. It was Coulter. He was the bastard who did that."

What the fuck was he talking about? I glanced at Ryth. She shook her head, not knowing a thing. She reached for her cell, pulled up her sister's number, and started typing.

"He wouldn't even take my damn call."

It wasn't like The Principal to be torn up about something like this. Maybe the sick motherfucker had changed?

"Look, I don't think he's even seen whatever you're talking about. He's dealing with some problems of his own."

"Problems?" His tone deepened. "What kind of problems?"

I swerved in and out of traffic, watching the rear-view mirror. "I don't know myself. He called and told me to go underground. Said that he's doing the same with Kat and the baby. Something's happened and it's a lot more than some doctored video. Look, we're heading underground. I'd suggest you do the same. You have the burners London sent, activate them and kill this one. We'll be out of communication until we're sure we're not being followed, or led into some kind of trap."

"Okay. Jesus...*okay*." He was finally understanding what was going on here.

"And Riven."

"Yeah?"

"Find that motherfucking Order and raze it to the goddamn ground."

"We're trying. Believe me, we're try—"

I was already reaching out to end the call.

"This is it, isn't it?" Ryth whispered, staring straight ahead. "This is really it."

There wasn't a goddamn thing I could do to comfort her. "I think so, baby. I think so."

ELEVEN

Helene

"IT'S NOT THE VIDEO." RIVEN TURNED AROUND AS HE lowered the cell in his hand. "Tobias is willing to bet Benjamin has no idea it even exists."

I took a step closer, waiting for him to continue. He closed his eyes for a second and exhaled hard, his brow furrowing before he opened his eyes. "He said something else is going on with the Rossis and it has to do with Kat and the baby."

"Kat and the baby?" I whispered. "What are you talking about? What does Kat have to do with any of this?"

"I don't know." He strode closer, those dark eyes boring into mine. "But we need to figure it out."

My mind raced, trying to find a connection. Knowing how secretive the Rossis were, there'd be no paper trail, nothing that could lead us to the information we needed. So that left me with one other choice...my sister.

"Ryth," I whispered.

"She's as close to Kat and Laz as anyone. So if anyone was going to know what this is all about, it'd be her."

Memories invaded my mind. Kat, holding their baby girl as she paced the hallway outside Ryth's hospital room after the attack at Coulter's mansion. She was panicked and desperate then, clutching her dark-haired daughter tight to her chest.

I'd never really had any cause to delve into who Katerina VanHalen was apart from what I'd seen in the news. She was rich, the daughter of one of the most influential men in the country. But Sebastian VanHalen had died suddenly in the months just after Kat left the VanHalen name behind and became a Rossi, exchanging diamonds and the celebrity lifestyle for guns and war.

I tried to make a connection. Money, maybe? I pressed the button and listened to Ryth's cell ring.

"Hey. Riven just called," she said carefully. "Is everything okay?"

"I need to know what's going on with the Rossis," I said, not as carefully. "In particular, Kat. Something is happening here and I need to figure it out."

"Helene, I can't—"

"You know I wouldn't ask," I pushed. "You're my sister and the last thing I'd *ever* do is ask you to betray your friend. But I have a bad feeling about this, Ryth, and right now, I'm betting you do, too. Just tell me what you can...and I'll figure out the rest."

There was silence for a very long time until slowly... "I don't know what is happening. Benjamin called Tobias and told him we needed to go underground, so that's what we're doing. We left the Parkland house behind, we're ditching the cells, and activating the burners. Ben said he's doing the same for Kat and her babies."

"There has to be some kind of connection here. Please, Ryth."

"Kat met Laz on some kind of island purposely built by and for the Cosa Nostra. Her father was rich and powerful and extremely influential. He had a lot of connections—"

I could hear Tobias in the background, warning her.

Please, just tell me.

"One of her father's very close friends was Haelstrom Hale. He and Kat were engaged for a while...until Laz came on the scene."

I stilled, my blood running cold.

"That's all I can tell you," Ryth said deliberately before she whispered. "The rest you'll have to figure out yourself."

The rest?

Oh, God. Oh...God.

A shiver raced through me as I lifted my gaze to Riven's.

"I have to go," Ryth added. "I'll contact you as soon as we're safe."

"Okay." I said automatically as Riven's brow creased. "Stay safe. I love you."

"I love you too."

Then the call was silent.

"What is it?" Riven urged.

My mind was spinning, my stomach churning so hard I thought I was going to throw up. "I...I..." The bedroom darkened, snatching all the color until there was nothing but gray.

"Trouble?" Riven caught me as I swayed, pulling me against him. "Talk to me. Tell me what it was."

I lifted my head. "Did you know Hale was engaged?"

He scowled. "Engaged? No."

"Well, he was." I slowed my breaths until slowly the colored hues inside the bedroom returned. "And you'll never guess who he was engaged to."

Riven stiffened, his eyes widening as he whispered. "No."

"Yes." I moved with him as he turned. "Kat VanHalen."

"Holy fuck." He ran his fingers through his hair, pacing the bedroom floor until he turned.

"I need to think," I murmured, focusing on the far wall. "And plan. I need to..."

I turned around and started walking.

"Where are you going?"

"To the command center!" I called over my shoulder as I raced down the stairs.

Hale was engaged to Kat?

Jesus...that changed *everything*.

I ran down the stairs and slammed through the door, racing for the stand-alone building that was an armory and a command center all in one.

"Helene, for Christ's sake!" Riven roared as I barrelled through the entrance and up the narrow flight of stairs to the room with the bank of monitors.

But it wasn't the computers I was interested in. I turned around, finding the wall that was crammed with names and pictures as they connected to The Order. That fever which burned inside me took hold as I stepped closer, pulled the pictures of Ryth, Vivienne, and me free, then took a step backwards and laid them on the floor.

"What the fuck are you doing?" Riven snapped.

But I didn't answer. I placed my picture down and surged forward again to pull Hale's free, ignoring the major players of The Order. My gaze skimmed Coulter's face. *Get her on the table...*I shook my head, pushing the horror away.

I was so close to figuring this out.

The Order.

I strode forward, grabbed a piece of paper and a pen, and scribbled the words The Order. But I stopped as I finished the r. It wasn't quite right. I reached up, grabbed another piece of paper and wrote the real monster behind this. *Haelstrom Hale.*

Whichever way you looked at this, it all came down to one person. The single driving force of one man. I placed the note in the middle, then moved to the board, pulled the image of my father from the wall, and placed it alongside Hale's.

The three of us surrounded my father. There was still a connection between them, one I couldn't quite work out. *Glioblastoma Multiforme is a fast growing and aggressive brain tumor. The diagnosis said six months and that was six months ago.*

The urgency to crack this was overwhelming, making my head throb at the base of my neck. I rubbed the tight muscle, until strong hands replaced mine.

"Talk to me." Riven's thumbs pushed into the points at the base of my skull, making me close my eyes with relief

"I don't understand the connection between my dad and Hale. I know about the fact that Hale was searching for our DNA and my father kept it safe...he kept *us* safe, but there has to be more to them. There has to be a darker connection."

"Then leave it. Move on to what we do know."

I opened my eyes and shifted my gaze to the name scribbled in black pen. *Hale.* "We know he was engaged to Kat."

"And?"

I moved away, leaving his magical fingers behind. "We know she kept it a secret and so did Hale." I picked up the pen and wrote *Kat engaged?*

"Keep going."

"And now she's having to hide." My pulse was thrumming, triggering that constant drilling in my head. I had to keep going. I was so close. *So goddamn close.* In my head, all I could see was her standing outside the door to Ryth's room, clutching her daughter tight against her chest.

The child was so beautiful, dressed in lilac that looked stunning against her jet-black hair and dark eyes.

Black hair.

Dark eyes.

Not like her mother's...because Kat was a redhead.

Not like Laz's either, come to think of it.

"What color eyes does Lazarus have?"

"Not really sure, never really stared longingly into them. Blue, I think?"

Blue...

Yeah, blue.

My heart was booming as it all slipped into place. A face rose inside my mind as I shifted my focus to the name *Haelstrom Hale,* the man with jet black hair and coal black eyes. "Oh my fucking *God.*"

"What is it?"

I spun around, meeting his stare. I couldn't quite believe it.

He and Kat were engaged for a while...until Laz came on the scene.

"She isn't Lazarus' child," I whispered. "She's Hale's."

Riven's eyes widened before he slowly looked back at the array of images and names. "Holy *fuck.*"

"They're going to ground because Hale's after them. He's going to take back what's his...right before he disappears for good."

"Jesus." Riven's voice shook. "You know what that means, right?"

"It means the Rossis are about to go to war."

"Grab your jacket." Riven barked as he turned and raced for the stairs. "You're going to need it."

"Where are we going?" I yelled as he hit the bottom.

"To the bastard who knew this all along. London fucking St. James."

Holy shit. This was a goddamn mess...and I just blew it all to hell.

TWELVE

Caleb
___

"WE DON'T KNOW WHO WE CAN TRUST WITH THIS." Benjamin Rossi lifted his piercing stare to mine as we sat in his black Escalade staring at the LionsDenz Motorcycle Clubhouse in the distance. "The others are so goddamn focused on finding Hale, they haven't even thought about what will happen if he slips away from them."

I glanced over to where the clubhouse sat waiting. The lights were on and music blared, reaching us through the windows. "We have to think bigger."

"Exactly, we play the long game and we cover all bases."

Benjamin was a master at the long game. After all, that's why we were here. Tobias and Nick might've taken out Amo and several leaders of the Death Valley Motor Cycle chapters, but others had gone to ground, men who did Hale's dirty work. That's exactly what Ben had been banking on.

A fight broke out in the club, two men going at each other as they fell out the front door and spilled into the yard. I watched them through the chain link fence as others came out, urging them on. But it was a movement in the dark that caught my eye as a shadow slipped along outside the fence and headed our way.

Alastair Alman. The name Ben had given me rolled through my mind. "You sure you can trust the guy?"

Ben focused on him as he cut across the street and headed our way. "I guess we're about to find out."

The Stidda Mafia leader shifted in his seat, his hand inching lower beside the seat as he reached over with his other hand and pressed the button to lower the window.

My damn pulse was pounding as the towering, tatted-up guy leaned into the window, eyeing Ben, then me. "Gentlemen."

"Get in." Ben gave a jerk of his head before the guy pulled away and stepped to the back door.

The window whirred, closing as Benjamin's guy climbed into the back and closed the door. The engine started, deep and snarling. The lights remained off as Ben turned the wheel, turning us around. As we circled, I lifted my gaze to the two bikers brawling in the yard. They were still at it. One was on top of the other, driving his fists down over and over again.

The barbaric nature of humans consumed me at that moment. We were beasts. All of us. Monsters living in a monstrous world. My chest ached, throbbing as Ryth's face filled me. I was a monster...for her.

The harsh silence lingered as we headed to wherever Ben had chosen for this meet. My focus narrowed on the guy in the back seat, a man Ben said could be trusted. But I hadn't stayed alive this long putting my faith in another.

Only family...

Always family.

My betraying father rose inside my mind. *Except for him. That fucker can stay dead.*

"You gonna like what I have to tell you," the asshole in the back muttered.

I turned my head, inhaled, and winced. "Christ, you fucking stink."

The asshole never flinched, just met my stare with a glinting glare. "When you lie with pigs, brother, when you lie with pigs."

I scowled. There was something about the asshole, something I didn't like. Ben hit the turn signal and spun the wheel, swinging us into a side street before he braked and pulled hard into an alleyway. I jerked forward until the seatbelt bit, cutting hard across my chest.

Fuck!

Ben killed the engine and climbed out, leaving me to follow. I scanned the alley, trying to get my bearings. We were in some part of Chinatown. A part of the city I wasn't familiar with. So how the hell did Rossi know where to go?

Keys rattled as the back door of the four-wheel drive closed behind me. Ben unlocked a door and pushed it wide before glancing my way. In the murky light, I caught the jerk of his head. "Inside, both of you."

I trusted him, so I stepped inside.

"There's a light switch on your left."

I reached out but hit a wall, then fumbled until I found the switch. A *click* and a dull yellow light filled the space, which was nearly empty. An old table in the middle of the room, apparently for us, and a few chairs that'd been pulled out around it. I moved in and the biker followed, then we waited for Ben to lock the door before he turned around.

"I told you to trust me, Mr. Rossi." The guy started. "Because I found what you're looking for. There's talk...talk of a Mr. H who's making plans to get out of the country."

Ben never flinched, just murmured. "Go on."

"The information wasn't shared with us, but there was one thing that was...it's a name, Ignatius Bremmer."

Ignatius Bremmer? Who the fuck was he?

"He's the man we're to protect. A lawyer who works for Hale."

"Why?" Ben asked. "Why you? Why would Hale go to a goddamn MC club like the Lions for that?"

Alastair fixed his gaze on the Mafia leader. "Because there's more of our kind than there is of yours," he said carefully. It came across as a threat. But, more than that...it came across as the truth.

"We shadow that guy, make sure he gets from point A to B with no trouble."

"To do what?"

Alastair gave a shrug. "Meetings with other assholes in suits."

"And you're sure that man will give me the information I'm looking for?"

The guy ran his grease-stained fingers through even greasier hair. "Yeah, I am."

Ben just gave a nod and exhaled slowly. "Okay. I believe you. Give me his name."

"Like I said, Ignatius Bremmer, he lives in Sureside, number 119, but he spends most of his time in his office in the city. We have men sitting on it twenty-four-seven, but lucky for you, I'm going to be one of those men."

Ben lifted his gaze. "When?"

"Tomorrow night."

"Just you?"

Alastair opened his arms, showing off his massive frame. "Just me."

Only then did Ben look my way. His dark eyes shone. That alone worried me.

"Tomorrow then."

Alastair grinned, showing yellow teeth. I winced and looked away. My damn pulse was pounding. This was really happening.

"Good job, Alistair. I appreciate your loyalty."

"I knew when you contacted me about the Lions it'd pay off." He sneered.

So that's it? He was a plant? I gave a chuff and turned back. Now it made sense why Ben would believe this guy. He'd had a man on the inside all this time. This was his man.

Ben stepped away and headed for the door. "I'll drive you back."

"Don't worry about it." He shook his head. "I'm good to make my own way, Mr. Rossi. I was plannin' on gettin' out of that place for tonight anyway. Let them assholes fight over a fucking woman, see if I care."

Ben gave a nod, then headed for the door again.

"Keep in touch," Ben said, shaking the biker's hand.

"Will do, Mr. Rossi. It's been a pleasure."

"Grab the light, Caleb."

I did, flicking it off and casting us into utter darkness.

One careful glance my way and Alastair turned around and left, headed back along the alleyway alongside the Escalade, and disappeared. We stood in silence in the doorway watching him leave.

"This could be a set-up." I said quietly.

"I guess there's only one way to find out, isn't there?"

The thought of only the two of us going in didn't sit well. "Do we bring in the others?"

"Yes. We all have a part to play in all this. But not that psycho. Get his brother, the mute. That way London can take care of Vivienne. God knows he needs it."

"And The Priest?"

Ben met my stare. "Yes...especially the Priest."

My stomach tightened as I gave a slow nod. "Consider it done."

THIRTEEN

Helene
_____

My hands shook as we pulled up outside London's house. I'd never been nervous about seeing him before, not like this, at least. I'd hardly slept after the revelation of Kat and the real father of her baby hit me. Instead, I stared at the ceiling, trying to figure out how in the hell could someone like Kat have had a child with a monster like Hale.

In the end, I came to the only conclusion I could. She had been forced to. I clamped my thighs together as we sat in the car. Still, the thought of that...the thought of *him* on top of me, forcing his seed inside me. Or, God forbid, him standing there while his team of doctors forced my knees apart and inserted his semen inside. A chill raced through me, making me shiver. Now we were faced with another problem, how the hell to tell London what we'd found out.

"We need to tell him, Trouble. He has a right to know." Riven murmured beside me in the driver's seat.

"A right yes, but we have no idea how this will impact my sister." I stared at the entrance to London's home. "She's so goddamn vulnerable, Riven. This could tip her over the edge."

Cars and motorcycles lined both sides of the street in this cul-de-sac. Black SUVs and gleaming Harleys in all different types. These were the men London had bought for our war. No doubt there'd be many more before this was done.

Riven reached over, gripped the back of my neck, and turned my head to force my gaze to his. "We're doing the right thing here." My damn lip trembled until I pinned it with my teeth. He fixed his focus on the movement. "Jesus Christ, you're sexy right now." His hold eased, his thumb finding my lower lip and dragging across the soft flesh. "You get this done, Trouble, and I'm taking you home. Our real home in the city. How would you like that?"

"Blackwood?" I whispered.

He gave a slow nod. Those dark eyes were already glinting with excitement.

Heat raced with his stare. I knew exactly the kinds of things he was planning. Memories of our first few days together rose inside my mind. If anyone knew the depraved things he'd done to me, he'd be the one tied up and beaten. But that was him, wasn't it. So controlled. So dangerous. My pulse thundered with the thoughts.

"You ready to do this," he asked.

For a moment, I'd forgotten why we were here. That's how much this man affected me. I gave a nod, then Riven climbed out of the four-wheel drive and I followed. God, I didn't want to do this. I inhaled hard as London's armed men stepped out, eyeing Riven, then me.

"Ms. King." One gave a nod.

I forced a smile, heading for the back of the house. "Gentlemen."

There were men everywhere, filling up the external garage until there was no room. I eyed London's gray Audi sitting outside as Riven made his way through the back door and disappeared inside.

I can do this.

I can do this.

I pushed through the door and headed down the hall. The armory door was open. One of Guild's men packed away a new case full of ammunition. I stopped, my gaze moving over the stacks of handguns and semi-automatic weapons. "Holy shit, he really is going to war, isn't he?"

Guild's man just met my stare. "Yes, ma'am. He really is."

Jesus. I turned away, hurrying after Riven as he stopped and spoke to someone in London's study. I slowed, catching Guild's voice, and gave him a smile when I reached the doorway. "Hey there, how's my sister?"

But there was no smile in response. He just stared at me with the most gut-wrenching look and said carefully. "She's doing well."

That didn't give me any confidence. Instead, it spurred me to leave them both behind and head for the east wing of the massive house.

"Viv!" I called as Colt stepped out of the doorway and into my path, stopping me cold. "Oh, hey." I glanced around him. "Where is she?"

"Resting. She's not to be disturbed."

Fear rose, causing me to focus on his unflinching stare. He was the same as his brother. Actually, he was the same as all the Sons. When he focused on you, there wasn't a moment of hesitation. He was a predator, honing in on his next kill. At that moment, I was glad we were on the same side.

"Is everything okay with her?"

"Colt." Came my sister's exhausted voice as she stepped into the doorway behind him. "It's fine."

"Sorry. I ah, didn't realize you were sleeping." I moved around the unflinching giant and wrapped my arms around her trembling body.

She shook all the time now. Her dark eyes were almost black, spilling into the creases around them. She looked haunted and exhausted and terrified all wrapped in one.

"You okay?" I pulled away and brushed the stuck strands of hair from her damp forehead. "You're not sick or anything, are you?"

"No." She gave a hint of a smirk and pulled away. "I'm not sick."

"London," Riven said behind me.

I turned, to find London's long strides carrying him toward us. "Riven," he said carefully, then turned to me. "I wasn't expecting you."

"Sorry," I said. "We should've called ahead."

"What's up?" London asked carefully as he stopped in front of Vivienne.

I moved back a bit, listening to that deep baritone voice soften as he stared into her eyes. "You okay, Wildcat?"

She gave a nod, but you could see she was lying, trying her best to ease everyone's fears. That reason alone made every male around her dangerous.

"We have to talk," Riven started.

"And it's not something that could've been discussed over the phone?" London inquired as he slowly shifted his gaze from my sister.

"No, it isn't."

The way Riven answered made everyone look his way. There was a graveness about it.

"Very well." London caressed Vivienne's cheek. "You look pale. Why don't I get Guild to make you some of those fluffy banana pancakes you love and some orange juice?"

Vivienne turned almost green. She shook her head. "No, no food."

"Ice chips, then?"

Viv gave a slow nod.

Jesus, is that all she consumed? No wonder they were frantic. No one can live on just ice, let alone a woman carrying twins under the strain of our traumatic world.

"Maybe you should head back to bed?"

"Don't keep me in the dark, London." She glanced my way. "You know how it upsets me."

"Fuck's sake, woman." His tone was desperate and pleading.

I'd never heard London plead. I hadn't even thought he was capable. But here he was, swallowing hard before he tried again. "Just...just please, for the love of God, be careful."

"I will." She caressed his cheek and stared into his eyes.

The moment seemed so intimate and raw. My cheeks burned before I glanced away.

"I will, I promise. Just don't shut me out, London. Whatever this is, I can handle it."

"The moment your pulse starts to race or you—"

"I'll leave. I promise."

I glanced at him, catching his gentle nod. "Riven," he called and headed for the gymnasium.

Riven looked my way. "Ah, we're going to do this in your birthing room?"

London stopped walking. "Unless you have somewhere else in mind?"

"No," Riven muttered, then followed.

We all did. I waited for Vivienne and walked beside her.

"Ten days," she muttered, waddling after them. "Ten goddamn days, then I can get these kids out and be goddamn normal."

"You can do this." I reached for her hand. "We will help you."

We made our way slowly into the gym. Vivienne took a seat and moaned with relief.

"Well?" London muttered. "What was so important?"

"The Rossis have gone to ground." Riven started.

London swiveled around, his glare instant. "Is he pulling his men?"

"Pulling his men? No." Riven answered. "It's because of Kat and the baby."

"Kat and the baby?" London snapped. "What the hell has that got to do with them?"

"Everything." I whispered. "Because Kat's baby is Hale's."

London froze. Vivienne's head snapped toward me.

"What?" she whispered. "What did you say?"

"Kat's baby is Hale's."

"No." She shook her head. "That's not right."

"She was already pregnant when Laz met her on the Cosa Nostra island and with a place like that, there's only a few reasons you'd go. One, to murder another. Two, to make a name for yourself, and three, to hide. I can't see someone like Kat waiting for either of the first two."

"I knew her father was associated with Hale," London murmured, running his fingers through his hair. "It makes sense."

"It makes sense?" Vivienne repeated and winced. "Jesus Christ, can you imagine how terrified she must've been? How... *sickened*. That poor woman. That poor woman."

"Which makes perfect sense why they're going to ground." Riven added. "Because they suspect, or have a reason to suspect, Hale is coming for them."

"Oh God." Vivienne whispered. "Do we reach out to them?"

"No," London answered. "We wait for them to come to us. The Rossis are ruthless, both of them. They won't just sit back and wait for him to tear their world apart. They'll be making moves of their own, and as long as we are fighting the same man, then we do nothing."

Doing nothing felt like hell.

Doing nothing felt like *abandonment*.

Riven glanced my way. His dark eyes told me the same thing my own mind was. He didn't like it. None of us liked it, but we had no choice. Until the Rossis called, we had to focus on our own battle.

The conversation moved into what men we had arriving. The list of allies was growing. Still, it wasn't enough.

You need more men, Principal, if you plan on surviving. The rogue Son's words replayed in my head and that panicked feeling returned as London and Riven talked.

We did need more men.

But we also needed to work together.

"Call us if you hear anything else," London murmured, then glanced my way before shifting his focus to Vivienne.

We all did, finding her brow glistening with sweat. I walked over to her, leaned down and pulled her against me.

"Ten motherfucking days," she whispered. "Then I'll be good."

I hoped to God she lasted that long. I hoped even more that we'd find Hale, then take the bastard and his vile men out and be done with all this. Then my sister could have her babies and we'd all just move on.

But as I pulled away, giving her a smile, a heaviness moved through me. I had a feeling it wasn't going to be that easy.

"Take care of yourself, Vivienne," Riven murmured as he placed his hand against the small of my back. "Please, reach out if you need anything at all, day or night. If you need your sister, I'll make sure she gets here in record time."

Her mouth dropped open, staring at him as though he'd suddenly grown a second head. As London moved to the doorway, Riven followed, leaving me behind.

"That's actually the sweetest thing he's ever said to me." She shifted her gaze to mine.

"Honey, that's the sweetest thing Riven's ever said to *anyone,*" I answered, ruffling her hair. "He means it, too. Day or night, call me."

"I will." She gave a smile.

As I left, Colt was there, hovering in the background, more in tune with her body than anyone could be. That unflinching stare met mine as I passed.

"Be careful," he murmured.

My steps stuttered. "I will." I said over my shoulder and was gone, heading along the hallway and outside.

Riven and London talked in hushed tones, until I neared. Then Riven headed for the car. When I climbed in and closed the door behind me, I just sat there.

"Holy shit," I whispered and slowly turned my gaze to him. "That just happened."

Riven started the engine before meeting my stare. "It did. Now we need to focus on the future and the things we can do to get this done." He turned his attention back to the road, pulled out, and accelerated. "Like finding Hale."

We did. That was my only priority now. Because my sister's health was deteriorating, that was easy to see, and I wasn't sure how much longer she could hold on. All I hoped was she made it out of this okay and the babies were healthy. But that fear... that fear festered, growing inside me. *Just hold on, Viv. Just hold on.*

The car turned, taking different streets as it made its way out of the opulent and deadly streets to a more secluded area with more trees and lush grounds until I lifted my gaze and saw the house in the distance.

Blackwood.

My pulse skipped, racing as I jerked my gaze his way. He never flinched, just reached up and pressed the button, causing the garage door to lift. This was the house he'd brought me to on the night of the abduction. The same house I'd fought hard to escape, going so far as to knock this man out cold.

But I hadn't run...I'd needed him.

I licked my lips.

Wanted him too, if I was honest.

He pulled the car in and killed the engine, waiting for the garage door to close behind us before he glanced my way. "You want me to carry you in, Trouble?"

He meant like that night, right after I'd cut my foot on the smashed headlight of his car. I shook my head and yanked the handle before climbing out of the car. I knew exactly why he'd brought me here. This whole fight to survive was consuming everything, including us.

I closed the door as Riven climbed out and stood beside the car, watching me round the front of the four-wheel drive.

"Are you reliving those moments?" he murmured.

I nodded as the thunder in my chest grew bolder. Flickers of images pushed in, his hunger and my desperate battle with my own sick need. I made my way through the house. It looked exactly the same, green and lush and breathtaking. I reached out and trailed my fingers along the thick, luscious green foliage of the indoor ferns as I headed for the kitchen.

My lips curled into a smile, remembering the look on Riven's face as he'd cooked me my first vegan meal of oat flour pancakes, then I'd told him they were dry.

"The pancakes, isn't it?" he murmured behind me.

I dragged my fingers along the counter, then stopped and turned around. "Yes."

He wasn't smiling, in fact he was scowling, no doubt reminding himself how he'd failed.

He hadn't. I just wanted him to believe that.

"They were perfect, you know," I declared. "The best I'd ever had."

One brow rose quickly "They were?"

I nodded. "They were."

"And yet you led me to believe they were dry and tasteless. I'm pretty sure your words were *'I've had better.'*"

Fear thrummed through me. His slow step was all predatory, making me instinctively step backwards. He knew how to ignite that adrenaline in me, how he made me want to run, and fight...and beg. He reached up and gripped my throat, driving me back along the hallway to the bedroom.

"You lied," he murmured. "And you know how that annoys me."

"Oh, yeah?" I jutted my chin higher, whispering. "So, what are you going to do about it?"

There was a long, slow, snarl with a twitch in the corner of his mouth. He drove me backwards through the room until I smacked into the foot of the bed. With his shove, I flew backwards and landed with a bounce. He was on me in an instant, grabbing my hand as he straddled me.

The cuffs attached to the bed above my head snapped around my wrist. I jerked and pushed upwards. "Riven, let me out of these!"

He grinned and grabbed my other hand. I fought him, bucked my hips and thrashed my body, but he was too strong for me.

The metal cuff clenched around my other wrist, splaying both my arms wide until I hung suspended. Riven breathed heavily, looking down at me as he pulled away.

"You still fight like a demon, Trouble."

Anger burned as I gripped the cuffs and bared my teeth. "Come closer and I'll show you just how much."

He smiled and reached out, brushing his thumb across my cheek. "You think I don't know how strong you've become with the help of my brother's training?"

I glared as he leaned closer, so close he could kiss me. But he didn't. Instead, he leaned up, and pecked me on the end of my nose.

"Boop," he murmured.

I lunged, slamming forward. *"Fuck you! Don't you goddamn BOOP ME!"*

His chuckle pissed me off even more. I lunged again. "Let me go, Riven, or so help me God..."

He gripped my ankles, pulling them until my head dropped and hit the pillow. "Go on." He climbed onto the bed and in between my legs. "Fight and spit and scream."

He ran his hands up my legs to the juncture of my jeans. His thumbs pushed in, rubbing along my crease. I writhed, moving out of his touch. He didn't even hesitate, just reached up, opened the button of my jeans, and grasped the zipper tab before I realized it.

The zipper slid slowly down.

"Riven!" I roared.

Cool air brushed my thighs as he dragged my jeans down. I kicked, slamming my boots against the bed. He slid his thumbs under the waistband of my panties and pulled. My breaths raced. My thrashing slowed as he tugged my panties to my knees, then even lower.

His attention turned serious. His ravenous stare focused on my pussy as he frantically tugged my jeans and panties down around my ankles, then moved in.

"Riven." I moaned as he ran his thumb along the soft flesh of my pussy.

"There's no being dominant with me, Trouble." His other hand joined in, rubbing up my lips until he massaged my clit. "I'm not Thomas."

"I know," I said, breathlessly as he rubbed back down, making me moan. "I know you're not."

"And so." He leaned down, parted the top of my slit, and sucked. "You'll lie there and take what I give you."

"Fuck you," I whimpered and closed my eyes.

His fingers pushed inside me. "No, Trouble. Fuck *you.*"

My spine curled as he stroked, then leaned down once more, his tongue finding that trembling, tiny nub and dragging it into his mouth. I rotated my hands and gripped the cuffs, the fight slowly sliding away.

"That's the way, Trouble," he murmured. "Look how wet you are."

I licked my lips and looked down as he lifted his head. His fingers shone as they withdrew, which made me whimper. "I need...I need to come."

"I know you do." He murmured, those dark eyes annihilating me. "You want to give in to the feel of my fingers and the slickness of my tongue. You would grip those cuffs and come against my mouth. But that's not going to happen, Trouble. You see, I need more than just my taste of you. I need to fuck this pretty pussy." He dropped his hand to the bed and pushed backwards, climbing from the bed as his gaze moved over me. "Fuck, you look so goddamn good right now."

I sucked in heavy breaths, watching him as he slowly peeled his shirt away and kicked off his shoes. "It's just like before." His fingers worked the button of his pants and slid them down, boxers and all, leaving the thick bulge of his cock to spring free. "You all tied up and helpless and me...in control."

Fire lashed inside me. I jerked my gaze to his, curling my lips. "If you unlock the cuffs, I'll show you how much things have changed."

He chuckled and moved to the foot of the bed, then grabbed one of my boots and yanked it off before moving to the other. One hard jerk and it, too, was gone, leaving me with my jeans and panties bunched around my ankles.

"I'm sure you'd love to show me just how unpredictable you can be, Helene."

God, I loved it when he said my name like that.

My breaths became panting. "Unpredictable and can still kick your ass."

His smile grew wider as he pulled my jeans and panties off, leaving me in just socks, bra, and shirt. "I'm sure you can." He climbed back onto the bed and prowled toward me. "But right now, I'm a little more interested in yours."

"What?" I jerked as he pushed my knees together and rolled me onto my side.

"You heard me." He said, his hand sliding over my ass until he dipped into the crease. He lowered his head, working the spittle in his mouth. Slick saliva ran down, tickling me, until he used that slick to push against the tight ring of muscle. "That's the way, baby...*breathe.*"

I tried to focus, releasing that tension as he pushed deeper. This wasn't the first time Riven had driven his fingers inside. He was working me, stretching me. Getting me ready for—

He reached over, tugged open the drawer on his nightstand. I couldn't see what he was getting. "Riven."

"Trust me, baby," he said and eased back, lifting my knee until I splayed wide for him.

"Trust?" I yanked on the cuffs, pulling myself upwards until he pushed harder against my ass.

"*Breathe*," he repeated.

I released a breath, slowly drawing another in and, at the height of that inhale...Riven pushed in.

"*Jesus fucking Christ.*" He groaned.

That tight ring of muscle burned as it stretched. I gripped the cuffs, holding on as he eased out.

"This ass is mine." He groaned, gently driving in once more. "You hear me, Trouble? Goddamn fucking perfect pussy and ass. I want to own every goddamn inch of you."

I closed my eyes and dropped my head back. Panic mingled with desire until I couldn't tell them apart. I was terrified and aroused all at once.

Stop.

Keep going.

My mind and my body were at war, but as he pushed harder, letting the thick head of his cock slide all the way in, I lost all ability to care.

"That's it." He purred. "Look at you taking me. Christ, you're a good girl. Open for me, baby. Make me proud."

Those words ignited something debased and desperate inside me. I rocked as he thrust, bearing down, releasing all the tension so he could force his way in further.

"You're so good, look at you taking my cock all the way in this pretty ass of yours. I'm going to fill you, Trouble. By the time I'm done, you'll be dripping."

A moan tore free, guttural and pathetic. My clit pulsed, desperate and needing. "Please," I begged. "Riven, for God's sake, *please.*"

"Fuck, I love it when you beg."

He pulled my knee higher. I looked down, watching his fingers finding that hooded nub. One brush and I jerked with the sensation. My ass clenched, gripping him as he slowly withdrew and thrust back in, only this time harder.

"Oh, *fuck,*" he moaned, his fingers brushing my clit once more.

My body trembled, stretched and throbbed.

"That's...*my...good...girl.*" He grunted, shoving his cock all the way inside, using me as only Riven could.

I wanted him to use me...anyway he wanted.

My body quivered, clenching around him. I closed my eyes.

"The hell you do," he grunted. "Look at me while I fucking own you."

I turned my head, meeting his stare.

"That's it." His lips curled as he thrust harder.

I couldn't hold on. That dark, consuming stare. The delicious stretch as he slammed his cock all the way inside and his fingers, the way they rubbed and slipped along my clit before pushing into my pussy. That tremble turned into a quake.

I cried out, gripping the cuffs as my body took over, clenching hard. White sparks exploded, and through the flickering glare, I saw Riven's desperate look of ecstasy. He bared his teeth, grunting as he drove all the way inside and stilled.

I felt everything. The thick head of his cock and the pulsing vein along his length as he came, filling me with warmth.

"Mine." He gasped. *"You understand that?"*

I sucked in hard breaths. If I didn't remember that before...I sure did now.

FOURTEEN

Thomas

THE LOW DRONE OF A VOICE LULLED ME, LEAVING MY MIND to wander. Images pushed in. Flashes of blood and a body...no, two bodies. One tied up, her legs splayed wide, deep welts so cruel against tender pale flesh that blood dripped from the wounds. Somewhere a cell rang and rang and rang, the nagging sound pulling me out of the memory.

I lifted my gaze and suddenly felt the vibration against my thigh. Not *a* cell, it was mine.

My fingers reached into my pocket. I pulled it free and stared at the screen.

Caleb.

Caleb? I scowled and swiped to answer the call. "Yes."

"About damn time you answered. I've been calling for the last twenty minutes."

Twenty minutes?

I stood in Hunter's living room, in front of the TV mounted on the wall. Next to it was a clock. But the numbers meant nothing. Nothing much did at the moment. I felt...lost. "Sorry," I said, suddenly remembering who I spoke to. "Caleb?"

"Yeah, Priest?"

"The Daughter," I murmured.

"Taken care of," he said carefully. "Just like you asked. So now it's time to repay the favor."

The TV droned as images changed on the afternoon news. I lifted my gaze to the screen as Cassius' face filled the space, black suit, white collar. His face in full view with the headline, *Local Priest Missing*.

I stared at that face. "What do you need?"

My pulse was booming as he started. "We have the name of a man working with Hale to help him escape the country on a private jet. We plan on stopping that from happening."

"When?"

"Tomorrow night. You, me, and Colt will meet with Benjamin Rossi and pay this guy a visit. If he knows Hale's whereabouts, then we track him down. But more importantly, we make it so he can't run. There is no escaping for him, not alive."

My breaths deepened as a flicker of rage tore through me. My fist clenched, still feeling the weight of the cross in my hand. I'd murdered a man in cold blood, a man of the cloth. My focus narrowed in on the TV in front of me and Father Cassius stared back. A man I'd respected. The man I'd killed.

"Send me the details and I'll be there," I answered, my voice distant.

"Already have...and, Thomas?"

"Yes?"

"Pull yourself together or we won't make it out of this alive."

I swallowed hard, unable to find the words to answer. But it didn't matter, because he was gone. I lowered my cell, found *message*, and opened the app. The details were there, date, time, and address.

You, me, and Colt will meet with Benjamin Rossi.

London's son was included in all this? For some strange reason, it felt on purpose. Me from our family. Caleb from his, and Colt from Vivienne's family. The three outsiders. I stepped to the TV and switched it off, then made my way out and up the stairs.

Pull yourself together or we won't make it out of this alive.

He was right. As tormented as I was, I had to get it together, or this would be all for nothing. Others were depending on me now. Others I loved and admired. There was no way I was letting them down. I unbuttoned my shirt and pulled it over my head as I walked into my room. The black suit and white collar still sat crumpled in the trash in the corner.

I kept moving, kicked off my shoes and unbuttoned my trousers, then replaced them with sweats and a dark t-shirt before I sat on the edge of the bed and pulled on my black sneakers, laces tugged tight. I pulled my hand away and that's when I saw it.

There was blood under my nails. The rusted brown mess etched into the corners. I shoved upwards, lifting both hands, then lunged for the bathroom, slamming my shoulder on the doorframe as I ran for the vanity.

Water gushed, splashing around the sink. My hands shook as I lathered and scrubbed.

Get it off.

Get it OFF ME!

I'd done that. I'd...*killed a man in cold blood.* Not just any man...a man of the cloth. I closed my eyes and rocked forward, reliving that moment in my head. *WHACK! You fucking WHORE! DO YOU KNOW WHAT GOD DOES TO FILTHY WHORES LIKE YOU?*

Panic boomed, casting flickers of white sparks in my eyes as I rinsed and lifted my hands. Water dripped from my shaking hands as I stared at the edges of my nails. The faint trace of blood was still there.

God will show me the way. My own empty words returned. *God will show me the way.*

I needed to get out of here. I needed to...*run.*

I stumbled out of the bathroom and lurched toward the stairs. Sparks still danced in my eyes as I staggered outside and turned to the mountain, then started to climb.

God will show me.

God will show me the way.

Rocks kicked out from under my feet as I climbed. I forced myself to focus on the movement as my feet found the trail I'd run over and over, until my breaths deepened and the burn of my muscles pushed in. When I reached the top, I stopped and just stood. My hands continued to shake, drawing my focus. I still saw the blood, even if it wasn't there. In my mind, it was. In my mind, I killed Cassius over and over again.

I lifted my gaze to the blue sky.

That ache I carried in my chest grew tighter.

Please, tell me I did the right thing.

I beg of you.

I searched the heavens, watching as a heavy, dark cloud blocked out the sun, casting me into the shadows. An emptiness filled me, one that seemed to push me further from God.

It was wrong, what I'd done.

I clenched my fists beside me.

I was wrong.

I WAS GODDAMN WRONG!

Agony tore through my chest with a sob. My shoulders curled as I closed my eyes. *You betrayer...you goddamn betrayer.* Warmth slid down my cheeks as I stood there, until a hand landed on my shoulder.

"Go away, Hunter," I said, my voice husky and thick.

Still the weight lingered, forcing me to open my eyes and turn around.

Only my brother wasn't there.

No one was.

Sunlight splashed across the ground at my feet, the afternoon rays finding a crack in the cloud. I stopped crying and stared instead as that pure luminescent glow brightened. Only, as it fell across the cracks in the mountain, it formed a cross.

A cross.

I lifted my gaze to the sky, finding that single perfect beam shining through and looked again. The cross was there, as plain as my own hands. But as I watched, it slowly dulled, faded, and disappeared altogether.

But it *was* there.

Right in front of me.

I stumbled forward, found the crevice in the stone the light had shone upon, and knelt. The rock was warm to my touch. Fingers splayed, palms pressed, I leaned down and closed my eyes as I pressed my cheek against the warmth.

He came to me.

He...came to me.

My chest trembled and my throat thickened until I could barely breathe. I stayed like that, with my face pressed against the mountain, shaking and crying, until the clouds moved on and the sun's rays dulled. But it didn't matter. I knew now. I knew that fighting evil was a battle worth getting bloody for, and Father Cassius *had been* evil.

To harbor that much hatred for another was evil.

To whip and mutilate and destroy.

I thought of Helene. My beautiful Helene.

To even *think* of doing something like that to her *was* evil.

And it was up to me to stop it, any way I could.

I lifted my face from the earth, brushed the bits of rock from my cheek, and rose. The sky was growing darker as I turned around and slowly made my way back down the mountain. With each step, I grew my focused. I was a fighter. Before,

I'd fought with prayers, but now I fought with fists and weapons.

Either way, I'd rid this earth of one evil at a time. By the time I made it back down, the others had returned from the city. Riven's four-wheel drive was in front next to Kane's Audi. My brothers had their own paths. Now I had mine.

Their voices reached me as I neared the house. But my mind wasn't on them anymore. It was waiting for the message...and a new sign from God. One I was ready for, more than ever before.

I PACED the floor of my bedroom, my focus divided between the clock on the bedside dresser and my damn cell. I'd waited all day, sat with my family last night after I returned from the mountain, and spent all day listening to Hunter strategize with his men. But now it was evening...and I'd had no call.

My boots muffled my steps, but still, I couldn't quell the thunder in my head.

Should I call?

I lifted my cell and pulled up Caleb's number, then my thumb hesitated over the icon. If I called him and he was with Ryth and the others, what then? I winced and lowered my cell, turning my focus to the room.

Buzz.

I wrenched the phone up.

Caller ID Caleb.

I answered it instantly. "I'm ready."

"Well, this is better than last time. I was worried you weren't up for the task," he murmured.

My focus shifted to the statue of the cross standing in the middle of my dresser. "No, I'm ready."

"Good. Then leave now and head to 105 Marketplace. I'll meet you there."

My hands were shaking, making it hard to grip my cell. "Okay, I'm leaving now."

"I don't need to remind you how important this is?"

"No," I murmured. "You don't."

"See you there, Thomas, and Priest..."

"Yes?"

"You might want to keep this to yourself. Just until we know what we're dealing with."

I gave a nod. "Okay."

I lowered my hand, the call now disconnected. This didn't seem real and yet, in my soul, I knew this was where I was always meant to be. I was now a messenger in the most brutal way. One from God.

I turned around, grabbed my jacket from the end of the neatly made bed, and headed for the door. Voices reached me from downstairs. The others were in the living room. The bitter, comforting scent of a fire made a pang in my chest. Still, I made my way downstairs, the thud of the last step hitting harder than I wanted.

"About time you joined us!" Riven called out as I stopped in the middle of the landing.

But I wasn't headed for them. Instead, I turned, grabbed Riven's Audi keys off the entry table, and headed for the door. By the time I stepped out and locked the door behind me, they'd know tonight would be different.

There'd be no *us* tonight. There'd be no anything.

I hit the button to unlock the car and climbed in behind the wheel. The door to the house opened as the engine started. They all stepped out, staring as I shoved the Audi into gear and backed out, turned hard, and headed away from our mountain oasis.

There was no tremble in my hands now, no doubt in my heart. Faith steadied me. My cell vibrated in the console beside me. I glanced at the caller ID, though I instantly knew it was my family.

An ache radiated through my chest. But as the pain grew deeper, the image of that sundrenched cross on the ground filled my mind. I was doing this for them...and for me.

They needed to trust me.

I pushed the sedan harder and headed into the city. Marketplace was on the edge of town, down near the water. It was a place of joy and laughter, with playgrounds and a towering Ferris wheel. A place for families, not a place for death. But that's exactly where I was headed.

I scanned the cars, searching for something Caleb would drive, and pulled into a parking spot across from a black Jeep Wrangler. The moment I reached to kill the engine, the Jeep's back-up lights flared. As the four-wheel drive backed up, I caught sight of Caleb through the window. He motioned me forward, wanting me to follow.

Where the hell was he taking me? I scanned the streets as we passed. Children held hands with their parents, eating ice cream as they walked along the sidewalk. But we quickly left them all behind and turned onto a street that took us nowhere, until he stopped outside a gray, nondescript building and the steel-gated garage door rose. Then he drove inside.

I followed, easing the Audi around a turn until I came out in an under-ground parking area. Headlights bounced against glass walls as Caleb parked. I caught sight of the Black Escalade the Sons drove and a sleek steel-gray BMW.

It wasn't until I'd killed the engine and climbed out that I saw them.

Colt.

Benjamin Rossi.

And Caleb as he climbed out of the Jeep and headed toward me.

"Thomas," he called as Benjamin and Colt headed toward me.

The moment felt ominous and charged. Goosebumps raced along my arms. I didn't know what we were in for tonight, where our violence would take us, or how many we might kill. What I did know was that this path of sin would be my salvation.

FIFTEEN

Helene

"WHAT THE FUCK?" RIVEN MUTTERED AS THE SOUND OF the front door closing gave a heavy *thud*.

I lifted my head, my lips burning from Hunter's raspy four-day growth. His hands were on my hips, pulling me harder against him as I straddled him on the sofa.

But the sound of the front door closing drew all our focus. Riven pushed up from the sofa across from us, his focus no longer on the way I fucked his brother. None of ours were. I pushed backwards, letting Hunter's hands slip free.

"Riven, where the hell is he going?"

"Hell if I know," he snarled as he headed for the front door.

I followed as the faint *thud* of the car door could be heard. Hunter and Kane were right behind me. Riven unlocked the door and stepped out, letting the cool night air rush in. I wrapped my arms around myself as fear pushed in.

"Did you piss him off?" Kane asked, glancing at Riven.

"Who the fuck knows?"

Headlights blinded us as Thomas turned the wheel, backed out of the driveway, and headed through the towering gate as it rolled open.

"Call him," Riven murmured, sounding desperate, and glanced my way. "He'll answer if it's you."

I turned around, pushed through the front door, and ran to the kitchen. *Where the hell are you going, Thomas?* My mind raced. Had I pushed him too hard the other day in his bedroom? He'd been acting strange since then.

Idiot!

I snatched my cell from the counter as heavy footsteps came behind me. My hands shook as I pulled up the contacts and swiped, calling his number.

It rang...

And rang.

Then went to voicemail. I spun, meeting Riven's dark stare. He gave a nod. "Call again, maybe this time he might answer?"

But that sinking feeling took hold, gripping me tight as I swiped and called again.

"The same." I shook my head as it was answered by that recorded message once more.

"Riven...*look at this,*" Kane called from the living room.

We left the kitchen behind and rushed to where Kane stood in front of the TV. He turned as we neared. "I saw this on before, Thom seemed mesmerized by it, muttering to himself."

I focused on the image of a man. A Priest.

"*Cassius.*" Riven glanced at Kane.

"He's from St. Augustine's."

Riven turned back, his eyes widening. "Now, that's not good."

We all lifted our gaze to the floor above and Thom's bedroom. Riven was the first to move, heading for the stairs.

"Riven, wait!" Kane called. "Let's not invade his space."

"Fuck *his space.*" Riven threw over his shoulder, taking the stairs two at a time.

He was right. This was no time for niceties. Not when the safety of those we loved was on the line. But what the hell did all this have to do with a missing Priest? And from Thomas's own church.

Riven pushed open the bedroom door and stepped in, expecting us to follow. The room was neat, neater than I'd seen it in a while. A quick scan of the space and Riven opened the door to the bathroom and flicked on the light. He was barely gone a second before he returned, then stopped suddenly, his head jerking to the corner. He stepped over to the wastepaper basket, reached in, and turned, holding his brother's black trousers and a white shirt...splattered with blood.

I swallowed hard at the mess, then moved closer to lift the shirt free. It wasn't just light spots of blood you might get flicking a cut hand...it was *drenched.*

"You want to fight about invasion of privacy now, brother?" Riven lifted his gaze to Kane.

Kane moved closer, reached up to grasp the edge of the shirt, and stared at the mess. "Fuck no."

"Someone must know where he's headed." Riven snapped.

My mind was racing, remembering the cagey way he'd acted when I'd caught him talking to Caleb. I'd known something was going on, something he didn't want me to know about. Was it London? Had London said something?

"I saw him with Caleb when we were at London's. They were talking, it looked serious," I said. "When I asked him about it, he got all cagey and secretive. Maybe London knows something?"

Riven looked pissed as he lifted his cell. "If that bastard knows what my brother has done, I swear to God, I'll ruin that square fucking jaw of his."

But the moment the call was answered, we knew something was very wrong.

"What is it, I'm dealing with a problem here!" London barked as Riven put him on speaker. Vivienne's worried tone slipped through in the background. "It's okay, Wildcat. We'll find him."

"What the hell is going on?" Riven snarled.

"Colt's missing. Took off about fifteen minutes ago, wouldn't tell us why. Vivienne is stressed."

Riven's eyes widened as he lifted his gaze to mine. "Us too, that's why I'm calling. Thomas took off just now, not saying a damn word."

Suddenly there was silence on the other side. "And you think Colt has something to do with it?"

"I think he's meeting Thom."

"Tell him about Caleb," I urged.

"Helene caught him talking to Caleb. We know he's been secretive lately."

"Benjamin goddamn Rossi's name has come up more than once and I saw him talking to Caleb. We know the Rossis have gone to ground. If he's using my goddamn son, I swear to God..." London growled into the phone.

"He needs to come back, London." Vivienne paced the floor. "It can't be like before. We almost lost him. We almost..."

London's voice deepened. "I'll make some calls. If he's with Caleb or the Rossis, I'll find out."

"We'll start tracking his cell from our end." Riven glanced at Hunter who gave a nod. "Call if you find anything."

"Will do, and Riven..."

Silence as he waited.

"I assure you, I had nothing to do with this."

"Just find my goddamn brother, St. James. Find him and bring him home."

He swiped and ended the call. I clenched my fists, trying to still the shakes, but there was no stopping whatever this was.

"If he's in trouble..." I whispered.

Riven stepped closer. "He's smart and capable, even if he is a little quirky. He'll be okay, just you wait and see."

But there was no truth in those words. Only the false ring of desperation in his tone. He didn't believe that, which only made me shake harder.

SIXTEEN

Thomas

HE WAS DRESSED FOR WAR. BLACK ON BLACK, WORN leather shoulder straps that criss-crossed over his thick chest were crammed with black handguns and loaded magazines. I'd only ever seen Benjamin Rossi in tailored slacks and open-collared shirts, looking like he'd spent all day in the boardroom.

But not tonight.

Tonight, he was made for terror.

A cell rang, the sound low and dangerous. Benjamin reached into his pocket and withdrew it, glanced at the caller ID before he swiped to turn it to silent.

"Your car is safe here, we'll all go in my Rover," he declared.

Colt glanced at the glistening black beast, then bent down and picked up a heavy duffel bag.

"We have weapons, son," Ben stated.

"I bring my own," Colt answered simply and headed for the vehicle.

I said nothing and followed, realizing I hadn't even thought of guns. The thick cross around my neck shifted as I turned and headed after the Son. But I'd made sure I had that. Tension grew inside me as Ben rounded the Ranger and climbed in, waiting for us to follow.

I said nothing as Colt heaved his bag onto the seat next to me and climbed in. The Range Rover's engine growled into life. Doors closed and we pulled out, heading back out of the empty parking area that no doubt belonged to the building the Rossis owned.

I was pushed back into my seat as we accelerated hard, driving back onto the city streets.

"Do we have information?" Colt asked. "Is that what we're doing here?"

Even he didn't know.

Ben glanced into the rear-view mirror and met his gaze before suddenly turning sharply. Headlights flew past and people were a blur before we turned again. That ominous, heavy feeling returned. So I shifted my focus out the window, hit the button, and rolled down the window.

Sirens wailed.

Someone screamed as a fight broke out. Drunken men threw punches. We'd driven past before I knew it, speeding through the streets before turning once more. The landscape only grew more violent, and a lot seedier. Harley engines roared, the jarring sounds so loud I jerked and pulled back, then reached for the button on the window, until I stopped and slowly pulled my hand away.

Over the tops of clubs shone a vision. The cross of what must've been St. Stewart's glowed in golden yellow, just like that vision of the cross that had spilled across the mountain at my feet. I pulled my hand back as we turned once more, pulling up on a darkened street outside the clubhouse of a notorious motorcycle club, Hells Saviors.

"You want to know what London's men are doing?" Benjamin said as the vehicle idled.

As we sat and watched, three four-wheel drives pulled up outside the clubhouse. The driver and the men in the back seat eyed us as they passed. A nod from one of them and I knew they were aware we were friends and not foes. They climbed out and, in a blur, all the men rushed into the building.

The sound of breaking glass was followed by a *BOOM!* Smoke billowed before a steady stream of men and women dressed in cuts staggered outside, coughing and spluttering. Then four of the eight mercenaries who'd gone in came out mere minutes later, dragging three heavy leaders of the club and threw them to the ground.

"That's what money buys," Ben murmured. "Men with guns terrorizing criminals. But that's not who we're after. Our target is a whole new breed of vile bastard, ones who hide behind the money and the law."

He shoved the Range Rover into gear and pulled out, leaving London's men behind. We turned once more and, as we headed toward the sleek, towering business buildings, I caught sight of the glow of the cross once more.

It was a sign. I was sure of it and, as we slowed and pulled into the parking lot of one of the most prestigious buildings in the city, I understood why.

"Are you sure you're in the right place?" I asked.

Colt just pulled a gun from behind his back, pulled back the slide, and lowered his hand. "Just tell me who I need to kill to find that fucker."

He meant Hale, I knew.

We parked in front of the bank of slick steel elevators. But there was already a car waiting as we pulled up. Two men climbed out, one scruffy and dirty, his seedy eyes scanning us dressed in leather cuts and grimy jeans. The other was a stark contrast, in a neat black suit. He adjusted his jacket as we neared.

"Any complications?" Ben asked as he neared.

"Not really. Once Alistair here let us inside, it was pretty fast. He caused a fuss at first, but we straightened him out."

I looked at the scruffy companion, trying to figure out where he fit in all this.

Ben glanced our way. "Alistair is undercover. He's a plant from the motorcycle club the Banks brothers, along with Colt and Carven, destroyed. I've had him working for me ever since, gaining the kind of information that doesn't make it online. Ignatius Bremmer is a master manipulator. Not only that, he is one of the lawyers behind The Order, helping it keep out of the courts for the vile things they do."

"He is who we're here to kill?" Colt asked as he readied the gun in his hand.

"No. We need information first. We need to know when and where Hale is running to. We get that and we'll have no further use for him."

That was all Colt needed. A nod, and the Son strode toward the elevator doors, then stopped and turned in front of them. "You coming, or do I have to torture this motherfucker myself?"

Ben gave a smile and headed after him without waiting for us to follow. But the moment we were inside the elevator, the Stidda Mafia leader changed. Gone were the brightness in his eyes and the remnant of a smile on his lips. He turned cold, so cold that goosebumps raced up my arms.

We rose all the way to the top floor of the building, and when we stopped Benjamin Rossi was the first one off the elevator, striding toward a set of frosted glass doors with the words *Bremmer Johnson* written in gold. Ben never slowed, just shoved his way through, passed the reception desk and headed for the hallway beyond it.

A man stood outside the door at the end, dressed in black. A Rossi man. He gave his boss a nod as we neared, opened the door for him, and stepped to the side. Why Benjamin wanted us here still wasn't clear. He had men to do his dirty work. Men to kill. Men to torture. But here we were, following him into the massive corner office to stare at a graying older man sitting with crossed legs on a seat behind a desk.

"Benjamin Rossi," he said slowly before glancing toward Colt, then me, and finally Caleb. "I see you've brought your lackeys with you."

Colt unleashed a low growl and took a step forward. But the asshole sitting in the seat looked like he'd met his fair share of bullies. He never flinched, never even registered the movement at all.

Benjamin reached around, pulling out some kind of USB device from his pocket. "You remind me of a man I once knew. Someone who assisted another slimy piece of shit like Hale. He too had limited conscience and a large bankroll. I didn't know the man he was helping to hide. It was just a job to me. One that paid very well." He reached around the computer on the desk and plugged in the device. Tiny blue lights flickered as data processed.

"What the fuck is that?" Ignatius wrenched his gaze to where Ben had released the device and straightened to his full height. Our presence might've been ignored, but that wasn't. *"Get that out of my computer now.* You're breaking the goddamn law here. I'm going to *ruin* you, Rossi! *I'm going to GODDAMN RUIN YOU!"*

But Ben just stepped around the desk to stop in front of him. He pulled out a pair of black leather gloves, sliding them on one at a time. "Yes, you very much remind me of that slimy fucker. He roared and spat, too, until I started on his teeth, pulling them out one by one."

The asshole couldn't take his eyes off those flickering lights on his computer. When he turned back, Ben had secured the straps of his gloves around his wrists. He lunged, grabbed Ignatius by the throat, and clenched. The move was so fast and violent it took the asshole completely by surprise.

He unleashed a cry and flung himself backwards. But it was pointless. Benjamin gripped his throat in a vise-like grip and drove him backwards until the chair tipped. "When I started gutting him slowly, he passed out, but not before he pissed all over himself. If I did that to someone I didn't know, imagine what I'd do to someone threatening my family."

Ignatius turned gray and shook his head. "I...I don't know anything."

"Are you prepared to bet your life on that?" Ben growled out.

Colt knew exactly what Ben needed, so he reached to his belt and stepped forward. The overhead lights glinted on the honed edge of the blade the Son held in his palm.

"Not only will I leave the entrails of the bastard who went after my family on the ground at his feet." Benjamin's tone was chilling as he gave that bastard his entire focus. "I'll go after his family, wives, mothers, children. I would kill and keep killing until I ended his bloodline." He glanced at the desk and reached over to grab a large picture, staring at the massive family all crammed into the one frame. "That's a lot of lives in your hands, Ignatius. I'd think very carefully before I spoke."

"You can't," the bastard whimpered, his eyes so damn wide I could see the whites all the way around.

Flashes of Cassius' terrified expression slammed into me.

"I can," Ben answered, leaning down. "So help me God, I can. Because I've done it before."

Ignatius unleashed a low, sickened sound and shook his head. There were tears in his eyes, thick ugly tears that slipped down his cheeks. My fingers clenched into fists. They were all the same...those *sinners*.

"Tell us what we want to know," I croaked, my breaths racing. "Or be prepared to meet God's wrath."

He shifted that watery gaze my way. "I...I know nothing. All I have is a contact. That's all, Haelstrom never gave me the details. He said he had to be careful, his cargo was too precious."

"Cargo?" Benjamin growled.

We *all* knew what that meant.

Kat and his daughter.

"Give us the name." Ben wrenched his shirt, dragging his gaze back. "You lie to me and I'll fucking destroy you."

"L-leroy Hay-Hastings." The lawyer blubbered.

Benjamin shoved him backwards so hard the chair skidded and slipped, then fell forward and landed upright.

"Where can we find him?"

He shook his head. "I...I don't know."

Ben flicked the knife upwards, leaving the lawyer riveted by the movement. "He's not a lawyer, some seedy bastard in Helenstown. That's all I know...*I swear, that's all I know.*"

Benjamin grabbed his shirt and yanked him forward. "And I believe you. You should thank your maker for that." With one savage slash, he dragged the blade across the lawyer's throat. Blood spurted instantly. I jolted, wrenching my focus to the smear on the knife before I looked back.

The lawyer's wide eyes were fixed on Benjamin as though he couldn't quite comprehend what just happened.

"W-what?" He spluttered, releasing a red torrent that streamed down his chest.

Benjamin was engulfed with the spurt as he stepped forward. It cut across his chest and dripped to the floor as he bent and wiped the blade on Ignatius' shirt, before he stepping back. "No one comes after my family and lives. You can die knowing this ends here, your family is safe."

But that meant little for him. He died like that, staring straight ahead. Just bled and bled and bled until the crimson mess had soaked into his shirt and stuck to his skin. Benjamin glanced at the USB in the back of the computer, then slowly peeled the glove off one hand and gave the blade back to Colt.

I tore my focus from that empty, dead stare and found the gaze of the stone-cold killer in front of me. "What do we do now?"

"Now we find Leroy Hastings," Benjamin said coldly, folding his gloves and handing them to his man behind us. "And we keep going until we find where this piece of shit is hiding. We give him nowhere to run and nowhere to hide. If I have to kill every man in this goddamn city to do it, then so be it."

I'd seen Riven kill out of pure desperation.

I'd even seen men shot in the head as he knelt alongside us on the filthy landing dock of The Order.

But I'd *never* seen anything like that.

Cold.

Mechanical.

Brutal.

Like he *almost* enjoyed it.

His man's phone chimed. The protector answered it before the second ring and lifted it to his ear. "Yeah? Yeah, okay. I'll ask. Hold on." He looked at Ben. "Do we need our escort?"

Ben scowled, then slowly glanced my way.

Why the hell did he look at me?

"Yes, have him follow."

He stepped around the dead lawyer as his man relayed the information on the phone. Ben checked that the USB was still processing, then said. "Tell the boys they can connect. Take them back to the garage. Call me once you have a location for Leroy Hastings." He glanced our way, meeting Caleb's stare. "Keep your cell close, I'll call when we have something concrete."

A nod from Caleb, and Benjamin turned and headed for the door, stopping only when he was alongside me. "You did well tonight, Priest. I didn't think you had the stomach for it. But you've proved me wrong. You remind me of my brother before he died, you know that? He was different from the rest of us, kinder, more considerate." His focus hardened. "But that didn't mean he wasn't capable of protecting those he loved, even if he demanded more from us emotionally than we were capable of. Keep that tenderness about you, son. It's a trait we all sacrificed to violence a long time ago, including your brothers. Protect it, cherish it, and I promise I'll do my best to keep you safe."

"Okay," I murmured, trying to keep up with what had happened.

Benjamin Rossi liked me, no, he more than liked me. He felt some kind of connection. Maybe it was all hidden under the ghost of his brother. Maybe it was a deeper yearning of his own soul. Either way, it looked like I had a guardian of sorts. His steps echoed and slowly faded as he strode through the door.

"Let's get you back to your cars," Benjamin's man said.

We all turned, until I stopped and looked back over my shoulder.

To the gaping wound and the bloody lips of a man who'd had so much to live for, but instead, he'd died protecting the Devil. Haelstrom Hale was pure evil. There was only one place for his kind, the same cold, empty place this man was finding his way to.

"Good riddance." I whispered as I turned and left the office and that building far behind.

"INCOMING," Colt muttered from the passenger's seat of the midnight blue Explorer.

Benjamin's man glanced into the rear-view mirror and caught the glare of headlights that flooded the car. "It's okay. It's our date for the night.

Our *date?*

I turned to look over my shoulder as the blue Land Rover pulled up alongside us. Through the dark tinted window, a hulking beast of a man took up the entire space behind the steering wheel. He turned his head and stared straight at me before he gunned the engine and drove out in front of us.

"Who is he?" I asked.

Ben's man met my stare in the reflection. "They call them Cerberus, the three-headed Mafia hound. If you ask me, they're ruthless sons of bitches. Ones you never want to piss off, if you get my meaning?"

I stared at the ominous shadow in the driver's seat and a sinking feeling gripped me. "Noted," I mumbled as we drove into the underground garage and pulled up alongside our cars.

The blue Land Rover followed us in but stayed back in the empty car spaces, the engine thick and throaty as it rumbled.

"He's going to follow you home, Priest." Benjamin's man glanced toward the car as we climbed out.

"Thomas," I answered as I closed the door behind me.

"What?"

I met his gaze. "My name is Thomas, not Priest. I'm not that... not anymore."

A slow nod and he gave a shrug. "Whatever you need."

Thomas, that's who I was. I reached into my pocket, pulled out the keys to Riven's Audi, unlocked it, and climbed in. I didn't start the engine right away, letting those words really sink all the way into my bones.

I wasn't a Priest. I couldn't be, not after what I'd done and all the things I was going to do.

But that realization didn't hurt as much as it should've. In fact, I felt free.

Freer than I'd felt in a long time. The cross around my neck shifted against my skin as I leaned forward and started the engine. I had my faith, and now I had my purpose, and it was bigger than ever before. When I drove out of the garage, that Land Rover followed and pulled in behind me.

I drove through the city, my focus divided between the streets ahead and the blinding headlights behind me. Cars cut in between us and each time they did, my pulse kicked up. But they quickly moved on, the cars thinning out as I continued heading out of the city.

He's going to follow you home, Priest.

Why?

Why me?

It seemed stupid having an escort, especially all the way out here.

I drove in silence, watching the road, and tried to push the events of the night from my mind.

Headlights shone, glaring in the rear-view mirror as two motorcycles overtook the Land Rover and closed in between us. I looked back as I started the climb up the mountain. The roar of the engines was very loud with them so near. I waited for them to overtake me, my focus more on the man behind the wheel of the Land Rover following me.

But as the road grew steeper, I realized the bikers weren't going to pass me. They sat between us, hugging each corner, gaining that little bit closer.

"Come on." I gripped the wheel tighter. "Just go *around.*"

The driveway to the house was up ahead, but I couldn't turn in, not with those assholes up my damn ass.

Crack!

I flinched as the side mirror exploded. "What the fuck?"

Headlights veered as the outline of a bike pulled out. In the reflection of his headlights, I caught sight of the leather vests and the patches they wore. They were bikers...like the ones from tonight. The ones London's men had bullied and beaten.

"Oh shit." I swung my focus back to the road and pushed the Audi harder.

Crack!

The passenger side window shattered and some glass flew in. I unleashed a roar as the car jerked hard across the middle of the road. *Get to the house...just get to the goddamn house.*

As more gunfire came, I knew I had no time left. I gripped the wheel, punched the brakes, and prayed.

SEVENTEEN

Helene
_____

THE CRACK OF GUNFIRE WAS SO FAINT IT BARELY
penetrated the silence. Still, I jerked my gaze up as Riven
glanced toward the door.

"Did you hear that?" He asked as he slowly rose.

I pushed up from the sofa as Hunter headed for the door. He'd
heard it and I'd heard it, too. When the faint *crack* came again,
it was louder. I rushed forward, with Kane right behind me,
rounded the opposite sofa and made for the door. It'd been
hours since Thomas left, hours spent worrying and waiting in
silent torment.

But as Hunter yanked open the front door, the shrill screech of
tires sounded. He was in trouble...*he was in trouble.*

"*Thomas!*" I screamed and ran like his life depended on it.

We all ran. Hunter had grabbed his handgun from on top of the
hallway cupboard. Riven's only weapon was pure rage as the
towering steel gate of the compound rolled open to reveal

Riven's Audi sideways, at a standstill, with the windows blown out.

Crack.

Crack!

CRACK!

The gunfire didn't come from Thomas, who was hunkered down across the front seat. Was he dead...*Oh, Jesus, PLEASE DON'T BE DEAD.* Hunter unleashed a roar as he swung his gun toward a dark blue Land Rover which was pulled up across the entrance of the driveway, with a massive brute of a man standing behind it.

That's when I saw it. Two motorcycles lay on their sides, with a body beside each. One guy was dead, his gun visible at the end of his outstretched arm. But another crawled toward his weapon, dragging himself forward inch by inch, until the towering beast of a man strode closer, lifted his gun, and fired.

CRACK!

I didn't even know him. I'd never seen him before, but I saw him now. He was dressed in black jeans and a black turtleneck, with a custom-made double shoulder holster criss-crossed across his powerful chest. When he glanced my way, I jolted. One eye was white and scarred, glinting in the night.

"You're welcome, Principal," he muttered.

"Alvarez?" Riven called the name like he wasn't sure if he was dreaming.

The towering male glanced toward Thomas behind the wheel of Riven's Audi. "Make sure he gets inside."

I was already running for him, cutting through the headlights to wrench open the driver's door. The moment he lifted his gaze to mine, relief hit me harder than anything I'd ever experienced before.

"Thank God! *Thank fucking God!*" I yanked him out, pulling him into my arms. I gripped him tightly, my heart booming so hard my chest was about to explode. "Are you okay?"

I pulled away, searching his vacant stare, and examined his body, running my hands over his arms and his chest, though I knew full well he didn't like to be touched. Still, I had to know. The moment after I'd checked him over, I pulled away.

"What the hell is going on here?" Riven jerked his gaze from the man he'd called Alvarez to his brother.

"Mr. Rossi sends his regards," the giant said, giving Thomas a slow nod.

One Thomas returned.

The huge man rounded his idling four-wheel drive and climbed back in as Riven headed for us.

"Want to tell me what the fuck just happened here?" he barked.

"No." Thomas shook his head. "Not really." He stepped around me, glanced at the others, and headed for the house.

"Not really?" Riven repeated. *"NOT REALLY? What the fuck!"*

He was angry, more than angry. Riven was scared, and that made him dangerous to everyone, even those he cared about.

"Goddamn asshole," he muttered as he approached his car. "Look at my car for Christ's sake!" He threw his hands up in

the air, glancing at the bullet holes and the smashed windows, then froze.

He took a step closer and reached out to press his finger against a neat hole, then stared at the driver's seat, doing what we were all doing. Mentally calculating how far his brother had been away.

It was too close.

It was *way* too close.

Riven looked at the empty space where the midnight blue Land Rover had sat moments ago, then jerked his gaze to the two dead bodies lying outside the gate. I saw the moment his fear turned to rage. His breaths deepened and his dark gaze turned terrifying. He left the open door of his car behind.

"Hunter," Kane called.

But our protector was already moving, closing in as Riven stepped outside the fence line and bent down. He grabbed one of the bodies and rolled it over.

"What the fuck does that even say? *LionsDenz?*" He lifted his gaze to Hunter. "Who the fuck is this guy?"

I stepped out from the car, watching as Hunter bent and rifled through the body's pockets, pulling out his ID. "Who knows, but you can bet your ass I'll find out."

I glanced toward the house.

"Go," Kane murmured. "He'll tell you what happened before he'll tell us."

I met his stare and started to shake my head before I stopped. He was right. For some reason, Thomas was more closed off around them, leaving me their only hope to find out what had happened.

I headed for the house, leaving them behind to search the dead and get rid of the bodies. My mind was racing as I stepped inside. I left the front door open, listened for movement, and heard the clink of glass in the kitchen.

Thomas was standing at the counter, gripping the edge, his head bowed, with a glass half full of Scotch beside him. I'd never even seen him drink alcohol before, let alone anything neat.

"Thom." I started.

He just shook his head. "I don't need you yelling at me, too. It's too loud...too *loud.*"

"I'm not going to yell at you." I reached out before I realized what I was doing and froze, my hand hovering over his shoulder.

He lifted his head. "You're not?"

"No." I soothed. "I'm not. I was worried, we were all worried. You just scared us, that's all."

He scowled, then grabbed his glass, stepped around me, and headed for the living room. That wasn't like him at all. Something had happened to him. Something had *changed him.* The sound of Riven's car came outside before switching off. Footsteps followed. I subconsciously counted the three of them before the front door closed.

"Brother." Riven started and stepped closer.

"I *don't want to be different.*" Thomas' voice trembled as he lifted his gaze. His amber eyes were dark now, so dark they barely looked like his at all.

"You want to talk to us, buddy?" Kane urged. "What made you think like that?"

The Scotch sloshed with his shudder. "Don't." He shook his head. "Don't fucking do that, Kane. Not with me."

Kane stepped closer. "Then tell us what happened and maybe we can find a way to ease your pain."

"*YOU CAN'T!*" Thomas bellowed. "*You can't ease my pain because it's MY GODDAMN PAIN!*"

We all stopped, stunned. Thomas was pale as a ghost and shaking. First it was the blood on the shirt. Then, it was secret conversations with Caleb. Now, it was sneaking out at night with Benjamin Rossi and others.

He lifted his glass and downed the contents before settling his stare on me. "I don't want to be different." He took a step toward me, dropping the glass as he got close.

It hit the plush rug with a *thud* before he was on me, grabbing me around the waist and pulling me toward him. My legs hit the sofa and I fell sideways, his hold around me the only thing preventing me from being hurt as we both fell onto the sofa.

His hard lips crushed mine. The bitter tang of Scotch burned on my tongue as he pushed his inside my lips.

"Thom..." Hunter murmured.

"Leave him," Riven urged. "He's got demons tonight. If she can ease him."

Thomas broke the kiss and pulled back to stare into my eyes. "Can you ease me, Helene?"

My pulse thundered, the aching need overwhelming.

"Will you let me fuck you?"

I glanced at the others as they stood there, watching.

"I want to use you, want to feel you. I want to lose myself in you." Thomas drew my attention back.

I met his stare. "Any way you need, you know that."

He gave a solemn nod, as though he was unsure, finding new ground as he went. He rose from the sofa to loom over me and reached for his shirt, pulling it over his head. His chest rippled and his softer stomach shook. I was so surprised, he didn't do this, not in front of the others, and not without me being the dominant one.

I leaned forward, pulled off my top and my bra, and slid my pants and panties low. Kane moved back as did Hunter, before they turned to leave.

"No." Thomas stopped them. "If I'm to be part of this, then I want you to stay. I want you to want her."

"Thom, buddy, you don't have to." Hunter explained. "We're all with Helene on our own at times."

"But not all the time."

"No. Not all the time."

Thomas gave a nod, that seemed to seal the deal for him. He was trying hard to be like his brothers without realizing he was special the way he was. But to refuse him now, even like this, could be damaging. He was too fragile, too raw. I eased toward the end of the sofa and ran my hands along his thighs as he worked the buckle of his belt and pushed his clothing low.

He might be a little softer in the belly than the others, but after a month of mountain running, his thighs were thick and rock hard. I shifted my focus sideways. As was his cock. The others in the room faded back, all except for Riven. He still stood close, watching as I slid my hands over Thom's hard muscles and cupped his cock.

"Do you want to be in my mouth, like the others?" I asked.

He didn't speak, those dark, empty eyes fixed on mine. I'd do anything to see the honey brown again.

Anything.

I lowered my head and parted my lips, my tongue seeking the smooth head before I took him inside, sliding my lips all the way down the shaft, until he unleashed a guttural moan.

The deep rumble only stimulated me further as he pushed harder until he hit the back of my throat. I sucked, drawing backwards and down again. Warm, smooth. I took him deeper until that sensation made my throat clamp and I had to force myself not to gag.

"That's enough," Thomas ordered.

Saliva trailed as I pulled back and lifted my gaze. He slowly knelt and ran his hands down the insides of my legs, grabbed my ankles and lifted my feet to the edge of the sofa. My knees parted, spreading my pussy open for him.

He seemed to freeze, or maybe he was taking his time as his eyes roamed down my body. A small blush rose as he settled his gaze between my legs.

"I'd never hurt you. You know that, right?" He met my stare.

Fear trembled. It was stupid. I *knew* that. Still, those kind of words were never spoken unless someone fought the need to do just that...or it was trauma from something else.

"I know that." I answered. "I trust you with my life as well as my body."

"But would you trust me with your soul?"

My mind raced, the thoughts frantic and unhelpful. *Too much noise.* Isn't that what he'd said before? It was too much noise. "Yes. Yes, I trust you with my soul."

He fell forward, wrapped his arms around me, and held me, or was it that I held him? Was he crying? I gripped hold of him as panic rose. He turned his head and kissed the top of my shoulder. "I promise I'll explain everything." He shifted his hips and slid his hands down until his fingers slid under my ass and he dragged me forward to meet his erection. "After this."

One hard thrust and he drove inside me. I didn't care about comfort or pain anymore. All I wanted was him. He pushed harder, drove all the way inside, and eased out.

"You need her," Riven urged. "Look how desperate she is for you."

Thomas pulled away, staring into my eyes. His own shone with unshed tears. But they weren't as dark now. Still not quite honey brown. But I'd take it.

"I *am* desperate for you." I murmured. "Anything you give me, I'll gladly take."

His brow pinched before he lifted one hand to the back of the sofa behind me and slammed his hips forward. I jolted with the brunt, then dropped my head backwards. "God, yes."

"I...*love...you.*" He growled, thrusting over and over, his pace intensifying.

"Look at how you join." Riven urged. "Look down, brother, watch as you give yourself to her."

Thomas did, easing upwards to find that juncture between us. I followed his stare, finding my knees spread wide. The thick dark bush around his cock crushed against mine until he rubbed my clit.

"My God, you're beautiful." Thomas's eyes widened as they met mine. "You're so fucking beautiful." His hand slipped from the headrest to around the back of my neck, holding my gaze to his as he drove inside me over and over and over.

My body jolted with the impact, then with one tilt of his hips, he hit just the right spot.

"Oh, right there," I moaned. "Don't stop...*don't you dare stop.*"

He didn't, focused on watching himself sink into me, and I watched him. He liked it...I liked that he liked it. That alone turned me on even more. The wave rose inside me, climbing and climbing...until I floated, crying out. "*Oh!*"

Then slammed back down.

Only as I did, sparks ignited. My body clenched, pulsing and pulsing, the friction of his shaft making that swollen nub pulse.

One sudden slam and Thomas stilled, dropped his head forward and closed his eyes.

"That's it, brother." Riven urged. "Give her everything."

Everything.

The word trembled inside me. Thomas panted, then slowly lifted his head.

"Thank you." He murmured, his dry lips catching on his teeth.

"You never have to thank me." My words were just as husky as his.

"Yes." He answered. "I do. I never want to take you for granted. I never want to lose a single second with you. I never want to be lost in myself again."

A brutal pang tore across my chest. I lifted my hand and cupped his cheek. "I love you for you, lost or not, lover or not. You don't need to be anyone else but who you are. I would give myself to you a thousand times over. Ten thousand if you'll let me."

His lips curled into a smile, making the darkness draw back just a little further. He eased back, sliding from me. I hated the cold he left behind. I hated all the cold they left behind. My body craved them like a drug. Still, Thomas grabbed my clothes and placed them on me before he collected his own and rose. His metal buckle clanged as he pulled his pants back on and I did the same, yanking my pants upwards and sliding my shirt on, leaving my bra behind.

"Do you want to start at the beginning?" Riven urged.

Thomas nodded as he turned around to face them. There wasn't a hint of embarrassment at what we'd just done. Only a surety, a comfort as he started. "I went to St. Augustine's the other night for guidance, and there I found Father Cassius. He spoke to me briefly before telling me he needed to leave. But he had a two-way radio with him, which I thought was strange."

Riven looked confused, same as the rest of us. "Go on."

"I thought I heard something...no, *someone*. I thought I heard someone on the radio. So, when he left through the rectory door, I followed him."

We all waited for this to make sense.

"He...he..." Thomas glanced my way. "He had a Daughter tied up and gagged, naked and spread-eagled at the end of the bed and he...*and he...he whipped her between her legs.*"

My stomach recoiled until the room around me bled away. I shook my head, swallowing bile, envisioning that.

"There was blood," Thomas croaked. "So much blood and she was screaming. I didn't even think. I just grabbed what I could and I—"

"You killed him," Kane answered. "You killed him to save her."

The tears that had threatened him before now trembled and finally slid free. "Protect her...no, I was far too late for that. She was ruined. Her body...was *ruined*. I called Caleb and told him what had happened. He came and got her and took her to a doctor, someone who won't speak to the authorities."

"That's what you were talking to him about?" I asked.

Thomas nodded. "That and we've been helping Benjamin Rossi."

"That's where you were tonight?" Riven added.

Thomas nodded. "Hale is planning to run. He's going after Kat and the baby and he'll disappear forever. Ben found a man who had information. But what he gave us was a name."

"Jesus." Riven rubbed the back of his head and turned away. "So you, what? Killed that guy?"

"Benjamin did, yes."

"And why the hell does he want *you* for all that?" Riven couldn't stop the anger from leaking into his tone.

Thomas flinched and anger moved back into his stare. "Why not me?"

"Because you're my goddamn brother." Riven snarled. "I've protected you from *all that*. Kept you from harm. Watched over you."

"And yet, here I am, involved in this one way or another."

"I didn't want this." Riven shook his head.

"He said I reminded him of his own brother. He said he'd protect me."

"And *that* out there was protection?"

"I'm alive, aren't I?"

"Barely."

Anger, desperation, and love filled the room, until Riven turned away and pulled his cell from his pocket.

"What are you doing?" Thomas took a step forward.

"Calling the sonofabitch myself," Riven said as he swiped. "If he wants to go around my goddamn back and use my brother, sure as hell he'll hear my fucking wrath."

"Riven." The faint voice came through the line. "I've been expecting your call."

"Have you just," Riven snapped. "Enough with the goddamn games, Rossi. You and me, we need to meet."

I couldn't quite hear what was next.

"What do you mean *all of us?* It's time? Time we all come together? Yeah, well. Let's just see about that. Name a time and place and we'll be there...and Rossi...*keep your fucking hands off my family.*"

EIGHTEEN

Riven

I scowled, glanced again at the address on the GPS, then lifted my gaze. Gigantic refrigeration trucks flew past us as we slowed at a commercial compound outside of the city, making the Explorer rock with the blasts of air. Hunter slowed to let a tandem tractor-trailer take the exit wide before slipping around him. The transport company straight ahead was spread out, loading docks and warehouses made the place busier than I'd expected. But then, what *did* I expect from someone like Rossi?

We pulled in through wide open gates and headed along the parking lot, taking up a space next to London's Audi. I winced as I scanned the sleek gray sedan. My own car was goddamn trashed, bullet holes peppered all the way along the side. Last night it hadn't looked that bad, but in the early morning light, I saw the extent of the attack. My brother could've been killed... that pissed me off more than anything.

We pulled up hard. I stabbed my seatbelt release and climbed out, listening to the roar of the trucks' engines and the piercing *beep...beep...beeps* as they reversed.

"Riven," Hunter called my name, drawing my gaze as he nodded toward one of Rossis' men standing outside a warehouse in the distance. "This way."

We all headed after Rossi's man and stepped in through what looked like some kind of mechanical workshop, then followed the guy to the back and slipped through a single door to an open expanse at the rear. Everyone was there. St. James, the sons, and even the bodyguard. I scanned the rest, the Bankses' with Ryth and the baby...Hell, even all the Rossis were here, Lazarus standing protectively next to his wife who held their two children.

My focus went instantly to the dark-haired little one. *Not all of them were theirs, remember?*

It's why we were there, right?

Now that the Stidda had skin in the game.

"Riven, Hunter, Kane, and Thom." Benjamin stepped forward, his gaze moving to my brother. "I'm glad you could make it."

Make it?

I still wanted to lay the bastard out for going behind my goddamn back. "Sure," I answered coldly.

Three massive bald bastards stood in the back. I recognized the white-eyed fucker immediately, and by the way he stared, he recognized me, as well. One small nod and Benjamin Rossi started.

"I'm sure you recognize everyone," he stated. "Except for Harper Renolt, London's hacker. To get everyone up to speed, a few of us have been tracking Hale's escape plan. Last night, we narrowed in on one of his associates and placed a device into their computer for Harper to gain access to their network. There we plan on tracking down his exact current whereabouts while burning any available resource he has to escape the country and go to ground."

"And almost killing my damn brother in the process," I snarled.

Thomas flinched, his cheeks reddening.

"That was unexpected." Rossi looked at Thom. "I told you I'd protect you and I failed. Please accept my apologies."

Thom nodded. Of course he did. But I wasn't so forgiving. I took a step forward as all heads turned to the thud of steps behind us. I glanced over my shoulder and found London's diamond assholes walking in. All fucking four of them, including the smug, self-righteous asshole who'd threatened me.

I glared at him as he walked past. He might be on our side, but that didn't mean I didn't want to drive my knee into his balls. Yeah, that's how low I was willing to go. The pompous prick must've read my mind. He jerked his gaze toward me as he strode by, giving me a look that told me the feeling was mutual.

"Helene," He murmured to my woman standing at my side. "So nice to see you again."

A twitch came in the corner of my mouth. *Keep going, buddy... keep fucking going.*

"Baron, Royal, Loyal, and Wolfe, and Miss..." Benjamin fixed his gaze on the young woman with them.

"Cloe," Baron answered for her, his hand protectively against the small of her back, and not in a fatherly way.

Interesting, very interesting.

"Cloe," Ben added. "Thank you for joining us. The Ares family?" He glanced at London.

St. James just shook his head. "Today is the funeral. I think they have enough problems of their own to deal with right now."

"Fair enough." Ben nodded, then turned his attention back to us. "We're closing in, but we need to move faster. London and Guild have their men pressuring the known gangs who work for him, but it's not enough. There's already been two attacks on my family. One two years ago, and another recently."

Surprise filled me.

All heads turned to Lazarus. His gaze was pure rage, clear, cutting...cold as ice. No wonder the redhead was fixed to his side. The baby mewled in her arms. The raven haired little one dressed in pastel lavender sat on the ground at her side, focused on scribbling with crayons on an open coloring book.

"What kind of attack?" London lifted his focus from Hale's child.

It looked like I wasn't the only one left out of the information loop.

"Hale has started proceedings to gain full custody."

"No," Vivienne whimpered, shaking her head. She was pale and shaking, her hands around her belly. "No, he can't do that."

Ben's expression only grew darker. "That's what we're trying to prevent. This is more than an outright attack, this is fucking sickening."

Kat's red eyes shone with tears. It looked like she'd been crying and hadn't stopped. It made me shift a little closer to Helene. The time for children for us was long gone. But that did little for the bloodthirsty part of my nature. I felt for Lazarus. To take a man's child was one thing. But to do what we *all* knew he wanted to do to this little one was a whole new level of sick disgust.

We needed to find him.

And we needed to find him *now*.

"Harper has been working ever since we gained access to find his location." London said.

But the moment my gaze found the hacker, he didn't fill me with confidence. Dark circles under his eyes only enhanced the desperate look. I'd seen that look far too many times.

"If he doesn't." I turned to the others. "What then? We keep going door to door until we've searched every goddamn building in the city? How long do you think that's going to take."

"It'll work." Lazarus forced the words through clenched teeth. The guy looked like he was about to rip someone's head off. I was quite partial to where mine was, but still, someone had to ask the question.

"What about Anna?" Kat asked, turning to him. "Please, Laz."

"She's a Salvatore, baby," he growled and stared straight ahead.

"No, she isn't," Kat whispered. "She's my friend."

Obviously there was bad blood between the two main Mafia families once more. I'd assumed they were over it, obviously not.

Tears spilled from her eyes. This was a whole new layer of tension.

"I can do it," Harper muttered, not convincingly. "I know I can do it."

Ben gave a nod. "Okay, now that everyone is on the same page, we need to work together here. We're closing in on the whereabouts of a Leroy Hastings, a slimy middleman who specializes in forged documents. The moment we have a location, Caleb, Thom, and Colt will be notified. We need all teams moving on this. We need to squeeze that sonofabitch out."

A cell beeped. We all glanced toward the sound.

Until it echoed around the room.

First St. James.

Then Lazarus.

Then Caleb...

Hunter's cell vibrated.

He glanced at the caller ID and answered it instantly. "Yeah?"

"The FBI?" London barked. "What the fuck are they doing in my home?"

His face went pale.

"A raid," Laz growled. "That *goddamn motherfucker.*"

"Get everyone out," Caleb demanded and started walking, heading for the doorway. "I'm on my way."

"They're tearing apart the house," Hunter murmured, meeting my stare, relaying the same information no doubt everyone in the room was facing.

It looked like Hale was stepping up.

Using the law to exact revenge in retaliation after what happened last night.

"Find that Hastings, Benjamin." I clenched my fist. "Find him and tear the bastard apart."

NINETEEN

Helene

"WHAT THE *FUCK?*" RIVEN MURMURED AS WE TURNED OFF
the highway into the driveway of the mountain house. "Yeah,"
he said into his cell. "They're here and it's a goddamn mess. Do
something, Reggie, and do it *now.*"

He lowered his cell from calling his lawyer and stared at the
four dark sedans parked outside the command center. Two of
Hunter's men were standing there waiting. One I recognized
instantly. Mark was his new second-in-command. A former MP
in the Marines. Apparently, he was as formidable in the law as
he looked, and that alone was slightly terrifying.

The moment we stepped out of the car, Mark headed over,
nodding to Riven before he turned to Hunter. "I tried to stop
them, but they had a warrant."

"It's okay." Hunter stared at two feds as they carried computer
equipment out of his command center and lowered his voice.
"Did you get everything squared away?"

"Yes, just in time. Another twenty minutes and we might've had a problem."

It looked like the call from the Rossi's lawyer was perfect timing. I hoped at least. I closed the car door behind me, then stared, stunned, as three more agents strode from the house carrying our personal things, including an armful of my t-shirts and underwear...

"Those are my clothes." I snapped and started forward. *"Hey! Those are my clothes!"*

One agent lifted his head, his gaze narrowing on me. He glanced at the two others and nodded. "Go ahead. I'll take care of this."

They took my things and stowed them in the trunk of one of the cars.

"Hunter Cruz?" The lanky asshole asked as he pulled a folded piece of paper from the inside pocket of his jacket and handed it over. "A warrant."

Riven snatched it, ignoring that it was for Hunter, opened it, and scanned the details. But it was the rest of us the agent looked at, Thomas in particular. I glanced at his FBI badge clipped on his pocket.

"Bremmer," I murmured, meeting his stare.

"Yes." His lips curled as he scanned all of us, settling on Thomas. "Thomas Cruz," he said. "We finally meet."

"Marcus Bremmer." Kane took a step forward, moving between the asshole and Thom. "Any relation to Ignatius Bremmer?"

"Yes," The agent answered. "He *was* my brother."

Ignatius Bremmer...the lawyer Ben killed last night. Oh, shit. Now it made sense.

Another agent strode from the house, this time carrying Thomas' clothes. His black suit jacket and white clerical collar were shoved into a clear plastic bag.

"I know it was you," Marcus Bremmer seethed in front of us, his gaze fixed on Thom. "The cameras picked you up outside the building." He stepped closer. "You might've had your men fry the servers inside the building but that doesn't mean you got away with this. I'm going to ruin you." He scanned the rest of us, stopping on Riven. *"Every. Single. One of you."*

We said nothing, even as they carried four firearms from the command center, cradled in the arms of one of the men.

"I have licenses for those." Hunter stepped forward, stopping them.

"Do you?" Bremmer answered, reaching around his back and pulled out a set of cuffs. "I'm sure your lawyer can argue that in front of the judge. Thomas Cruz, I'm placing you under arrest on the suspicion of firearms trafficking, anything you say will be..."

What?

What did he just say?

Thomas?

He had *nothing* to do with this.

"The hell you do!" Riven lunged, slammed into the agent, and knocked him to the ground.

"They aren't his guns!" Hunter bellowed. *"They're mine. They're registered to ME!"*

Chaos erupted as two of the other agents dropped whatever was in their hands and rushed forward, throwing themselves into the fray.

Fists swung. Marcus Bremmer took Riven's blow on the cheek. I watched his head snap backwards, his eyes rolling, before they swung back, narrowed with chilling rage.

"Get him the FUCK OFF ME," he roared.

Hunter grabbed his brother, as did Mark, and pulled him off. *"Hey!"* The towering mountain snapped, forcing Riven's gaze to his. "We'll take care of this, okay?"

"Handcuff him!" Bremmer swiped the red mark on his cheek and winced as his other hand gestured at Thom.

"Hands behind your back," one agent demanded, his shirt crumpled, his eyes wide.

But Thomas didn't fight, just stared as Bremmer pushed himself up from the ground and brushed the dirt from his trousers. Then Thom extended his arms, his wrists together.

"No." Bremmer stopped the agent. *"Behind his back."*

"He's not a goddamn risk!" I barked, desperation roaring through me. *"He's a priest, for fuck's sake!"*

"Priest, huh?" Bremmer just smiled, a cruel, calculating sneer as they pulled Thomas away from us. Bremmer's cell chimed, causing him to drag it out. I saw the screen just as he answered. Riven shrugged Hunter and Mark off him, sucking in hard breaths as he murdered the asshole agent a thousand times with his stare. But it was the caller ID that chilled me.

"Yeah?" Bremmer answered, that icy stare fixed on me.

My pulse was pounding as I stepped forward.

H?

That's what was on the screen. Just a single *H.*

Was that Hale?

I turned to Riven, who stared as Bremmer mumbled into his phone and turned away, striding for a sedan.

"Did you..." I whispered.

"What?" Riven scowled.

"The ID on that call. It had *H.* As in..."

"Hale."

I lunged, racing after them as they pushed Thomas in the back seat of the sedan. "Don't say a word!" I yelled, pressing my hands against the window. "Do you hear me? *Don't say a word. We'll get you out of this."*

Car doors opened and closed.

The engine started.

Thomas turned to stare at me, his hands secured behind his back. But it wasn't fear I saw in his eyes. It was resignation.

"We'll get you out," I promised. *"We'll get you out."*

The sedan pulled away, slipping from my touch. I stared at the rear window as he left, knowing in my gut what I'd seen. It was Hale that had called Bremmer. I knew it.

It was Hale.

TWENTY

Thomas

"GET IN." BREMMER SHOVED MY SHOULDER DOWN UNTIL my knees buckled.

"*NO!*" Helene roared and lunged forward as I hit the back seat. "*NOO!*"

Thud.

The car door closed beside me, leaving my mind to freeze. *This was bad...this was bad.*

Bang!

Helene slammed her hand against the window, making me flinch and jerk my stare to her. There was panic in her eyes, desperate, bared-teeth panic. It pulled me away from the disconnect my mind desperately wanted. *Stay here...just stay here. We're in trouble, don't you get that? We're in serious fucking trouble.*

"*Don't say a word!*" she yelled. "*Do you hear me? Don't say a word. We'll get you out of this!*"

186

The driver's door closed as I gave a small nod. I tried to hold on to her, focusing on her wide eyes and her wind-scattered hair as the sedan pulled away.

I shifted, looking back through the rear window at my brothers. Riven yelled at someone on his cell, his fist clenched around it as he raged. Hunter stood beside his second, staring at me. But it was Helene who drew my focus back as she ran forward, chasing the car as we left.

The car bounced, jarring me. I tensed my thighs as we turned hard and I flew sideways, slamming my shoulder into the door. Agony followed, plunging all the way up into my neck. But I didn't have time to cope before I was thrown backwards into the seat.

Bremmer said nothing as he drove. Just met my gaze in the rearview mirror. I pressed myself against the seat and glanced at the seatbelt hanging down beside me.

"I don't have my seatbelt on." I turned to the rear-view mirror as he looked away. *"You didn't put my seatbelt on."*

An icy sensation rippled deep in the pit of my stomach. There was something very wrong here and it was more than the steel wrapped around my wrists and the law. I shifted, glancing back at the dark blue fed sedan behind me, then the two in front as the faint *tick, tick, tick* of the turn signal filled the space.

We turned right, spearing off from the others. The car bounced hard against the rocks, kicking up dust as we headed down some road I'd never seen before, one that took me away from the city.

That sickening wave of nausea grew more intense as I stared at the long, empty stretch of road lined with towering pines.

"What are you doing? Where are you taking me?"

Bremmer met my stare in the rear-view mirror, but said nothing.

This was bad...*this was really bad.*

I glanced at the lock on the door, then the hatred in his gaze. The car slowed, braking before we skidded hard and swung around. I flew across the seat, cast one way then the other, as the car swung back to face the way we'd come and stopped.

The driver's door was shoved open and dust billowed in, filling the car in an instant. My own door was flung open, then I was grabbed and hauled out, falling to the ground at his feet.

"Get up."

My mind raced and filled with all the scenarios where you'd take someone handcuffed down an empty road.

"I said *get up!*"

He yanked the cuffs until the metal ground against the bones of my wrists. His other hand found my throat, clenching tight. I coughed and gasped, drawing in dust-choked air. Flashes of memories slammed into me, of London St. James towering above me as he kicked and punched, driving his brutal knuckles into my face over and over as he shouted. *Where is he? WHERE IS MY SON?*

"GET THE FUCK UP!" The FBI agent roared above me.

I shoved upwards, slamming back against the car.

Crack!

My head impacted with the car. White, hot stars detonated behind my eyes, blinding me.

"The guns *aren't mine*." I croaked as the steel cuffs screeched against the paintwork. "You have to believe me. They...aren't... mine."

I tried to lift my head, finding him shrouded in shadows. Bremmer sucked in hard breaths, straightened until he blocked out the sun, and reached for his gun.

No!

GOD, NO!

He dragged it out of his holster.

The gun was all I could see. It was London all over again.

I shook my head as terror punched through me. I jerked my hands, but they slammed against my back. With me unable to protect myself, he lifted the gun and swung.

Crack!

My head slammed backwards. My lips split against my teeth. Blood bloomed as I lay there against the car, dazed.

Bremmer's harsh breaths wheezed as he towered over me. "I'm going to tell you once, do you understand? Because if you don't do what I tell you to do, we're going to have a problem. I'll go after your family, starting with that brunette back there. I'll arrest her, throw her in the males' cells. How do you feel about that?"

I shook my head as tears threatened.

I didn't understand. I didn't under—

He lunged, then yanked my shirt until my gaze snapped to his. "Are you hearing me, *Priest?*"

I didn't kill your brother...I didn't—

"You're to back off Hale. Do you hear me? *Back the fuck off Haelstrom Hale.*"

I froze, my mind unable to comprehend.

The shadows around his face brightened until I stared into those hateful eyes. "This is a warning and it's the only one you'll get."

Wait...wasn't this about his brother?

Bremmer's cell chimed, drawing him away. He reached into his pocket and pulled it out, swiped, and lifted it to his ear. "Yeah," he gasped. "Message given and received, loud and clear."

He looked down at me and I saw the emptiness in his soul.

The utter gaping hole where his soul should be.

"I understand." He said. "I'll call you as soon as it's done."

As soon as it's done?

As soon as what's done?

I shook my head, staring as he lowered his cell and ended the call.

"Don't do this." I shook my head. "You don't need to do this."

He took a step forward. All I saw was the gun, and that panic came roaring back. Only now I didn't have Riven to save me.

Bremmer leaned down with the gun in his hand. Even if I'd dared to try to fight back, I couldn't. Not physically at least.

"Your brother is dead," I started, trying to keep the shake from my voice. "And yet you're doing Hale's dirty work. Why? Money, power? Does he have something over you?"

"Shut up."

"He's using you." I licked my lips and kept going. "Once he's done, he'll leave you behind. Even if you didn't love your brother, you still have something you love." I glanced at the badge on his pocket. "Your job, your career. Are you really willing to risk that for a man like Hale?"

He pushed the gun under my jaw, those empty eyes glinting with hunger. "Keep going. I'd love nothing more than to splatter your brains all over the side of my car."

I froze as the muzzle pressed harder. The faint scent of gun oil filled my nostrils. It had been cleaned, and recently. He slowly pulled away and straightened until he slid it back into his holster. One glance down to my crotch and he gave a chuff. "Didn't wet yourself. Usually men like you piss themselves."

Men like me?

He was telling me something.

He was telling me he'd done this before...many times.

"Now get the fuck up." He leaned over, grabbed my arm, and hauled me upwards.

My head throbbed and my mouth was swelling, causing me to swallow my blood. Still, I shoved upwards and leaned against the car until I caught my breath. He yanked open the back door and jerked his head.

I stumbled backwards, then dropped down, hitting the seat before I swiveled around and lifted my feet inside.

Thud.

The door closed behind me. He climbed back in, yanked his door closed, and started the engine. There was a chilling silence between us as he drove, one that only grew colder as we headed back along the isolated road to the mountain highway. I looked left, to the stretch of road as it rose steeply. My home was up there and my family. Yet I'd never felt so far away from them as in this moment.

Fear moved in, but instead of withdrawing into myself, I focused on the man in front of me. He wasn't just a sinner, he was a pawn in the Devil's work.

"You will die, you get that, right?" I winced as pain radiated through my jaw. "Men like you don't make it out of this."

He glanced into the rear-view mirror and pushed the car harder, picking up speed as we made for the city, not saying a word. But I knew he'd heard me, and that only strengthened my faith. I gently worked my jaw, focusing on him as I sat with my hands grinding against the seat back.

We left the mountain far behind and headed into the city, pulled into the driveway beside the FBI building, and stopped at the massive steel doors to the underground garage. *Where they bring prisoners.* Was that my fate now? To be imprisoned for a crime I didn't commit?

But I had killed...hadn't I?

The steel doors rose and we pulled inside, coming to a stop near a set of double doors. Two of the agents who were at the house were there, waiting. Bremmer switched off the car and climbed out before opening the back door.

"Get out," He commanded.

I glanced at the agents and slowly turned, slid my feet out, and rose. My knees shook, but it was my face that was the worst. One eye was swollen nearly shut and I wasn't sure my jaw wasn't broken. I couldn't tell from the punishing pain in my face.

"Move." Bremmer pushed me toward the doors.

I stumbled and slowly headed for the agent who stepped to the side, pressed his badge to the scanner, and opened the locked door. The sound of steps echoed along the hallway. I was shoved forward until I stopped at a reception counter, eyeing a group of men dressed in expensive suits. Two turned, glanced my way, then scowled.

They stepped forward, heading for us.

"Agent," one called. "Jameson Hutch, I'm representing Mr. Thomas Cruz. I'd like a moment with my client," he muttered, scanning my face, then stepped forward, grasped my jaw gently, and winced. "I expect a full report of his injuries, as well."

Bremmer stepped forward, his lips curling as he glared at the lawyer. But there wasn't a thing he could say. The doors opened behind them and two men and a woman headed my way. But they weren't the usual suited up lawyers, in fact, two didn't even wear suits. The young, brooding male glanced at who had to be his lawyer and nodded, motioning him forward.

"Jameson," the lawyer nodded to the man who'd announced himself as my lawyer, then turned his attention to the two agents beside me. He gave a smile as Bremmer's cell rang. "I suggest you answer that, Special Agent."

Bremmer scowled, glanced at the caller ID, and flinched, answering it instantly. "Sir?"

Whatever was said on the other end was short, sharp...and to the point.

"I understand, sir," Bremmer responded. "No, sir. My investigation has led to—. Yes, sir. I understand, sir. I'll have the paperwork taken care of. Yes, I can see you in your office this afternoon. Okay. I'll see you then."

He lowered his cell, his cheeks burning. Sparks of hostility exploded in his eyes as the two young people stepped forward.

"Thomas," The guy called my name. "Finley Salvatore, and this is my wife, Anna. We're friends of Lazarus and we're going to escort you out of here."

The woman gave a soft smile and stepped closer, then reached up to gently touch my cheek. "Let's get you looked at, okay?"

I fought the panic inside, not even knowing these people.

"It's okay," Anna said softly. "We're just here to get you out of here."

I didn't know these people, yet...they seemed to know me.

"Okay," I answered.

"Let's get out of here," Finley murmured, glancing at his lawyer, who gave a nod.

Bremmer yanked my arms up hard as he unlocked the cuffs. My hands dropped hard, leaving my shoulders to howl with the strain. Still, I lifted my hands, rubbing the feeling back into them.

"I'll be watching you," Bremmer muttered. "Just remember what I said."

"And what was that, Special Agent?" Finley's lawyer snapped. "I'm sure the Director would be as interested as I am to hear about it."

But Bremmer remained tight-lipped, glaring at me as I took a step and headed out of there with the Salvatores at my side.

"Thank you," I murmured the moment we were out.

Anna gave me a smile. "You're very welcome. I'm just sorry you had to experience all that."

"My family?"

"Meeting us at our property. Our guard can have a look at your face there."

I gave a nod as we stepped out of the double glass doors

"You're the one Kat asked for, aren't you?" I murmured, heading for the waiting Explorer against the curb. "The hacker they call the Ghost."

That soft smile eased, leaving a formidable stare behind. "The Ghost?" she answered, giving me a wink. "Sorry, I don't think I've ever heard the name."

She was, I knew it in my gut. I climbed into the back seat and watched her round the rear of the car and climb in. Finley watched her like a hawk, only climbing into the passenger's seat after she was inside.

I realized I'd just met a whole new level of Mafia.

One who not only had connections.

But the strength to make them kneel.

TWENTY-ONE

Helene

THE CAR SKIDDED HARD, PULLING UP AT THE TOWERING gates of an enormous compound. I yanked the handle, shoved the door open, and lunged out.

"*Helene!*" Riven roared from the driver's seat as the guard stepped out from the guard hut, armed to the teeth. "*Helene, for Christ's sake!*"

But I didn't stop, not even when the gate rolled open far too slowly, leaving a gap barely big enough for me to slip through. My shoulder slammed against the edge, then I was running, pushing the pain away as I raced for the house. The front door opened in the distance and Thomas raced down the long stretch of stairs, and ran toward me.

I thought I'd lost you.

Tears streamed down my face.

He ran, then slowed. But I didn't, slamming into him hard enough to knock him backwards. He grabbed me as he stumbled back a couple of steps before righting himself. But he didn't pull away. He just buried his head in the hollow of my neck. His body was hard and warm, but his emotions were tender as he murmured. "I thought I was gone for good."

I shook my head and pulled back so I could cup his face, and forced his gaze to me. A couple came out of the front door of the house as I held his face, examining the red swollen cheek and eye and the busted lips.

"Motherfucker," I spat. *"I'll fucking kill him."*

Car doors opened and closed behind us. The rush of heavy footsteps followed as the sound of a car grew closer in the distance.

"Thom," Riven called as he neared.

Riven gripped his brother's shoulder with one hand and raised his gaze upwards, surveying the damage. Silence followed as Riven's eyes darkened and a twitch came at the corner of his mouth.

More cars drove into the compound. I turned, to see London's Audi and the Sons' Explorer. But there were more. Two sleek, powerful sports cars were followed closely by two very imposing four-wheel drives.

"London," The young male called from the entrance of the house. "Vivienne, so nice to see you again."

My sister slowly made her way toward us, holding onto her belly with one hand and Colt's arm with the other. The Son was more than her strength, he somehow soothed her. No wonder she'd been panicked the night Thomas and Colt had disappeared.

Lazarus and Kat climbed out of their car, opened the back doors, leaned inside, unfastened the child seats, and pulled out a gorgeous baby and their perfect dark-haired little girl. Flashes of Hale assaulted me. Standing over me. Leering. Those infernal eyes shining with sick satisfaction. My skin crawled as they closed the doors and headed toward us. Now more than ever, I needed to understand how a woman like Kat could have had a child with someone like Hale.

Three more cars drove in. I recognized Harper, the computer programmer London worked with, and Guild behind the wheel. Nick was behind the wheel of a silver Explorer, with Tobias in the front and my sister, her baby, and Caleb in the back seat. The other car was a Land Rover, one I knew instantly...Benjamin Rossi.

He stopped and climbed out, his bodyguard moving instantly toward him as the rest of my family followed, climbing out and bringing my nephew with them. Ryth gave me a haunted smile as she headed my way. Within minutes, the entire front yard was filled with the most dangerous men I knew. My own father tried to push into my head. I hadn't seen him since that night at Harmon's and all he'd left me was that medical report. That goddamn report that had ruined it all.

Why couldn't he have let me hate him?

Why couldn't he have just let me forget?

"Baby sister." I crossed the front walk and grabbed her in a hug, leaning close to kiss my nephew's cheek.

"Benjamin." The young male called from the front door, drawing my focus.

I swallowed more than breathed as the air turned choking with distrust.

"Finley." Ben answered stiffly, striding toward him.

Finley...as in, Finley Salvatore?

Now it made sense.

But he didn't greet Lazarus as he and Kat neared with their children, just clenched his muscled jaw, staring at the man who had been his best friend.

"I guess you'd all better come inside." He said finally before he turned and headed into the entryway.

I held Thomas' hand and followed them inside. The place was massive, with towering ceilings and stunning woodgrained furnishings. You could tell this was real money, a lifetime of terror and every dark deed known to man spread out in front of me. The Salvatores were dangerous. If I hadn't known that before, I sure did now.

They led us to the rear of the house, where thick steel-lined walls separated the vulnerable from the safe. I glanced at the heavy locks, then around the inside of the massive room.

"Don't worry." Finley glanced our way. "Once inside, no one else can hear us."

He glanced at the two bodyguards inside. One was packing up a massive medial kit as we entered. He glanced at Thom, then me. Was he the one who'd cleaned up the cuts on Thom's face and his split lips? A swell of appreciation followed as he cleared the space.

Everyone stepped inside the room, which was the same size as a small apartment before a guard pressed a button and closed the heavy reinforced door.

Clunk.

The lock snapped shut.

But it was Benjamin and Lazarus Rossi I watched. They were still, so very still, almost chilling. The hairs at the back of my neck rose.

"Um...do you have somewhere I can work?" Harper heaved his bag with him, looking from Lazarus to Finley.

Anna was the one who nodded. "Sure," she said carefully. "Let me get you set up."

They stepped to the side and began setting up Harper's laptop. I could hear them talking as she asked questions and he answered as best he could. Still, there was tension in his tone and a look of defeat in his eyes as he pulled out a chair, sat down in front of his laptop, and started working.

Anna left him, turning to the rest of us as Finley started. "So, now that the Priest is out, you want to explain what the fuck is going on?"

He might've not said any names, but we all knew who he was talking to. Anna moved to Finley's side as Lazarus glanced at Kat. Still, he waited.

"Don't let business come into this." Finley growled. "This is personal. Whatever trouble you're in, Anna and I want to help."

"Fine," Lazarus snapped and took a step forward. "The only problem, *brother*, is that, to me, business *is* personal. I asked you before to get involved by sending your men out to help, and what were your words to me? That's right, *this isn't something we want to be associated with.*"

Finley scowled and shook his head. So that is what they were fighting over? "You asked me to send a heap of my men down to some bikers' bar on the edge of town. We were in the middle of one of the biggest cross-country arms hauls we'd ever made. I couldn't spare the men."

Lazarus unleashed a snarl and turned away, his gaze finding Kat. Just looking at her seemed to calm him a little. "Your men were supposed to find those working for Hale, the man trying to take away my child."

"What?" Anna cried, her eyes widening as she turned to Kat.

Kat just held their son tighter.

"Talk to me." Anna headed for her. "Kat, please."

"He came after her and Sophie," Lazarus answered for her.

"What?" Anna shook her head, her hand moved to her mouth. "*No.*"

Lazarus' gaze narrowed in on her, those blue eyes glinting. "Now he's using the law to go after sole custody, right before he takes her for forever. The men I asked for you to squeeze were men Hale was using to gather all the Daughters who'd escaped. He's rebuilding, and he's trying to use *my* daughter to do it."

"Jesus," she croaked, her voice trembling. "Jesus Christ."

She spun around, her wide eyes finding her husband. The utter devastation in his eyes said it all.

"We have a back door into his lawyers' servers, trying to find the location where he's at now, but we can't seem to crack it."

Anna spun back. "That's the firewall you're trying to break?"

Harper met her gaze and nodded.

"Without that information, Hale is going to escape. We need to cut off any method of escape, find the bastard, and kill him."

Anna turned back to Kat, then crossed the rest of the room to grab her in her arms. "And you couldn't come to me?"

Kat's eyes shone with tears right before they spilled down her cheeks.

"Oh, babe." Anna hugged her close. "You're my goddamn blood. Do you hear me? I don't give a fuck what these men have going on, you can always come to me."

Kat unleashed a sob as she wrapped one arm around Anna, the other still clutching her son.

"Man, you should've said." Finley headed for Laz and gripped him by his shoulders. "I had no idea this was going on."

Laz just scowled. Stubborn asshole.

"We need to know where Hale is," London spoke as he stepped forward. "Because Kat and her children aren't the only ones in danger here. All of us are. The attacks on our families and now the FBI. Because all of this...is only the beginning. A man like Hale leaves only devastation behind. The moment he gets on that plane, he's *gone,* and he'll never come back. If you think it's hard now, trying to find him in the city, think about how hard it'll be trying to find him in the entire country...or the world, for that matter. Hale will run and run and run."

"He's right," Riven agreed. "We are going to find that motherfucker and we are going to *kill* him. So, you're either with us, or you're...against us. There is no middle ground here. There's no sidelines anymore."

The words hung heavy in the air as all the men took in each other. This was the line in the sand. Enemies or allies. It came down to this moment.

I held my breath, waiting.

Anna released Kat and turned around, meeting everyone's gaze. "You're right. You're so very right. No more dick measuring, boys, no more of these games. You come for my best friend, my *blood*, you're already dead. Whatever it takes, Fin."

He just stared at his wife, but it was Laz he spoke to. "Whatever it takes."

"Right." She left Kat's side and headed for Harper. "Move over, let's burn this fucking thing to the ground."

Harper met her stare. "It's a lock-tight firewall with tripwires and the kind of kill features that will bring the entire law establishment down on us."

"I seem to have a lot of experience with that," she answered as he slid out of his seat.

She took it instead. "Step aside, let's see how fast we can break this, shall we?"

Beep.

We all turned to Ben as he grabbed his cell. He answered it instantly. "Yeah, any update? You found him?" He lifted his gaze to Caleb, who gave a nod. "Don't make a move until we're there. Sit on him. Don't let the bastard out of your sights. He's going to run, I just know he is. He's going to run."

He lowered his cell. But it was Laz who turned to Kat, swiping the tears from her cheeks with his thumbs. "I won't let Hale near you or our Daughter." His voice croaked. "On my goddamn life, do you hear me? *On. My. Goddamn. Life.*"

Ben stepped closer, grasping his son's shoulder. There was pain in his eyes, pain hearing Laz's words. "It won't come to that, son. Take my word on it. It won't come to that."

"Then go." Anna tore her focus from the screen, her fingers still flying across the keyboard faster than I'd ever seen anyone type before. "Find that asshole. I'll get this cracked."

Ben met her focus and gave a nod before she turned back to the scrolling prompts flying across the screen.

"Caleb," Ben called. "Colt. Thomas. You ready to finish this?"

My heart hurt when Thomas took a step, then glanced at me over his shoulder and answered. "Yes. We end this tonight."

TWENTY-TWO

Thomas

———————

THE ENGINE ROARED AS WE TOOK THE CORNER HARD. Headlights from the oncoming traffic blinded me.

"What do you mean *you lost him again?*" Ben roared, wrenching the wheel as we tried to overtake a slow-ass Toyota that pulled out in front of us. "*Goddamnit! Motherfucker!*"

His rage permeated the interior, seething and festering until flashes of the rectory returned. *Filthy fucking cunt. It deserves to be beaten. Open your legs, Daughter. Open them or I'll shove this cane all the way in your—*

"A?" Ben snapped. "You there? We've lost him. Call me when you can. I need a location for this guy." He glared at the traffic, then finished. "Call me when you can."

He hung up the call and focused on the traffic. "We need that motherfucker..." He glanced into the rear-view mirror at me. "We need that key."

Streets passed by in a blur. He seemed to know where he was going, turning hard into an alley before bottoming out as we exited.

His cell rang, the caller ID displayed on the console. *Lazarus.* Ben leaned forward and pressed the button to answer the call.

"Do you have him?" Laz sounded desperate, his heavy steps thudding in the background. Behind that were voices, frantic voices. I caught London's voice barking commands.

"No, not yet," Ben snapped.

"Anna is almost there, she's so close. We have the men gathering. The moment she has the location, we're moving. Leave that's fucker, we'll go after Hale ourselves," Laz urged. "We don't need him anymore.

"I can't, son." Ben pushed the car harder. "We have to put an end to *any* means of escape. I can't let him come for my family again. I *won't* let that happen. I need to finish this. We cut off *every* head of the goddamn snake. We *will* get him, Laz. Do you hear me? He will *never* touch your daughter. Not while I'm alive."

He yanked the wheel as a message flashed. "I gotta go, son. I'll call as soon as I have him."

"Okay, but Dad, hurry."

Laz ended the call, leaving Ben to his answer. "Alastair, talk to me."

"I have him." His voice was low and hushed. "We're running."

"Where are you?"

"We're...wait a second. The bank of units behind Galveston Road. They're distributors, hardcore motherfuckers. You don't want to come here."

"Drug runners?" Ben shook his head. "Fuck. That's all we need."

"I think I can get him out of here. If I can lead him south, you can wait for us at that empty warehouse off Walker's Lane. You know the one?"

"I know the one."

"Give me twenty minutes and I'll take him there. Be there, and you can get what you want."

Ben wrenched the wheel and punched the accelerator. "We'll be there, and Alastair? Don't let me down."

The call ended. I gripped the armrest, sliding with the turn as we headed south.

"Whatever happens, we get that information, then we get the hell out of there. If Anna has the location, we move and keep on moving. We have a narrow window here."

He sounded desperate, more than desperate. He sounded on the edge. His wide, dark eyes shone in the mirror. The swipe of his hand across his mouth was nothing but nerves. He shifted his focus back to the road, driving through the backstreets where thugs and lookouts were sitting in parked cars, watching everyone who drove past.

We were close to the drug runners, that was easy to see.

"Eyes up, boys." Ben urged as he slowed but kept on driving.

Colt said nothing. The Son didn't even react as two men stepped toward his side of the car and lifted their shirts to reveal big silvery guns in the waistbands of their boxers. He just looked away, focusing on the road ahead. But I had a feeling those men wouldn't like it if we pulled over...not one bit at all.

"Up ahead." Ben glanced into the rearview mirror. "I'm dropping you, Colt, and Caleb off at the corner. I need you to make your way down in case that fucker slips past us again. Keep your eyes up and stay together."

Wait...he was dropping us here?

I glanced over my shoulder at the seedy apartment complex and its criminal guardians as Ben slowed the four-wheel drive.

"I'll call you if there's any trouble." Ben said as he met my stare and reached to grab something from under the seat before handing me a gun. "I don't need to remind you what's at stake here."

I stared at the weapon as panic rose. But Colt yanked the handle, pushing the door wide before we even pulled to a stop. *Fuck.* "No, you don't." I answered Ben and grabbed the gun.

We all climbed out, quietly closing the door behind us. Ben was gone in an instant, heading further away.

"Keep close, Priest." Colt muttered as I slipped the Glock into the waistband of my jeans and pulled my shirt over it.

He didn't have to tell me twice. I glanced at Caleb, then hurried, haunting the Son's steps, following him along the rear of the houses before we found a small walkway that led to the street in front and slipped down it. My pulse boomed as I kept walking. It was dark here, too damn dark.

Busted streetlights gave us little to go on. But Colt didn't seem to even notice. Instead, he scanned the shadows, found his way between parked cars, and crossed the street. A long bank of empty warehouses sat behind a towering, rusted-out chainlink fence. We headed for a visibly open tear before Colt glanced over his shoulder, then yanked the corner up.

I slipped underneath, wincing as the sharp edges caught my shoulder. Fabric ripped, making me mutter a curse before I was through. Thorny bushes crowded the side of the massive warehouse. In the distance there was a set of stairs that led upwards. Headlights cut through the far end of the lot that seemed to take up half a block. Colt glanced my way and jerked his head, motioning me to follow.

The closer we got, the more I saw. There were lights on at the end of the building. Goosebumps raced as we hunkered in the shadows, then hurried forward. I *felt* them inside more than heard them. Colt pulled his gun free, keeping it at his side.

I winced and reached for my own. I didn't want the gun. But I didn't want to be killed, either. I worked my jaw, reaching up to touch my swollen lips. One attack was more than enough, and I sure as hell wasn't going to die here if I could help it. So I gripped the patterned steel grip and lowered it by my side, following Colt.

Voices echoed, raised ones.

We pushed ahead, slipping under the overhang to hide ourselves. As we came closer, we heard them. A deep, gruff voice followed. "Keep calm. We wait until the team is here and then we move. You go out there now and you might as well give yourself over to the goddamn Rossis, you want that?"

The answer was a second or two of silence before. "No." The second guy, who had to be Leroy Hastings, answered a little loudly.

"Then we wait."

We slowed at the stairs before Colt yanked his gun upwards, finding movement where I saw nothing but darkness. Barely a heartbeat later came two shadowy figures. Ones the Son seemed to know because he didn't shoot them.

Benjamin neared from the opposite side, then climbed the stairs soundlessly. He was fast and focused, his gun raised in front of him, two hands around the grip, swiveling to scan both sides as he reached the landing.

"*How much fucking longer?*" Leroy hissed.

"Almost here," the growl followed.

Benjamin jerked his gaze to us, then motioned right with two fingers. Colt was a ghost behind me, soundless and swift as he swept around Ben and moved toward the dark doorway at the far right. I followed, keeping my weapon low.

Two loud thuds and the door flew inwards with a *crack!* Ben and Caleb were inside in an instant. Screams and shouts followed, before a *crash*. We could hear running. Movement came from the window between us and the door where they'd just entered before the one in front of us was yanked open in his hasty escape...and there was Leroy Hastings, slimy little fucker.

He stopped instantly and lifted his gaze to Colt, who crowded the doorway and stepped in, pushing him back into what looked like a darkened office.

"What?" Leroy whispered and shook his head.

He was little, sparse hair stuck to his head in a sheen of sweat. One I could smell from here. I winced with the fetid stench of body odor and turned my head.

"You run and it'll only make this worse, Leroy." Ben stepped into the doorway, shrouded by the faint yellow hue. "Now, why don't we go back inside and have a nice little chat?"

"You...just stay the fuck away from me." Leroy stumbled backwards, slamming into Colt. I stepped inside the door, closed it behind me, and guarded the doorway.

"Move," Colt growled, the predatory sound reverberating through the air.

Leroy had no choice but to stumble toward Ben, who grabbed him by the arm and led him back the way he'd come. One hard shove and Leroy stumbled back into the filthy office area of the warehouse. There was a half-eaten pizza that'd turned hard and cracked, the cheese, once yellow, was now a foul molded brown. I quickly looked away, resisting the urge to gag. But the rest of the place wasn't any better. Overflowing ashtrays and empty cola cans littered every inch of the desk, and the table next to him was crammed full of papers and faded yellow manila envelopes.

"Sit." Ben drove him down onto a busted swivel chair that scooted backwards until it hit the desk. "Now, you know why we're here."

Leroy just wrenched his gaze to a shadowy figure that stepped out from the darkness in the far end of the office.

"Well?" He barked, his eyes widening. *"Aren't you going to do something?"*

My pulse was booming and my palms were sweaty as I gripped the gun and raised it. The male that strode toward us was tall and lanky, wearing leather cuts littered with motorcycle club patches. Ones that told me he was dangerous.

"Watch out." The words left my lips.

But Ben didn't care about the biker, in fact he barely gave him a sideways glance. "Alastair," he murmured.

"Just like I said, Mr. Rossi," the biker muttered, glaring at Leroy. "All tied up in a nice neat bow."

"I appreciate it," Ben muttered, straightening. "Now, I'm going to ask this once, Leroy. Where are Hale's new documents and where is he running to?"

Leroy just glared at the biker. "Fuck you, Rossi."

Ben lunged with a roar, grabbing him around the throat and bellowed in his face. "I will *fucking murder you. Do you get that? I will fucking DESTROY everything you have.*"

Leroy flinched, paling as he leaned as far away from the Mafia leader as he could. The smelly, weedy asshole shook his head, his eyes wide. "No. Don't *you* get that? I tell you what you want to know and I'm as good as dead."

Ben's reaction was swift, he lifted his gun and pressed it against Leroy's temple. "You think I'm joking here? Either way, you're a fucking dead man. The only difference is you *might* have a chance at evading Haelstrom but you have *no* chance at evading me."

A dog barked in the distance, drawing my gaze to the doorway but no one else moved, just me. Inside instinct shifted, morphing into a beast of its own. Something *felt wrong*. Just like it had felt wrong in the church with Cassius.

Through the broken metal slats in the window, a shadow shifted.

"Ben," I croaked, then jerked his way. *"Ben!"*

BOOM!

The sound reverberated as the door was thrown open and the space was invaded as powerful, muscled bikers surged in.

Crack!

Crack!

CRACK!

Gunfire exploded all around. Caleb opened fire. Colt lunged, taking out the biggest of them. I wrenched my gun upwards, my finger poised on the trigger...but I didn't fire.

That instinct was screaming in me, making me swivel as the biker Ben had called Alastair lifted his gun behind Ben's back, his dark eyes glinting as he took aim at the back of Ben's head.

"NO!" I screamed, my finger jerking the trigger.

BANG! BANG!

Two shots sounded, slamming Alastair backwards, but only one shot was mine.

Ben dropped to the floor in an instant, blood splattering over Caleb in front of him.

Colt roared, *bang, bang, BANG!*

Two more men dropped. Caleb shot two more. But there were more of them coming. I couldn't look away from the dark crumpled form on the floor as I stumbled forward. *Please, God... please, GOD!*

The heavy thud of steps boomed like thunder along the stairs and headed toward us. I was grabbed and hauled backwards, the bestial glare of Colt right in front of me.

"We have to move now!"

A light caught my gaze. Ben's cell lit up, the caller ID visible clear across the screen *Lazarus*.

"No...*no*...*no*...*no*...*no*." The words repeated.

But the Son gave me no other option. He opened fire at the door allowing Caleb to slam against me and drive me back into the far office. I couldn't think. I couldn't even fight, leaving Caleb and Colt to unleash shot after shot into the office as we sank back into the darkness, and I yanked open the far door.

Two men lay on the landing outside the main office, bathed in the ugly yellow light as they pressed their hands against the blood flow of their wounds.

"Move, Priest," Caleb barked as he shoved me down the stairs.

I stumbled but kept on my feet somehow, letting me career down stair after stair until I staggered back into the dark.

"Are there more?" Caleb barked.

Colt swung his gun, then lunged, quickly leaving us behind.

"No." I shook my head, the image of Ben's unmoving body burning in my mind. "We have to go back. *We have to go back.*"

"Listen!" Caleb grabbed me and roared. "There could be more of them coming. Do you understand? *There could be more here."*

But it didn't matter. It wasn't my life I thought about.

I'll take care of you, Thomas. Ben's words echoed. *I'll protect you.*

He'd saved me from the FBI and those men who'd tried to kill me. Men dressed in leather just like they were.

"I'm not leaving him up there." I wrenched my arm out of Caleb's hold. "Not in that filthy place. He needs to come with us."

I lunged for the stairs and climbed them as fast as I could.

My knees were shaking almost as much as the gun in my hand. I took aim and swiveled to the two men lying outside the office. One was slumped down, his eyes glazed and empty. The other just wheezed an awful wheeze, watching me as I neared.

His gun lay just out of reach. I kicked it away as I neared, leaving it to topple over the landing and fall to the ground with a clatter before I stepped back inside. One scan and I found Leroy Hastings dead with a neat bullet hole in the middle of his head. But I didn't care about him. Not anymore.

Alastair was still alive, wheezing, lying on top of a mountain of files as he stared at the ceiling. He never looked my way as I neared and knelt beside Ben's body.

"It wasn't personal."

I jerked my gaze to Alastair.

"Just business," he muttered.

I rose and moved closer, to stand over the man who'd killed Benjamin Rossi. "Everything is personal," I murmured. "But you can tell that to God."

I lifted my gun, my hands no longer shaking as I took aim and pulled the trigger.

Bang!

His body jerked and then stilled...forever.

Ben.

I turned around and knelt, pulling him over. There was blood over the back of his head, but it was nothing compared to the massive hole in the front. Wide, unblinking eyes stared up at me as his cell rang again. *Lazarus.*

"Please, Father, give me strength," I murmured.

Beep.

Lazarus: Dad, we have him. We have Hale.

Agony ripped through my chest at the sight. I reached down, grabbed his cell, and slipped it into my pocket before I gripped Ben under his arms and hauled his body upwards.

There was no way I was leaving him here.

No goddamn way.

TWENTY-THREE

Helene

My knuckles screamed with agony as I twisted my fingers, driving punishing pressure into the joints as chaos filled the room. The moment Anna lifted her head from that keyboard, looked at us and said '*I've got him. I've got Hale,*' everyone went into a frenzy.

Everyone but us, that was.

Vivienne stood motionless.

Ryth was the same.

And me.

We seemed to gravitate toward each other, standing in the middle of the room as orders were barked into cell phones and an army of mercenaries was whipped into motion. Like the eye of a violent and terrifying storm, we were silent and still, staring at the heavy steel door, waiting for those we loved to return.

Where is he?

They should be back by now.

They should be well and truly back.

Lazarus gave a snarl. "Answer your goddamn phone, Dad." He sounded desperate before he ended the call and swiped someone else's number, who answered. "Where the *fuck* is my father? What do you mean *he's not with you?*"

A faint voice drifted from his cell. One I couldn't hear well enough to know what was said.

A shiver raced along my spine. Vivienne still held her belly as she slowly took a step forward. The sound of heavy footfalls came barely a heartbeat later, thudding, pounding. A hard *thump* against the door drew the guard. On the monitor was Colt.

"Open the door." Vivienne urged desperately. *"I said, open the damn door."*

Lazarus' voice nagged at the edge of my senses as he barked commands into his phone. There was something wrong. Something all three of us felt in the core of our beings. The locks gave a *clunk* as they withdrew and the heavy steel door swung inwards, drawing everyone's stare.

Colt was there, striding through, heading straight for the only one he cared about. Vivienne threw her arms around him, burying her face into the hollow of his neck. Only then did I see it...*blood...lots of it.*

"Colt." Ryth's voice shook as footsteps came again.

Only this time there was no waiting. Caleb strode through the door, heading straight for Ryth. His eyes were wide and haunted as he wrapped his arms around her. This time there wasn't blood just on his shirt...it was *all over him*. One side of his face was splattered with deep rusted freckles. My knees shook.

"No." I whispered, knowing in my head it was someone close to him who had been shot. Someone very...*very* close.

Then he was there, stepping slowly through the open door. But Thomas didn't come to me. He stopped just inside the doorway, his gaze frozen on Laz. The world slowed down to an aching crawl.

I saw the scowl on Laz's face as his brow furrowed before grief slammed violently into him. He slowly lowered his hand, the voice on the other end of his cell forgotten.

"No," Laz whispered and shook his head. "*No.*"

"Lazarus," Thomas said carefully.

But the Mafia son just lowered his gaze to Thomas' bloodstained hands. *"Get the fuck away from me."*

He turned away, giving Thomas his back.

"Your father—" Thomas started.

Lazarus just lunged for him, flying across the room. Spittle flew from his mouth as he roared. *"SAY ANOTHER GODDAMN WORD AND I'LL KILL YOU!"*

Everyone moved. Riven lunged for Thomas and Tobias sprang for Laz, pulling him away.

"Easy," Tobias growled to Laz before jerking his gaze to Thomas. "You'd better be real right now, Priest. 'Cause you're about to unleash something that cannot be undone."

Laz released a sickening, tearing sound, and jerked himself from Tobias' hold. Then he threw his hand out as his knees buckled. Kat rushed forward, still clutching her baby on one hip, and grabbed him around the waist.

"No," her voice was raw as she shook her head. *"This can't be happening. This can't. Be. Happening."*

Approaching footsteps resounded as two guards carried in the dead body of Benjamin Rossi...and the entire room froze. All but Laz.

He tore away from Tobias and Kat. *"DAD, NO!"*

Finley's men lowered Ben's body to the floor. Laz dropped to his knees. The *thud* as he hit was brutal. His fists were clenched so tightly they were white. His wide eyes stared at the massive exit wound before he reached out with shaking hands and pulled his father onto his lap.

His head bowed as he rocked forward.

A low, keening sound tore free.

"It was a setup," Caleb said as he stepped near. "There was no way..."

"Who..." Laz stared wildly around. "Who killed him?"

There was silence.

He wrenched his gaze towards Caleb. *"I said, WHO KILLED HIM?"*

"Alastair," Thomas answered.

Lazarus bowed his head. "Did you kill him?"

The way he said it was half desperation and half rage.

"Yes," Thomas answered. "He said it wasn't personal, that it was business. There's only one business here...and that's Hale."

The answer was a slow, careful nod. "He was so sure, so goddamn sure. If he'd only listened. If he'd only—" He stopped, his fingers shaking as he gently slid his dad back to the floor. He stiffened as he looked down at his father, even his breath slowing. I saw the change, the way his shoulders relaxed as he buried his pain deep inside.

"Laz," Kat urged as she took a step forward, the look in her eyes tormented.

"Call everyone," His tone was empty as he lifted his gaze to Finley. "I want *that* motherfucker dead."

There was a moment of silence before Finley stepped forward. "I will, brother. I will."

"Baron and his brothers are on the way." London strode forward, moving to Vivienne and Colt.

"It's time," I whispered. "It's really time."

Riven's dark eyes found mine. "Yes," he answered. "It is."

"Ah, guys." Anna muttered loudly. "You might want to see this."

None of us wanted to move. Our heads stayed bent, gazes helplessly locked on Benjamin's body lying on the floor in the middle of the room. But it was Lazarus who turned away first, leaving his father behind.

Only then did we force ourselves to move and head to where Anna still typed.

"So, I was able to find my way in the back door of this network," she started, lifting her gaze to Lazarus and Finley as they neared. "Only it's not just a network of lawyers, is it? It's so much more than that. This, here." She tapped the screen. "Is a GPS coordinate. When I brought this up, I found nothing."

"What do you mean, nothing?" Lazarus snapped. "I thought you said you had him?"

"I do. But it's not what you think. The main ping is here...but when I infiltrated this device, it opened a whole network of smaller servers spread throughout the city."

"The city?" London moved closer.

"Yes." She lifted her gaze, meeting his. "They aren't hiding out in some fortress in the mountains. They're everywhere."

"Everywhere?"

Anna bought up a new map, one that had bright red dots scattered across the middle of the city.

"He's been hiding right under our noses?" London snarled. "That motherfucker. I bet he's been laughing at us. I bet he's fucking *howling* with glee."

"He's not gonna laugh for much longer." Lazarus turned his head to Finley and gave a nod. "Is he?"

"No, brother," Finley answered. "He's not."

TWENTY-FOUR

Riven

___

Don't go. Kat's pleas still replayed in my head. *Please, Laz, not like this.*

But the Mafia leader didn't listen. Because I don't think he heard her at all. Instead, he grabbed his weapons then strode for the door.

The rest of us followed and climbed into the cars before we hauled ass out of there, heading for the marker Anna had given us in the middle of the city.

Headlights bounced against a brick wall in front of us as the black Explorer skidded sideways when it braked facing the alleyway we'd been led to. *Jesus fucking Christ,* Laz was a goddamn animal as he shoved out of the Explorer two cars ahead, his head down and moving fast, without a damn vest.

I guess he didn't need it. The man was bulletproof by rage alone.

But Tobias was right behind him, lunging out of the Mustang as it stopped on a dime with Nick behind the wheel.

"Brake," I snapped at Hunter, desperate to be there, too. I'd be fucking damned if they were finishing Hale without me. My hand clenched around the weapon at my side. *"Hunter, fucking stop!"*

The heavy Hummer didn't respond well at all, the grab of the brakes slamming me toward the dashboard. With a snarl, I drove my hand against the dash to keep from being knocked the fuck out and jerked a glare at my brother.

With one yank of the handle, I shouldered the door open and lunged. But Thom was already moving fast, taking me by surprise.

Bright flashing yellow lights blazed as a garbage truck backed into the alley in front of us. Two men on the back jumped down, grabbed the overflowing cans, and hauled them into the air.

But I was around them in an instant, gripping my gun and running with my younger brother at my side.

He's here...Hale is fucking here!

I bared my teeth and slammed my boots harder against the pavement, surging forward as the alley branched right behind the row of shops. The flare of headlights came from the other end of the alley and the powerful shadow that was Finley Salvatore headed our way, with several others behind him.

Bang! The heavy thud against a door came as I turned right and found them outside a row of doors. *Bang!* Lazarus threw himself against one at the end of the alley before he stepped backwards and lifted his gun.

Both he and Tobias unloaded.

Crack!

Crack!

CRACK!

Their shots were still echoing when Tobias lunged this time to slam his muscled frame into the damn thing. Still, the door didn't budge. It didn't even crack.

"*FUCK!*" Lazarus roared.

I slowed, scanning the row of doors as the sound of car engines came.

"*What the fuck is this?*" Lazarus whipped around, bellowing as Finley stopped beside him.

"This doesn't feel right." Tobias voiced what I felt.

I scanned the row of doors, finding a dull shine in the crack of the door. Instinct kicked in, nagging at me as the heavy thud of footsteps came racing along the alleyway behind us.

Thud!

Finley slammed his shoulder against the door.

I swung my stare to Hunter, who scanned the rows of doors beside me. He scowled, sensing what I sensed.

"*Lazarus!*" London roared behind us. "*STOP!*"

The alley door to our right opened. Shadows spilled out, moving like a plague. I lifted my gun as that chilling feeling took flight, and took aim as one man slammed into Lazarus, lifting him off his feet.

Carven and Colt rushed forward, like a thunderous wave crashing against the army that came.

Crack!

Grunt!

I squeezed off a shot—*Boom!*—and hit one of them in the shoulder. He spun backwards, stumbling before he righted himself and whipped a sickening glare my way. I knew what they were...mechanical, terrifying hunters.

They were Sons.

"Hunter!" I roared as I rushed forward.

Two of them had Lazarus, one drove his fists into the Mafia leader's face as the other yanked a glinting blade into the air. With a roar I lunged, driving my shoulder into the guy, trying my best to knock him sideways. But he was ready for it, turning to swing back around and drove the blade into my shoulder.

I unleashed a roar as pain plunged deep.

Bang!

Lazarus stumbled backwards, his gun kicking as it fired, hitting the Son in the center of his chest, dropping the bastard where he stood. The alley erupted in gunfire and screams. But the screams didn't come from the mechanical, trained killers. They came from us.

Thomas unleashed a roar behind me. I swung, to find him lifting a heavy gold cross above his head before driving it back down. The same cross that was in his bedroom. I knew it was there...but how in the Hell did he bring it here? A Son was on the ground behind me, his sickening, rage-filled stare pinned on me.

One look and I knew my brother had just saved my life. I met Thom's stare and nodded.

Caleb and Nick had taken back-to-back stances, each firing to pick off one after another of the bastards who came for us.

The white-eyed scarred fucker came from somewhere behind me, charged in to fire and dropped one of the Sons. But he was hit in kind, the shot clipping his shoulder to throw him backwards. I'd seen the guy take on four goddamn bikers on his own. But not even he was prepared for the onslaught of these bastards.

More of them came, throwing knives like words. I ducked sideways, but Alvarez Cross of the Cerberus brothers wasn't so goddamn graceful. He took a knife in his thigh, and another in his stomach.

"Get back!" I screamed and clutched my gun, staring at the carnage as they took Lazarus' bodyguard down. I yanked my gun upwards, swallowing the wave of pain that ripped like lightning through my shoulder, and squeezed the trigger.

Lazarus was down. Finley too. Hunter unleashed a bellowing roar as he took out two of the Sons.

But there were too many...*we were going to die in this alley.*

"Get them!" I yelled, pointing to Laz and Fin.

I fired my gun and strode forward, then kept on firing, making the fuckers dodge and run.

But it only gave us a second of reprieve. Still, it was what we needed. Hunter lunged for Fin, who was the closest, and swung his massive fist around to connect with the Son who had Fin on his back.

Crack.

The brutal blow was sickening. But it did the job. The Son flew sideways, slammed against the ground, and struggled to rise. I lifted my gun and stumbled to the side, then drove it down with all I had, cold-cocking the bastard on top of Lazarus as I shoved out my other hand.

He was dazed, still he grasped my hand and let me pull him upright. Hard, ripping coughs came as he clutched his throat and tried to breathe. But there was a look of pure rage burning like neon fucking lights in his eyes. The kind of rage that didn't care if he was killed or the rest of us, for that matter.

Only I sure as hell cared.

"*Go!*" I shoved him backwards. "*Grab your man and GO!*"

I swung back around, not wanting to take my eyes off these fuckers for a second, to see Alvarez grab one of them by the throat and lift him until his feet dangled in the air. One sickening *crunch* and he just dropped the bastard to fall.

They didn't deserve this. A vein in my temple pulsed as rage and regret filled me. They were killers...but they were nothing more than robots, trained from childhood to kill while they were useful, but ultimately to die. My gun felt heavy as I lifted it and fired at them again...so goddamn heavy.

They didn't deserve this.

But *we* needed to survive.

I clenched my jaw, hatred seething inside me. Laz grabbed his bodyguard, pulled him upwards, then heaved him over his shoulder, stumbling at the weight. Fin was next, staggering toward them before he swung, firing his gun at the rest of the bastards as Tobias lunged to drive his fists into one, over and over, in a killing rage.

"Come for my family?" He raged, his eyes wide and wild. *"I'LL SHOW YOU WHAT HAPPENS!"*

Bang!

Bang!

Bang...bang...bang...bang.

Nick and Caleb still fired, one after the other, the sound ricocheting off the walls until it was all I heard. I was grabbed and pulled backwards. Panic roared until I found the familiar eyes of my brother.

"Let's go!" he bellowed, firing a shot behind me.

But the Sons were leaving, slipping back behind the steel doors to leave us behind. I stumbled, then turned, to find Laz and Finley lurching along the alley toward us. Alvarez was driving three of the Sons backwards.

"You go." I nodded to Fin, who cradled his arm and tried to stop the bleeding in his neck at the same goddamn time. "Get him back. We'll follow you."

There wasn't time to acknowledge anything I said as Fin's leg buckled and sent him crashing to the ground. Hunter lunged, grabbed Finley Salvatore, and all but carried him to his car.

"We need to go." I turned to Alvarez and met that unflinching stare. He gave a nod, glanced over his shoulder to the place where we'd almost died, then started forward.

Headlights shone, blinding me as I reached the Explorer. The others pulled up hard, and London was the first one out, with his buddy, Baron, right behind him. It had been only a matter of minutes that we were in that alley with the Sons of The Order. But it felt like it had been a lifetime.

London raced around the front of the Audi. "Colt and Carven?"

I just shook my head. "I don't know. It was...like nothing I've ever seen."

There was a flare of panic in his eyes before he shifted his focus to the alley. Loyalty to his sons drove him forward. He lifted his gun and charged, heading back to the fucking deathtrap we'd barely escaped.

Alvarez stopped and turned to watch London and the diamond asshole disappear. I did the same as guilt and loyalty forced me to turn.

"Fuck," I grunted.

Alvarez turned to me, and I knew he felt the same. We stumbled back into that alley, limping, bleeding, and cursing, jerking our weapons toward anything that moved. But there was nothing but bodies outside those false doors. London checked each one, before meeting my stare. "Where the fuck are my sons?"

I shook my head, trying to make sense of what had just happened. "They came out of nowhere. Carven...and Colt, they saved our asses, driving them backwards." I lifted my gun to the door. "They're in there. They're all the way in there."

London rose from the ground and moved closer, his hands moving over the door. "It's steel."

"All of them are."

"There's no way in?"

"Not unless you have a key."

He turned around. "So you're saying my sons are in there, fighting a goddamn army of trained killers by themselves?"

I froze, my pulse booming. "Yes."

TWENTY-FIVE

Helene

THE ROOM WAS A VACUUM OF SILENCE. FEAR LACED WITH hope as we all stared at the heavy steel doors in the Salvatore house. There was no laughing or chatting, not even from the new influx of men who'd arrived to crowd the room. These men didn't pace, nor did they rage. They didn't need to. The sharp *snap* of racking slides and loading fresh magazines was the only call to war we needed.

The Baldeons and the Bernardis I recognized as two of the main Mafia families. The other men who came in were either mercenaries or allies of the Salvatores or the Rossis. But there was a couple who stood at the edge of the gathering that I didn't know, a striking older man everyone nodded when they entered and a stunning raven-haired woman next to him.

She glanced my way and gave me a hint of a smile. One that said friend and not foe. I nodded back, knowing we needed as many allies as we could get.

"Where are they?" Vivienne groaned, shifting her weight from one swollen foot to the other. She should be sitting down and resting, not standing there, panicked and desperate, staring at an empty doorway as we waited for those we loved to return. "They should be back by now."

"Easy," I urged. "We have no idea what waited for them."

It was just supposed to be a scouting mission, but by the look in Lazarus' eyes, we'd all known it was much more than that.

Ryth just clutched Ali to her chest as he slept. How he could in this madness I had no idea. Still, she swayed her body from side to side, rocking him in her arms, and waited.

I grasped Vivienne's hand and placed my other on Ryth's shoulder, connecting with them as my focus shifted to Anna, who'd spent her time hunched over her laptop, gathering as much data on this new map she'd found as she could.

But it was Kat who stood in the middle of the room in utter silence, her empty eyes fixed on the steel door in front of us. It was her silence we all felt, her *vacuum* of grief sucking us all in.

Her raven-haired daughter clung to her leg, looking up at her with those big dark eyes, ones which looked just like her father's in the worst way possible. But Kat didn't acknowledge her. She barely noticed the baby in her arms. Just that door. That *motherfucking door*.

"They're coming in now." The crack of the two-way made all three of us flinch.

I held my breath as the creak of the front door sounded and grunts and moans of agony tore through the air. Ryth was the first to move. Hugging her son to her chest, she raced forward.

Like a crashing wave of desperation, we all followed, tearing through the house. I paced my steps with Vivienne, catching sight of Lazarus and Finley stumbling in with blood all over them.

"Oh fuck." Vivienne croaked. *"Oh fuck! London? LONDON!"*

London came in behind them, along with Riven and Hunter who looked like hell. There was blood all over one side of Hunter's face and he was limping badly. Riven looked just as bad, his shirt soaked with blood and stuck to his body, moving in a way that couldn't be good. But it was Thomas who called to me. Sweet, perfect, Thomas, who was now carrying a cross like a weapon, his face also splattered with blood.

Vivienne stumbled forward, wrapping herself around her lover as best she could with her belly in the way. "Where are they?" She glanced behind them. "Where're Carven and Colt?"

I took Riven's weight as she shook her head, screaming. "No... NO!"

"They're *not dead,* Vivienne..." London gripped her chin, forcing her gaze to his. *"Did you hear me? They're NOT dead."*

"What the hell happened?" I turned to Riven as Tobias and Nick lurched in arm-in-arm, looking shell-shocked. Caleb sucked in hard breaths, as numb as his brothers.

The agony in Riven's stare said all I needed to know. Whatever had happened must have been very bad. He gave a shake of his head. "Hale wasn't there, but the Sons were. Waiting for us."

"Waiting for you?" My pulse sped as my mind was filled with terror.

"Yeah."

No wonder they'd barely survived. I let him lean on my shoulder as we stumbled back inside that room.

Lazarus crossed the room, heading straight for his wife. He wrapped his arms around her. She held him, still in silence. Both of them shell-shocked and empty.

"So then where are they, London?" Vivienne's voice broke. *"Where are my men?"*

Desperation was a fist around my heart, squeezing and clenching as I helped Riven into the room. One of Finley's men was ready, pulling out his medical kit and giving instructions, motioning for Riven to sit while he triaged everyone's injuries.

But it was Viv that worried me the most. I glanced over my shoulder at her, watching as she shook her head. Her face was pasty, her once red lips now almost gray. London winced as he left her side and made his way to the medic, who checked his shoulder and side, but his focus was on her.

This couldn't be good for the babies, not this much stress. She needed the Sons. She needed Colt.

I left Riven with the medic and headed for her. "Vivienne, baby. Look at me."

"I can't leave them out there." Fresh tears shone in her eyes. *"I won't. Not again...not after last time."*

When she'd almost lost them to this goddamn war. She shook her head and took a step backwards before turning to leave.

"Vivienne!" London yelled as she walked through the door. *"Goddamnit!"* He pulled away from the medic, leaving his shirt to fall into place.

"I'm not finished." Finley's medic called.

"It doesn't matter," he muttered, limping after her. "Nothing does, apart from her."

We all watched them leave. But it was the faint roar of an engine which had me running. I left Riven and the others behind, racing to the front door to find dust kicking up in the early morning sunlight as the Mustang tore away, leaving London behind.

"What the fuck?" Nick snarled, striding past to make his way down the stairs. "She took my goddamn car!"

I won't leave them...not after last time.

We all knew where she was going. She was going back there, to that same alley where they'd all almost died. The Explorer roared to life in an instant. I was already sprinting, with Riven and Thomas fast behind me, yanking open the back doors and lunging inside.

"Move it!" London roared, shoving the four-wheel drive into gear.

My men followed, Riven in the passenger's seat, with Thomas beside me. I barely had time to grasp the seatbelt before I was slammed backwards against the seat as we headed after her.

"Goddamn woman!" London groaned. *"She's going to be the fucking death of me."*

He wrenched his panicked stare to Riven, who never said a word. But he didn't need to. The moment London jerked the wheel, heading along the straight stretch of road, we caught sight of her in the distance.

"I didn't know she could drive a stick," Riven murmured.

London just shot him a sorrow-filled glare. "She can't...not well, at least."

I winced.

"Poor Nick," Riven finished.

I couldn't care less about Nick or his damn car. I just wanted my sister safe. But she had other ideas. London gunned the Explorer, pushing the four-wheel drive harder as we headed toward the city.

"How does she know where to go?" I asked.

London met my gaze in the rear-view mirror. "It was on Nick's GPS."

"Shit." I eased back as up ahead, the Mustang turned left.

"She'll be okay," Thomas murmured, drawing my gaze. "God is on our side."

"It didn't look like it," I answered. "Not by all the bullet holes and knife wounds."

"But we all came back, didn't we?" My mind raced as he shifted his gaze to the road ahead. "We all came back."

They did. For that, I was so very thankful.

"She's fighting for those she loves, just like we were."

"Fighting is one thing, putting herself in danger is another," London growled. "She is my fucking world. If anything happened to her..."

"It won't." I shook my head and reached out to grasp Thomas' hand. "It won't."

TWENTY-SIX

Colt

HUNT...HUNT THEM.

Then kill.

The Beast was hungry, ravenous for blood. I hunched my shoulders, driving my body harder. Heavy steps thudded against the concrete tunnel under my feet. Carven was a blur beside me, his nearly white hair fucking neon in the dark as we left the alley far behind. The moment the doors opened and Hale's Sons spilled out, we'd known this was the only way to reach him. So we'd fought. We'd killed, and at the first opportunity, we'd pushed through those open metal doors and plunged into the darkness.

"Move...your...fat...ass," Carven snarled beside me as he surged ahead.

My chest burned.

My breaths were like razors.

Still, I pushed harder and let that savage part of my nature rise. Because it wasn't him I focused on...it was the three up ahead running away from us. The three Sons who were leading us to the only one we really wanted. The one we hungered to tear apart...*Haelstrom Hale.*

I unleashed a growl and pushed harder, hurtling toward them... and slowly gained ground.

"'Bout...*fucking...time.*" Carven jerked an unhinged grin my way and dropped his hand, palming a blade.

Only, I sensed movement in front of me, coming fast. I drove my fist through the air and into my brother's shoulder, pushing him hard away from me. He stumbled to the side as the first of Hale's Sons stepped out of a small alcove and lunged.

I dropped my shoulder and met the swing of his fist with brute force. His feet left the floor as I drove him into the air, then down again, hard.

Thud.

His body impacted with the floor as two more of them came in fast. Steel slashed through the air, forcing me backwards. I lunged, driving myself back again and again and again, until there was nowhere else to go. Agony sliced through my shoulder.

That pain triggered the savage monster inside me. Walls trembled before they came crashing down and the Beast was unshackled.

NO!

He roared, clawing upwards, and instead of moving backwards, he slammed into Hale's Son and drove him back. I couldn't hold on, slipping further and further away into that emptiness. But I didn't fight him this time.

Instead, I gave him the one thing he needed...

The memory of her.

KILL THEM. *Kill them. Kill them.*

Hard breaths. The slash of pain. One that whipped my gaze toward him. The male stopped, scowling as I just continued forward. Blood. Agony. They only made me stronger. I clenched my fists and drew them upwards as an image slammed into me.

My Wildcat.

Big and round with my offspring.

Her hair whipped in the wind, wild and free.

"They want to hurt me," she urged, her hand resting against our babies. *"They want to kill what's yours."*

My lips curled back as my focus narrowed in on the male in front of me. One who shook his head and glanced at the other one at his side. My brother grunted, the clash of steel sharp and brutal in the dark. But I didn't focus on him.

Carven could take care of himself.

It was *her* I thought about as I stepped forward. *Her* that ripped through me like adrenaline.

"What the fuck?" One of them muttered before I lunged.

My fist drove up, connecting fast and hard with his stomach. With an *oof,* he doubled over. But I was already grabbing him by the throat and lifting him until his feet dangled and kicked as he wailed.

The bite of cold steel pressed against my temple. "Put him down *now,*" the other Son commanded.

My muscles quaked, driving the pain into my elbow as I slowly turned my head to meet the Son's stare.

He flinched with the connection, then murmured. "What the fuck *are* you?"

"Not Son," I grunted. *"Killer."*

"No, he isn't. He's my goddamn brother." Carven sucked in hard breaths and pressed the tip of his blade into the back of the other Son's neck. "Now, how about we play a little game. Let's see if your finger can pull that trigger faster than I can drive this blade through your fucking spine."

There was a flicker of panic before his lips curled.

"That's what I figured." Carven reached around and took the gun from his hand, then he shifted that piercing blue stare my way before glancing at the male in my hands. "Take your time, brother. Do what you have to do."

I turned my focus back to him. To the one who wanted to *hurt her.*

"Mine." The word was a growl that rumbled in my chest as I squeezed. *"My female. My mate."*

Feet kicked. Fists swung, landing against my cheek. My head was snapped to the side by the blow and my elbows howled as I clenched my fists, driving all my hate and desperation into my grip until, with a roar, his neck went *snap* and Hale's Son was no more.

"Goddamn, Beast." Carven jerked his stare my way.

I sucked in hard breaths and stared at the male in my hands as I let him go, letting him crumple to the floor.

"You aren't one of us," The male Carven pressed his knife against spoke. "What the fuck are you?"

"Something your kind made," Carven spat. "Now, you and I are gonna have a nice little chat while my brother comes back to us." His stare was desperate. "Right, Colt?"

No.

Not yet.

Not ready.

I swung my stare to the darkness up ahead. I could feel *him* up there. The man we were hunting...and so could Carven. My brother's focus shifted with mine.

"He's up there waiting you know," Hale's Son croaked. "He made you. You belong to him. You feel it, right? That need to belong. You finally found it. You never belonged to St. James. You belong with us. *We* are your family."

I swung my glare toward him. Heavy breaths consumed me as I took a step forward until I almost towered over him and leaned in until my chest hit his and he was forced to breathe my air.

"Easy, Beast," my brother urged. "Easy."

Rage howled inside me, hating the fact I felt what he'd said. It thrummed inside me, like a pulse I couldn't quite find. I wanted to strangle that pulse...I wanted to tear it out.

"I will find him," my words rumbled in the back of my throat. "And he won't like what he created one bit."

Colt pushed in, not desperate or demanding. Comforting. I eased back, letting him take hold. Knowing I didn't have to take control. He hated and raged just as I did. I slipped away, melting back into the shadows, waiting to return to her.

A keening call tore from my chest, resounding in the darkness.

My Wildcat...my mate.

She was close.

"WHAT THE FUCK kind of sound was that?"

I shook my head, my senses dull...until one last surge of the beast ripped through me. I saw everything. His mind. His senses...and in that clarity...two heartbeats behind us. I turned, whipping my gaze to the darkness. To another alcove deeper in the tunnel we'd come from.

Vivienne's face rose in my mind. Confusion filled me. Through the connection of the Beast, she felt close...real damn close. I stared at the two dark blurs racing back along the tunnel behind us, and an overwhelming *need* to follow filled me.

I took a step backwards.

"Colt? What is it?"

With every second, that howling desperation grew louder until it was undeniable.

"She is here," I croaked. "And they know it. They're going after her. They're—"

A low snigger came from Hale's Son in front of me, right before Carven slammed his fist down on the hilt of the knife, driving the tip all the way into the hunter's neck, severing his spine instantly. He dropped to the floor, but I had already spun around and was driving my body forward in the dark.

They knew where she was.

And they were going after her.

I ran, pushing myself harder than ever.

Carven matched my strides.

"Go!" I roared. *"Save her."*

He needed no encouragement, his own terrifying need for her driving him forward. The cracks in the tunnel beside me were a blur. My pounding steps were sledgehammer blows. Still, I needed harder, faster.

GET TO HER NOW!

The Beast howled.

Carven pushed harder, charging along the tunnel back to that alley. Fear pushed in. Why the hell was she here?

Crack.

Crack.

Crack.

The faint sound of gunfire pushed me harder. Sunlight splashed against the floor of the tunnel. Screams outside pushed in. A woman...*was it Vivienne?*

Carven turned right and lunged. I knew where we were. The metal doors at the end of the alley. The walls blurred, rage was all I saw as I barrelled right and all but threw myself out through the open door and into the alley.

Riven and Thomas were fighting one of the Sons, unleashing the kind of violence that was sickening. But I didn't care about them...I turned my head.

London was there.

Carven too.

Two Sons stood between them and Vivienne...

My Vivienne.

Her hand went to her belly. Her wide eyes fixed on me. There was a look of relief as she met my gaze. But she shouldn't be relieved. No, she should be fucking terrified.

"Easy." London lifted his gun as the Son in front of her pulled his blade.

The bastard said nothing, but he didn't need to. We all knew exactly what he intended to do with that honed razor's edge.

"Make a move and I'll drop you where you stand," Carven growled.

But I didn't wait for that to happen. I lowered my head and strode toward him, watching as the Son's eyes widened in surprise.

Mine.

The Beast snarled, still hovering close to the surface.

If you don't kill him, then I will.

He didn't need to say it twice. The other Son lunged, aiming for Carven, as I took a step forward and leaped. The burning slash of the blade drove all the way into my side. Still, I slammed the Son sideways and away from the woman I loved. That searing agony drove deeper. I didn't need to look down. I didn't even feel the blade at all.

All I felt was the Beast...and rage.

I drove my fist onto his face as the alley erupted with the roar of gunfire. The Son's head snapped back as blood spilled from his curled lips and stained the front of his teeth red. I unleashed again...and again. Each blow hit harder than the last, until the bastard who'd threatened my mate buckled and fell to the ground.

"Five seconds," he said, staring up at me. "And I would've gutted her like a fish."

A guttural roar ripped from my chest, burning as it took flight. Inarticulate screams echoed through the alley from the others as I slammed my fist into his face over and over until his eyes fluttered shut. Still, I didn't stop, falling forward to straddle his body.

His face was crushed, the white of bone visible through his split nose. I couldn't even see his eyes.

Until with one more savage blow, his head rolled backwards... and that's where it stayed.

I stopped, my fists throbbing at my sides. My breaths consumed me.

"Colt."

Her voice pushed into the red haze. I lifted my gaze from the mess of his face to hers. To my beautiful Wildcat. The woman I watched over...the woman I loved.

"Baby," she said carefully reaching out to brush her hand against my cheek.

I closed my eyes and tilted my head, desperate for every soft brush of her fingers and every soothing word from her lips. The faint *thudthudthudthud* of our babies' heartbeats called to me. She was the only one who could turn the Beast in me to a mewling, purring thing. I reached out, wrapped my throbbing hands around her waist, and pulled her gently to me.

My head tilted as my ear pressed against the swell of her belly. I closed my eyes, those racing throbbings both soothing.

"I wasn't going to leave you there." She dropped her hand, her fingers sliding through my hair. "Never again"

I nodded, because it was all I could do.

There was no anger.

No rage.

Just knowing she would do anything to find me.

And I'd do the same...to protect her.

"We found him," Carven's voice pulled me away from the sounds of my children. "We found Hale."

"Where?" London growled.

"In the tunnel...you follow that to the end and you'll find him. But he has Sons. Lots and lots of Sons, and they're waiting. They're waiting for us."

"Then it'd be rude of me to fucking disappoint, wouldn't it?"

I lifted my head and turned to the man who was the closest thing we'd ever had to a father, and spoke. "Yes. Yes, it would."

TWENTY-SEVEN

Helene

_____

"MINE!" THE ROGUE SON'S FINGERS ENTWINED IN MY hair, wrenching me backwards until I slammed against his chest. *"Do you hear me, Daughter?"* He roared in my ear. *"YOU BELONG TO US!"*

No...

NO!

Fire lashed my scalp until the tears came. Through the haze, Vivienne pressed her body against the wall as another of Hale's Sons moved toward her.

There were too many of them. Four had raced from the open doors at the end of the alley; two made for Vivienne and two came for me. London was fighting as hard as he could, howling with rage as he slammed one of them against the wall. But these weren't just normal men. No, they were killers.

My head was yanked back, wrenching my focus from London and my sister to the Son who'd lunged across the open space and taken us by surprise. One minute, I was hurtling into the alley to save my sister and the next, I was grabbed and spun so fast my mind couldn't catch up. He pressed me against his hard body.

Only, the second Son who headed my way wasn't so lucky.

Riven stood between us, his gun aimed in the center of the Son's chest.

"Make a move, motherfucker." Riven growled, sucking in deep breaths, his gun pointed rock-steady at the Son's heart. "And I'll put a hole right through the middle of you."

The Son just grinned, until he glanced down at me and that smug smirk faltered, even as the hold across my chest grew tighter.

"You know she's coming with us," The bastard murmured. "Either way."

Warmth rushed through my veins, the trembling, feeble feeling of connection writhed under my skin and made me feel panicked. I didn't like it, not the way they made me feel, or what they wanted me for.

Then the Son in front of Riven lifted his hands. "Sooner or later, she'll be ours, Principal."

Riven unleashed a savage snarl. "Call me that again, I dare you."

It was Coulter's mansion all over again. The way they'd hurt us and used us, stabbing and cutting, forcing us to breed.

"Get the fuck off me!" I bucked, slamming my head backwards as I aimed for his face.

But he was far too fast, reaching around to grasp me by the throat.

"You can't win, don't you understand that? You. Can. Never. Win."

Movement came from the open metal door. Carven was a blur of neon white hair and rage as he lunged for the two attackers crowding Vivienne. But it was Colt who bellowed like a bull and charged, slamming into another Son.

"You belong to Hale." The sick words were snarled in my ear as the Son holding me drew me back.

Get her on the table.

The words plunged deep into me.

I froze, my gaze fixed on Riven and the gun in his hand, until CRACK! The sickening sound shattered the hold on me, causing me to release a startled scream as the Son who held me lurched sideways before falling to one knee.

As Colt unleashed sickening blows into the rogue Son he held, Thomas strode forward. The bright morning sun glinted off something metal in his hand as he lifted his arm and swung.

CRACK!

The blow hit hard, tearing the rogue Son's hold from my throat. He crumpled instantly, falling to the ground until Thomas stood over him.

"God is in my hand!" Thomas roared. *"MY RIGHTEOUS, VIOLENT HAND!"*

As he swung, I saw what he used as a weapon. It was the heavy gold cross he prayed to, now splattered with blood.

CRUNCH.

I couldn't look away, frozen by the sight of that kind, beautiful, awkward man as he swung that holy weapon, and I realized he wasn't the man I knew, not anymore. This Thomas was terrifying, filled with rage and pain until there was nothing but vengeance left.

"You do not touch her." He stared down at the male with the side of his head caved in and raised his weapon once more. *"You do not touch what belongs to us."*

Swing.

Drop.

CRUNCH.

The Son's head snapped sideways. Thomas knelt, his glazed eyes fixed on nothing. Heavy breaths sounded as Thomas rose, still holding the cross coated with brain matter and etched with dark strands of hair.

"Easy." Riven warned the other Son as he watched the attack. "I'd love nothing more than to end you." He glanced at Thomas. "Brother, you okay?"

Those once soft brown eyes were now dark with rage. I'd seen Thom look like that once before and he'd come back to me. But as he shifted that merciless stare my way now, I knew that Thomas was no more. This man standing before me, wielding the cross as his weapon of choice, was just as dangerous as his brothers.

"Vivienne," London croaked and stumbled forward.

"I'm-m o-kay," She stuttered as she staggered sideways to wrap her arms around Colt.

Riven took a step forward and pressed the muzzle of his gun against the last rogue Son's head. "All that's left is to end this one."

But it was Vivienne who commanded my attention. She tightened her arms around Colt, burying her face against his chest. Blood was spreading across his side, but he didn't seem to notice.

"We found him." His deep voice resounded, bouncing off the walls of the alley. "We found Hale."

London jerked his head upwards, his eyes darkening. "Where?"

"Wherever that tunnel leads." Carven pointed to the open steel door as he approached us.

London took a step toward the door.

My mind was reeling, trying to put it all together. The dead Son in front of me called my focus and something inside howled at his death. It was that connection, that aching sense of the familiar. I lifted my head, meeting the gaze of the Son who was still alive.

He felt it too, that ache in the pit of his stomach that had no name...but a knowing.

"No." I shook my head and stepped toward Riven. "Put the gun down."

Anger and a cutting, cruel pain flared in Riven's dark eyes. "What the fuck did you say?"

My stare was pleading. I prayed he trusted me. "I don't want you to kill him."

He turned and took a step toward me, glaring with jealousy. "You *what?*"

"I want to take him alive."

There was a flicker of amusement as he jutted his chin out. It was pride. One I wanted desperately to exploit anyway I could.

I met Riven's stare, urging him with my eyes alone. I didn't know if he heard me or if he was too stubborn to know I'd never hurt him, but he turned away, lowering his gun. "Then he's all yours, Helene. Do with him what you wish."

He left then, giving me his back. That hurt more than anything.

The Son gave a *humf* before Thomas stepped forward and lifted the cross, placing the blood splattered, matted with strands of hair weapon under his chin. "I wouldn't be so quick to smirk if I were you."

The Son's smile fell away before Thom drove the cross against his throat and growled. "Get up carefully and move."

"Wait," London said as he stared at the open doors, then glanced over his shoulder. "We can't just leave it like that."

"No...*Hell, no.*" Vivienne shook her head as she pulled away from Colt. "You take a step through that door, London St. James, and you'd better push it wider, 'cause I *sure as hell* am not going to stand here for another minute without you." She turned to Colt and Carven. "All of you. Where you go, I go. You got that?" There was a mumble until she swung her savage gaze to London. "I said, *you got that?*"

There was a twitch at the corner of London's mouth. One I almost took for a smirk.

"Yes, pet." He moved back toward her and pulled her against him. "We stay together."

"You got that right." Her voice shook.

"You really going to take him with us?" London looked at me.

Carven and Colt just glared at the Son. It didn't take a lot to know they wanted to gut him and leave him behind.

But we had an opportunity here, one we hadn't had before.

"Yes," I answered. "I'll take responsibility for him. He can be my prisoner."

Carven gripped his knife and took a step forward. "One wrong move and I'll kill him, you got that?" He swung that icy stare my way.

I swallowed hard. "Loud and clear."

TWENTY-EIGHT

Helene
_____

"YOU WANT TO *WHAT?*"

I held my ground, staring into the endless pit of rage that was Tobias Banks. "I want to keep him prisoner."

His lips curled, baring his teeth, as he swung that stare toward the rogue Son. "No fucking way. No Son stays alive." He jerked his head toward Carven and Colt. "Unless it's those two."

"Thanks for the clarification," Carven muttered, glaring.

I stood in front of Hale's hunter, protecting him with my body alone. He stood handcuffed behind me, guarded by Thomas and London, with a cross and a gun making him think twice about twitching.

"I say he does." I held my ground, not once looking my sister's way.

She shook her head, that same look of revulsion and pain in her eyes. The last thing I wanted to do was hurt Ryth. But I had this feeling and it wasn't that sickening connection I felt between us. It was that dangerous, fragile, hope...

"He doesn't live," Tobias urged.

"I say he does."

Tobias shook his head, glancing behind me to the Son. One look. One breath and it'd all be over.

"T," Caleb murmured to his brother.

But Tobias didn't answer, nor did he look away, just glared at the male behind me. Glared and glared and glared.

"T," Caleb called again, this time grabbing his brother's arm gently. "We can use him. Find out what he knows and get to Hale that way."

My pulse thundered. Did he understand? *Christ, I hoped so.* He glanced at the Son behind me. But whatever he saw didn't fill him with confidence. His brow pinched with a frown.

There was no way the Son would be intimated. Not by a man...but maybe...he would be by a Daughter. I looked at Ryth and Vivienne. One looked terrified and the other pissed. My pulse raced, knowing if there was anyone who could get the information we needed from this hunter, it was me.

Tobias turned away. "This is on you, Helene. Any blood he spills, you'll wear. I hope you understand that?"

I did and it terrified me.

"Move." London pushed the Son away from the others.

I met every stare, the looks of disappointment, pressed lips, hard swallows, grinding teeth. I felt it all as I turned away and froze. Riven was there, watching my every move. Slowly, he stepped to the side, allowing us to pass.

Finley Salvatore led us to a room, much smaller than the massive panic room we'd made into a command center. He pressed in the code and the steel door opened. "This code disengages the locks until you lock them again. I'll give you the code and *only* you. You can use this room however you choose."

He watched Thom and London push the rogue Son inside and force him to sit against a wall. "I hope you know what you're doing, Helene," He murmured, then grabbed his cell, typed out a message and held it up in front of my face. 6767, the code filled the screen before he lowered his hand, turned, and walked away.

London was next. "I need to see Vivienne."

"Of course." I answered.

The way he said it made me feel like shit. No one wanted the Son here, least of all me. I knew what it meant...

The others would torture and even try to kill him, and they'd force me to watch it happen. I stepped into the room as Thomas rose, looking down at the Son now secured to the wall by a chain.

"Outside, Helene," He murmured, giving me no choice but to follow.

I met the Son's stare and that same feeling of belonging filled me. His dark eyes softened with the connection. Whatever it was I felt, I knew he felt it too. But I followed Thomas outside the small room, meeting one of Finley's bodyguards.

"Ten years in the military police. If he knows anything, I'll get it out of him." He said, glancing at the room.

Could I trust him? I wasn't sure. I needed him, that I knew.

"Nothing will happen, unless he forces my hand. You have my word." The guard urged.

I had to trust that...for now.

Raised voices came from the main room where everyone waited. I headed back in with Thomas, finding the dull roar quieting the moment I stepped inside. Heads turned my way. No one wanted to see me, not after bringing the enemy through the door. But it was Vivienne and Ryth who broke away and headed toward me.

"It's okay." Vivienne ran her hands along my shoulders and pulled me in close. "I know what you're doing."

I held her, meeting Ryth's stare.

"We can't do it," My sister murmured in my ear. "So it has to be you." I pulled away, finding desperate compassion in her stare.

"Thank you." Ryth said and smiled.

"You feel it too, right?" I asked. I had to know...desperate to find out it wasn't just me. "That connection to them."

Ryth eyes widened. Vivienne glanced over her shoulder to where Colt and Carven stood. "Yes." She turned back to me. "It's like fate, like you've known them your entire life even though you've only just met. I don't believe in past lives or alternate realities. But if I did, it'd be like this." She turned back to me. "There is a connection between us, one only we can feel. If there's a way to exploit that connection to end this and be rid of Hale once and for all, then we need to do everything we can.

If that means you need to form a connection with this Son, then I'll do everything I can to help you." She looked at Ryth. "We both will, but we can't be part of it...you understand that, right?"

My sister spoke of fate as though it was a tangible thing, but fate, to me, was a hunter just like a Son. One always hunting, desperate for a connection. I'd known it the moment I stepped into the path of Riven's car and the moment I'd made the decision to become a Daughter in The Order. But my fate wasn't just tied to the men I loved and the Sons...it was also tied to the two women standing in front of me.

I felt their connection as clearly as I did the Sons'.

"The attack from the tunnels was a damn mess, but this is bigger than that. Whoever he has hiding his tracks is good." Anna's voice rose above the groans and mutters of revenge, calling my attention. "He's good, Fin. He's really good. But I need to be better."

"*We* need to be better," Harper added. "We need to break this code and find a way into this system. We need to figure out where that bastard is hiding."

Anna ran her hands through her hair and turned to Kat. "I'll find him. Believe me...I'll find him."

"The moment you do, we're ready."

I met my sisters' panicked stares. But what if she never did? What then? There was no way in hell I was waiting for the moment both of them looked at us, defeated. Hale had escaped once before by pretending he was dead. We all knew he wasn't...because monsters like him don't die. They infect. They possess...and they live on through reputation alone.

"I can't wait for that." I murmured and turned away. "I just can't."

I walked out, leaving those I loved behind. I needed quiet. I needed me. My pulse raced as I headed out of that room and sought a darkened, quiet hallway, one where I could think. My steps blurred as I paced, the movement sanely comforting.

I'd spent my entire life pretending.

First, I was the daughter to a stranger, content to be alone.

Then I was a sister with a loving family.

After that I was a meal to a group of violent and dangerous men...and through them, I became a pawn for The Order. So what was a little more pretending?

"You give too much of yourself." I stopped walking and slowly turned around, meeting Thomas' stare. He strode toward me, powerful and sure, slid his hand around the back of my neck and forced my gaze to his. "Too damn much."

An ache bloomed in the back of my throat. I wouldn't cry. Not now. Not here. There wasn't time for that. But as Thomas pulled me closer, that knot of pain moved into my chest.

"We all sacrifice." My words were thick and husky.

"There's sacrifice, and then there's you."

I gripped his arms, holding on as he pulled away to stare into my eyes. "The moment this is over, you aren't sacrificing a single thing ever again, do you understand me? Not. A. Single. Goddamn. Thing. You'll have nothing but happiness. Nothing but safety and love. Nothing but puppies and rainbows and all the vegan food you can eat. I'll make sure of it."

My lips curled with a soft, sad smile. The way he said it made me a little scared. Thomas was quickly turning into a man I both desired and feared. But not for myself...no, for others, and I had a feeling this was only the start for him.

"We're heading to the mountain, gathering supplies, and getting some sleep. Everyone is going to do the same, leaving time for Finley's man, then Lazarus, to work on Hale's hunter."

I held my breath, panic rising inside me.

"They now understand how important he is and they're smart, really smart. These aren't your normal men and we need to trust them. I don't understand this connection you seem to have with them, neither does Riven, but if anything, Finley and Lazarus will set the scene. You can use this to your advantage. Let them try their best and if it's not good enough, then you use what power you have over him."

There was that word again...*trust*.

"Are you ready to do that?" He implored.

I had no other choice, did I? At some point they needed to understand one plan just wasn't enough when you were dealing with a snake like Haelstrom Hale. You needed more...as many as you could get. There was a fragile pleading in Thomas' tone, one I heard loud and clear.

"More than ready." I answered, tilting my head to rest my cheek against the inside of his arm. "I'm ready to be with you... *all of you.*"

He gave a smile. "I was hoping you were going to say that."

Footsteps resounded. Doors closed and the faint growl of engines starting sounded. Thomas glanced past me as the steps stopped nearby. I turned around, to find Riven, Kane, and Hunter.

"You ready, Trouble?" Riven said carefully.

He didn't need to ask twice. We left the Salvatore house and climbed into the four-wheel drive before we headed home. Thomas reached out to grab my hand as I sat between him and Kane in the back seat. Hope filled me, scared and helpless, a scurrying, fleeting feeling. Like it wasn't quite sure yet.

I guess none of us were.

All we had was this moment...this gathering before the storm.

We were closing in. That I knew.

I met Hunter's stare in the rear-view mirror.

He felt it too.

The end...

Was finally here.

TWENTY-NINE

Thomas
___

Headlights bounced against the glass panes of the front door. The towering mountain loomed dark and ominous behind the house I'd come to find familiar. As familiar as any other place we'd lived in. Only, this house had purpose...and a future. I turned my head, finding the moonlight caressing the perfect planes of her face. A future with the woman we'd all fallen for...*Helene*.

The four-wheel drive pulled up hard, the tires skidding on the loose gravel. As the towering fence closed behind us, Hunter killed the engine and we all climbed out.

Thud.

Thud.

Thud

Thud.

One by one the doors closed. Hunter was the first to move, his gun aimed by his side as he moved toward the house and pressed the buttons to unlock the doors before moving in. We were taking no chances, not anymore. Hale was getting desperate, sending his army of honed killers after us, desperate to take out as many of us as he could.

Because that's just what pathetic, weak, vile men like him did. But he wouldn't win...not now...not anymore. We were gathering an army of our own, one that had a lot more at stake.

Hunter disappeared inside. Riven followed, his own weapon raised and ready, leaving Kane, Helene, and me outside. I didn't like it. Not standing here waiting for someone else to protect and control. I was tired of being a passenger, tired of being the one to be protected instead of the one protecting. I gripped the heavy cross in my hand. The one I'd taken from my room as a reminder of the kind of man I was...the one I now used as a weapon as I headed for the door of the house.

"Thom." Kane called my name as I pushed the door wider and stepped inside.

But I didn't answer, just headed deeper into the darkness. My senses were more alive than they've ever been in my entire life. There was no panic now, no anxiety. No constant drone of the repetitive words and phrases in my head, beating me into submission. There was just action now, the breath filling my lungs, the heavy weight of the cross...and that hunger that burned white hot inside me.

This was who I was, the man who stepped into the house, listening to the weight of Hunter's steps above him, and felt the undeniable thirst of rage.

"Brother." Riven called in the dark. "Everything okay?"

I met his dark, empty stare and stilled. For a long time, I'd seen Riven as damaged, corrupt, and ruined from that fateful night our sister had been taken. But now, standing in front of him in the murky gloom, I saw him more clearly than I ever had in my entire life. He wasn't corrupt, or damaged. He was...selfless.

A memory resurrected. That day at The Order when Coulter's man had found Helene and tried to rape her. I'd fought as hard as I could, but I was hurt and weak, spiritually more than physically. I'd had a distorted sense of right and wrong and through that lens, I'd seen my brother as he attacked with savage ferocity, wrapped his arm around the guard's neck, and choked the life from him without a second of hesitation.

"Thank you," I answered. "I don't think I've ever said that."

Lights came on overhead, and the sound of footsteps from the others grew closer. I didn't have to turn around to know they were all there listening.

"For what?" Riven shook his head slowly. "You've got nothing to thank me for. In fact, you should hate me for the things I've put you through."

The brutal hand of London St. James.

The attack of the Sons.

The neverending fight...for survival.

I stepped closer and grabbed his shoulder. "And yet, here we still stand."

He scowled, pain flaring behind his unmerciful stare of anger.

"Here we still stand," Hunter echoed.

"Here we stand," Kane followed.

"Here...we stand," Helene murmured, moving closer. She curled her hand around my arm, then ran her other along Riven's.

Need rose inside me, seething and aching. My balls tightened as I looked from her to him. Her breath caught as she met my gaze and then turned to him, slid her hand around the back of his neck, and pulled him close. The kiss took me by surprise, not because he grabbed her and pushed her backwards until she pressed against the wall. But because I was suddenly aroused by the intensity of them, by the way he gently gripped her throat, forcing her head backward by the pressure of his thumb under her jaw, and the way she released a moan, giving herself completely into him.

I moved before I realized it, tugging her shirt upwards until it dragged over the swell of her breast. I couldn't stop myself as I yanked down the cup of her bra and lowered my head. Warmth brushed across my lips as I opened them, drawing her nipple inside my mouth.

"Oh...*God,*" She moaned.

Then Kane was there, moving to her other side, reaching around Riven to turn her mouth to his. He kissed her, taking her completely.

"Maybe we should," Hunter moaned, "take this upstairs."

I licked her nipple, feeling the soft flesh tighten and pucker.

"You want that, Trouble?" Riven urged.

"*Yes.*" Her answer was a rush. "Yes, I want that."

Riven lifted her, allowing her to wrap those long legs around his waist as he carried her back through the house and up the stairs. The *thud, thud, thud* of his boots echoed before the rest of us turned and followed.

With each step, we moved faster, until we were taking the stairs two at a time, until we all stopped at the entrance to Riven's room. Helene pulled her shirt over her head, then reached around and unhooked her bra.

I was captured by the light bouncing off her body and the sheer beauty of her. The red scar line from her attack was still angry and raised. But it was healing. Just like her...she was healing.

I headed inside the room, kicked my boots off, and dropped the cross, letting it hit the floor with a *bang*. They all flinched and glanced down at the bloodied weapon. But they said nothing as Riven jerked his shirt over his head and unbuckled the belt on his pants.

Kane and Hunter moved deeper into the room and kicked off their boots, undressing until we all stood there naked and unmoving. The silence spoke volumes between us. We didn't want to break the spell, and didn't want to go back to our reality.

The reality that this could be our last night together...forever. One of us might be killed in the upcoming battle. In fact, there was a high probability we'd *all* be killed. As much as we didn't want to think about it, it still hung heavy in the air.

"Trouble," Riven started, his voice husky.

"Don't," she whispered, shaking her head. "I don't want to talk. I just want to love...so love me."

Riven's pants and boxers hit the floor as I unbuttoned my cargos and pushed them free. Kane and Hunter moved together, both now naked and desperate. There was blood smeared all over

Riven's side, one rectangular dressing on his ribs and one on his shoulder. His injuries were the worst of ours. Stabbed and beaten. None of us were unscathed, but right now, we didn't care.

Riven pushed Helene backwards, holding her steady, and eased her down onto the bed. He kissed her, and so did Kane as he grasped her hand and kneeled on the bed, then lowered his head to kiss her breast. My breath caught, knowing exactly how she tasted to him, how warm she felt, and how desperate he was.

Hunter lowered himself to her thigh, wrapping one massive arm around her leg.

"Thomas," she called my name. I jerked my head upwards to meet her stare. "Come to me."

I rounded the other side of the bed and climbed on. There was blood on my chest, a heavy smear I hadn't seen before, and when I reached for her, there was still blood on my hands... images slammed into me. That was Ben's blood. Ben's...*blood*.

I closed my eyes and felt the room sway.

"It's okay," She murmured. "We're all damaged here, all bloodied and broken. There's no need to hide between us."

Her words forced my eyes open. My brothers all looked at me, but it wasn't out of horror. It was comfort.

"We're all in this together, brother," Riven added. *"All of us."*

Kane gave a nod. "There's no hiding, no pulling away. No one else will understand you better than us, and no one will love you more than her."

He was right. I knew he was right. I might feel alone in my anger and pain, but I wasn't...because I had them.

"Kiss me." She urged, drawing my gaze. "Love me and let me love you. Take what you need from me. All of you, I want you to take what you need, anytime you need it. My body and my heart are yours."

I'd never known the kind of selflessness like her before.

Even after all she'd been through.

She still gave and gave and gave.

Which only made me love her more.

My pulse boomed as I lowered my head and my eyes closed as our lips touched. So warm, so giving. Her mouth parted for me, letting me take all I wanted to take. In a rush of desperation and desire, that wall inside me came crumbling down. I pounced on her, my bloodied fingers gripping her jaw as I rose above her, taking more, moving deeper, plunging my tongue into her mouth.

Movement came from the corner of my eyes. My brothers slowly eased away, allowing me to move on top of her. My hands gently gripped her face, my mouth claimed hers until her breath rushed from her nose, leaving me to tear away and move down.

Her fingers slipped through my hair as I kissed her breasts, moving from one to the other, licking her nipples until I sucked the smooth flesh taut.

"Oh, God," She moaned, opening her legs for me.

I wanted it all, every inch, every second. But that ravenous hunger inside me wouldn't wait. I reached down, sliding my fingers along her slit and plunged inside. Her hips bucked with the invasion. I lifted my gaze, staring into her eyes. "This is what I want."

"Yes," She groaned. *"Yes."*

I lifted my knee, climbing in between her legs, then lowered my hips. My hand went to my cock, gripping the rigid length. I was so ready for her...*achingly ready.* There was no need for handcuffs this time, no binding or shift of control. We could play with that later. Right now, there was just this. I lowered my body against hers, aiming myself to slide into her warmth.

Her beautiful, consuming warmth.

It was like coming home as I pushed in. To a place I'd always dreamed of and never had.

A slow thrust and I drove all the way inside her. Her hands gripped my shoulders, pulling herself upwards. "Fuck me, Priest. Fuck me like your life depends on it."

I held her stare, bucking my hips until I drove in harder. All that tension. All that pain, it all melted away. There was just her, the way her breath caught with every violent push. The way her eyes shone with hunger. The way her lips met mine as she lifted herself higher to kiss me.

"That's it, baby," She urged, then bit her lower lip.

The sight of that did something feral inside me. I lowered my hands, gripped her hips and slammed against her. The rush collided with the feel of her body as slick sounds came between us. It was all I could do to hold on and even as my balls tightened, I knew it was a lost cause.

Sparks ignited behind my eyes. I clenched my jaw, driving in one last time as the rush exploded, leaving me to drop my head and bury my face against her neck. Her scent enveloped me and it was all I needed...all I wanted. "I love you." I gasped. "I fucking love you."

Her fingers moved deeper through my hair, her hold around my shoulders pulled me closer against her. "I love you too. I love you more than anything. Nothing can touch us here, at this moment...nothing can touch us."

"Except us." Riven urged. *"Only us."*

I lifted my head, finding the warmth and the hunger in her eyes. There was us...always us and as I kissed her, then slowly pulled free, I realized I couldn't be prouder.

THIRTY

Helene
___

"Looks like it's our turn." Riven eased closer, pulling my focus toward him.

I hesitated, searching for the flicker of pain or horror in Thomas' stare. But it didn't come, instead he smiled and eased back. "I think I'm going to enjoy this."

"You're not the only one." Riven murmured as he grabbed my side and pulled.

I flipped over. One minute I was staring up at him, the next, my face was buried in the bedding.

"On your knees, Trouble."

Jesus...when he said my name like that, I knew I was in for it. His arm slid around my waist and lifted, easing my lower half upwards. I clenched my fist in the sheets and glanced over my shoulder. All of them watched as Riven ran his hand over the curve of my ass.

Slap.

I bucked with the sound. But there was no pain, just the slow caress of his hand over the burn until his lips met my flesh. "I don't think we've shared with the others how good you've been lately, have we?"

My pulse raced as he lifted those dark eyes to mine.

"Hunter might be the one pushing you to run up the damn mountain, but I've been the one pushing you in other ways. Want to share with them, precious?"

My body reacted without my mind. My head nodded, knees slid against the sheets, already desperate to feel him.

"Oh fuck." Hunter growled.

"Yes, *oh fuck.*" Riven slid his hand between my thighs, his fingers pushing into the slick his brother left behind.

I couldn't get pregnant, not by them. Safe. Secure. Protected. They gave me everything and took nothing. Warm, wet trails came from his touch as he moved higher, sliding over my ass before he stopped, then slowly pushed in.

"That's it. That's the girl."

The pressure grew and grew and grew. As exhausted as my body was, it wanted this, craved this, coming alive as he pushed his finger in deeper before sliding it out.

"Two now, baby."

I closed my eyes and exhaled slowly, the pressure building until there was the burn.

"If you don't get in there, brother, then I sure as hell will." Hunter's deep growl was predatory, which only made me push back against the thrust.

"You'll need to wait your turn." Riven pushed against me, forcing me to turn back.

I knew what was coming. My body opened and my breaths raced. I forced myself to focus on my fists, on the feel of the sheets between my fingers and the slide of his hard cock between my thighs as he coated himself, then pushed the head of his cock in.

The hard ring of muscle clamped tight, forcing him back out. With a low growl, he eased back in, the tip pushing in and out, gaining ground with every thrust.

I unleashed a moan, lifting my head as the bed dipped hard.

"Let me underneath her." Hunter slid closer, grasping me around the waist lifting me in the air. I hit his hard chest, his powerful thighs forced my legs wider until the tendons between my legs felt the stretch.

"Oh, *Jesus.*" Hunter groaned as the head of his cock brushed my core, gently pushing in as he shifted.

I looked down at him then gently gripped his jaw, forcing his gaze to mine. The connection ignited as he eased the thick head of his cock all the way inside me. My pussy stretched, taking in his massive length, and at the same time, Riven pushed back inside my ass, then slowly retreated.

I dropped my head, my body consumed by the feel of them.

"That's it." Riven grunted. "Open your body for us."

Hunter slowly thrust, the invasion matched by Riven as the head slipped inside. I panted and dropped my head, my whole focus on the slight burn of my ass as he pushed in deeper, rubbing against his brother inside me.

Hunter thrust, which made Riven moan, then ease out, only to drive in harder, pushing my body to its limit. They were all I could feel, stretching, aching, making me rock my hips with the lunges, desperate for more.

"Kane." I turned my head, finding him watching. *"Please."*

He gave a smile and skirted the bottom of the bed, climbing up onto his knees. We'd never been all together before, not like this...*Jesus, not like this.*

Kane cupped my cheek, then lowered his head, staring directly into my eyes. "If you could only see yourself right now."

I shivered with the sensation of them, overwhelmed and at the same time craving more. Slick sounds came between us. I lowered my head, grunting as Hunter picked up pace. I wasn't going to last like this...not long at all. I slid my hand down Kane's chest to the firm ridges of his stomach, then lower until I cupped him.

"Oh *fuck,*" He moaned.

My spine curled as I lowered my head. My lips met the slick skin of his rigid cock as I opened my mouth and forced him all the way inside.

"Sweet Jesus," He groaned and grasped the back of my head, following the movement as I eased away and then drove my head down harder with the thrust.

I closed my eyes, pinching them tight as my body clenched and quivered.

"Hold on, baby." Riven grunted, thrusting all the way deep inside. "Just...*hold...the...fuck...on*."

But I couldn't, one last thrust of Hunter's cock sent me over the edge. I opened my mouth, driving down on Kane as my body took over, quivering and clenching. White sparks ignited. I held on, driven upwards by Hunter and slammed forward by Riven.

"*Fuck*." Riven grunted before he stilled.

Warmth filled me, a delicious wave of ecstasy slamming into me. Kane's hold on my head grew stronger as he kept thrusting. Hunter gave a growl, slamming into me as Riven slipped free, and ran his hand along my back. "That's it, Trouble. Fuck, you look like trouble right now. Take him all in."

I drove down as Hunter gave a grunt, his cock kicking inside me. Kane's balls tightened. "That's it...*that's fucking ittt*."

Their warmth filled me, spurting down my throat and inside my pussy. I swallowed, brushing my thumb across the mess as he eased free.

"Take it all in, precious," Kane murmured.

I licked my thumb, meeting his intense stare as he leaned down. His hold was softer, caressing my cheek as he kissed me. "Such a good girl."

My pulse was booming, thundering in my head a little louder with the praise. I'd do anything for them...*be anything*...just for one more smile and whisper of pride.

"Baby." Hunter gripped my hips, his heavy breath a blast as he rose and kissed my breasts. "You are fucking incredible."

My core pulsed, like a ticking engine as it cooled. Kane released his hold, leaving me to look down at his brother.

"If I wasn't starving before, I'm goddamn famished now."

"Me too," Thomas added.

"And me." Riven pulled away, bending to grab his pants from the floor before he stopped and looked my way. "Baby?"

I willed my body to move, easing from straddling Hunter's massive thighs and slipped from the bed. "Food sounds delicious," I answered, unable to remember the last time we all ate.

We all went downstairs, cooked and laughed, even if the sound was a little strained. When our bellies were full, we climbed the stairs once more. Hunter went to his room, Thomas and Kane to theirs. I followed Riven into his bathroom where he waited, bare chested.

I stopped in front of him, staring into his eyes as he pulled the clothes from my body and then his own. We showered, taking the small moments together to love and touch each other in silence. When we were done, he switched the shower off, then grabbed a towel.

We needed no words, just each other's presence, until I couldn't hold back any longer. "You know what I need to do, right?"

"I know."

He might. But that didn't mean he liked it. In fact, as he tied a towel around his waist and walked into the bedroom, picking up the pillows we dislodged from us earlier, he grew colder.

"If it was you who could use and exploit someone, you'd have no problem doing that."

"That's right." He turned, threw the pillow high against the headboard, and met my gaze. "If you think you'll come out of this unscathed, then think again. This is going to torture you. This is going to—"

I crossed the room, naked, and brushed my fingers along his cheek. "I'm already tainted, already tortured. We all are and if this can get us closer to the end, then I'll use whatever connection to him I have."

"I don't like it."

"I know you don't."

"If he tries anything." The warning was loud and clear.

He wasn't worried about the Son hurting me. He knew he wouldn't. No, there was only jealousy burning in his stare.

"He won't. Because I won't let him."

"He's a dead man either way." Riven's dark eyes glinted.

I knew that. Still, it weighed on me.

"HE'S SAID NOTHING." Finley glanced at the door. "My men worked on him all night. Hell, even Tobias stayed back to have a go."

I glance at Tobias, standing next to Ryth. They both still looked like hell, and he held his bloodied fist carefully by his side. I knew exactly what kind of 'conversation' he'd had with the Son.

"You're not going to get anything out of him," Finley added, drawing my focus back. "Not anymore."

"Can't or won't?"

He didn't answer. I guessed that was reply enough. "Shit," I muttered as I turned away.

"Don't even bother," Finley called.

But I would, because we had a lot riding on this. I scanned the massive room we'd taken over in the Salvatore mansion and saw way too many suits for my liking. They all milled around London, some of them on their cells as they called in favors or sent money. But they were here to fight, and that meant something.

Vivienne caught my eye. Her weak smile looked sad as she stood next to London. This was taking a toll on all of us, but especially her. I lowered my gaze to her belly. God, she must be in pain. But she said nothing as she glanced London's way when he spoke to her.

His guarded stare met mine before he gave a slow nod. I greeted him with one of my own before I turned around and slowly headed for the door. It was time to see what kind of damage I was dealing with.

"Trouble." Riven waited for me outside the room, leaning back against the wall. "You're still going through with this?"

If there was a way I could get through to the cold, calculating killer and get information on how to get to Hale, then I'd do almost anything.

"Don't try to change my mind." I said and walked past.

He shoved off the wall and followed as I turned along the hallway and headed for the smaller, secure room. A guard stood outside, scowling at the sight through the open door. I stopped, glanced over my shoulder to Riven, and shook my head.

But he didn't leave, not right away, until I stepped up to the guard and said, "Thank you, I'll take it from here."

What was it with these men? The guard turned his scowl toward me, but I ignored it as I walked through the door and into the room.

The Son sat on the floor in almost the same spot I'd left him last night. But then he lifted his busted face and found me through the slit of one swollen eye.

"Daughter," He croaked. "Told you you'd come back."

"Jesus Christ." I jerked forward and sank to my knees beside him.

I didn't even think about how dangerous he was at that moment, nor did I care how close I was. I grasped his jaw carefully and turned his head. His cheek was split open, by the gaping wound it looked like from a ring of some kind. But Tobias didn't wear a ring, not that I remembered at least.

"Why do you care, I'll be dead soon anyway."

The way he said it hit me hard. My chest tightened and my fingers trembled. I swallowed hard. "Don't say that."

"Why not? It's true, isn't it?" He glanced at the open door. "It's only a matter of time. Doesn't matter anyway. I'm good to go now...now I've seen you."

Surprise hit me. I froze, my fingers still curled against his bloody cheek. It wasn't love that I felt...but it was something. "What is it that connects us?"

He gave a soft shrug.

"You know what I'm talking about, don't you? You feel this, right?"

He didn't answer, but that piercing stare never wavered. He felt it.

"We were created in a lab, then handed over to those who ran the orphanages. They kept us together for a while, did you know that? Sons and Daughters, in the same place. Just long enough for us to understand we were connected somehow. Maybe it was what they did to us when the eggs were fertilized, maybe it was that soul-sucking place. All I know is that when they broke us apart, it was the most brutal day of my entire life. Far worse than today...however it plays out."

He was talking about his expected death.

And still, the day he was ripped away from the Daughters had hurt more.

"Why?" The word slipped free.

"Because they kept us alive after. When I die, I'm free, free of this world and their control."

That ache moved higher, thickening my throat until it was painful.

"You'll never get in, you know that, don't you?"

The words were so quiet I barely heard them.

"Get in?"

"The warehouse where Hale is...or he was, at least."

I shook my head, hating how my voice was choking. A tear slipped down my cheek and I turned my head, swiping it away.

"Unless I tell you how."

I swung my gaze back to his. To that slither of darkness between his bloodied swollen lids. Panic rose instantly, making me shake my head and look toward the door. "Don't then."

"Don't?"

"Don't tell us. I know it's crazy. It's all we want, all *everyone* wants. To get inside and put a bullet in Hale's head and every other bastard who stands with him. But you and I know what will happen if you do."

His focus never wavered. "They'll kill me."

The tears came again, warm and slick, only this time I didn't brush them. I left them and nodded slowly.

"Still it'd be better than you leaving. Better than never seeing you again. Better than never feeling this right now, this connection."

"I do feel it."

The smile was more of a wince as his split lip widened. "Yeah, I feel it too."

He lifted his hands, now cuffed in front of him, and his rough thumb brushed my cheek. "There's a door," he said. "On the northeast side of the warehouse that's not far from the private airfield. The door is small, you'd miss it really, trying to break down the main doors. It has a keypad, the code is sixteen-oh-one. You get in that door and it'll take you straight down a hallway to where Hale's private quarters are. He's running, I know that. But he wants his daughter first, the one he fathered with the woman whose husband did this to me."

"Lazarus."

He nodded slowly.

"He's going to come for the child and he's going to unleash all the Sons to do it. There's no stopping it...unless you get to him first."

Get to him first.

Get to him first.

It's all that filled my mind.

"You're going to have to hurry, Daughter. If you want to catch him."

I pulled my hand away and shoved up from the floor. *Hurry... hurry...hurry.* We now had a code and a way in. All we needed was a location.

"Run, run, run," He murmured.

I spun around and lunged for the door. All I could think about was Kat and that precious dark-haired little girl. I couldn't let that happen. I couldn't...

I slammed through the doorway, sidestepped the guard lingering outside and raced down the hallway.

"Anna!" I roared. "Anna! *I have a code and a—*"

Bang!

I stopped and spun around, staring at the open door of that room...with my heart breaking in two.

He'd killed him.

He'd...KILLED HIM.

"No...no...no...no." Anguish tore through my chest. *"We have a way in,"* I croaked. *"We have a way to Hale."*

THIRTY-ONE

Helene

BANG!

I flinched, my knees trembling as I drooped in the doorway. Vivienne's eyes widened as I whispered. "We have a way in... we have a way in to Hale."

The thud of heavy footsteps sounded behind me and for a minute, I didn't want to turn for fear of who I'd find holding the gun. But I didn't need to look because movement came from the corner of my eye as the bodyguard headed straight for the man he was loyal to..._Lazarus Rossi._

The Stidda Mafia leader looked savage. His blue eyes were vibrant and cruel, cutting almost, as he met my stare. There wasn't a flicker of compassion in that glare, just a pitiless, unforgiving look before he turned away.

"Trouble." Riven stopped at my side.

He lowered his hand, his fingers caressing my arm quieting and comforting. "I'm sorry."

I swallowed the pain, blinked away the tears, and forced my voice louder. "He said a private airport."

"What?" Anna lifted her head from the keyboard.

Her fingers were still moving, punching in codes that raced across the screen as next to her London's IT man, Harper, did the same.

"He said, there's a warehouse next to a private airport."

Anna shook her head, then punched in a few new commands and lifted her stare to the screen in front of them. "This is all the points we've tracked where the tunnels lead to so far."

I froze, my focus on the map displayed with a mess of red dots. There were just too many of them. Too many to count, let alone search. It was like a needle in a haystack. Where could we start?

"Private airfields should be listed, but not always, especially when you're dealing with someone like Hale. If he can get access to the government military bases, then he can hide a damn airfield...somewhere out there is the warehouse we need." She stared at the mess of red dots like we all did. "There has to be another map, another plan somewhere."

"The map," Thomas murmured as he turned to Kane. "The one we took from Coulter's study."

"You mean the one we almost died for?" Kane's eyebrow rose.

"I have that." Hunter stepped forward, pulling his cell from his pocket. "It's a digital copy. What's your email address and I'll send it."

Anna gave him the details, hovering over her keyboard before she hit the button and displayed the map on the screen. I'd looked at that more times than I could count, we all had scoured over every inch of it. Part was topographical, the other was a layout of a building...but what building, we'd had no way of knowing.

There's a door. At the northeast side of the warehouse that's not far from the private airfield. The door is small, you'd miss it really. You get in that door and it'll take you straight down a hallway to where Hale's private quarters are.

The Son's words came back to me. "It's a warehouse, Hale's warehouse."

"That right there looks like a navigation code." Anna zeroed in on a faint number that was printed in the corner of the map. One so faint, you'd easily miss it. In fact, we had missed it, all of us.

Anna focused in and sharpened the numbers before glancing at Harper. But he was already on it, punching in the details, and all of a sudden, the map of the red points from the tunnel narrowed down to three...

Three little red dots, all of them so close they were almost on top of each other.

"Gotcha." Harper muttered.

An icy feeling rushed through me. He was there...hiding behind a single door in a massive warehouse. The screen changed, pulling up a satellite view. We stared down at... nothing.

"There's nothing there." Nick snapped.

Anna shook her head, confusion and panic pushing into her stare. "It's there...*it's right there.*"

"Maybe it's gone." Fin looked at his wife.

"Gone? How can a building that size just up and disappear?"

He shook his head. "I don't know." He stared at the screen. "But it's not there."

"It is." She sat forward, typing in more commands.

The view narrowed in, moving toward the private hangar and the closed gates. But the moment the camera swung back, there was...*something*.

"Wait," London snapped, striding forward. "Move back."

Anna glanced his way, then shifted the camera back the way it'd come.

"Did you see that?" He glanced around the room. "Do it again, only slower."

She did, panning the camera over very slowly this time, until the air shimmered. It was gone in an instant.

"Holy shit." Came a mutter somewhere behind us as Anna tried again, only this time, stopping mid-motion and revealing a towering building that had somehow blended in with the environment, leaving it completely hidden.

"Jesus Christ." Nick snapped. "What the fuck is that?"

It was Hell, that's what it was.

"That's some high-tech shit right there," Harper muttered beside Anna.

"If that's the outside, I can't imagine what the inside is like." Fin shook his head.

He looked scared now. We all looked scared.

"There's only one way to find out," Lazarus glanced at his man. "Looks like we have our target."

"Gotcha," London growled, stepping closer until he was right in front of the screen. "You piece of fucking shit."

Movement came, slow at first, until the room was a flurry of movement. Calls were made, a lot of calls. I turned around, finding Riven first, then Hunter, Thomas, and Kane. They all waited, dodging towering armed men as they hauled bags over their shoulders and grabbed their guns. We had enough men to form a small militia, armed to the teeth, savage in their hunger.

It was our hunger too. But my men sidestepped those leaving and headed my way.

"We stay together." Riven ordered, glancing around at everyone else. "Because we have no idea what we're in for."

They all looked at me. I knew exactly what they were thinking...more like remembering. The tunnels under Coulter's mansion were one thing. But what Hale and Melanie had done to us at that place would haunt me forever.

"We stay together," I whispered as a shiver raced through me.

Hunter grabbed his pack and heaved it over his shoulder. "Then let's get that motherfucker once and for all."

We all followed, allowing Hunter to lead the way as we made our way out to the front of the Salvatore house. They were all waiting, standing outside four-wheel drives and military trucks, ready to invade.

"The Son told me how to get in," I said as we headed toward the Explorer. In the corner of my eye, the driver's door was opened and one of the soldiers climbed in behind the wheel. "He told me the small door to the—"

BOOM!

I was lifted off my feet and thrown backwards. Air was all I felt, rushing against my face before the sudden bone-crushing impact as I hit the ground. Agony roared through me, stealing my air and my thoughts. Screams came a second later, before the deafening sound of gunfire and the ear-splitting yell from one of the men as he bellowed. *"We're under attack!"*

THIRTY-TWO

Riven
_____

BOOM!

I was slammed backwards, colliding with something big that gave a heavy grunt before I hit the ground. Car alarms started, the piercing wails barely puncturing the dull roar in my ears. I shoved up slowly, my thoughts scrambled, until a murky sound came.

I lifted my head, watching one of the Salvatore guards raise his gun, take aim, and fire. *What the fuck...just happened?* Inch by inch, I turned my head, to find a wave of armed men heading toward us. No...not just heading...hurtling our way.

I shoved upwards, panic pushing the muffled pressure in my head away until the roar of the attack rushed in. I grabbed my weapon, scanning those around me as Hunter climbed to his feet beside me. I grabbed his shoulder. *"HELENE! FIND HELENE!"*

Screams continued to invade as we were slammed by men who moved faster and sleeker than anything I'd ever seen. I

292

wrenched my gun upwards, taking aim as one of the men lunged over the front of someone's Audi and hurtled towards me.

Crack!

Crack!

My finger squeezed the trigger and the gun bucked in my hand. The shot hit him in the shoulder as he lunged for Kane, spinning the bastard like a top until he slammed backwards.

Crack!

CRACK!

Hunter opened fired as more of the men came, spilling around the cars to attack with a kind of savage ferocity I'd never seen before. Knives whipped through the air, spinning end over end. One flew right past me, hitting someone standing behind me.

I wrenched my gaze over my shoulder, to see one of London's buddies with the hilt of the blade sticking out of his shoulder. He looked down, snarled, then wrenched the thing free. I swung back, firing shot after shot, and moved with Hunter as he lunged to grab Helene, protecting her with his body and racing for cover.

A flash of neon blond hair tore across my vision as Carven, with Colt close behind him, lunged and slammed into three of the fuckers. At the height of the impact, I saw what was happening...it was *Sons against Sons once more.*

Hale had sent them.

He'd sent them to kill us.

I unleashed a roar as I strode toward them, emptying the clip before I collided with one. Blows on blows as my head snapped sideways. I couldn't keep up, couldn't even protect myself. Agony roared in my side and it was only my sheer self-preservation instinct that allowed me to lash out fast enough to grasp the wrist which held the blade as the savage glare from a Son met mine.

"Going to kill you," He grunted. "Right before we take what's ours."

He meant Helene...

He meant all of them.

Helene.

Vivienne.

Ryth...

And the baby.

The goddamn baby!

BOOM!

The Son's head exploded in front of me, blood and gray matter splattering my face. I turned and found Hunter starting to lower his sniper rifle, but then he swung around and kept firing. But a sickening feeling washed through me. There was more to this...more to this outright attack.

I spun around, finding Colt and his brother deep in the fray and caught sight of Finley Salvatore, Lazarus Rossi, and Tobias Banks all fighting alongside each other. If they were out here... that only meant one thing.

The women were inside.

I spun around. *"ROSSI! He's after the kid!"* I screamed and lunged.

I don't know if he heard me. I didn't have time to see, just raced toward the open door of the house, praying to God I wasn't too late.

Screams greeted me, guttural howls of agony and piercing, shrill, panicked sounds. The kind that chilled me to the bone. I forced myself to move, running for that secured room.

"NO!" A male roared up ahead.

I turned the corner and came face to face with terror as a Son stood over one of the guards, stabbing him in the chest over and over with savage, bloody blows. The poor bastard had never had a chance. Instantly, I raised my gun and took aim as screams came from inside the room, slipping through the barely open door. It was obvious the guard had been trying to close it when he was attacked. Now the poor bastard was dead.

The Son lunged through the open door. I heard the heavy thud of steps right behind me before the bellow came. *"KAT! KAAATTT!"*

"Laz!" She screamed back as I charged through the door and into the room.

There were two of them. One had Kat separated from the others, advancing as she shielded her daughter, who was shrieking in terror, clinging to her mother's leg in sheer panic. But the other one had Anna around her neck, strangling her.

"Motherfucker!" Laz roared behind me.

My mind screamed to head for Kat and their child, knowing they were the real reason the Sons were here, but the gurgling, choking sounds from Anna called me. She kicked, her feel flailing in the air as she slowly lifted the gun in her hand.

The Son clenched harder as she dangled in mid-air. Her eyes bulged and her face burned bright red. She had no strength left to stop him as he reached out with one hand and tore the gun from her grasp.

"HEY!" I roared as I charged across the room, slamming into both of them and knocking her free.

Her gasping, choking sounds followed as the Son stumbled, then righted himself before slowly turning toward me. I was in trouble. I knew that even as I swung my gun upwards, my finger, squeezing the trigger. He moved faster than I was prepared for. One second, I was standing, and the next I was flying backwards with agony roaring through my chest.

The slash of a blade came. I did my best to duck and as blood roared in my head I looked up into the eyes of death and prayed *please, God...help me.*

He lunged, driving a killing blow under my jaw. All I saw were stars until the faint sound of gunfire broke in...then next, there was nothing but the swirling room and dark shadows moving into my view.

"You alive?" Finley Salvatore asked above me.

I tried to answer, but all I could do was stare upwards.

"Blink twice if you hear me."

Blink.

Blink.

"You're okay." Finley reached out his hand.

It took all my damn strength to meet it. One powerful yank and he pulled me upwards. The darkened room sharpened into focus. Anna was doubled over, her hand clutching her throat as she coughed and wheezed.

"He would've killed her," Finley murmured. "That's what she said...he would've killed her if you hadn't stopped it."

I kept sucking in deep breaths, the feeling slowly coming back into my body.

"You have my loyalty for that." The head of one of the most powerful Mafia families pledged.

The weight of that hit me. I gave a nod, glancing at Anna before I turned to Kat and Lazarus Rossi. The Stidda Prince, "now King" flashed across my mind, rose upwards, his fists a goddamn mess...but that was nothing compared to what was left of the Son lying dead at his feet.

He sucked in harsh breaths and lifted that rage-filled gaze to me. Shrill wails came from the child clawing at her mother's leg, trying desperately to get away.

"*Laz,*" Kat snapped. "*Please.*"

In an instant he changed and stepped over the Son's body to bend and grab his daughter, then coaxed her head down against his shoulder and away from the gruesome sights. He cradled her with bloody hands, moving away from the others.

"Hale...wanted her." I croaked. "It was her all along."

Lazarus stopped and slowly turned, those blue eyes igniting.

"He's never going to stop. You know that, right?" I met that terrifying stare.

"It will," he answered coldly. "When he's dead."

That was the only thing that would stop him.

He left then, still cradling his daughter, and waited at the door for his wife and their son before he stepped through.

"There's nowhere safe," I said and looked at Finley. "Not with us *or* without."

He scowled, then looked at his wife, who pulled on a shoulder holster and seated her weapon before making her way to the gun safe secured to the wall for more.

"At least with us they have a chance."

I jerked back to him as London St. James strode through the door. *"Vivienne!"* he roared, his face smeared with blood.

But she wasn't there, nor was Ryth.

"In the safe room," Anna croaked, still coughing and wheezing a little. "We secured them inside before we came back here. We thought they were the ones they wanted."

London spun around and lunged, heading for the door...and his very pregnant wife.

THIRTY-THREE

London

THE SAFE ROOM...GET TO THE SAFE ROOM!

I plunged through the steel door, slamming my shoulder hard on the edge as I scraped through. But I didn't stop, not even as agony barrelled through my neck, spearing into my jaw. My boots gripped tight as I turned the corner hard. The child's screams from back in that room resounded in my head.

"Vivienne!" I roared. *"VIVIENNE!"*

"London!" Her voice was faint from behind the closed steel door. I stared at the keypad and the red blinking light. *"The code...GIVE ME THE GODDAMN CODE!"*

Finley's response was instant, letting me punch the number into the keypad and wait as the door gave a *click*. Suddenly, my ash-gray world had one spark of color...and it was her. I stumbled into that small, secure room and glanced at Ryth holding the baby before I turned to the woman I loved.

My Wildcat...my *future*. "Baby," I choked and lurched forward to grab her in my arms.

She wasn't real until she was there, all bony limbs and belly. She dropped her head, breathing hard and fast, but it was the trembling in her body I felt more than anything.

"Are you okay?" I pulled away to stare into her eyes.

Tears brimmed, then fell to course down her beautiful, gaunt cheeks. She was still the most beautiful woman I'd ever seen in my entire life. The *only* woman I wanted more than anything in the world...including my own future. I dropped my gaze as my hand moved to her belly, finding warmth.

"Yes." She whispered.

"And the babies?" I searched her gaze.

Those tears were still spilling. She couldn't speak...not for a minute, and it was in that minute that my world ground to a halt. Then under my palm I felt it, a tiny *kick*. My throat thickened, making it impossible to be anything other than humble.

"They're okay." She whispered. "They're okay."

"Never again." I pulled her against me. "Do you hear me? *Never. Again.*"

The familiar thunder of heavy steps resounded along the hallway outside the room. Carven and Colt yanked the door open wider behind me and hurtled in.

"Wildcat." Carven groaned, gasping in hard breaths.

He was coated with blood...*no, bathed in it.* Those deep blue murderous eyes softened as they settled on her, then lowered. "Are you hurt?"

She shook her head. "No."

"The...the babies?"

"They're okay."

"*Ryth!*" Tobias roared. "*Ryth!*"

"*Here!*" she called.

I stepped aside, but the Sons didn't, causing the hurricane that was Tobias Banks to snarl and shove past them. Carven staggered sideways, slamming into me as Tobias grabbed Ryth and yanked her against his chest. "*Jesus Christ. Jesus fucking Christ.*"

"*T!*" Nick's roar echoed in the hallway.

"*Here!*" Tobias called, staring down at her as he caressed his son's face. "*She's in here!*"

Then Nick and Caleb flew into the cramped, tight space, pushing us further to the side and against Vivienne. I wrenched my gaze toward them and glared. "Maybe take this outside?"

Caleb was the one who noticed me crammed against my wife's belly and nodded instantly.

"T," He muttered. "Let's take this outside."

We all shuffled, until finally I could breathe and help my wife out of the room.

"*Finley!*"

I glanced along the hallway to where Finley Salvatore was striding away. He glanced my way before he kept going, but it wasn't long before I saw her. His wife, Anna, charging after him.

"I'm coming with you whether you want me to or not."

I winced at her tone, knowing instantly what the poor bastard was in for. One glance her way and that same anger, that same desperate yearning burned in her eyes. We didn't leave each other behind. Because no matter how many men we had...the ones we loved weren't safe...*anywhere.*

Their raised voices echoed along the halls of their home. No matter how firm the ground he thought he stood on, it was quicksand.

"You think I'm safe here? Look at what just happened. You and I are a team, aren't we?"

"Not in this case."

"You've seen what that...Hale is capable of. You know the kind of men he's sent after Kat, are you ready to take the chance we're safe? Look at me, Fin. *I said, look at me! I want you to tell me you're willing to risk my life and Kat and their child's life on this."*

He was fighting a losing battle. One I knew all too well. I glanced at Tobias, then Nick and Caleb, watching as each of them winced. We'd all fought that war. No doubt the head of the Salvatore Mafia would come to the same conclusion we all had. The only one we knew for certain. We loved, we fought, and we died...together.

"Baby," I started.

"I don't want to hear it," Vivienne answered as she turned and grabbed a black shoulder holster she'd carried with her, then shoved it against my chest. "Just help me put this on."

I stared down at the fistful of weapons pushed against my chest, then met my wife's determined stare. "Don't be a hero, London. Not now."

One careful nod and I took the guns, then helped settle the thick webbing of the holster in place. The moment she was armed, she gave us a weak smile. From the deep murmurs coming from Finley Salvatore and his wife, it sounded like they'd also come to the same conclusion.

"We stay together," I murmured, meeting Viv's stare. "You stay behind me no matter what."

"I stay behind you," she answered and for once, I believed her.

I glanced at the Sons, they would be our weapons. "We have a location." I met their stares. "We know where we're going. We know now what we're dealing with." The heavy weight of dread settled deeper.

Footsteps came from that secured room at the back of the house. Kat, Laz, and the remaining Salvatore guards came out of the room. We all headed toward the front of the house, waiting until the rest of the men came back to advise the coast was clear.

There had to have been fifteen or twenty Sons who'd come after us. How many that left waiting in that fucking warehouse, I didn't know. I didn't like it, not one bit. I turned to Baron as he headed toward us, the rest of the Lawlor brothers in his wake.

"Are you ready?" I met his stare.

"Ready," he answered, then glanced at Vivienne. "We'll be in the lead."

They would be. One nod and he turned around and left, taking his brothers with him. Car engines started and we waited for the explosions to come. But none did.

"The Ares', have you heard from them?" Baron asked.

I shook my head. "No."

"Maybe someone should give them a call."

I waited until they'd left before I grabbed my cell.

"London?" Vivienne murmured.

"Just give me a second." I stepped away and swiped the number for Silas Ares. I was loath to make the call, remembering the blood-splattered study I'd walked into on the day he'd found both his parents murdered. That was barely weeks ago...weeks, and still this fucking thing wasn't done.

"St. James." The voice on the other end was empty and cold.

"I'm calling to see if you've made a decision. We could do it with an alliance."

"It's not our war."

"It is if you could see how much—"

"No."

Jesus, he was cold. Cold and hollow.

"The Salvatores and the Rossis are here, they—"

"I don't care," he answered. I swore I heard crying in the background, muffled, choked crying before Silas Ares murmured. "Don't call me again." And hung up the call.

Then there was silence. Anger burned deep inside me and it had little to do with his tone. *It's not our war.* My thoughts turned to his sister and the way his mother had protected her. Not his war? He was wrong...so very, very wrong.

THIRTY-FOUR

Helene

HUNTER PUSHED THE FOUR-WHEEL DRIVE HARDER, sweeping around one of the other trucks to push in front. That stony-faced look of determination and rage burned in his eyes. Eyes that flicked up to the rear-view mirror to meet mine and in an instant, I felt the vehicle slow, as though he'd forgotten for a second what was at stake here.

"Go," I urged. "*Go.*"

The Hummer surged once more, gaining ground.

"Trouble," Riven called from the passenger seat. "Your weapons."

I looked down, finding Kane trying to fix my holster as I seated my Glock against my chest.

"We're to stay together." He demanded. "No one is to be a damn hero, we get in and get out before any of the others even know we're there. How hard can it be to kill one fucking asshole?"

Too goddamn hard.

If it was easy, it would've been done by now.

Hunter glanced at his cell as we skirted the city, taking the back roads. But the moment we were thirty minutes out, we seemed to gather company.

"Incoming." Thomas murmured from across the other side of the back seat.

I shifted, my guns in my holster slamming into Kane as I looked behind us. There were more vehicles, spilling in from every direction, north and south to join the convoy to end Haelstrom Hale and his fucking Order.

Beep.

"Yeah?" Riven answered in front of me. "Understood."

In the side mirror, a truck came roaring past, overtaking us. Riven glanced at Hunter and motioned back with his head. We slowed a little, letting the truckload of paid mercenaries take the lead. Dust kicked up as they took a hard left. Three more trucks behind us followed them.

"Stay on the course, brother," Riven murmured.

We headed for the towering fence that bordered the private airfield and followed it along to where the guard hut and the entrance were. Tires skidded from the four-wheel drive as we turned hard. I caught movement inside that confined space as the guard stepped out, the automatic rifle in his hand raised. But before Riven could even get the car door open, the *pfft* of a sniper's shot filled the air.

The guard never had a chance, falling where he stood, allowing Riven to climb out and flank the front of the car before he made his way inside the hut. Seconds later, the towering gate rolled open. Other vehicles flew past as trucks followed, barrelling inside. Riven hurried back to climb inside before we took off, following the others through.

I glanced behind us, to find London's Explorer, and beyond them, Tobias was at the wheel of their midnight blue Land Rover. Our vehicle bounced hard, jerking my focus back.

"You know what to do, Trouble?"

I gave a nod. "I know."

"You get separated from us, you head for London and the Sons, got it?"

"Got it."

"And if...if anything bad happens, you get yourself to DeLuca. He'll take you to the safehouse."

"Nothing bad is going to happen." I could barely get the words out.

Hunter spun the wheel, throwing me against the door.

"No, it won't," Hunter growled.

But Thomas and Kane were silent as they looked at me. Nothing bad was going to happen...because I didn't think I could endure one more death...or any more heartbreak.

We pulled up inside a thick line of trees and Hunter killed the engine. Others did the same, Vivienne and her men beside us, Ryth and hers next to them. The trucks of armed soldiers quickly emptied and the moment I cracked open the door, the sound of gunfire filled the air.

"We're on." Hunter scanned the trees, pulling his weapon free.

Car doors closed. My pulse was racing as Riven turned toward me. "Remember."

"Stay together," I answered for him, meeting his gaze as he adjusted my holster and the rest of the others made their way around the car.

Hunter scanned the trees, but then turned back to me. I was all they cared about. I was all they saw and I didn't have to listen too hard to know my sisters were being treated the same.

"You two move ahead." London ordered. "But not too far. Vivienne."

"I know. Stay at your back."

"Yes, my love. We are your shield, do you hear me? *We. Are. Your. Shield.*"

My chest throbbed with the words as I glanced over to where London brushed her hair from her face and kissed her. She reached out to brush Carven's hand. He reached behind and grasped her fingers for a second before he was gone. But Colt... Colt was the one standing still, staring as London stepped away.

"I'll be okay," she said quietly, her eyes brimming with tears.

"We have to go," Riven called me away.

I quickly met her stare, then glanced over the front of their car to where Ryth held her son against her chest. Nick and Caleb were in front of her, with Tobias striding ahead.

We're going to be okay.

We're all going to be okay.

I followed Hunter and Riven, leaving Thomas and Kane to flank my sides as we pushed through the trees. The sound of gunfire was growing faint now. Men swept in all around us, running forward with their guns raised.

Roars followed and the sound of gunfire filled the air again, causing me to pull my weapon free. I'd fought for my life before —I glanced at Hunter, with his sniper rifle resting against my shoulder—and I'd fought for them. But this...this was war on a whole scale I wasn't prepared for.

Click.

Something sounded under my foot. Hunter stopped instantly and swung around. His eyes widened before he lunged. I was hit and knocked through the air as the sound of rapid fire exploded around me.

Screams followed, guttural screams before the deafening sound of gunfire fell silent. I sucked in hard breaths, the heavy weight of Hunter pressing down on top of me. He lifted his head, scanning the trees behind us before he turned his attention to me. "You okay?"

I gave a slow nod as he rose.

"*Goddamnit!*" Kane barked.

Hunter shoved upwards, letting me follow. I rushed forward, finding blood seeping into the arm of Kane's shirt. The sound of tearing fabric filled the air as Hunter ripped the shirt open. "It's just a scratch."

"Jesus *fucking Christ,*" Kane bellowed.

But Riven was the one who strode to where the automatic machine gun was waiting. One of London's men rose from behind the weapon, the pin and something else in his hand. He met our gazes and gave a nod. "This place could be filled with automatic turrets, we need to be careful where we step."

No shit.

I glanced behind us to where Vivienne and her men stared at us with wide eyes, until in the distance...the thunder of footsteps sounded, growing louder.

"Riven," I murmured, swinging my gaze toward the rumble.

"Easy, baby." He took a step to place himself in front of me. "Easy."

The army of men that had come with us urged us forward, gathering speed.

"With us, Helene." Hunter pushed forward, raising his weapon.

I took a step, desperate to be ahead of Vivienne. "Go." I lifted my weapon, moving ahead. *"Go."*

We surged forward, our pace picking up as the crack of gunfire came, and as we charged through the trees toward that goddamn warehouse, I finally saw what we were up against.

There was an army.

A whole fucking army.

They stood around the shimmering *thing.* Sunlight bounced off the walls, blinding me. I blinked into the glare as Hunter squeezed off a shot, *crack,* then swung the muzzle, firing again.

Kane was next, then Riven, and the deafening sound of gunfire filled my ears. Hale's men were everywhere. Men dressed in leather cuts, others dirty and sweaty. They were nothing but bullet catchers.

I raised my gun, my finger squeezing the trigger until the gun kicked in my hand. In an instant, it all came back to me. The rush. The fight. The collision of all I was and all I had been. I unleashed a roar. Hunter jerked a look at me over his shoulder. Pride and love burned in his stare as he turned back.

Our men collided with Hale's men with a deafening *THUD*. Hunter lunged, slamming into a big-ass biker. Fists and rage were all I saw. I swung my gun, squeezing off a shot as another biker came for those I loved. Behind us, London roared. But I couldn't look back at him. I couldn't risk taking my eyes off those in front of me.

Crack!

Crack!

Crack!

Every hard step was a blow, tearing through my ankles and into my knees. I kept up with Hunter and Riven, veering left along the mammoth shimmering monstrosity this thing was. It wasn't a warehouse. It was a goddamn spaceship buried in the ground.

There's a door. In the northeast side of the warehouse that's not far from the private airfield. The door is small, you'd miss it really, trying to break down the main doors.

The door. My steps faltered, skidding hard.

"What is it?" Kane, slowed meeting my gaze.

I sucked in hard breaths, scanning the glimmering walls as each angle caught the sun. No wonder we couldn't see it from above. But we saw it now. We saw it and wanted to *burn it to the ground.* "The door...there's a door." I scanned the walls, desperate to find any kind of entrance, and kept running. "There's a small door, we need to find it."

"A door?" Kane jerked a panicked gaze my way, then jerked his gun up and squeezed off a shot, hitting a guy in the center of the chest. "What goddamn door?"

I stopped, scanning the wall, searching for any way inside, but there was none. There was no fucking door. I lunged, driving past Riven and Hunter as they took aim and fired.

"Helene!" Riven barked. *"HELENE!"*

I couldn't wait, my mind raced as I made for the corner of the building, desperate to find a way inside.

"Goddamnit!" Riven roared.

The heavy thunder of my heart was deafening. I scanned the wall in front of me, then turned back...it was only then that I caught the gap in the mirrored wall. It was larger than the others, drawing my focus like a star in the sky that shone brighter.

"Helene!" Riven grunted. *Bang!* "We have to go *now.*"

We have to go.

We have to—

I surged forward, my heart driving into my throat as I skimmed my fingers along the smooth, glittering surface. "Go...go where, Riven?" I murmured. "There's no way inside. There *is* no way inside."

No without this door...

There was a smaller gap, one I pressed.

Click.

A section swung inwards, showing a keypad instead. My heart *boomed.* But the others weren't calling me anymore. They were silent, giving all their focus to the fight. The jarring sound of gunfire faded as I stepped closer to those numbers. Flickers of a memory rose. One I didn't want or need in this moment. Still, all I saw was the sensor on that safe in my father's destroyed study. The one which had held that report. The one I'd tried so hard not to think about. But here it was...pushing to the surface *now.*

"Trouble!" Riven barked. "Gonna need you to do something here."

I stared at that keypad.

Medical report for Weyland King.

My fingers trembled as they lifted. In the back of my mind, the numbers *sixteen oh-one* echoed. I pressed the first digit one, six —*CAT Scan evaluation, Glioblastoma Multiforme, Grade IV.* My fingers shook so damn hard I couldn't press the buttons.

"Baby," Kane urged.

I squeezed my eyes shut, trying desperately to force the image of that report away, then opened them once more. Zero-*one.*

There.

It's done.

I stared at the keypad, waiting for the click. But it never came. *Nothing came.*

Agony roared across my chest. I stared at that keypad, waiting for the red blinking light to turn green. *Glioblastoma*

Multiforme, Grade IV...Glioblastoma Multiforme, Grade IV... Glioblastoma Multiforme, Grade IV.

"Helene?" Kane urged.

Crack!

Crack!

CRACK!

It was all I could hear, until that tiny voice inside my head pushed through. *Betrayed once more.* My throat thickened, so tight I thought I was being strangled. I shook my head and stepped closer. Maybe I put in the wrong code? Maybe I fucked up. I pushed in the code once more.

One.

Six.

Zero.

One.

Nothing. *There was nothing.* "No." I shook my head. "No...no... no."

Movement came from the corner of my eye.

"Look at me." Kane's finger under my chin forced my gaze to his. There was dirt on his cheek and his normally perfect hair was dishevelled. Dressed in cargos, boots and a black t-shirt, my Teacher was more like a soldier. Still, that didn't stop him from dropping everything to keep me together.

"They lied." I forced out the words. "They *all* lied."

Crack!

Crack!

"Then we'll find another way in," he said carefully. "We do it on our own. We are a team, you hear me? Whatever happens out there, you have us. We're not going anywhere. *We're with you.*"

Tears blurred his face as the light on the keypad in front of us turned from red to green and the door gave a *click,* opening itself.

Kane jerked his gaze to the door, then shouted behind us. *"Boys."*

They all turned and glared at us, until they saw the door. It hit me at that moment that it opening hadn't come from the code. Kane stepped forward, grabbed the smooth edge of the door and opened it wider. I lifted my gaze, sweeping along the glinting wall and upwards. High above us was a camera...one so small you could easily miss it.

"What the fuck?" Riven muttered as he brushed my shoulder, opened the door wider, and peered inside.

But a chill raced along my spine. Someone was watching us... *no, someone was watching* me.

"Riven, *wait—*" I barely got the words out before he stepped into the darkness.

It was too late.

Far too late.

To stop this now.

316

THIRTY-FIVE

Vivienne

"PET?" LONDON CALLED ME AND PUSHED FORWARD.

I jerked sideways, one hand holding my belly and the other a gun, lifting it high in the air as I took aim. *Bang!* The kickback was strong. Still, the shot hit its mark, bringing one asshole to his knees in front of Carven. He took him out with one slash of his knife across his throat, killing him instantly.

Blood shot high, then welled over the gash before he fell face down, leaving us to step over him and keep going. There were too many of them spilling from around this ugly fucking thing in front of us. Too many for us to wade through.

"*Son.*" Came a snarl from our right.

Out of nowhere they came, three Sons spreading out to attack us. Carven and Colt were at the front, surging forward to slam into two of them. But that left one...and he came for us.

Grunts followed as Carven slashed and punched. But each blow he gave was met with one just as fast if not faster. His brows creased with the effort, unleashing all he had. But these warriors were strong and trained...and there were too many of them.

Crack!

A shot came from out of nowhere and slammed into the third Son who'd come to attack us. He stumbled backwards but didn't go down. No, he righted himself and surged forward. But as London readied to attack, three massive men slammed into them. I caught sight of the towering hitman London had called Alvarez and two others just as big and dangerous. The Cerberus brothers. Three men who did the Mafia dirty work. Three men you didn't want to mess with.

Powerful blows landed, driving the Son down.

Crack!

Alvarez fired his weapon, killing the male instantly. He slumped to the ground and for a second, I felt...*loss* at the sight of his dead body in front of me. I knew there was no way out of this for them. It was either kill or be killed. Still, knowing they had no choice but to attack hit me harder than I was prepared for. *That could've been Carven or Colt.* I shifted my focus to my twins, each of them fighting with all they had. The only difference was, *my* Sons fought for survival and love, not for a leader who was a monster.

Alvarez lifted his head, then glanced back at us over his shoulder. One nod from London and he left with the brothers, pushing further into the horde of Hale's henchmen.

"We can't get through." London scanned the mass of men fighting in front of us. The Lawlor men were there, driving powerful blows into a mass of bikers, dropping one after another. "Not through there, are least."

Movement came from the right. Hidden further back from the trees where the three Sons had come from there was a door, one that was open, leading into darkness. "There," I shouted, lifting the gun and pointing to the door. "There's a door."

Carven rose from a Son, the blade in his hand dripping blood. "I'll go."

"No," I shook my head. "We stay together, remember?"

He didn't like it, clenching his jaw, but he nodded.

"We need to be prepared for whatever comes in there, Pet. You prepared for that?" London glanced my way.

"It'll be no different than what's out here," I answered, staring at that open door and the hell that waited for us inside. "We need to get in that building, London. We haven't come this far...to just come this far."

"That we haven't, Pet, that we haven't." He took a step, nodding to the twins.

Carven and Colt pushed forward, and we headed for that gaping wound, desperate to carve this cancer out for good this time. The hinges howled as Colt pushed the door open. He slipped inside, followed by his brother, then London allowed me to push in behind him.

"Vivienne, take my hand, baby." London's deep rumble came before a brush at my arm.

I grasped his hand and stepped inside, following the familiar thud of boots. It was a tunnel. The same tunnel Carven had told us about? It had to be. But all the way out here? The tunnel must've taken...*forever to build.*

Rage seethed inside me. I gripped London's hand and my gun and pushed forward.

"There's more coming." Carven murmured.

"Behind me, Pet."

I stepped behind London, releasing his hand to find my weapon as we moved deeper into the darkness, until we came to another door. It was too easy. It felt...too damn easy.

"London."

He kept walking.

"London."

He stopped as Carven reached out and grabbed the door.

"It's too easy."

From beside each door, they came, two Sons moving fast. The *slash* of a knife was instant. Carven gave a *grunt* before he unleashed a snarl and drove one shadowed bastard back against the wall. Colt grabbed the other and slammed him backwards. The *BOOM* of gunfire was deafening, making me scream out. Colt's roar followed, the bellow half man and half...*beast.*

I couldn't keep up with them. They spun, slammed, and fists flew, but from whom I didn't know. I lifted my gun and took aim, until London grabbed my hand and pushed it down. "No."

Grunts and fists, and the desperate grappling for life were all I saw and heard, hating how fucking *useless* I felt, until someone groaned *"No"*, and fell.

My world stopped as my eyes widened. I stared into that darkness, stared until they blurred into one and another body dropped to the floor.

Crunch.

The third body dropped.

My eyes adjusted to the gloom and found the silhouette of Colt as he sucked in hard breaths and turned toward me. The whites of his eyes were all I saw, glistening in the dark.

"Baby," Carven called my name and took a step toward me. "You okay?"

In a rush, my world started again. My pulse raced and my breaths were panting. It was all I could do not to pass the fuck out.

"We're okay." Carven took a step toward me. "Look at me. We're okay. We have to keep going."

I gave a nod and moved when he turned, pulled open the door, and stepped inside. For a moment, it was even darker, pitch black. Still, we kept walking, shuffling until a weird pulsing light slowly brightened the hallway, growing brighter the deeper we moved. I glanced at London and found him scowling. We relied on the twins, following them. Carven was ahead, sweeping his gun around corners as we moved deeper until we came to a cracked open door where that pulsing light came from.

For a second, I froze. I didn't want to go in there, didn't want to see what hell waited. But it was Colt who pushed the door wider and stepped inside.

"Colt," London warned.

The Son stopped, glancing over his shoulder but it was me he spoke to. "I can feel them."

Feel them?

He turned back, instinct leading the way. We had no choice but to follow. Carven stepped in next, leading the way as he let London, then me inside. It was some kind of airlock arrangement, leading to another door. One that was locked. Colt tried the handle, letting the hard *thud* echo through the space.

"We need an access card," London said as he moved to the secure keypad.

"You mean one like this?" Carven lifted his hand.

A blood-splattered card was in his hand. One jerk of his head and Colt moved aside, leaving his brother to sweep it across the sensor. The tiny red light turned to green, signaling the door was open. Colt pulled the handle and wrenched the heavy steel door open. *What the fuck was in there?*

The scent of cleanliness hit me instantly, bitter alcohol and filtered, cool air. Colt stepped inside, but through the hiss of air came another sound, muffled and quiet. But the more I focused on that sound, the more I realized what it was. A chill swept through me as I stopped walking.

London jerked his gaze to me. "What is it?"

"That's cries I hear. Cries from women...lots of women."

He swung back, moving faster. We all did, heading to the far side of this. Carven slammed the card against the scanner on the wall and, as Colt yanked the second door, we saw what hell waited for us. A terrifying, sickening hell that was their lives.

The room expanded to a floor of cages and medical equipment. A woman was cuffed in place on one of the beds, her wide eyes fixed on us as we neared.

"No." She shook her head. "Don't hurt my baby."

I froze at the words, my eyes shifting to the bump of her belly. Revulsion slammed into me, tearing a sickened sound from my throat. There were machines everywhere, beeping and pulsing. This place looked like something out of a horror movie. Half science. Half hospital.

"Easy now," London urged. "We're not here to hurt you."

Those cries grew louder, so loud they were all I could hear. My pulse was racing, that cold, empty feeling met and swirled with the fevered rush of adrenaline. I scanned the row of doors at the end of the fucking horror room, finding movement in the small glass panels.

"Get them out of there." I shook my head and stumbled forward.

It could be Ryth in there.

It could be Helene.

Or me...it could be me in there.

"London..." I swung my gaze to him, desperate. *"Get them out now."*

He stepped forward, grabbed the card from Carven, and slammed it on the scanner of the first door. It opened with a *clunk* as he stepped to the next. I moved forward, slowed at the woman cuffed to the bed, and touched her arm. She flinched at the contact, pulling away from me.

"It's okay." I moved closer. "I'm a Daughter, just like you."

She stopped fighting and her eyes widened as her lower lip trembled. "Y-you are?"

I gave a nod as more doors were opened. "Yes, baby. I am. Carven..." I swung my gaze to him.

"Already working on it, baby." He growled, searching the room for anything he could use to get her free. He moved to a desk, swept aside pages and keyboards to snatch a set of handcuff keys from the mess, and strode back to me. I grabbed them, my hands shaking so bad I couldn't get the key in the lock.

A wounded sound vibrated in the back of my throat.

"It's okay," she whispered, her focus fixed on me.

Tears welled as I shook my head, finally driving the key into the lock. "No, it isn't." I twisted, unlocking one hand, before I rounded the machines connected to her body. "None of this is okay."

The rest of the cell doors were unlocked now as I unsnapped her last cuff. She rose carefully, her hand moving to her belly.

"I'll get these off her." Carven started unhooking the monitor leads.

She helped, pulling the cords free, and peeled the tape off her arm before yanking the plastic catheter from the vein in her arm. Blood flowed instantly.

"Shit," Carven snarled, lunging to grab a wad of gauze and slap it over her arm. "You could've waited for me."

No. No they couldn't.

I stepped toward those open cell doors, watching the women still standing inside in terror. How long they'd been held here, I didn't know. My throat thickened until the ache was all I felt. A *kick* came deep in my belly, making me lower my hand and press against my side comfortingly.

But it was the women that called me. These women I hurt for, deep in my soul. My words were thick and husky, but I was desperate to connect with them as I moved to the first door. "It's okay. You're safe now. You're safe."

They all stared at me, most were desperate, some were full of hope. I opened my arms, pulled one against me, then moved to another. She clung to me, wrapping her arms tightly around my neck. Her thick sobs filled my ears. I held her, staring at all of them. But one stood separate from the others, cramming herself as far back in the shadows as she could. I patted the Daughter's arm around me and gently pulled her back.

"Follow them," I urged. "We're going to get you out of here."

But it was the Daughter huddling in the gloom who called me. I stepped toward her, reaching out. "I won't hurt you."

She pulled away, causing me to stop. "I'm Vivienne," I murmured. "I'm a Daughter, just like you."

She shook her head. "No. Not like me," she whispered.

"Why?" I stepped closer. "Why am I so different?"

"It's not you who's different." She whispered and slowly took a tentative step forward.

All I saw was beauty. Big voluptuous curves, round perfect cheeks, deep natural red lips which only accentuated her big, dark, doe eyes. "It's me," she finished.

I shook my head. "No...*no.*" I wrapped my arms around her.

I could only imagine the kind of terror she must've endured. They'd *all* endured.

"My name is Melantha," she murmured.

"Well, Mel, we're going to get you out of this hell. What do you say to that?"

She smiled, revealing perfect dimples. God, my heart ached for them. I stepped away, leaving Colt to urge them forward. "You need to be quiet, help us to get you out of here," he urged.

They touched him, brushing their fingers along his cheek. One even moved closer and wrapped her arms around his powerful chest. He just froze, turning panicked eyes to mine. I gave him a soft smile and nodded. They needed him, even if it was just the idea of him. They trusted him, because he was a Son.

"Keep moving," London pushed. "We're going to get you out of here. But you need to be careful. There's a lot of men out there. Men who want to hurt you."

The Daughters were wary of him, giving him a wide berth as they made their way to the door.

"This way." Carven led them out.

I moved from one cell to the other, helping them out. They touched me, my face and my belly. Their eyes were so full of hope it was heartbreaking. "It's okay," I urged. "Hurry, it's okay. We're getting you out of here."

It was all I could do not to break down in tears. These women deserved so much more than a life in a cell, being used as nothing more than a vessel. They were human...they were real.

Rage rippled through me. My baby kicked. I knew instantly which one it was. My boy was a force to be reckoned with. I glanced at Colt, just like his father.

It took too long, but we got all the Daughters out of those cells, urging them through the rooms and back out into the dark hallway.

"I'll lead them through the tunnel and be back," Carven urged.

"We'll wait here," London answered.

Their steps shuffled, their hands reached for me. They were scared and desperate. "It's okay," I whispered. "Go, follow Carven. He's going to get you out of here. I promise we'll take care of you. I promise."

Those words hit me hard and my heart climbed into my throat. They left, held onto each other for comfort, and followed Carven as he led them out of there. I knew the carnage they'd witness. The bodies and the blood, and I only hoped once they were out they wouldn't all run.

You're a Daughter, right? You belong to us.

Those words resurfaced from the attack outside the restaurant on the night Colt had been taken. I now knew there were other rogue Sons hunting Daughters. Who they worked for I didn't know. All I knew was it was a dangerous time to be female and owned by The Order.

We waited, standing in the dark while the scuff of their bare feet grew fainter and finally ended. "London, I'm scared for them and for us."

"A few more minutes, Pet. A few more minutes and I promise we're out of here. Just need to find him. You give me that and we're done."

Boom!

The sound made me jump and cry out. I stumbled sideways, slamming into Colt. His arms were around me in an instant and my baby kicked...*hard.*

"Oww." I doubled over with the sudden pain. *"Easy."*

But he wouldn't settle in there, just kept rolling and kicking, which would've been fine if there was only one of them. But he never kicked his sister, no, he unleashed his karate blows on my insides instead. I caught my breath, then slowly released it as London stepped toward the sound.

I'd missed the heavy thud of steps, but Carven's deep growl cut through the air. "I heard it from outside."

"We have no idea where the fuck that asshole is," London snapped.

"Only one way to find out." Carven brushed past me, his fingers gentle as they skimmed my arm. "Stay close, baby."

I intended on doing exactly that, following them along the hallway, until it branched out. There was a low light spilling from floor lights now that led in a different direction. The place was a maze. Still, we followed Carven as he led the way.

Bang!

The sound of a door echoed like a shot along the hall, causing Carven to grip his knife and surge ahead, then turn left, heading further into the belly of this beast. Colt followed, barely a step behind. A cry was followed by the sound of blows.

Crack!

A shot came. London pushed me backwards as shadows came from further along the hallway in front of us.

"Baby." London urged me back and stepped to the side, directly in front of me as two Sons appeared.

I gripped my gun, ready to kill, as London strode forward, lifted his gun, and fired. *BOOM!* The sound was deafening as he fired once more and rushed forward to meet the killers head-on.

One Son went down, but he didn't stay there for long, shoving upward as London clashed with the other bastard. London fought, but he was slowly earning crippling blows to his kidneys. I pushed backwards, horrified, and lifted my gun, taking aim.

Only I didn't feel the air shift behind me. Nor did I feel the wall at my back slide sideways. But I heard the sickening voice of my nightmares as Haelstrom Hale murmured in my ear. "Now we don't want to pull the trigger, do we, Vivienne? You wouldn't want to kill the man you love."

His hand wrapped across my mouth and he wrenched me backwards as he gripped the gun, then pressed his finger around mine as he took aim at London and fired.

Bang!

All I saw was London stumble forward before I was dragged backwards.

"*London!*" I screamed behind Hale's hand. "*LONDON! NOOOOO.*"

THIRTY-SIX

Ryth

"There's no way in." Caleb fired his gun. *Bang!* "No. Goddamn. Way. In."

There wasn't. I lifted my gaze, stared up at the shimmering walls, and cradled Ali against my chest. Tobias fired, *Bang! And* killed another of Hale's men who skirted the corner of the warehouse and ran straight toward us.

Ali bucked and unleashed a wail. I spread my fingers over his face, tilting my face to kiss his cheek. "Shhh...it's okay. It's all going to be okay."

Tobias scanned the walls, then the grounds. I'd lost sight of Helene and Vivienne after the first attack and now...we were alone.

"I'm going to fucking destroy this place." Tobias growled, turning to glance at us before focusing on something in the distance.

Nick and Caleb fired, downing as many men as they could. But Tobias left them both behind and strode past me. I turned, holding Ali with one hand as Tobias headed for a group of soldiers hired by London and his buddies.

They swung their weapons, taking out two more assholes from the other side of the building. I caught Tobias' snarl, but I couldn't hear what he was saying.

"Princess." Nick grunted, firing his gun. "Stay close now."

I shifted closer but my attention was on Tobias as one of the soldiers opened his duffel bag and pulled something out and handed it to the man I loved. A short conversation and the soldier gave a nod, leaving Tobias to stride back toward us.

The closer he came, the more I realized what he had in his grip. It was a *bomb*.

"We can't find a way inside, then I'll make one." He growled as he went past me and fixed the device waist high on the mirrored wall. "You might want to all step back here."

Nick and Caleb jerked their gazes to their brother as he fixed the massive wad of C4 explosive to the wall. But I was already walking backwards before I turned and lunged toward the safety of the soldiers.

"*T!*" Nick roared as he grabbed me. "*You are one crazy motherfucker!*"

We made it to the safety of the trees, where Tobias and Caleb met us. I turned my back, cradled Ali tight against me, and covered his ears as Nick covered mine.

"*Now!*" Tobias barked.

One of the soldiers held a trigger, scanned the area, and pressed the button.

BOOM!

The explosion was deadening, even through Nick's firm grip on the sides of my head. But Ali didn't cry out, not this time. Nick's hands slid free as he turned, then we all did, and stared at the gaping hole in the side of the building, one that'd lead us inside.

"Boom," Tobias muttered as he lifted his weapon and moved closer.

"Stay here, baby," Nick urged, leaving me behind.

Tobias, Nick, and Caleb neared the gaping hole. The sound of glass crunched under their boots before Tobias stepped through the massive hole to disappear inside. My pulse throbbed in my temples, growing louder before he returned. "It's all clear."

Wild horses couldn't have held me back. I rushed forward, meeting Nick as Caleb stepped through. The two soldiers followed as I stepped over the jagged shards and into some kind of office. But we didn't stay long.

"Let's get this motherfucker." Tobias led the way.

He was more savage than I'd seen him in a long time. A pure killing machine. One driven by the need to protect those he loved. My body still ached from his love, both he and Nick had been ravenous last night. I'd known it was different when Tobias pulled me into the shower with him, tracing the tattoo low down on my abdomen. I wanted to remove it, but he wouldn't let me.

It's not time yet, little mouse.

Now I knew what he meant by that.

He needed to see it one last time. To burn it into his mind, and use it as he charged into the hallway of this building. I held our son tight and followed them inside.

Crack!

Crack!

One of the soldiers fired behind us. I cried out, hurrying forward as Tobias turned right. The lights were bright above us, glaringly bright. The hum of the lights were so loud they sounded like cicadas. We turned again, moving away from that irritating sound and deeper into the belly of the place.

"You two head that way." Tobias commanded. "I'm after the goddamn communications room, so I can tear this place to the ground."

"Here." One of them reached into his bag and pulled out another hunk of C4 explosive.

Fear pushed through me. I trusted Tobias, more than I trusted anyone. But the sight of that explosive around our child was enough to fill me with dread. He took it and nodded to them before they turned and left.

"The comms room?" Caleb said. "You think that's a good idea?"

"Is it going to stop his escape or ruin his goddamn plans?"

"Maybe," Caleb answered.

Tobias turned around and started walking. "That's good enough for me."

He swept his weapon around the corner and pushed on. Nick was behind him, scanning the other way as the hallway branched out.

Boom!

The sound ricocheted along the hallway, which only made Tobias push harder, until he was almost running. Nick went after him, leaving me to hurry with Ali...until I slowed, then stopped. Something nagged at me, worming its way through my mind. I turned around, and saw a lone figure standing at the end of the hallway. A figure I almost didn't recognize...except for those eyes.

Washed out green.

Green like I saw every day when I looked in the mirror.

Only that man...he was a stranger.

He took a step forward, agony filling his eyes.

"No." I shook my head. "*NO!*"

I closed my eyes.

"Ryth? *Ryth!*"" Caleb grabbed me to him, looking behind me. "What was it?"

But I shook my head and turned, staring at the same place he was...only my father was gone. *Like he wasn't there at all.*

Only he was. He *was* there. I cradled my son and stepped away from Caleb, moving in the opposite direction.

"Ryth, *no.*" Caleb called.

"Baby?" Nick was next.

"What the fuck was it?" Tobias pushed past me, heading further back into the hall until he stopped, then turned around.

"I..." I started. "I thought I saw—"

"*Who?*"

I met that implacable stare. "My father."

I saw a flicker of fear as he froze. "Your *what?*"

I wanted to shake my head. I wanted to say it was a lie, just a figment of my imagination, a remnant of the deep scar he'd left on my heart. But it wasn't a lie. I knew it wasn't. "He's here... *there.*" I stepped forward.

Tobias' lips curled in a sneer. "Yeah? Then let's find out where the sonofabitch has been all this time."

He left us, striding forward, his gun raised. All I could see was my father's death. I wanted that more than anything. To see him hurt, begging for his life. Begging forgiveness. That's what I wanted.

Because he'd hurt me.

He'd betrayed me.

Just like Mom.

That old pain resurfaced as we headed along the hallway, turning right at the end. We moved, our steps thudding like the beating of my heart until we came to the end and two doors, one left and the other right.

"Which way, little mouse?" Tobias turned toward me.

I stared at them, then lifted my finger. *Left.*

"Right it is." He yanked the handle and shoved, but the door was locked. The red light blinked. Tobias swore, then turned to the other door and smacked the handle.

Click.

The lock went green, causing Tobias to turn back, glance at us, and then open the door. My heart leaped as he stepped through. But Nick was there, stepping around me, touching Ali as he followed his brother inside.

Then Caleb went, leaving just me. Part of me wanted to turn away and just not know. But that haunting stare stayed with me, dragging the agony of betrayal back to the surface.

"Holy shit," Tobias snarled.

I looked down at our son, at his perfect gray-green eyes, ones he carried from my bloodline, and stepped through that open door into a world of machines.

There were rows and rows of servers. I moved between the towering stacks, finding Caleb first, then Nick, and finally Tobias. He spun around, his eyes shining with excitement. "I say it's the perfect place to put this."

In his hand was that hunk of C4. One that would tear this place apart.

"We need to get you and Ali safe first." He glanced at his son.

"I can help with that."

I stiffened at the soft murmur. One I hadn't heard in what felt like forever.

"You? You MOTHERFUCKER!" Tobias unleashed a roar.

Movement came all around me. I was grabbed and pushed to the side, spinning to see Tobias grab my father and drive him backwards until his head slammed against one of the rows of servers with a *thud.*

But my father didn't fight back. Instead, he stood motionless as Nick rushed forward to search his jacket and his pockets. "He's clear," He called, staring my father in the eyes.

He didn't look like my father.

Not the one I knew.

This man was gaunt and weak, sallow looking. He shifted that piercing stare to me once more, then slowly lowered it to my son. "Ryth."

"No, you fucking *don't,*" Tobias growled as he stepped to the side, blocking his view. "You don't get to look at her. You don't get to look at *anyone but me.*"

The pain I'd suffered at the hands of our family was nothing compared to Tobias'. His own father had not only sold me out, but then he'd tried to make amends, ultimately dying in Tobias' arms. That hurt more than anything.

"I'm here to help," my father said quietly. "Just let me help you, son."

I winced at the word.

"Don't you *dare* call me that. I'm *not your son* and *that woman there* isn't your daughter. You lost that right when you fucking betrayed us."

"I tried—"

"You sold your own fucking DAUGHTER TO A RAPIST!"

Ali unleashed a scream, kicking and thrashing in my arms. I stumbled backwards, clutching my son. I wanted to see pain in my father's eyes. I wanted to see anything but *utter helplessness.*

"Are you going to deny it?" Tobias towered over him, his fists clenched like he wanted to beat my father to death with the fistful of explosives. He'd do it, too.

"How can I?" The words were almost a whisper. "It's the truth."

Tobias sneered. "You *vile* piece of shit. Nick...cuff this bastard to the server there. He needs to die along with the rest of this place."

Nick glanced at me, then shook his head. "Not going to do that, T."

Tobias' rage was a beast of its own, making him wrench that hateful glare toward his brother, until he saw me. Then he stopped, his big chest heaving.

"It's her dad," Nick urged. "Regardless of what he's done. I'm not going to watch her see him die, we know what that feels like, right?"

My beautiful tornado of pain flinched, that rage dying down to an inferno as he turned back to my father. "No, we're not going to do that. She just won't watch."

"It won't matter anyway," My father said. "I'm dying."

Tobias gave a *huff.*

"I have maybe a couple weeks left."

Tobias froze.

That icy sensation grew along the back of my neck as I took a step forward, brushing past Caleb and Nick before I placed my hand on Tobias' arm. His anger was a direct result of the love he felt for me. He'd destroy everyone and everything which hurt me. But this pain wasn't something that could be destroyed...just completed, before I moved on.

I met my father's familiar stare. "I hope you find the peace you've been looking for in your next life."

"Ryth, *baby*."

I shook my head as tears welled in my eyes. "*Noooo*. No, you don't get to call me that. You don't get to—"

"Dad?"

The call was deep, wounded. I spun around, finally heeding the thud of footsteps, and found Helene standing in the doorway. Her gaze went from me...to our father.

"You?" Riven pushed past her, those killer eyes fixed on our father. "You *fucking bastard!*"

There was no stopping him as he lunged across the room faster than anyone expected, shoving Tobias and me aside to get his hands on our father.

"*I'm going to FUCKING KILL YOU!*"

Tobias grabbed me and steadied both of us before he turned, shoving Riven hard. "*Hey! You fucking asshole!*"

"Riven," Helene called, making the vengeful male turn around and face her.

She strode closer, easing him aside. But she didn't give our father her attention. No, not at first. Instead, she focused on me, moving closer to hug me and brush her fingers across Ali's cheek. "You okay?"

I gave a nod, my heart swelling with her love. She might not've been the sister I'd wanted throughout my childhood. Hell, she wasn't even a normal sister now as an adult. But there was a love between all three of us. One that had been etched by blood and pain. One stronger than I'd ever realized until that moment as she turned to our father.

"I'd ask you why you're here, but I realized I really don't care." He opened his mouth to speak, until she cut him off with a wave of her hand. "Don't bother. Your diagnosis means little to us now. All I want from you is closure. So, say what you need to say to us, then leave. We can't wait to forget you ever existed."

Agony roared across his eyes. He reached into his pocket, making Riven grab his wrist.

"Easy." He warned.

But our father didn't carry a weapon, not one we could see, at any rate. He pulled out a small black thumb drive. "This...this is worth everything."

Helene stared at the drive in his hand.

"The files in the Vault were corrupted. We didn't know that at the time, but I had my man try to crack the codes to release the information. He couldn't and in the end, I realized there was no way for you to survive this without more. There are more Hales involved in this. More than you could ever know. They hide behind badges and plaques. They hide behind the greatest house we know. There're no laws that can touch them, no amount of money that can force them from the dark where they hide. There is no winning this war without this." He lifted the device, his voice cracking. "And there was no getting this unless you were on the inside. He had to think I was part of all this. I had to find some way to earn his trust."

"So you just fed your daughters to those men to do it?" Riven spat. "You fucking *disgust me.*"

"Yes." Our father answered as tears filled his eyes. "I did and if I had to do it again, even if it caused me this, I'd do it again."

"You really are a bastard." Tobias shook his head.

But our father just looked at us, desperately holding out that goddamn drive. Helene stared at it, then turned and gave him her back.

"Please." He begged. "You wanted an ending, right? You wanted closure from me, this...this is your closure."

She turned, her eyes shimmering. My throat thickened at the sight. I reached out and brushed her arm. She'd suffered so much for us. *Too much.* I dropped my hand and stepped forward, taking the drive from his hand.

"Thank you, Ryth. Thank you, I—"

Crack!

The blast was deafening, making me cry out and stumble backwards, cradling Ali as I gripped the drive. In the blink of an eye, our father dropped to the floor where he lay with a gunshot wound in his skull.

Roars followed. I stumbled backwards and clutched Ali even closer. Helene was there, lunging in front of me as the server room filled with men...and one woman.

A woman I'd seen before.

Riven's sister.

"You-" *CRACK!* "Fucking *bitch!*"

Crack!

Crack!

CRACK!

The roar of gunfire was all I could hear. Helene fired her gun, taking down one of the men as they skirted the servers and came for us. Tobias and Nick disappeared, leaving Caleb to stand guard alongside my sister.

Choked sounds of death and roars of rage filled the room.

"You bitch!" Riven bellowed. *Crack!* "You fucking die, you goddamn *bitch.*"

I trembled with rage as I lowered my head and kissed my son's cheek. This is all there was for us...this is all—

Until suddenly there was silence.

Cold, empty silence.

I lifted my head, to find Caleb and Helene standing side by side, watching for movement.

"Is it over?" I asked.

Footsteps sounded, heavy and hard. They were followed by another and another...until Tobias rounded the towering metal shelves. There was blood all over him. Blood that splattered over his face and ran down his hands. Nick was the same...as was Riven and his brothers who followed closely behind them.

"Baby," Riven croaked, but Helene was already moving, lunging into his arms.

Tobias wrapped his around me, pulling me close. "It's over," he said, his face buried against my neck. "It's over."

I hugged him back, sobs tearing free as I shifted my gaze to our father. "He's gone."

There was pain in Tobias' eyes as he met mine. "Yes."

Still, I needed to see. I let him go and stepped around him, making my way to where my father lay. His wide eyes were fixed and empty. Whoever he was or had hoped to be was no more. So many questions remained unanswered, but I guess there wasn't an answer to them. I could ask why forever and still feel pain.

My fingers clenched around the device. I opened it and turned, finding the slew of bodies between us and the door. The soldiers had paid well...and so had Riven's sister, lying with her arms open, on top of the men she'd used.

But none of them were Hale.

He was still out there.

Until he was dead, this wouldn't be done.

"We need to find him," I whispered. "And kill the sonofabitch."

THIRTY-SEVEN

Vivienne

"VIVIENNE!" London screamed as the hidden door slammed shut.

Boom!

BOOM!

The sound of his fists was deafening, filling my ears. But it was my breaths I focused on as Hale kept his hand clamped over my mouth and blocked my nose. I bucked, thrashed my arms, and stumbled backwards, trying to keep from falling. A hard *kick* came from inside me as Hale jerked me back along the dark hall and through a doorway.

I lashed out, clawing for a hold on the frame as I passed.

"No, *you don't.*" Hale grunted and yanked me hard, tearing my hold free.

"NO!" I screamed, lunging to claim my hold once more.

"Let go, you fucking BITCH!"

He dragged me backwards and kicked the door closed. But the moment he tried to slam his card against the scanner to lock it, I spun around. *No...no...no...no.* If he locked that door, it was over. If he locked that door, I was as good as dead. I wrenched my head backwards, then slammed forward, clashing hard with his. Agony ripped through my skull, plunging into my neck, but his hold on me loosened and I leaped away.

Panic was all I felt as the faint crackle of a two-way radio carried through the destroyed study.

"The jet is ready, Mr. Hale. The pilot is starting the engines."

Hale jerked his gaze toward the sound, his eyes widening before he turned back to me. There was a sickening hunger in his stare, one desperate to destroy what he could. That gaze carried down to my stomach. I recoiled, curled my spine, and covered my stomach with my hands as the two-way crackled once more.

"We can't get to the child, Mr. Hale. The Rossi men are everywhere, cutting us down all over. We're trying, but we're being slaughtered out here."

Hale winced at the words. But he didn't turn those beady eyes away from my belly. I could almost see the thoughts racing through his head.

"No," I whispered and took a step backwards, cradling my belly. "No."

"I want an heir." His words were a throaty rattle like the fucking snake he was. "If I can't have my own," he lifted his gaze to mine. "Then, I'll take yours instead."

My knees shook. My heart was hammering, driving fear through my veins. "No." I shook my head. "You can't have them. You can't have my babies."

My belly rolled and *pushed.* Quivers rippled deep inside me before my baby stilled.

Hale took a step closer as the crackle of that two-way sounded again.

"Awaiting your command, Mr. Hale. Do you want us to keep going after the child or call it?"

Hard, consuming breaths expanded his chest as he took another step closer.

I moved backwards, desperately scanning the mess of the study for a weapon. A small bag was open. Stacks of papers were scattered across the desk underneath it. He was running, that was for sure. Only now, I stood in his way. He stepped even closer, pushing me until I hit the wall.

Fight.

I glanced at the door, but he clucked his tongue.

"I wouldn't try that if I were you—"

I lunged, driving my body as fast as my legs would allow toward the door. But I wasn't anywhere near fast enough, leaving Hale time to grab me around my stomach and haul me back.

"No! NO!" I screamed, then opened my mouth and latched onto his hand, biting down as hard as I could until I tasted blood.

"Fucking BITCH!" Hale screamed.

The blow was instant, connecting with my jaw until it tore my teeth free. Agony followed, jarring into my neck. Only, I didn't have time to attack again. I was dragged instead, around the end of the desk and toward the chair.

"FUCK YOU!" I stumbled, falling against him. *"FUCK YOU, YOU SONOFABITCH!"*

He yanked me harder, one arm in a stranglehold around my throat and the other hit the desk. I didn't see it until it was too late. My vision focused on the white sparks dancing in my eyes and missed the shine of steel...until he lifted his hand and I saw the blade.

"No...no...no...no."

"You won't give me what I want?" He grunted, lifting the blade as high as he could. *"Then I'll take it for myself."*

My baby bucked inside me, kicking and pushing until, in one final *shove,* he drove deep into my belly as the knife arced down. I shoved backwards, throwing myself to the side. Hale let me go...watching me stagger. Warmth slipped down... trickling out of me.

Until I looked down...and saw the hilt of the blade.

Buried deep inside me.

Movement came from the doorway. I slowly lifted my head, my world slowing to a crawl as London and the Sons shoved the door wide, before freezing, staring at me with the knife in my belly.

"My babies." I whimpered before my knees buckled, sending me crashing to the floor.

THIRTY-EIGHT

London

I stepped forward, took aim at the sonofabitch who had held my son, and squeezed off a shot.

Crack!

FUCK YOU!

FUCK YOU ALL TO HELL!

The shot hit him in the shoulder, spinning him around. It was all Carven needed to gain the upper hand, driving the blade of the knife deep into his chest with a savage snarl. But there were more of them coming, spilling out of a doorway along the hall like rats on a sinking ship.

And they were rats.

All of them.

"*London!*" The muffled sound came from behind me.

I took too long to turn...too long to see the real threat...and it wasn't from the trained killers headed our way. It was behind me.

Vivienne was being dragged backwards. For a moment my mind froze, fixed on her wide eyes and the hand across her mouth before I saw him. The beady, glinting fucking eyes. The cruel, bloodless smirk on his face...*that motherfucker Hale!* She was gone in an instant as the false door slammed closed between us.

"*Vivienne!*" I lunged along the hallway, slamming my hand against the wall, before I pushed back and screamed her name. "*VIVIENNE!*"

"*No...no...LONDON!*" Her muffled scream reached me.

Behind me the *boom* of a shot tore through the air. But I didn't stop. Not even when Carven's brutal scream of pain followed. I fixed on the sound of her, as the desperate muffled sounds of her fighting and thrashing slipped further away, until they disappeared.

Get to her.

Get to her.

GET TO HER!

I drove my fist into the wall. "*FUCK!*"

That image burned in my head. Her eyes were wide...*and that bastard's arm wrapped around her throat as he dragged her backwards.*

I spun around, scanning the hallway. There had to be a way to get to her...

I lunged, running back the way we'd come, my focus searching for a goddamn crack in the wall. Carven's scream came, punching through my chest like a goddamn fist. But I couldn't turn around. I couldn't save him, not when Vivienne and our babies were at stake.

I'm sorry, son.

I skimmed my hand along the wall until I came to the corridor turning right, pushing faster until I was running along the hall. A faint scream was borne from somewhere deep in the walls, growing closer. I stopped, tracking the sound and tried to quell the booming of my heart, desperate to hear.

Was it her? Was that...*my Vivienne?* The sound came again. Only this time it was clearer, and my stomach dropped in an instant. I charged forward, desperately searching for those sounds. Her screams were louder now, just out of reach. I stopped and scanned the wall. *Where...where WAS SHE!*

One shove of my hand and the false panel gave way to another hallway and her piercing shrieks grew louder, coming from the room at the end of the hall...until in an instant, they stopped.

"VIVIENNE!" I charged, dropped my shoulder at the sight of the door, and collided.

BOOM!

The door flew inwards...there she was...standing in the middle of the room on the other side of a desk, her wide eyes unblinking as they turned to mine. My focus was drawn downwards, to where her hand pressed against her side...and the hilt of a blade buried deep in her belly.

"My babies." She whimpered before her knees buckled and she crashed to the floor.

Rage.

Rage was all I became.

Bitter like ash.

Empty as the Devil's soul.

I lunged, lifted my gun in one hand, and slammed the other against the desk, catapulted myself clear, and fired.

BOOM!

Hale slammed backwards, blood instantly seeping through his shirt.

"No." He shook his head as I drove the gun under his jaw.

"*I promised you I'd be the last face you saw before your death. I'm here to collect on that promise.*" I forced the words through clenched teeth and pulled the trigger.

BOOM!

Blood splattered across the wall as his head snapped backwards.

"*Vivienne!*" Carven screamed her name.

I turned my head, finding him standing in the doorway. His intense blue eyes were wide, fixed, and full of rage. He turned that rage to the man I held upright and lunged. Colt was right behind him, his blue eyes now filled with the Beast.

Screams were all I heard.

Brutal, sickening roars of rage and pain as Carven shoved me aside, plunging his blade into Hale's neck. I stumbled backwards, and turned toward the woman I loved.

"Pet..." The word was weak and pathetic, slipping free as I dropped to my knees.

The *crunch* of bones behind me made my stomach clench. My hands shook as I pressed against the wound in Vivienne's belly, trying to stem the blood.

"London!" Helene screamed.

"WE'RE IN HERE!" I roared.

I was frozen, unable to do a damn thing but stare at that weapon plunged deep into the woman I loved and push against the bleeding.

Crack!

Rip.

My sons continued to tear Hale apart as movement came from the doorway. In an instant the room was filled, Helene and Riven, followed by Ryth and the Bankses. They stopped, staring as I slid my hand under her knees and gripped her around the back.

"We need to get her to the Doc!" I screamed and drove my body upwards. But they still didn't move, frozen by the thing sticking out of her, until I jerked my gaze toward them. *"Somebody fucking HELP ME!"*

Movement came from the corner of my eye. But it wasn't her sisters. Colt unleashed a low, wounded sound and stumbled forward. He slid his hands underneath her, taking her weight, his focus riveted on the knife.

That keening sound grew more desperate as he turned his gaze to her wide stare...until her eyes rolled back in her head. I pushed forwards, shoving them aside. *"Out of my fucking way!"*

Helene and Riven stumbled sideways. Ryth turned and ran, lunging in front of us. *"Tobias...TOBIAS! HELP THEM, PLEASE!"*

We ran along that corridor with Ryth and her brothers in front, guiding our way out of there. Carven's scream haunted me until I heard the thunder of his steps as we pushed toward the front of the building. The faint *boom* of gunshots grew louder.

"Move!" Carven screamed.

I lunged aside, letting him shove ahead until he bowed his body around her and pushed past into an area that looked like a bomb had gone off.

"What the fuck?" Riven growled.

But I didn't have time to care, just keeping my gun upwards, taking aim at anything that goddamn moved. Colt carried her out of there, his powerful body cradling hers against him. Those guttural sounds came from him, desperate to connect to our children...and the woman we loved.

"DOC!" Carven screamed. *"FOR FUCKS SAKE, DOC!"*

"Here!" Came the call from the line of cars near the treeline.

DeLuca rose from patching a hole in one of the gunmen, his gaze turning to Vivienne in Colt's arms, and froze at the sight of the knife. That *wasn't what I wanted to see.*

He took a step backwards, motioning weakly to the opened tailgate of the four-wheel drive in front of him. Colt carried her closer and eased her inside.

"How long has she been out?"

Colt looked at me. I shook my head. "A couple of minutes."

Doc pressed against her belly, and worked his stethoscope into his ears.

"Well?" I growled.

He listened, pressing over her body, then moved to her chest. "We need to get her to a hospital *now*." He straightened. "She needs surgery now, London."

My feet moved on their own. "Is she going to survive this?"

He shook his head. "I don't know. No one could."

Carven was already moving, lunging for our car.

"You're coming with us, Doc. Tell me no and I'll...I'll—" I stuttered, unable to find the words.

"Of course I'm coming." He answered.

Relief hit me like a goddamn truck as the four-wheel drive backed up hard and braked. The driver's door was thrown open as Colt lifted her once more, carrying her gently toward the opening back door of our Explorer.

Doc grabbed his kit, hauling it up before he turned to the guy he'd been working on. "Keep that dry and clean and you'll be fine. See me tomorrow if you get worse."

I didn't waste a second heading after them and climbed into the passenger seat.

"Baby?" I turned, watching Colt cradle her against him.

Her eyes fluttered open, her gaze wavering. *"My babies."* She whispered as the doc closed the door behind him and Carven punched the accelerator, throwing me against the seat.

Dust and stones kicked up, pinging under the four-wheel drive as we skidded and surged ahead.

"It's okay, Vivienne." Doc pressed his hand against the wound, then tore open several packets of gauze to try to stem the flow. "I need you to stay with me here, can you do that? Can you stay here?"

She gave a slow nod, but as I watched, the color drained from her face, leaving her ghastly pale.

I was going to lose her.

I tore my gaze away, my fist clenched tight around the door handle. In the side mirror, movement came. A car skidded hard, then raced to catch up with us. The moment the dust settled I saw who it was... Guild. Then came another car behind him...and then another. Before long, the stretch of cars behind us was all I could see.

I'd never been a man of prayer.

Not even when my son was taken and tortured nearly to death.

My fists were my salvation.

My rage was my church.

But I closed my eyes now.

And I prayed.

If you're up there. If you're listening, don't take her. Don't take the one good thing you've ever given me...no, you've ever given us. I beg of you. If you have to take someone, take me instead.

I don't know how long I stayed like that, while my world seeped away from me one drop at a time.

"Take us to Mercy," Doc murmured. "I have a team on standby."

I opened my eyes, finding the city skyline rushing toward us. Carven pushed the car harder, taking the corners wider as we hurtled closer. Seconds felt like hours. Minutes like days. I risked a glance behind us to where her bloodless lips were parted, and her breaths were fast and shallow.

"She's going into shock." Doc shifted, pulling her legs upwards, until her feet were in the air.

"Get the fuck *out of my way!*" Carven screamed at the traffic.

I hung on, we all did, as we turned hard once, then once more, hitting the driveway of the hospital with a *jolt* then tore toward the entrance. Tires skidded. I slammed forward as he hit the brakes, throwing my door open wide before we'd even come to a stop.

They were waiting for us, yanking open the door before Doc pushed out.

"Female, 20 years old, currently thirty-nine weeks pregnant with twins. Has extensive injuries to her..."

I zoned out, unable to look away from the knife in her belly. That fucking knife...*what the hell had happened in there?* The doctors lifted her gently onto the stretcher, nodding at the nurses to rush her inside.

"The babies." I stepped forward and grabbed the doctor's arm. He stopped, then met my stare. "If it comes down to it, she is the priority here."

There was a slow nod. He never winced, never missed a beat as he said, "Let's hope it doesn't come to that."

Then they were gone, leaving us standing there as the other cars pulled up and those who loved my wife stepped out. I stared at those closing double doors for too long. My body couldn't move, waiting on signals my frozen mind couldn't give.

"London." Ryth called my name.

I shook my head and, as tears blurred my vision, I turned away, giving them my back.

"Hey." Ryth's small hand grabbed my arm, stopping me. I looked down at her hand. "Whatever happens, we're going to be there."

I swallowed that hard lump in the back of my throat as Carven and Colt headed inside, following DeLuca.

"Thank you," I answered, then headed after them.

Flashes of images assaulted me as we headed for the bank of elevators. The knife in her belly. Her wide, unflinching eyes...then it was that *bastard*. That *goddamn bastard* who stared at me as I drove the gun under his jaw and pulled the trigger.

"London."

I turned my head, finding DeLuca. He stared at me, searching my face as he reached out with a wipe in his hand.

"There's blood all over you."

I stared at that wipe, then took it as the elevator doors opened. My body moved automatically, stepping inside as I dragged the cleaner over my face. Carven was silent, staring at the closed doors. Colt was motionless, standing at the back. None of us were speaking.

"They'll take her straight into surgery. We won't find out anything for a while. I've arranged for you to have the entire doctors' break room to yourselves. You can grab coffee or something to eat, or just even rest while we wait."

It wasn't for us. I knew that. It was for all the other patients and their families. Out of sight and out of the wrath of our rage. At that moment, I didn't care. I gave a nod as the elevator came to a stop and the doors opened. I caught the movement as I stepped out. Vivienne was on a bed, her belly a mountain partially hidden under a white blanket as they rushed her through a set of double doors.

"Gentlemen," DeLuca urged. "This way. I'll get you some clean clothes and some coffee."

I stared at those double doors before I turned. "Come on, boys," I urged, heading after DeLuca.

They wouldn't leave without me. Maybe they wouldn't even leave if I did. Who could blame them? I followed the doctor to a break room marked *Staff only,* pushed open the door and headed for the sink.

London!

LONDON NO!

Her screams resounded in my head as I hit the faucet with shaking hands and bent over, splashing water on my face. The echo of steps was faint in the hall. DeLuca went out, guiding Ryth and her stepbrothers in as I grabbed a towel and switched off the water.

"What happened?" Caleb asked.

What happened?

Carven and Colt looked at me. They all did...but I turned away, giving them my back. I couldn't look at them, not now. "I don't know." My words were a choked hiss. "I just don't know."

Silence grew behind me.

Empty silence.

Not a scrape of a shoe, or a drag of breath. Not even a cry from Ryth's son, now asleep in Nick's arms. There was *nothing*. Maybe this was how my life would sound now? Empty, vacant...until she came back to me.

The door opened and someone eased their head inside. "Doctor, can we see you for a moment?"

I spun at the sound, watching a nurse dressed in surgery gear glance my way.

"What's happening?" I asked.

She forced a smile. "Just the Doctor, that's all."

"I'll be back as soon as I can." DeLuca strode toward her. "Wait for me, London. Just wait."

He was gone in a heartbeat, leaving us all alone.

"Okay, looks like we're going to be here for a while. So, we need coffee." Helene murmured and headed for the cupboards.

Doors opened. The hiss of the coffee machine sounded. Still, I couldn't look away from that door. Not even when she pushed a cup into my hands and urged me to drink.

A nurse came in, handed out a stack of fresh scrubs, and motioned for us to change. I did, making my way to the bathroom at the side, then returned while the others followed.

Ryth and Helene left, returning minutes later with whatever they could scrounge from the vending machines. Sandwiches and bottled water were laid out on the table. Still, I clutched the cup of coffee until it went cold, unable to take my eyes off that door.

Then it opened.

And my entire world shifted.

DeLuca walked in, cradling a tiny bundle in his arms, one that mewled and cried out, stopping the entire room cold. He glanced at Carven and Colt, but slowly made his way toward me, dressed in the same surgical scrubs like the nurse wore before.

"London." He gave a weak smile. "I'd like you to meet your daughter."

My daughter?

I stared at that bundle in his arms. My pulse boomed as her little arms flailed in the air and she unleashed a cry. Colt stepped forward, mesmerized by the sight, and reached for her. But he stopped suddenly, turning to find me instead. "She's calling for you."

I shook my head as agony roared through my chest. "No... not me."

"Yes." He stepped to me, stopping directly in front of me. "Can't you hear her? She needs you, she needs her father."

Her tiny wails were piercing, like needles into my brain. I took a step before I knew it, moving around Colt to the doctor. She was so tiny, all bright red on one side of her face. I looked up at the doc.

"It's okay, that's just from being pressed against her big brother." DeLuca lifted her. "Colt is right, she's calling for you."

"Not me...no."

"Yes, London," Tobias answered. "You. She needs you now."

I flinched with a vulnerable growl, unable to take my eyes off her. She was beautiful, with dark hair and big round eyes. Her tiny fingers stretched wide as she flailed. I reached for her hand, letting her wrap those fingers around my finger. She quietened instantly, her shrieks deepening to cries.

"See, look how she needs you. If you can just—" Doc started.

But I cut him off by moving closer and taking her from his arms. She bucked, wailing louder for a second. But I knew, as soon as I held her, I knew. They were right. They were all right. She settled as I cradled her tighter.

"Skin on skin is best. She needs that right now."

"Vivienne." I croaked her name, my eyes filling with tears. "Please tell me..."

"She's lost quite a bit of blood and there are..." he stopped. "Other complications here."

Fear hit me. "What *kind* of complications?"

He didn't answer but he looked at Colt. "I'm going to need the three of you to come with me."

The floor dropped out from under me. Colt emitted a pained cry, and slowly shook his head.

"This way." DeLuca reached for him.

Carven wrapped his arms around his brother, guiding him as DeLuca turned and headed for the door, opening it wide for me.

"We'll be here," Ryth whispered. "We'll be right here."

I cradled my newborn daughter in my arms, gave Ryth a nod, and followed them. I didn't know what we were walking into... all I knew was it was about to change my life forever.

THIRTY-NINE

Vivienne
___

BEEP.

Beep.

Beep.

The faint sound pierced my mind, dragging me from the darkness. The icy rush of air was instant, filling my lungs, the sudden chill drawing me higher. My eyes fluttered open and blinding light flooded in. The moment I was awake, I felt it, a crushing weight that was settled on my chest. Something was wrong...*very wrong.*

"Pet..." London called. "You're awake."

That *beep...beep...beep...*of the machine sped as the darkened blurs inside the room sharpened. Carven stood on one side next to me, his fists clenched tight around the steel rails. It was a hospital. Stark white, high up so that the sun flooded in enough to hurt my eyes.

How in the hell did I get here? But my attention shifted to London on the other side, cradling something in his arms. But there was no Colt. *Where was he?*

"Colt..." I croaked, my throat bruised so bad I winced.

I reached up, gripped the rails and tried to pull myself upwards. But the moment I moved, agony plunged through my belly, making me catch my breath.

"Easy, Vivienne." DeLuca stepped closer. "You've lost a fair amount of blood. You need to be gentle with yourself now."

Blood?

I jerked my gaze to the mound of bedding on top of me. Bedding that should be higher...much higher. Images assaulted me. A knife buried deep in my belly...and the face of the man who'd put it there. "No...*noooo...*" I whimpered. "My babies. Please, my babies."

London stepped forward. My pulse pounded as my gaze was drawn to the tiny bundle he cradled in his arms and a surge of love burst from me. I reached up, my fingers aching to touch, knowing instantly it was *her.* My daughter. My soul. "My son?" I croaked and touched her perfect cheek. "Where is my boy?"

But there was no answer.

Not from the doctor or London. The room went quiet, so quiet. Only that *beep...beep...beep* of the machine filled the room. So quiet the air grew heavy.

"London..." I fixed my gaze on his agonized stare. *"Where is my son?"* He just looked to DeLuca for guidance.

"The knife caused extensive damage. One inch deeper and we wouldn't be here talking to you now. I need you to understand how serious it was. It was only a miracle you survived at all. The blade cut through the muscle, aimed at where your daughter was. Only she'd been pushed hard to the side and upwards, which resulted in some pressure on the side of her body, nothing that won't disappear in the next few weeks. But your son, Vivienne. Your son took the blow."

That knife plunged into me all over again.

Carving not into my stomach, but my heart.

Only this time I couldn't see it.

"My boy..." Tears welled in my eyes, spilling over instantly. "Where is my baby boy!"

London shifted to the side, then I saw him. Colt was standing at the end of the room, his head bowed, his back to me. That low, throbbing call resounded in his chest. A softness. A connection. One only he had. He turned then, holding a bundle in his arms.

I didn't care about the pain. Didn't care about myself at all. I pulled myself upwards with all I had, until Carven grabbed me, gently lifting me until I sat upwards.

"The stitching will heal. He'll be left with one helluva scar, but he survived and because of him, so did you and his sister."

I couldn't even see him, I was crying so hard. When Colt laid him in my arms, I unleashed a sob that shook my entire body. *My boy...my beautiful, protective boy. He saved us, even before he was born. How could I love him more?*

I blinked the tears, quickly swiping them away until I looked down into the most beautiful blue eyes I'd ever seen. They were the eyes of his father. That deep rumble came from Colt again, the sound making our son stretch and yawn, tilting his perfect face for me to see the white dressing that stretched from one side of his jaw and all the way across his mouth, then above his lip and upwards, stopping just under his eye.

"Oh fuck." I sobbed. "Oh, Jesus. What the hell have I done to you?"

"Nothing." Colt answered and stared down at our child. "He did this to protect you. To protect the both of you."

I looked at our daughter, then held open my arms as London eased her next to her brother. They were perfect. Dark hair, big eyes. Only my boy was far bigger, lazily stretching out until his hand smacked hers. You'd think she'd cry or buck or something. But she didn't, she stretched out just like him, until it wasn't just their hands that touched, but their feet and legs too.

"They want to be together." Carven's eyes widened. "Look at them, they just want to be together."

"Against their mom." London added.

"And their fathers." I turned from Carven to Colt, then London. "All three of them."

FORTY

Helene
___

"She's okay." London stood in the doorway of the doctors' break room cradling a baby in his arms.

No.

Not just *a* baby.

My sister's baby.

"Oh, thank *fuck*." I bent at the waist, bracing my hands on my thighs. *"Thank you, Jesus. Thank you."*

Riven was there beside me, wrapping his arm around me, steadying my body against his.

"And the babies?" He asked.

I looked up, finding London's eyes darkening. "They're okay. They *will* be okay."

Those words hit me hard, forcing me to straighten and step forward. "What do you mean by 'they *will* be okay'?"

"Our son...he suffered extensive damage from the attack."

I froze, feeling the warmth rush out of me. The knife. That's all I could see. I hadn't been able to push it from my mind. The blade buried deep in my sister as Colt carried her from the room...and after that what was left of Hale after the twins were done with him.

Those were two images I *never* wanted to see again in my life. Those sickening, terrifying images. But now we were living with the aftermath...and we had two little humans to love.

"Can we..." I glanced at Ryth and she gently nodded. "Can we see her?"

I waited for what felt like an eternity until he answered. "Yes, she's been asking for you...both of you."

Ryth's eyes widened, then she glanced at Nick and their son asleep in his arms.

"Go." He urged. "Go see your sister."

I stepped forward, leaving Riven and the others behind, meeting Ryth as London turned and headed back down the hall. I couldn't walk fast enough, reaching out for my sister's hand. My heart sped the moment our hands connected. This was the moment I'd wanted my entire life. This connection. This...*love*.

London stopped at a closed door and gently knocked. It opened almost instantly and DeLuca was standing there. He smiled at me, then Ryth as he stepped out. "I'll leave all of you for a moment, let you have some space."

I didn't even see him leave, all I wanted was my sister. I stepped inside and glanced at the others and the baby in Colt's arms before I turned my focus to my sister.

"Baby." I moved closer.

Her eyes were red. I could see she'd been crying.

"Helene." She burst into tears again, holding out her arms. "Ryth."

We rushed forward and I rounded the bed, grabbing her in my arms on one side as did Ryth on the other.

"Fuck, you scared the shit out of me." I croaked.

"And me."

I pulled back, looked into her eyes and swiped away her tears. "Are you okay...really okay?"

She gave a nod. "Yes, I will be at least."

"Fuck, I was scared." I hugged her again. "So fucking scared."

Her thick, heavy sobs filled my ears. "I was too, but it's over, right? Please, tell me it's over."

I bowed my head, feeling her body shake and quiver. "It's over." I whispered, watching Carven and Colt tear Haelstrom Hale apart in my mind. "It's all over."

She clung to us. "Thank God."

She'd never know the things they did for her. The *sheer* animal brutality those two men had been pushed to. I hoped to God she never did. I lifted my head and found Colt across the room, cradling his son in his arms, and a shiver of fear coursed through me.

"I need to see these babies." I croaked. "After all, I am their aunt."

"Me too." Ryth leaned forward, kissed Vivienne on the cheek and straightened. "Me too. I cannot wait to show them so much love."

I rounded the bottom of the bed and moved to London first, with his daughter in his arms. We all knew who the fathers were and the moment I saw her, I knew they were one hundred percent true. Big dark eyes stared back at me as she pursed her lips. She looked just like London.

I touched her cheek, then met his stare. "She's perfect."

He gave a careful smile. "They both are."

While I left Ryth to fuss over Vivienne's daughter, I moved to her son, finding him in Colt's protective arms. "Can I...?"

He didn't want to, that was easy to see. But he did, holding out his son without saying a word.

I looked down at the dressings taped across his little face and my heart went out for him. "Oh, fuck..."

Vivienne pushed herself upwards. "The knife was meant for his sister...and me. But he pushed her aside and he took the blow himself."

My breaths froze as my heart boomed. *He took the blow? As in...the knife.* "Oh, Jesus." I looked down into those big blue eyes and saw...*love*.

Ryth neared, touching his cheek. "May I have a hold?"

I looked down. "Of course." Then I gently handed him over.

We loved, cradling the babies and hugging our sister, staying until slowly the others came in. Riven, Hunter, Thomas, and Kane moved to my side. Ryth's stepbrothers stood at hers while London explained what had happened.

At first it was unbelievable, but then, what part of this whole thing wasn't.

Then Vivienne winced and DeLuca scanned the room. "I think that's it for today. Maybe pick this up tomorrow?"

I gave a nod, then kissed Vivienne and Ryth on the cheek. We all walked out of there, numb and empty as we climbed into the Explorer before we headed for home. Although, when we turned off the highway and through the gates, it didn't feel like home. Not anymore.

Still, we went inside but my steps were heavy as I walked up the stairs and into Riven's bedroom. I pulled off my clothes and left them to drop at my feet as Riven came closer.

There were no words as he undressed and headed into the bathroom. Hot water spray filled the room with steam. I stepped in, wrapped my arms around him and rested my head on his chest.

"It's done, Trouble," He murmured. "It's done."

Hard shudders tore through me. I gave in, letting all the emotions flow through me. I cried, then sobbed, letting him wash me until I was numb and empty. When I stepped out into the bedroom, they were waiting for me, naked, with wet hair and towels around their waists.

"We just want to sleep," Hunter murmured. "Please."

I rounded the bed and slipped in, holding the sheets up for them to climb in. We slept that night huddled up together, and in the morning, we woke late, cracked open our eyes and reached for each other. Only Riven wasn't there, nor was Thomas.

The nightmare of the last few days lingered in the back of my mind, but I grounded myself in the moment, in the touch of Kane's hands and the roughness of Hunter's beard. Thomas stepped in and watched from the doorway as Kane gripped my thighs, opened my legs, and positioned me with my back against his chest.

I held his brother's gaze as Kane pushed inside and slowly filled me. Lazy thrusts made me more awake. My body responded, warming and softening, leaving me to grip his thighs. Still, Thomas never moved, his gaze fixed on mine.

"Christ, you feel so goddamn good." Kane grunted, thrusting harder.

I bit my lip, a rush of need slamming into me. They were the only thing I wanted to feel now. Nor terror, not pain...not hopelessness or rage, just them. As Kane unleashed a low, guttural grunt and spilled his warmth inside me, Hunter's hand found mine, lifted it to his lips, and kissed me.

Kane's heavy breaths spilled warmth against my shoulder as Hunter rolled over, and climbed on top of me. The movement slipped Kane free as Hunter's big hands gripped my hips. Those dark, haunted eyes consumed me as he pushed inside.

I reached up, holding his face. He was my protector, my savior, my man in the mask. "I love you," I whispered as he slowly pushed all the way inside. My eyes fluttered with the sensation, deepening my tone to a moan. "God, I love you."

"I love you, Helene." He lowered his body, his arms a cage around me as his hands clasped mine. "I love you so goddamn much."

That rush pushed to the surface, making me open my legs wider, hungry for him. I bit my lip as my body quivered, clenching tight as he slammed home. I gave myself to him, bucking my hips upwards as I cried out. "Harder."

He obliged, unleashing powerful thrusts until my body stilled and *throbbed*. White sparks collided behind my eyes as Hunter gave one last grunt and stilled deep inside me.

"Jesus...*fucking Christ, you feel good.*" Hunter's heavy breaths were a blast against my ear, sending shivers along my neck.

The bed dipped hard as he slowly slid down to collapse beside me, but this man mountain wasn't done. Because now, he wanted to snuggle. The weight of his arm dropped around me, dragging my back against his chest.

"Fuck, I need coffee," Kane murmured as he rolled from the bed, grabbed a pair of boxers, and pulled them on. Thomas was gone from the doorway, but from the kitchen the delicious smell of coffee and pancakes rose.

"Oh," I moaned, my belly coming instantly alive.

One deep chuckle and Hunter pulled his arm away. "Go," He murmured, closing his eyes once more. "Save me some, at least."

For the first time in a long time, I smiled, feeling that fragile feeling of happiness. I moved slow, rolling to the side as Kane left the room. I grabbed someone's shirt, I think it was Riven's, and pulled it on before I headed for the bathroom, used the toilet, and tugged on clean panties.

The smell was intoxicating, drawing me to the kitchen where fresh coffee and Riven's delicious pancakes waited. He turned around as I neared and slid a fresh stack of fluffy deliciousness onto a plate next to a steaming cup of brew.

"You know, I could get used to this." I said and yawned.

Those dark eyes were fixed on mine. "Good. My plan is to feed you enough so you'll never think about wanting anything else."

I smiled as I rounded the counter and slid my arms around him. "I missed you this morning."

There was a quirk in the corner of his mouth. "I'm sure my brothers kept you busy enough."

I scowled. "That's not the point."

"No." He leaned closer. "It *isn't.*"

His kiss was sweet and soft, unlike the man. There was nothing sweet about Riven, not at first. But now...now, as he wrapped his arms around me and pulled me close, there was potential.

The sound of chatter pushed in, some kind of interview.

"Did you see this?" Kane broke into our moment.

But as Riven broke the kiss and lifted his head, I realised it didn't matter.

From now on, our lives would be these moments. We were free...we were finally free. I turned my head, finding Kane staring at his cell. "They're calling yesterday a rival motorcycle gang attack."

I pushed away from Riven and reached for my coffee. "Of course they are, how else can they explain what really happened?"

"They can't," Riven answered. "And so it gets chalked up to this and is swept under the rug."

I sipped the slightly bitter brew and closed my eyes as I swallowed. Flashes of terror pushed in. Death waited for us... but it didn't come, not yet. "It doesn't matter." I shook my head. "Not anymore."

"No." Riven wrapped his arms around me from behind. "Not anymore."

But that desperate need to push it aside didn't arise like it should've. Not that day or the few days that followed. As hard as we tried to lose ourselves in each other, the weight of responsibility weighed us down.

We slept.

We fucked.

We fucked a lot.

And on the fifth day after the attack, I woke to a message on my cell.

Ryth: Vivienne's out and wants to see us.

Finally. I smiled and rolled over, to find Riven watching me. "She's out." I almost felt giddy with relief. "And she wants to see us."

"Then, my beautiful seductress, what are you waiting for?"

Nothing. I was waiting for nothing. I jumped up, raced for the bathroom, and showered. Murmurs reached me as I washed and rinsed. Riven walked in naked and stepped into the shower behind me. I kissed him, but left him to shower. By the time I stepped out, the others were ready, dressed in neat casual, even

Hunter wore an open-collared shirt and black trousers that pulled taut against his massive thighs.

"You look incredible." I smiled at them. "So incredible."

I pulled on a dress, something I hadn't worn since the day I'd stepped in front of Riven's car. They all stared, swallowing hard, as I climbed into Explorer and we headed for the city.

THE HEAVY STEEL gates of the Salvatore mansion opened, allowing us to drive inside. I stiffened at the sight of the house and the armed guards patrolling the perimeter, not having expected to be back here. But while Vivienne and London were getting their new house on the upper east side of the city set up, we were all meeting here.

It wasn't quite a baby shower.

Nor was it a coming home.

It was a celebration of life, of living and surviving, of forging new paths, I guess. But as I turned to grab the big basket that Thomas handed me, I realized that for me, it was about family and friends, and putting the past behind us.

"You ready for this?" Riven asked as Hunter pulled up and switched off the ignition, leaving us to climb out together.

I took a breath and lifted my gaze to the front door as the Salvatore guard opened it, waiting for us to step through. "More than ready."

Laughter spilled out before we even reached the first step and my God, that sound was alien and perfect all at once. The insistent wail of a baby followed, making me quicken my steps and rush through the door. They were all there, all of them. Tobias, Nick, and Caleb, and little Alias Banks in my sister's arms, then Vivienne. My beautiful, defiant Vivienne.

I handed Riven the basket, shoving it against his chest before I lunged and rushed forward as she slowly pushed up from the sofa and stepped toward me.

"Hel," she called.

I wrapped my arms around her and hugged her tight. "Fuck, it's good to see you."

She gripped me fiercely, holding on. "It's good to see you too."

I couldn't help it, tears welled in my eyes and slipped down my cheeks. I pulled away and looked into her eyes. "Are you okay?"

She looked tired and weak. Underneath that was a flicker of fear. One I saw in my own reflection.

"I will be," she answered.

That was the best answer we could give. *We will be.* I smiled and turned to London and Colt, each of them holding a baby. "Right." I smiled, swiping away the tears. "Let's see these kids."

If I said I didn't feel a pang of regret from not having my own as I held them, I'd be lying. But this life, this kind of love and devotion wasn't meant for me. But that didn't mean I wouldn't be the most kickass aunt there was.

I held each of them, pulled them close, and inhaled their perfect scent before kissing their foreheads and handed them back. Alias was next, as I pulled Ryth against me, kissing her cheek. "Love you, little sister."

"We love you," she answered.

"Very...very much." Vivienne added, coming closer.

I fucking sobbed, cried and laughed, hugging them hard like I couldn't get enough of their embraces. How the three of us had come to stand there like this, I'd never know. But we did, and for that I was so very grateful.

We stayed for hours, laughed and drank, eating from platters until the babies went down for naps. Then there was just silence. It wasn't awkward at all. Just comforting as everyone settled down. Finley and Anna held hands at the end of the table. London had his arm around Vivienne's shoulders, rubbing the knots from the base of her neck. Ryth sat on Nick's lap, with Tobias and Caleb on each side of them.

I turned to Riven, his fingers entwined with mine as Kane rested his hand on my thigh. Hunter stood at the back of the room, his eyes twinkling, fixed on me. Thomas was somewhere, walking, praying, finding his own way to salvation.

This was home.

More home than any house in the mountains or in the city.

People. *My people.*

They were home.

When the sun dipped and the day bordered on dusk, we rose, weary and sated. Then we kissed and hugged, said our goodbyes, and climbed back into the cars. Only we didn't head for the mountain. Instead, we made for Riven's house, climbing out of the Explorer as Hunter parked in the garage.

Bang.

The car door slammed shut, echoing in the space. I flinched at the sound, remembering the crack of gunfire. The thud of steps followed me until a nagging feeling made me stop and turn around. Riven was first inside, making his way through the house with Hunter behind him, leaving Kane and Thomas behind me.

But there was no Thomas.

"What is it?" Kane turned around.

"I'm not sure." I left him there and headed back to the garage, to finds Thomas standing in the open garage door staring out at the street.

"Thom?" I called. He didn't turn around, just stared at the shadows at the end of the drive with his fists clenched at his side. "What is it?"

He shook his head, then turned to me, that pained stare full of torment. "Nothing." He forced a smile, caressing my cheek. "Nothing for you to worry about, at least."

But I did worry, even when he took my hand, pressed the button, and waited for the door to close. I worried a great deal. I guess I always would.

FORTY-ONE

Thomas

SHE DIDN'T SEE HIM.

Not the demon who'd followed us home, then hid in the shadows parked in his car at the corner of the street. I wanted it to stay like that. I'd give *anything* for it to stay like that. God knows she deserved some peace.

"Thom? What is it?"

I forced a smile, unclenching my jaw and took her hand. "Nothing." I answered. "Nothing at all."

I pressed the button and waited for the door to close, making sure the demon stayed outside as I led her deeper into the kitchen. I pretended. I was getting good at that, pretending when it mattered most.

Contentment made her sleepy. She'd had her fill of champagne and food, and was now content to rest.

"You go." I urged her, nodding to Kane, who yawned for the fourth time in as many minutes. "I'll be just a minute."

"You sure?" She murmured.

I brushed her cheek and leaned down, kissing her softly. "Positive."

She didn't fully believe me. Still, she nodded and left. I waited for a moment, making sure she was gone before I reached for my cell and pressed the number, waiting for it to be answered.

I didn't have to wait long.

"Priest," Caleb murmured as I went to the front door of the house and stepped outside.

"We have a problem."

"What kind of problem?"

"An FBI kind." I closed the door gently behind me, making sure the door locked.

"At your house?"

"Riven's one in the city."

"Jesus Christ. We knew this might happen."

My stomach sank as I stayed behind the towering shrub, my focus fixed on the gleam of light bouncing off the car window in the distance. "Yes, we did."

"I'll call Colt and be right there...and Priest...don't do anything stupid."

"I won't," I answered, fighting every instinct I had in me.

I hung up the call, watching the sonofabitch who'd put a gun to my head sit across the road from where my family slept. I knew he was there. I'd seen him before at the mountain, perched high up, had followed his car as it slowed outside our drive.

They wouldn't leave us alone. Even now in the wake of Hale's real death and the destruction of The Order. Still, he kept coming. Protecting a ghost...or was he? That nagging thought filled my head. Because why else was he here?

Beep.

I looked down to my cell.

Caleb: Two streets north.

I stepped out, pushed my hands into my pockets and hunched over, keeping to the shadows. Agent Bremmer never noticed me, not when I slipped around the rear of his car and headed north. But I noticed him, hunched down behind the wheel.

Why was he here?

What was he planning?

Headlights flashed once in the dark up ahead. I quickened my steps toward the four-wheel drive and climbed into the back.

"We've done some digging and found his address." Caleb said from behind the wheel.

"Good." I tugged my belt low. "I think it's time we paid him a visit."

The engine started, we turned hard without the headlights on, worked our way around him, then headed to a quiet part of the city where we slowed down outside a lowset dark brick house. No car was in the driveway. No evidence anyone else lived there at all.

"Single from what we found. Had a girlfriend but she left him six months ago. Now he lives and breathes the badge." Caleb pulled the car in and parked further down the street.

"A version of it at least," I added. "One that protects the corrupt."

Caleb lifted his gaze to the rear-view mirror. "Are you ready to hunt now, Priest?"

Those words haunted me.

"Yes." I pushed open the door. "I am now."

Colt handed me a gun. Any other time, I might've recoiled from the weapon. But not anymore. I took it and slipped it inside the waistband of my jeans at the small of my back. Together we headed for the FBI agent's house. Colt picked the lock, getting us inside in minutes. I readied myself for a dog, but it looked like the agent didn't even have that.

His house was sparse. The study and bedroom were the only rooms which looked lived in. Microwavable meals in the freezer, the cupboard bare except for coffee and creamer. This man was a wasted life, one which needed an ending.

"Over here," Caleb called softly.

Both of us headed over, stood in front of the makeshift desk in the living room, and stared at the transcript sitting in front of the printer.

"They're names," Caleb said, pulling sheet after sheet forward. "And instructions. These are men he's been paid to protect. Men *Hale* paid him to protect."

"Jesus fucking Christ." Colt glanced at me.

He rarely spoke, but when he did, it was exactly what I was thinking. We stood there for ages, pulling apart all the documents, gathering what information we could until headlights cut through the window, blinding us for a moment before they were gone.

A car engine died and the *thud* of a door followed.

"Grab that chair," Caleb murmured. "Colt, you know what to do."

But the Son was already moving, cutting across the door to stand at the side as the jingle of keys came. Bremmer never stood a chance as he opened the door and stepped inside. Colt moved fast, wrapped his thick arm around his neck, and squeezed.

Seconds was all it took.

Seconds for the keys to fall and hit the floor.

Seconds for him to be out cold.

Colt dragged him to the chair, leaving Caleb to search his pockets and grab a set of cuffs he used to secure the agent's wrists behind the chair. Now all we had to do was wait for him to wake. He slowly opened his eyes, his head rolling to the back until Caleb cleared his throat.

"Who's there?" Bremmer snapped his head upwards, seeking us in the dark.

Caleb stepped closer. "The names beside your printer. Why do you have those?"

"Who the fuck are you?"

"It doesn't matter. The names...why do you have them?"

He scowled. "Do you know who I am? What kind of trouble you're in just by breaking into my goddamn home?"

"The kind of trouble that won't see the light of day if you're dead." I said slowly, stepping forward. "Will it, Bremmer?"

"The Priest?" He stared at me. "You? You're behind this?"

I reached around and pulled the gun free. "Are they Hale's partners? Men who are involved with The Order? Is that your job now? Covering the tracks and hiding men who buy and abuse those women?"

"Fuck you."

Fuck me?

I stilled, rage burning in the pit of my belly. Flashes of that room at the rectory rose to the surface. Blood...so much blood.

Are you ready to hunt now, Priest?

The moment those words filled me, I lunged, grabbed his shirt, and shoved him backwards so hard the chair rocked on two legs. "I don't think you understand who you're dealing with here." His eyes widened as the surge of rage fought against the need to keep the bastard alive.

"You kill me and the entire FBI will be on your doorstep."

"Not if they don't find the body." I snarled. "Besides, this whole fucking place stinks of corruption. I think the FBI will be quick to close this as a missing person. Look how fast they shut down the attack at the warehouse. Was that you? It reeks like you."

He shook his head.

"Names," Caleb prodded. "You lie and we'll find out."

"They'll kill me."

I dragged him closer. "How does it feel to have a gun pressed against your head?"

His shook his, his eyes wide. There was no Hale now. No big names to keep him safe. I pulled backwards, leaving his chair to drop back to the ground.

"Here is how this is going to go." Caleb stepped closer. "You will provide us with the names and details of the men you're paid to keep clean. At any time we feel you've betrayed us, you're a dead man. Nod, so we know you've heard us."

His lips curled into a sneer. Hate raged in his eyes.

I released my hold and stepped backwards.

"Nod." Colt growled a deep, animalistic rattle in the back of his throat.

A sound that'd terrify anyone.

Bremmer gave a slow nod.

"Good," Caleb turned. "We'll be in touch, Agent Bremmer. Oh, and one more thing." He stopped. "We so much as feel you're following us again, and we'll take it as a direct attack. Do you understand what I'm saying?"

"Yeah."

"Good," Caleb answered. "Gentlemen."

The agent's gaze never moved from me. The heat stayed with me as I followed Colt and Caleb back out of the house and headed for the car. Bremmer would give us names, that was for certain. How long he stayed alive to do that was a whole other flip of the coin.

Until then we would hunt.

And we would kill.

Destroying The Order one sick motherfucker at a time.

"You good, Priest?" Caleb asked as we climbed in.

"Yeah," I answered. "I think I am."

Now...we hunt.

FORTY-TWO

Ryth

Sunlight washed across my face as I stepped out of the Mustang. Nick closed the door, then rounded the front, holding out his hand. "You ready for this, Princess?"

Ready? No, not really.

But it still needed to be done. I gave a nod and lifted the bunch of flowers in my hand. Yellow sunflowers and red roses with faint sprays of baby breath. It was a cheerful array, conveying a feeling I wasn't in tune with.

"I'm right here." His big hand clenched around mine, giving me all the strength I needed.

He took the first step and I followed. My heels sank in the soft grass, forcing me up to my toes as we crossed the front of the grounds. A fresh clump of dirt squashed under my step and the heady smell of the earth filled my nose. The sunlight wasn't warm anymore, it wasn't beautiful or calming. It was harsh and hollow and cruel.

Yes. That's what it was...cruel.

I glanced at the rows of tombstones, then the fresh dirt spread out on top.

"Row two fifteen, it's this one here."

I forced a smile and gave a nod. But inside I was pulling away, retreating into the memory of Alias this morning. He was smiling now, kicking his little legs in the warm bath, watching everything around him. A pure joy to be around. My heart gave a flutter when I thought about him, which was exactly what I needed.

"There he is."

I lifted my gaze and sunlight caught my eye, blinding me for a second before it passed and I stepped closer. Fresh earth and a clean headstone.

Weyland King...

My father.

I stopped at the base of the grave. My heart boomed, emotions a whirlwind inside me.

Please, Ryth. Please take it.

For a split second, I was back there in that room, in the seconds before the *crack* of the gunshot sounded. My hand clenched around the base of the flowers, just like it had around the USB he'd given me. A USB that was worth dying for. One I'd given to the best person to not only investigate, but keep its secrets safe. Only my father was already dying at that time, wasn't he? I just didn't know it yet.

He was dying, and instead of spending his last few months with us, he'd chosen to spend them with Haelstrom Hale.

"You okay, Princess?"

I gave a nod, my emotions conflicted. "Is it strange to love him and hate him all at the same time?"

"Strange? No, baby. It's not strange. Your father was a deeply complicated man. One who made his own decisions in life without thinking about the consequences or how they might impact on those he loved. I guess in a way, you have to just be okay with it being fucked, that's all. It's all fucked."

It was all fucked.

I hated it, but that didn't change the outcome. He was gone. Hale was gone. Now, it was time to move on with our lives however we could. "Goodbye, Dad, I hope you find peace where you are now."

Nick wrapped his arm around my shoulders as I pulled one red rose free from the bouquet and stepped forward. "Goodbye, Dad." I said and laid the rose at the base of his tombstone.

Nick stepped away and I followed, heading further along the rows until we came to another fresh grave. There were too many for us to count. This war was relentless.

I left my father's grave behind, heading for the one we'd come to see, and stopped at Benjamin Rossi's stone. This man had been more of a father than my own. He'd protected and fought for us. Then he'd died for us, doing all the things a father should have. A lump rose in the back of my throat, hard and throbbing, filling me with an ache I couldn't swallow.

I bent, placing the flowers down. "Thank you, Ben, for everything."

Nick stayed quiet and unmoving, but I could tell he hurt for this man. We all did. When I turned around and reached for his hand, there were tears in his eyes.

"Now, how about that chocolate shake?" His voice was thick and husky.

"I don't really know. I just want..." I met his stare. "You."

A nod and we left the cemetery, heading toward our old house. Nostalgia hit me as we drove familiar streets and finally turned, creeping past our old house until we turned right. The sight of our old park hit me hard. My chest ached at the sight as he pulled the Mustang in and parked.

"Do you think you'll ever sell the house?"

"Do you want me to?" He glanced my way. "Because if you do..."

"No." I shook my head, shifting in the seat. So much had changed now and still...nothing really had. We were together and now finally we were safe. As much as I wanted to move on from the painful memories of my father, there were just some things I didn't want to leave behind. Including the memory of when we first met. "No, I don't want to."

"Then I won't. Whatever you want, Princess. You know that."

I did. I knew that well. I stabbed the button to release my belt and turned in my seat, climbing over the gearstick. "And what if I want a trip down memory lane?"

His chuckle was instant as he grabbed me and pulled me close. "I thought you'd never ask."

I kissed him and grazed my fingers along his stubble before I pulled away, easing back to my seat. Those dark eyes glinted when they looked at me, watching me slowly pull the bottom of my sundress higher.

"Jesus fucking Christ, little sister. You're gonna make me come all over myself like a goddamn teenager again, aren't you?"

My lips curled as I eased my thighs apart, my finger sliding under the elastic of my sheer lace panties. "Only if you behave."

A low, guttural sound erupted just before he lunged. But I knew him now. I knew him better than anyone would. My hand instantly went for the door handle before I yanked hard and pushed out of the car, tore across the grass ahead, and raced for the trees.

"Goddamnit, Ryth!" He roared.

My pulse rocketed at the sound. Fists pumping, my legs stretched and drove my body toward the trees until I was snatched out of the air.

"You gonna make me run, Ryth?" He growled, turning me around until we both fell to the ground. "Goddamnit," He grunted.

He tried to be angry, but he wasn't, not when he pressed me back into the grass and leaned down. Hard breaths punctuated his words. "I'm always chasing after you, always..."

"Desperate for me," I answered for him.

There was a tiny scowl, then his mouth collided with mine, kissing me so deep it stole my mind. His hard body pushed, slowly rubbing, his hips grinding until I felt the hard outline of his cock before he pulled away.

"You want to fuck me, Nick?"

"Princess, I *always* want to fuck you," he growled. "I never wanted anything more."

He lowered his head and his kiss was softer now, turning from the man who wanted inside me to the man who wanted to take his time. Kissing, licking, until I was a quivering wet mess under him.

"I'm going to take you home and you're going to keep that goddamn dress on while you ride me." He groaned. "What do you think about that?"

Think about it?

It's all I thought about.

Him, Tobias, and Caleb.

My family.

Forever.

"Then do it," I murmured. "And if you come nice and deep inside me, we might make a sister for our son."

His eyes widened. "You want that, baby?"

I reached up, caressed his face, and stared deep into his eyes. "Yes, Nick. I want that."

"We have to be careful now." He searched my stare. "It's not like it was before, but we still have to be safe. The new house... the new...opportunities."

The desire gave way to a flicker of fear. I knew what opportunities he was talking about. Ones that were born from loyalty and this time they weren't just loyal to me...now we were loyal to the Rossis.

"Take me home, Nick. Let's love each other as hard as we can until the end."

"Until the end, baby," He murmured, kissing me one last time before he slowly rose and pulled me up with him.

Together we went home. Our new home. One that filled me with fear and love, all at the same time.

FORTY-THREE

Tobias

THE SOUND OF THE MUSTANG'S GROWL GREW CLOSER, pulling me away from the conversation in front of me.

"T," Laz muttered. "Are you with me, brother?"

I jerked my gaze to his, finding pain in his blue eyes. "All the way."

"Because I need you." He stepped closer.

Freddy stood at the back of the room next to Caleb. On the wall, movement came on the black and white monitor. Tiny arms and legs kicked, pushing the blanket from his body for the tenth time. My son, Alias Banks, occupied as much of my attention as his mom did.

"I know." I turned back to my best friend, my brother-in-arms. The man I'd die to protect...and who'd die for me. "As we need you."

Car doors slammed closed outside. My body came alive just with the thought of her, her sad eyes and perfect lips. Christ, those sundresses she'd been wearing lately sent me wild. I wanted under them, my hands sliding up her thighs and between her legs.

"Tobias."

I pulled my attention back to the head of the Stidda Mafia in front of me, knowing full well if I was any other male, I'd have been shot in the head by now. Fuck, that woman was going to get me into trouble...even deeper than I was in now.

"You take out the guards. I need Nick on the wheel," Laz urged.

"That wasn't the deal." I shook my head. "You get me...and only me."

But this Laz shook his head. *This* Laz demanded more. No, he demanded *everything.*

"I need you beside me, to be my right-hand man taking over the company. I need you hungry, T. I need you so fucking hungry even the Salvatores are scared."

"They are already." My voice deepened as savage rage rippled inside me. I lifted my gaze to his, finding that same spark of anger. "Everyone is."

Laz stepped closer as her footsteps rang out from the foyer and headed along the hall toward me. This was the price we paid to keep her safe—the monitor hovered in the corner of my eye— the price *I* paid to keep everyone safe. "I can drive the cars, Laz."

He shook his head as she stepped into the room, and it took all my fucking willpower not to go to her.

"With the Banks brothers at my side, we'll be unstoppable. Not only will we end this fucking Order, we'll make sure that no one touches us again. This is what I need, Nick." He glanced at my brother as he followed her inside.

His hair was dishevelled and there was a leaf stuck to Ryth's dress. Looks like they'd had fun. A little *too much fun.*

"Tobias," Ryth murmured my name before she glanced at Laz. "What's going on?"

Laz shook his head, but he didn't look at her. He knew exactly what he was asking, because he asked the same thing of himself.

"You get me, Laz. That was the deal. You get me because if anything happened, if this all went wrong..." *She'd still have protection.*

"We need Nick," Laz pushed. "He's the best wheelman I know. He's faster, more agile. Hell, he can drive almost anything."

"I can," Nick answered. "And yet you're talking about me like I'm not in the room."

"The intel is solid," Laz said. "We know which gang worked for Hale, so we take them out. The only MC gangs that will be left in the city will be the ones loyal to *us.*"

"Can you be sure about that?" Nick stepped forward, cutting across the room to stand next to me. "Sure enough to risk our lives?"

I resisted the urge to look at Ryth, knowing she must be recoiling inside. That USB her father gave her was more than just a who's who in the depraved world of The Order. It also had details in Lazarus' world that couldn't be ignored. A world that was now becoming ours.

"Aldolfo Martinez is a goddamn snake. His MC is done and his time is done. The moment he gave his allegiance to Hale was the day he sealed his fate. If you think I'm going to mourn his loss, you're very much mistaken."

"Mourn?" I murmured. "No. But we cut off one head and three more fill its place. We need to make sure who they are and how bad they want retribution."

"We make it so they don't come looking. We make it so they don't think about retribution at *all*. We kill the fuckers. Those... slimy fucks who think riding their goddamn bikes and spewing their shit is going to save them. Tonight, they'll find out no one will save them. We burn their clubhouse to the ground...with them inside."

"So why do you need me?" Nick asked.

"It's a three-pronged attack. You take out the Master of Arms. We take the clubhouse. Freddy and Alvarez Cross and his brothers wait in the wings to exterminate. We get this done and we make a statement."

"That's a pretty clear statement," Nick murmured.

"Anyone who doesn't stand with us is against us," Laz ended. "The only question now, *brothers*, is...are *you* with me?"

"NICK, how are you doing? Are you in position?"

"Five more seconds." Nick's voice barely smothered the growl of his untraceable Mustang. "I have the bastard in my sights."

We sat in a four-wheel drive in a parking lot across from the LionsDenz MC Club under a shroud of darkness. It was late... or early, depending on how you looked at it. I just wanted this to be done, so I could be home. "You tell me who I need to kill and they're as good as dead."

The Mustang's engine roared in the background of the call. If we thought this was going to be easy, it wasn't. The Master of Arms of the LionsDenz wasn't just a nobody. He was the son of Marcus Diaz, head of the small but brutal Mafia seat in the south.

Marcus had a reputation of cutting off hands when it came to those who took from him, running a gambling operation that was worth hundreds of millions. He was mostly quiet and kept to himself. But after tonight, that was about to change.

I yanked open the car door and climbed out.

"One minute." Nick grunted. I could hear the squeak of the window as he rolled it down.

To make a hit out in the open was brazen as fuck, but for who it was...it was goddamn suicidal.

"Mask," I snarled.

"Already down, brother."

I could hear it as I made for the edge of the building, the rush of the air, the muffled tone. I tucked the gun in the waistband of my jeans and made for the rear of the building. The music was still blaring, the fight that broke out when we got there was all over. Pity. I would've enjoyed the look on their faces when I walked in, took aim, and fired.

The screech of the tires came from my cell, I turned the volume down, listening to the roar of the wind before *CRACK! CRACKCRACKCRACK!*

My brother's hard breaths filled the speaker. "It's done," he muttered. "Jesus fucking Christ, it's done."

They were the only words I needed. "Talk soon, brother," I said quietly, then pressed the button and ended the call.

Get it done.

Just do what it takes and get it done.

In my head I saw the back of Ben's head...bloodied, *and brain fucking exploded.*

I grabbed the fence at the rear of the compound and lifted myself higher, climbing fast until I reached the razor wire, then grabbed the cutters in my pocket. Two seconds. I watched the rear door of the club, hating it took me that long.

Snip.

I was over, heaving my legs until momentum took me and I hit the ground with a *thud.* My steps were fast and quiet as I pulled the gun free and opened the rear door. I was lead on this but not because I had something to prove, because Laz and Freddy wanted them running, right before we killed them all.

Cheers and laughter filled the air. I glanced right and left, leaving the kitchen alone to head for the bedrooms. Aldolfo Martinez was a fat, ugly fuck. One who liked them young...*very goddamn young.* Young enough to be a present from Hale himself, fresh from The Order.

There were four doors, three along the hall on the right, and one at the end that was cracked open. Moans came from that slip of darkness...and they didn't sound pleasurable in the least.

"Suck...*it.*" Came the snarl.

A cry followed, soft, short, coming from someone who knew crying got you nowhere. I grabbed the handle, my focus on the thud of steps deeper in the club heading away as I pushed the door open and stepped inside.

The sick fuck was on the edge of the bed, naked, with his gut almost on his thighs. He had a fistful of her hair, shaking it until he made her dance. Christ, there were bruises all over her. Big, thick ones...the size of a goddamn fist.

All I saw was Ryth.

Ryth, bruised and beaten.

Ryth naked like they wanted.

"She can't suck what she can't find you fat, ugly, fuck," I muttered, as I lifted the gun and fired.

CRACK!

His head snapped backwards before the rest of him fell. I swung around as she fell, crumpled into a ball, and curled herself tight. "You might want to get yourself out of here. This place is about to go up in flames."

But she didn't move. Not even when I headed for the door. I stopped in the doorway and looked back. "Did you hear me?"

She never moved, just curled her knees tighter to her chest.

"Fuck." I spun around, searching the room...there was nothing...*nothing.*

Until I lunged for the bed, grabbed that ugly ass motherfucker, and heaved him upwards. The thud of boots sounded. Faint cries of *"turn the music down! I heard a gunshot."* followed.

I pushed and heaved, wrenching my focus to her dark eyes. "You want to live? *Then...help...me."*

That seemed to work, she slowly shoved upwards as I rolled Adolfo onto his front and kept pushing. She grabbed him from the other side, yanking him toward her until he fell from the bed and hit the floor. One yank and I ripped the sheet free. "Put that on."

It was bloodstained and filthy, but she wrapped it around herself as someone called out. *"Alfie! You okay in there?"*

I moved fast, yanked open the door, and lifted the gun at the same time. "Just fucking peachy I'd say."

Crack.

Crack!

CRACK!

Screams erupted as they went down. One asshole charged me, grabbed me around the waist, and drove me against the wall. All that did was trigger something dangerous inside me, something I tried to hide from the world...

The real me.

I drove my fist upwards and connected with his jaw. *Crunch.* His head snapped backwards, and I was moving, firing the gun, feeling the rush as it kicked in my hand. I lost count of how many I killed...I lost count of it all. They ran like I knew they would, hurling themselves out of the front of the building where Laz and Freddy waited.

She tore past me, the bloodied sheet flapping wildly as she tripped and fell.

"*Stop!*" I lunged and grabbed her, my fingers almost slipping from her arm as I lifted her from the floor and turned away. "You don't want to go out there."

Crack, crack, crack, crackcrackcrack. Gunfire followed. The young woman kicked and bucked, fighting me as I turned around and grabbed a bottle of Scotch on the counter, lifted it high, and slammed it down.

Crash.

I found another.

And another, until the floor glistened with the fluid before I reached into my pocket...pulled out a lighter, and flicked it. Then she stopped fighting, turning her tear-filled eyes toward mine.

"For Ben." I murmured and tossed it high, until it landed on its side.

The bar erupted in a *whoosh.* But I was already moving, heading out the back door...desperate to be home.

The growl of the engine kicked and spluttered. Nick was already waiting, with the chain on the gate now cut.

"Who's this?" He jerked his gaze her way.

She gripped my waist. "Have no fucking idea."

"She a whore?"

"No," she whispered as I half-carried her through the gate. "I'm not a whore...I'm a Daughter."

He stared at her as the sound of shattering glass came from the clubhouse behind us. His eyes widened. "What the fuck are we going to do with a Daughter?"

The only thing we could.

"We call London," I answered and hurried her toward the car. "He'll know exactly what to do."

FORTY-FOUR

Vivienne

"I DON'T KNOW WHAT TO DO." LONDON STARED AT THE young woman wrapped in a bloody sheet in Tobais' arms.

"She's a Daughter, isn't she?" Tobias muttered desperately. "So," he lifted her like she was nothing, pushing her into London's chest. "She's all yours."

"She's not a goddamn sack of potatoes, for Christ's sake," I snapped, stepping close to brush her filthy hair from her face. "She's a person."

"Look, we just can't..." Tobias licked his lips.

"Colt." I called and glanced over my shoulder. "Can you please take her inside?"

One nod and my beautiful lover moved forward, took her from Tobias, and carried her inside.

"Really, you two ought to be ashamed of yourselves." I tutted as I turned around.

"What the hell did I do?" London muttered and pointed to Tobias. "He's the one dropping and running."

I just shook my head and slowly made my way inside, heading to the kitchen.

"Drink," Colt's careful command rang out. "You're dehydrated."

I stepped inside and rounded the counter. "Sweetheart, my name is Vivienne. This is Colt. We're going to take care of you, okay?"

She was so small, naked, filthy. Her hair was matted and oily. God only knew what kind of injuries she had. We'd found one more like her. A Daughter from The Order sold to a cruel sonofabitch that was killed in the attack at the warehouse. But there was no doubt we'd find more of them.

I gently brushed her hair from her face, but stopped when she flinched. My heart hurt as I watched her take the opened bottle of water from Colt and sip it, licking her cracked lips.

"We'll get you looked after, okay?" I lowered my hand. "I promise."

Fear shimmered in her big eyes. She drank, consuming the entire bottle.

"Do you need a doctor?" I asked carefully.

DeLuca was fast becoming someone we could trust entirely, responding to our calls no matter the time. Most of the time now, he came with his stepsister, leaving her to help out at the monstrous mansion located on the outskirts of the city we'd somehow acquired from one of London's friends.

It was a temporary fix to a growing issue. *Where the hell do we put them and what do we do with them?*

She shook her head. "No, no doctor."

"What's your name, honey?"

"Elena." She swiped the back of her hand across her mouth as the familiar thud of London's boots came from deeper in the house.

"Okay, Elena. I'm going to take you to a bathroom and get you some clean clothes while Colt here whips you up some eggs. Does that sound good?"

She nodded hard as her belly gave a howl. Jesus, she must be starving.

"Then we'll take you to a place where you can rest and recover."

She stiffened. "You're selling me."

"No." I moved closer, cupping her cheek and lifted her gaze to mine. "I want you to hear me. You'll *never* be sold again. Do you understand? Never again. That part of your life is over. There are others like you. Daughters like me and my sisters. Ones we rescued, just like you. When you've showered and had something to eat, we'll take you to them and get you settled. But know this, we're here to help you, to take care of you..." *until we can figure out what to do.*

"He's dead," she whispered. "The man who owned me. He's dead and I'm glad."

She was softening to us, not cowering like a beaten dog. She didn't even pull away when I wrapped my arms around her and pulled her close. She let herself be held and rested her head on my shoulder. I met Colt's hard stare and whispered. "Me too, sweetheart. Me...too."

I took her to the spare room we had set up and gathered some of the clothes we'd purchased for the others, then I found sweats and some jeans, as well as one of the packs Doc and his sister had brought us. It was small, but was filled with all the essentials as well as tampons and pads, band-aids and painkillers.

"Here." I placed the stack on the bathroom vanity. "There're fresh towels and plenty of hot water, so take all the time you need. I'll be out here if you need anything."

She gave a nod, but she was reeling. Her body was shaking so hard her teeth chattered.

"Everything is going to be okay now." I murmured. "Just you wait and see."

It was like a blow to my chest when I turned around, closed the door, and left her. I stood there, waiting until I heard the quiet, hard sobs, then I forced myself to leave, swiping away my own tears in the process.

The nursery was quiet and soft amber light spilled out from the cracked-open door. The door I'd closed barely an hour ago. I knew he was in there, watching over them like he always did. I pushed open the door and stepped inside, finding my protector standing over her crib.

I slid my hand in his, lowering my head to his chest as Colt slid his arm around me, pulling me tight against his side.

"She will never know that life," he said carefully, watching her open-mouthed sleeping. "I promise you now."

"I know."

He turned to me. "Her world will be sunshine and daffodils and eating ice cream in all the flavors. Her world will be the hard decisions between pink or purple, or royal blue, for that matter. She will stay awake wondering how butterflies are made...and she will never hear the name Haelstrom Hale in her entire life."

That ache in my chest grew bolder as I caressed his cheek and repeated. "I know."

SHE LOOKED up through the side windows at the looming moon hanging heavy in the sky. I think she was expecting betrayal, after all...that's all she'd had her entire life. But not this time. I glanced over my shoulder as she met my gaze. London flicked his eyes to the rear-view mirror and kept driving.

"There're more Daughters out here," I murmured. "They do all the cooking and the cleaning, but we have a team of men who patrol the grounds, just so you're aware. I don't want you to worry about them. They are loyal and trustworthy. They aren't going to approach you unless your life is in danger, okay? So you have nothing to worry about."

"Unless you call cleaning at three a.m. chaos," London muttered.

I cut him a glare.

"What?" He looked my way. "It's true, they clean at three a.m. What kind of person does that?"

One who's been controlled their entire life.

London slowed the four-wheel drive at the turn-off, stabbed the button, and rolled down the window, then waved at the guard sitting in his car hidden by the bank of trees. One flash of headlights from the guard acknowledged he knew we were coming.

We might've found them a temporary house to live in, we might've even supplied them with food and drink and all the entertainment we could. We might've even helped them feel safe, as safe as they'd allow themselves to feel. But the Daughters of The Order we'd rescued were far from healed.

A lot of them had suffered things beyond comprehension and if vacuuming carpets at three a.m. made them feel comforted in any kind of way, then I say let them vacuum.

Lights twinkled through the trees up ahead. Shadows cut across the drive, the flash of a gun and the careful pace told us instantly who it was. London braked, pulled up carefully, and there was Guild. His focus shifted to me and there was an instant smile. "Good to see you're up and about. As bossy as ever, I hear."

"A little *too* bossy," London muttered under his breath.

"Oh don't worry, Guild." I glared at London. "I won't be taking over from you."

"Good to hear it," he chuckled. "I doubt London could handle it if it was both of us." His attention shifted to the back seat. "Hi there, I'm Guild. We're going to get you settled right in. You're going to love it and I'm pretty sure some of the others have just started a movie and have cooked enough popcorn to put a movie theater to shame. I'll meet you up at the house."

London gave a nod as Guild turned and headed for the glaring bright lights of the beautiful and expensive mansion. The place had been empty when we'd first stepped in. Cold and empty and strange. Now, it was vibrant and full. London drove the Explorer toward the house, parking out front.

"This place is real?" The small voice came from the back.

"As real as you can get it." I yanked open the door and climbed out.

Guild was there in an instant, holding my hand, letting me lean on him. I'd be lost without the man...we all would.

"Here we are." London opened her door.

She climbed out, clutching the bag with clothes and essentials against her chest like a shield. A lot of them did that, refusing to let anything go until they felt safe. She would eventually.

The sound of a vacuum started upstairs, even though it was almost morning. London cut me a look that said 'I told you so.' One I ignored as we led her up the stairs, following the heady scent of freshly made popcorn.

Her steps were careful as she followed Guild, climbing the steps to the front door.

She'd make it here.

She'd find solace and hopefully peace.

In the meantime, we'd protect them and care for them as much as possible. Because it wasn't just those vile men from The Order we needed to worry about. It was the Sons. They were out there, hunting for them. It was only a matter of time before they found where they were and they'd come.

That thought chilled me to the bone.

She stopped at the front door, then looked over her shoulder to where I stood with London. Her mouth quivered giving us a sad, sorrowful smile.

"Thank you." She mouthed as Guild opened the door.

Laughter and voices spilled out. The sound made my chest swell with pride. They might have a long road ahead for healing...but at least now they'd found the path. One which would lead them on a journey of self-discovery.

"I wish there was more we could do." I murmured as Guild closed the door behind them. "We need to protect them somehow. We need to keep them safe."

"What else can we do?" He gave a chuckle. "It's not like we can marry them off."

My breath caught, and I slowly turned to him.

The smirk on London's lips fell away. "No." He shook his head. "Wildcat, *do not look at me with those eyes.*"

"Why not?" I whispered, my mind racing. "It's not like they'd be sold like they were at The Order. You have many powerful and rich friends. Men who could provide and protect."

He turned to me. "I have dangerous friends, Vivienne. You really want to subject those women to a life like that?"

"You once said yourself it takes a monster to know another. That you were that monster. Look how you fought for me...how you saved me."

"And almost cost you your goddamn life."

I moved closer to him, leaning my body against his. "But it didn't. Because I'm right here. Think about it. You have a lot of acquaintances." I glanced at the house. "And we have a lot of Daughters to protect. All I'm asking for is an introduction. If it doesn't work, then it doesn't work."

"You ask too much." His tone was throaty and full of desire.

I pressed my body tighter against his. "Please...*Daddy*. Do this for me."

"Jesus." He looked away.

But I knew the battle was won. His body spoke for him.

"You're going to be the death of me, you know that, right?"

"And what a beautiful death it is," I whispered, looking up into his eyes.

FORTY-FIVE

London

THE WOMAN WAS INSANE IF SHE THOUGHT THIS WAS GOING to work. My friends marrying Daughters of The Order? Number one, they wouldn't know how to handle them. Not without this blowing up in all our faces. And two, who the hell wanted to be married to a stranger after what these women had been through? I know I wouldn't. I'd want to be as far from men like me as possible.

No normal woman would want that.

But they weren't normal women, were they?

They were trained for men like me. Created to be used and cast away.

But if they were treated right, if they were honored and protected...who knew what kind of future that would give life to. I pulled the Explorer into the driveway and headed along the back, catching sight of the guard we had patrolling the grounds.

"I think this could work, London," Vivienne murmured for the tenth time.

I turned the key, killing the engine before I turned to her. "Why don't we just think on it and we can discuss it in the morning?"

She stifled a yawn, but she didn't fool me. I brushed the back of my knuckles along her cheek. "Tomorrow, Pet. We've done enough for today."

"It *is* tomorrow," she retorted and climbed out of the car. "I want to explore this, London. I want us to draw up some names, potential suitors."

I unleashed a groan and climbed out, locked the doors, and followed her into the house. But the moment she was inside, she went quiet, yawning loudly. I turned around, picked her up gently, and carried her to the bedroom. "Sleep first, then we'll discuss it later, deal?"

Her eyes closed as she dropped her head against my shoulder. "Deal."

The woman was so goodhearted she didn't know when enough was enough. But I did, so I took her to our bedroom and eased her onto the bed before I carefully pulled the bedding down. "The twins will be awake before we know it. Colt and I will take first shift, then it's all yours."

She nodded as she kicked off her shoes and slid under the sheets. "Just a nap," she murmured.

"Yes, Pet. Just a nap."

Whatever it took to get her to rest. Her eyes were closed before her head hit the pillow. By the time I reached the door, she was out cold, her soft, heavy breaths staying with me as I pulled the door closed and headed for the one place that'd occupied my attention in the days since the attack at the warehouse.

I stepped into my study and eased into the chair before I hit the mouse and logged in. Tiny blue lights flickered on the USB as it booted up. The USB Ryth had given me.

That thing...that thing was dangerous in the wrong hands.

Not only did it have names.

It had everything.

I'd been consumed by the data, sifting through all the different folders of Hale's entire operation, and I'd barely scratched the surface. The screen lit up as I scrolled through the names of those who'd sent money to Hale. It was all there, dates, amounts, even secret offshore bank accounts. Everything for me to plan an attack. With the right person behind it, we could launch a financial attack and bleed them all dry.

Lucky for me, I knew the best of the best.

Both Harper Renolt and Anna Salvatore were more than excited to start, and so was I.

Footage.

My fingers stopped the mouse at the folder and my heart pounded. I'd purposely stayed away from that section, scared of what I might find. If I saw my Vivienne forced to be with another man, I might just become that savage bastard once more.

But eventually I'd have to open that file...and take my chances with what I found inside.

Click.

The mouse clicked before I knew it, opening up folders and folders, all listed not by names at first but by years. I sat there, stunned. "Jesus fucking Christ."

I started with the current year, but didn't see a name I knew, and moved out. The thought of spying on these women revolted me. They'd suffered enough, let alone a stranger watching them perform intimate and degrading acts. I clicked out and moved to the next one, then the next...this one would've been around the time of Vivienne and Ryth.

E...

Evans...

Only Vivienne's name wasn't there.

Castlemaine.

Fuck, there was Ryth.

There was no way in hell I was clicking that. I scrolled upwards.

Ares.

My pulse boomed. *Ares?* I checked the date. That wasn't right. They'd adopted Angela when she was a child. Part of me didn't want to, but I had to know. I opened the folder and stared at the two names.

Angelica and Meredith.

Meredith Ares?

"What the fuck?"

I was too far gone now, no longer able to backtrack. I opened up the folder and clicked on the latest file, freezing at the date. It was the date of her death. The video waited, daring me to press play. That bastard in me rose to the surface. I needed to know.

Click.

"You want your husband to know about us?" The deep growl came from behind the camera.

Tears silently slid down Meredith's face as she slowly shook her head.

"Then take off your blouse, Meredith. It's either you or your daughter, and both of us don't want that, do we?"

I leaned closer. *Who the fuck* was *that guy?*

His voice was so fucking familiar and yet...I couldn't quite place it.

On the camera, Meredith Ares lifted her hand. Her fingers shook as she unbuttoned her blouse. "How many more times must we do this? You've got what you wanted. I've told you everything I know of my husband's dealings. You have enough to wipe us all out." Her voice turned thick as she lifted her head, her pain so fucking clear. "I'm begging you, please don't make me do this."

"Clothes...*off.* I want you to lay back and spread your legs. I want us to record just how perfect your cunt is before I fuck you so hard I destroy it. Then when you're full of my cum, you can get dressed, get your Daughter, and go home. I'm sure her training will be done by then. It sounds like Angelica is quite the natural when it comes to giving head."

"Holy...*fucking shit.*"

This...this was the kind of thing that destroyed worlds.

And families.

There was no way I could sit on this. I pulled out my cell, scrolled, and pressed the number I was told to never call again... and prayed it answered.

"St. James." His voice was slurred. "I told you to never call me again."

"You'll want this call." I said carefully knowing I was staring at a ticking bomb. "I have information about your mother."

Bedsheets shifted, and in an instant he was lucid. "What kind of information?"

I stared at the woman on the screen as she undressed and laid down on the bed, naked. "The kind of information that could rock your world."

Silas Ares

"THE KIND of information that could rock your world." The low growl filled my ear.

I glanced over my shoulder to the shadowed figure under the sheets and rose. Faint memories came back to me. Some fucking club where I was smashed off my face. A woman who was very available. I didn't even remember her name.

Still, I rose and made my way out of the bedroom, closing the door behind me. "Speak."

There was a heartbeat of silence. London St. James wasn't used to others talking to him like that. But right now, I didn't give a fuck.

"You didn't want to be involved in the war with Hale and the Order." He said as I walked along the hallway where our bedrooms were located. Theo's door was open and his bed still made. "I think that was a mistake."

"Oh yeah?" This fucking guy was starting to piss me the hell off. "How's that?"

My gaze moved to the bedroom further along the hall. My sister...*Angelica*. The word 'sister' stuck in the back of my throat like a bone.

"Because I have in my possession a recording...of your mother... on the date of her death...having sex with a man who's not your father."

I froze outside Angelica's door.

My pulse thundered.

My world darkened.

"You want to say that again?"

Fucking bullshit.

Fucking BULLSHIT. This motherfucker was going to say anything. He was going to say—

"I'm watching the recording right now. It's her, your mother and another man...and not only that...your sister, Angelica she was there...she knows *everything*."

She knows everything?

That brutal burn of rage plummeted inside me, carving all the way through pain and loss as I snarled. "Does she just. Send me the recording, London...no more lies. No more secrets. I want the truth...*and I want it now.*"

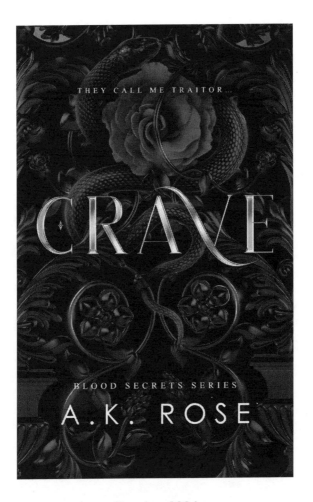

Coming 2024

We had the perfect life.

A family built on greed and fortune.

Two parents madly in love.

Then, we had *her*.

The sister we never wanted.

The stray...

The problem.

The liar.

In a single night, she *destroyed* our family. Now, we don't just stand over stand one casket, we stand over two.

With our father gone, it falls upon me to *uncover the truth.* Now I find out the truth starts and with her.

There's nowhere for her to run now.

No *mommy* to protect her. No *dad* to send her away.

Together my brothers and I will pry the truth from those poisoned lips.

I'll make her talk, then I'll make her scream, until I don't just become accustomed to the taste of her lies.

I crave them...

And her as well.

Made in the USA
Las Vegas, NV
30 November 2024

12987500R00234